STEEL RESOLVE

B.J. DANIELS

CALCULATED RISK

JANIE CROUCH

MILLS & BOON

Calculated Risk © 2019 Janie Crouch

ISBN: 978-0-263-27425-7

0719

MIX
Paper from
responsible sources
FSC™ C007454

STEEL RESOLVE

B.J. DANIELS

This one is for Terry Scones, who always brightens my day. I laugh when I recall a quilt shop hop we made across Montana. She was the navigator when my GPS system tried to send us through a barn.

Chapter One

The moment Fiona found the letter in the bottom of Chase's sock drawer, she knew it was bad news. Fear squeezed the breath from her as her heart beat so hard against her rib cage that she thought she would pass out. Grabbing the bureau for support, she told herself it might not be what she thought it was.

But the envelope was a pale lavender, and the handwriting was distinctly female. Worse, Chase had kept the letter a secret. Why else would it be hidden under his socks? He hadn't wanted her to see it because it was from that other woman.

Now she wished she hadn't been snooping around. She'd let herself into his house with the extra key she'd had made. She'd felt him pulling away from her the past few weeks. Having been here so many times before, she was determined that this one wasn't going to break her heart. Nor was she going to let another woman take him from her. That's why she had to find out why he hadn't called, why he wasn't returning her messages, why he was avoiding her.

They'd had fun the night they were together. She'd felt as if they had something special, although she knew the next morning that he was feeling guilty. He'd said he didn't want to lead her on. He'd told her that there was some woman back home he was still in love with. He'd said their night together was a mistake. But he was wrong, and she was determined to convince him of it.

What made it so hard was that Chase was a genuinely nice guy. You didn't let a man like that get away. The other woman had. Fiona wasn't going to make that mistake even though he'd been trying to push her away since that night. But he had no idea how determined she could be, determined enough for both of them that this wasn't over by a long shot.

It wasn't the first time she'd let herself into his apartment when he was at work. The other time, he'd caught her and she'd had to make up some story about the building manager letting her in so she could look for her lost earring.

She'd snooped around his house the first night they'd met—the same night she'd found his extra apartment key and had taken it to have her own key made in case she ever needed to come back when Chase wasn't home.

The letter hadn't been in his sock drawer that time.

That meant he'd received it since then. Hadn't she known he was hiding something from her? Why else would he put this letter in a drawer instead of leaving it out along with the bills he'd casually dropped on the table by the front door?

Because the letter was important to him, which meant that she had no choice but to read it.

Her heart compressed into a hard knot as she carefully lifted out the envelope. The handwriting made her pulse begin to roar in her ears. The woman's handwriting was very neat, very precise. She hated her immediately. The return address confirmed it. The letter was from the woman back in Montana that Chase had told her he was still in love with.

Mary Cardwell Savage, the woman who'd broken Chase's heart and one of the reasons that the cowboy had ended up in Arizona. Her friend Patty told her all about him. Chase worked for her husband, Rick. That's how she and Chase had met, at a party at their house.

What struck her now was the date on the postmark. Her vision blurred for a moment. *Two weeks ago?* Anger flared inside her again. That was right after their night together. About the same time that he'd gotten busy and didn't have time, he said, to date or even talk. What had this woman said in her letter? Whatever it was, Fiona knew it was the cause of the problem with her and Chase.

Her fingers trembled as she carefully opened the envelope flap and slipped out the folded sheet of pale lavender paper. The color alone made her sick to her stomach. She sniffed it, half expecting to smell the woman's perfume.

There was only a faint scent, just enough to be disturbing. She listened for a moment, afraid Chase might come home early and catch her again. He'd been angry the last time. He would be even more furious if he caught her reading the letter he'd obviously hidden from her.

Unfolding the sheet of paper she tried to brace herself. She felt as if her entire future hung on what was inside this envelope.

Her throat closed as she read the words, devouring them as quickly as her gaze could take them in. After only a few sentences, she let her gaze drop to the bottom line, her heart dropping with it: *I'll always love you, Mary.*

This was the woman Chase said he was still in love with. She'd broken up with him and now she wanted him back? Who did this Mary Savage of Big Sky, Montana, think she was? Fury churned inside Fiona as she quickly read all the way through the letter, the words breaking her heart and filling her with an all-consuming rage.

Mary Savage had apparently pretended that she was only writing to Chase to let him know that some friend of his mother's had dropped by with a package for him. If he confirmed his address, she'd be happy to send the package if he was interested.

But after that, the letter had gotten personal. Fiona stared at the words, fury warring with heartbreaking pain. The package was clearly only a ruse for the rest of the letter, which was a sickening attempt to lure him back. This woman was still in love with Chase. It made her sick to read the words that were such an obvious effort to remind him of their love, first love, and all that included. This woman had history with Chase. She missed him and regretted the way they'd left things. The woman had even included her phone number. In case he'd forgotten it?

Had Chase called her? The thought sent a wave of nausea through her, followed quickly by growing vehemence. She couldn't believe this. *This woman was not taking Chase away from her!* She wouldn't allow it. She and Chase had only gotten started, but Fiona knew that he was perfect for her and she for him. If anyone could help him get over this other woman, it was her. Chase was hers now. She would just have to make him see that.

Fiona tried to calm herself. The worst thing she could do was to confront Chase and demand to know why he had kept this from her. She didn't need him to remind her that they didn't have "that kind" of relationship as he had the other times. Not to mention how strained things had been between them lately. She'd felt him pulling away and had called and stopped by at every opportunity, afraid she was losing him.

And now she knew why. If the woman had been in Arizona, she would have gone to her house and— Deep breaths, she told herself. She had to calm down. She had to remember what had happened the last time. She'd almost ended up in jail.

Taking deep breaths, she reminded herself that this woman was no threat. Mary Cardwell Savage wasn't in Arizona. She lived in Montana, hundreds of miles away.

But that argument did nothing to relieve her wrath or her growing apprehension. Chase hadn't just kept the letter. He'd *hidden* it. His little *secret*. And worse, he was avoiding her, trying to give her the brush-off. She felt herself hyperventilating.

She knew she had to stop this. She thought of how good things had been between her and Chase that first night. The cowboy was so incredibly sexy, and he'd remarked how lovely she looked in her tailored suit and heels. He'd complimented her long blond hair as he unpinned it and let it fall around her shoulders. When he'd looked into her green eyes, she hadn't needed him to tell her that he loved her. She had seen it.

The memory made her smile. And he'd enjoyed what she had waiting for him underneath that suit—just as she knew he would. They'd both been a little drunk that night. She'd had to make all the moves, but she hadn't minded.

Not that she would ever admit it to him, but she'd set her sights on him the moment she'd seen him at the party. There was something about him that had drawn her. A vulnerability she recognized. He'd been hurt before. So had she, too many times to count. She'd told herself that the handsome cowboy didn't know just how perfect he was, perfect for her.

Fiona hadn't exactly thrown herself at him. She'd just been determined to make him forget that other woman by making herself indispensable. She'd brought over dinner the next night. He'd been too polite to turn her away. She'd come up with things they could do together: baseball games, picnics, movies. But the harder she'd tried, the more he'd made excuses for why he couldn't go with her.

She stared down at the letter still in her hands, wanting to rip it to shreds, to tear this woman's eyes out, to—

Suddenly she froze. Was that the door of the apartment opening? It was. Just as she'd feared, Chase had come home early.

At the sound of the door closing and locking, she hurriedly refolded the letter, slipped it back into the envelope and shoved it under his socks. She was trapped. There was no way to get out of the apartment without him seeing her. He was going to be upset with her. But the one thing she couldn't let Chase know was that she'd found and read the letter. She couldn't give him an excuse to break things off indefinitely, even though she knew he'd been trying to do just that for the past couple of weeks— ever since he'd gotten that letter.

She hurried to the bedroom door, but hesitated. Maybe she should get naked and let him find her lying on his bed. She wasn't sure she could pull that off right now. Standing there, she tried to swallow back the anger, the hurt, the fear. She couldn't let him know what she was feeling—let alone how desperate she felt. But as she heard him coming up the stairs, she had a terrifying thought.

What if she'd put the letter back in the drawer wrong? Had she seen the woman's handwriting on the envelope? Wasn't that why she'd felt such a jolt? Or was it just seeing the pale lavender paper of the envelope in his sock drawer that had made her realize what it was?

She couldn't remember.

But would Chase remember how he'd left it and know that she'd seen it? Know that if she'd found it, she would read it?

She glanced back and saw that she hadn't closed the top dresser drawer all the way. Hurrying back over to it, she shut the drawer as quietly as possible and was about to turn when she heard him in the doorway.

"Fiona? What the hell?" He looked startled at first when he saw her, and then shock quickly turned to anger.

She could see that she'd scared him. He'd scared her too. Her heart was a drum in her chest. She was clearly rattled. She could feel the fine mist of perspiration on her upper lip. With one look, he would know something was wrong.

But how could she not be upset? The man she'd planned to marry had kept a letter from his ex a secret from her. Worse, the woman he'd been pining over when Fiona had met him was still in love with him—and now he knew it. Hiding the letter proved that he was at least thinking about Mary Cardwell Savage.

"What are you doing here?" Chase demanded, glancing around as if the answer was in the room. "How the hell did you get in *this* time?"

She tried to cover, letting out an embarrassed laugh. "You startled me. I was looking for my favorite lipstick. I thought I might have left it here."

He shook his head, raking a hand through his hair. "You have to stop this. I told you last time. Fiona—" His blue gaze swept past her to light on the chest of drawers.

Any question as to how he felt about the letter was quickly answered by his protective glance toward the top bureau drawer and the letter from his first love, the young woman who'd broken his tender heart, the woman he was still in love with.

Her own heart broke, shattering like a glass thrown against a wall. She wanted to kill Mary Cardwell Savage.

"Your lipstick?" He shook his head. "Again, how did you get in here?"

"You forgot to lock your door. I came by hoping to catch your building manager so he could let me in again—"

"Fiona, stop lying. I talked to him after the last time. He didn't let you in." The big cowboy held out his hand. "Give it to me."

She pretended not to know what he was talking about, blinking her big green eyes at him in the best innocent look she could muster. She couldn't lose this man. She wouldn't. She did the only thing she could. She reached into her pocket and pulled out the key. "I can explain."

"No need," he said as he took the key.

She felt real tears of remorse fill her eyes. But she saw that he was no longer affected by her tears. She stepped to him to put her arms around his neck and pulled him down for a kiss. Maybe if she could draw him toward the bed...

"Fiona, stop." He grabbed her wrists and pulled them from around his neck. *"Stop!"*

She stared at him, feeling the happy life she'd planned crumbling under her feet.

He groaned and shook his head. "You need to leave."

"Sure," she said and, trying to get control of her emotions, started to step past him. "Just let me look in one more place for my lipstick. I know I had it—"

"No," he said, blocking her way. "Your lipstick isn't here and we both know it. Just like your phone wasn't here the last time you stopped by. This has to stop. I don't want to see you again."

"You don't mean that." Her voice broke. "Is this about the letter from that bitch who dumped you?"

His gaze shot to the bureau again. She watched his expression change from frustrated to furious. "You've been going through my things?"

"I told you, I was looking for my lipstick. I'm sorry I found the letter. You hadn't called, and I thought maybe it was because of the letter."

He sighed, and when he spoke it was as if he was talking to a small unruly child. "Fiona, I told you from the first night we met that I wasn't ready for another relationship. You caught me at a weak moment, otherwise nothing would have happened between the two of us. I'd had too much to drink, and my boss's wife insisted that I let you drive me back to my apartment." He groaned. "I'm not trying to make excuses for what happened. We are both adults. But I was honest with you." He looked pained, his blue eyes dark. "I'm sorry if you thought that that night was more than it was. But now you have to leave and not come back."

"We can't be over! You have to give me another chance." She'd heard the words before from other men, more times than she wanted to remember. "I'm sorry. I was wrong to come here when you weren't home. I won't do anything like this again. I promise."

"Stop!" he snapped. "You're not listening. Look," he said, lowering his voice. "You might as well know that I'm leaving at the end of the week. My job here is over."

"Leaving?" This couldn't be happening. "Where are you going?" she cried, and felt her eyes widen in alarm. "You're going back to Montana. *Back to her.* Mary Cardwell Savage." She spit out the words as if they were stones that had been lodged in her throat.

He shook his head. "I told you the night we met that

there was no chance of me falling for another woman because I was still in love with someone else."

She sneered at him. "She broke your heart. She'll do it again. Don't let her. She's nobody." She took a step toward him. "I can make you happy if you'll just give me a chance."

"Fiona, please go before either of us says something we'll regret," Chase said in a tone she'd never heard from him before. He was shutting her out. For good.

If he would only let her kiss him… She reached for him, thinking she could make him remember what they had together, but he pushed her back.

"Don't." He was shaking his head, looking at her as if horrified by her. There was anguish in his gaze. But there was also pity and disgust. That too she'd seen before. She felt a dark shell close around her heart.

"You'll be sorry," she said, feeling crushed but at the same time infused with a cold, murderous fury.

"I should have never have let this happen," Chase was saying. "This is all my fault. I'm so sorry."

Oh, he didn't know sorry, but he would soon enough. He would rue this day. And if he thought he'd seen the last of her, he was in for a surprise. That Montana hayseed would have Chase over her dead body.

Chapter Two

"I feel terrible that I didn't warn you about Fiona," his boss said on Chase's last day of work. Rick had insisted on buying him a beer after quitting time.

Now in the cool dark of the bar, Chase looked at the man and said, "So she's done this before?"

Rick sighed. "She gets attached if a man pays any attention to her in the least and can't let go, but don't worry, she'll meet some other guy and get crazy over him. It's a pattern with her. She and my wife went to high school together. Patty feels sorry for her and keeps hoping she'll meet someone and settle down."

Chase shook his head, remembering his first impression of the woman. Fiona had seemed so together, so… normal. She sold real estate, dressed like a polished professional and acted like one. She'd come up to him at a barbecue at Rick's house. Chase hadn't wanted to go, but his boss had insisted, saying it would do him good to get out more.

He'd just lost his mother. His mother, Muriel, had been sick for some time. It was one of the reasons he'd come to Arizona in the first place. The other was that he knew he could find work here as a carpenter. Muriel had made him promise that when she died, he would take her ashes back to Montana. He'd been with her at the end, hoping that she would finally tell him the one thing she'd kept from him all these years. But she hadn't. She'd taken her secret to the grave and left him with more questions than answers—and an urn full of her ashes.

"You need to get out occasionally," Rick had said when Chase left work to go pick up the urn from the mortuary. It was in a velvet bag. He'd stuffed it behind the seat of his pickup on the way to the barbecue.

"All you do is work, then hide out in your apartment not to be seen again until you do the same thing the next day," Rick had argued. "You might just have fun and I cook damned good barbecue. Come on, it's just a few friends."

He'd gone, planning not to stay longer than it took to drink a couple of beers and have some barbecued ribs. He'd been on his second beer when he'd seen her. Fiona stood out among the working-class men and women at the party because she'd come straight from her job at a local real estate company.

She wore high heels that made her long legs look even longer. Her curvaceous body was molded into a dark suit with a white blouse and gold jewelry. Her long blond hair was pulled up, accentuating her tanned throat against the white of her blouse.

He'd become intensely aware of how long it had been since he'd felt anything but anguish over his breakup with Mary and his mother's sickness, and the secret that she'd taken with her.

"Fiona Barkley," she'd said, extending her hand.

Her hand had been cool and dry, her grip strong. "Chase Steele."

She'd chuckled, her green eyes sparking with humor. "For real? A cowboy named Chase Steele?"

"My father was an extra in a bunch of Western movies," he lied since he had no idea who his father had been.

She cocked a brow at him. "Really?"

He shook his head. "I grew up on a ranch in Montana." He shrugged. "Cowboying is in my blood."

Fiona had taken his almost empty beer can from him and handed him her untouched drink. "Try that. I can tell that you need it." The drink had been strong and buzzed through his bloodstream.

Normally she wasn't the type of woman he gravitated toward. But she was so different from Mary, and it had been so long since he'd even thought about another woman. The party atmosphere, the urn behind his pickup seat and the drinks Fiona kept plying him with added to his what-the-hell attitude that night.

"How long have you two been dating?" Rick asked now in the cool dark of the bar.

"We never dated. I told her that first night that I was in love with someone else. But I made the mistake of sleeping with her. Sleeping with anyone given the way I feel about the woman back home was a mistake."

"So you told Fiona there was another woman." His boss groaned. "That explains a lot. Fiona now sees it as a competition between her and the other woman. She won't give up. She hates losing. It's what makes her such a great Realtor."

"Well, it's all moot now since I'm leaving for Montana."

Rick didn't look convinced that it would be that easy. "Does she know?"

He nodded.

"Well, hopefully you'll get out of town without any trouble."

"Thanks a lot."

"Sorry, but according to Patty, when Fiona feels the man pulling away… Well, it makes her a little…crazy."

Chase shook his head. "This just keeps getting better and better." He picked up his beer, drained it and got to his feet. "I'm going home to pack. The sooner I get out of town the better."

"I wish I could talk you out of leaving," Rick said. "You're one of the best finish carpenters I've had in a long time. I hope you're not leaving because of Fiona. Seriously, she'll latch on to someone else. I wouldn't worry about it. It's just Fiona being Fiona. Unless you're going back to this woman you're in love with?"

He laughed. "If only it were that easy. She's the one who broke it off with me." He liked Rick. But the man hadn't warned him about Fiona, and if Rick mentioned to Patty who mentioned to Fiona… He knew he was being overly cautious. Fiona wouldn't follow him all the way to Montana. She had a job, a condo, a life here. But still, he found himself saying, "Not sure what I'm doing. Might stop off in Colorado for a while."

"Well, good luck. And again, sorry about Fiona."

As he left the bar, he thought about Mary and the letter he'd hidden in his sock drawer with her phone number. He'd thought about calling her to let her know he was headed home. He was also curious about the package she'd said a friend of his mother had left for him.

Since getting the letter, he'd thought about calling dozens of times. But what he had to say, he couldn't in a phone call. He had to see Mary. Now that he was leaving, he couldn't wait to hit the road.

MARY CARDWELL SAVAGE reined in her horse to look out at the canyon below her. The Gallatin River wound through rugged cliffs and stands of pines, the water running clear over the colored rocks as pale green aspen leaves winked from the shore. Beyond the river and the trees, she could make out the resort town that had sprouted up across the canyon. She breathed in the cool air rich with the scent of pine and the crisp cool air rising off the water.

Big Sky, Montana, had changed so much in her lifetime and even more in her mother's. Dana Cardwell Savage had seen the real changes after the ski resort had been built at the foot of Lone Peak. Big Sky had gone from a ranching community to a resort area, and finally to a town with a whole lot of housing developments and businesses rising to the community's growing needs.

The growth had meant more work for her father, Marshal Hud Savage. He'd been threatening to retire since he said he no longer recognized the canyon community anymore. More deputies had to be hired each year because the area was experiencing more crime.

Just the thought of the newest deputy who'd been hired made her smile a little. Dillon Ramsey was the kind of man a woman noticed—even one who had given her heart away when she was fifteen and had never gotten it back.

Dillon, with his dark wavy hair and midnight black eyes, had asked her out, and she'd said she'd think about it. If her best friend Kara had been around, she would have thought Mary had lost her mind. Anyone who saw Dillon knew two things about him. He was a hunk, and he was dangerous to the local female population.

Since telling him she'd think about it, she had been mentally kicking herself. Had she really been sitting around waiting to hear from Chase? What was wrong with her? It had been weeks. When she'd broken it off and sent him packing, she hadn't been sitting around moping over him. Not really. She'd been busy starting a career, making a life for herself. So what had made her write that stupid letter?

Wasn't it obvious that if he'd gotten her letter, he should have called by now? Since the letter hadn't come back, she had to assume that it had arrived just fine. The fact that he hadn't called or written her back meant that he wasn't interested. He also must not be interested in the package his mother's friend had left for him either. It was high time to forget about that cowboy, and why not do it with Dillon Ramsey?

Because she couldn't quit thinking about Chase and hadn't been able to since she'd first laid eyes on him when they were both fifteen. They'd been inseparable all through high school and college. Four years ago he'd told her he was going to have to leave. They'd both been twenty-four, too young to settle down, according to her father and Chase had agreed. He needed to go find himself since not knowing who his father was still haunted him.

It had broken her heart when he'd left her—and Montana. She'd dated little after he left town. Mostly because she'd found herself comparing the men she had dated to Chase. At least with Dillon, she sensed a wild, dangerousness in him that appealed to her right now.

Her father hadn't liked hearing that Dillon had asked her out. "I wish you'd reconsider," he'd said when she'd stopped by Cardwell Ranch where she'd grown up. She'd bought her own place in Meadow Village closer to the center of town, and made the first floor into her office. On the third floor was her apartment where she lived. The second floor had been made into one-bedroom apartments that she rented.

But she still spent a lot of time on the ranch because that's where her heart was—her family, her horses and her love for the land. She hadn't even gone far away to college—just forty miles to Montana State University in Bozeman. She couldn't be far from Cardwell Ranch and couldn't imagine that she ever would. She was her mother's daughter, she thought. Cardwell Ranch was her legacy.

Dana Cardwell had fought for this ranch years ago when her brothers and sister had wanted to sell it and split the money after their mother died. Dana couldn't bear to part with the family ranch. Fortunately, her grandmother, Mary Cardwell, had left Dana the ranch in her last will, knowing Dana would keep the place in the family always.

Ranching had been in her grandmother's blood, the woman Mary had been named after. Just as it was in Dana's and now Mary's. Chase hadn't understood why she couldn't walk away from this legacy that the women in her family had fought so hard for.

But while her mother was a hands-on ranch woman, Mary liked working behind the scenes. She'd taken over the accounting part of running the ranch so her mother could enjoy what she loved—being on the back of a horse.

"What is wrong with Dillon Ramsey?" Dana Cardwell Savage had asked her husband after Mary had told them that the deputy had asked her out.

"He's new and, if you must know, there's something troublesome about him that I haven't been able to put my finger on yet," Hud had said.

Mary had laughed. She knew exactly what bothered her father about Dillon—the same thing that attracted her to the young cocky deputy. If she couldn't have Chase, then why not take a walk on the wild side for once?

She had just finished unsaddling her horse and was headed for the main house when her cell phone rang, startling her. Her pulse jumped. She dug the phone out and looked at the screen, her heart in her throat. It was a long-distance number and not one she recognized. Chase?

Sure took him long enough to finally call, she thought, and instantly found herself making excuses for him. Maybe he was working away from cell phone coverage. It happened all the time in Montana. Why not in Arizona? Or maybe her letter had to chase him down, and he'd just now gotten it and called the moment he read it.

It rang a second time. She swallowed the lump in her throat. She couldn't believe how nervous she was. Silly goose, she thought. It's probably not Chase at all but some telemarketer calling to try to sell her something.

She answered on the third ring. "Hello?" Her voice cracked.

Silence, then a female voice. "Mary Cardwell Savage?" The voice was hard and crisp like a fall apple, the words bitten off.

"Yes?" she asked, disappointed. She'd gotten her hopes up that it was Chase, with whatever excuse he had for not calling sooner. It wouldn't matter as long as he'd called to say that he felt the same way she did and always had. But she'd been right. It was just some telemarketer. "I'm sorry, but whatever you're selling, I'm not inter—"

"I read your letter you sent Chase."

Her breath caught as her heart missed a beat. She told herself that she'd heard wrong. "I beg your pardon?"

"Leave my fiancé alone. Don't write him. Don't call him. Just leave him the hell alone."

She tried to swallow around the bitter taste in her mouth. "Who is this?" Her voice sounded breathy with fear.

"The woman who's going to marry Chase Steele. If you ever contact him again—"

Mary disconnected, her fingers trembling as she

dropped the phone into her jacket pocket as if it had scorched her skin. The woman's harsh low voice was still in her ears, furious and threatening. Whoever she was, she'd read the letter. No wonder Chase hadn't written or called. But why hadn't he? Had he shown the letter to his fiancée? Torn it up? Kept it so she found it? Did it matter? His fiancée had read the letter and was furious, and Mary couldn't blame her.

She buried her face in her hands. Chase had gone off to find himself. Apparently he'd succeeded in finding a fiancée as well. Tears burned her eyes. Chase was engaged and getting married. Could she be a bigger fool? Chase had moved on, and he hadn't even had the guts to call and tell her.

Angrily, Mary wiped at her tears as she recalled the woman's words and the anger she'd heard in them. She shuddered, regretting more than ever that stupid letter she'd written. The heat of humiliation and mortification burned her cheeks. If only she hadn't poured her heart out to him. If only she had just written him about the package and left it at that. If only…

Unfortunately, she'd been feeling nostalgic the night she wrote that letter. Her mare was about to give birth so she was staying the night at the ranch in her old room. She'd come in from the barn late that night, and had seen the package she'd promised to let Chase know about. Not far into the letter, she'd become sad and regretful. Filled with memories of the two of them growing up together on the ranch from the age of fifteen, she'd decide to call him only to find that his number was no longer in service. Then she'd tried to find him on social media. No luck. It was as if he'd dropped off the face of the earth. Had something happened to him?

Worried, she'd gone online and found an address for

him but no phone number. In retrospect, she should never have written the letter—not in the mood she'd been in. What she hated most since he hadn't answered her letter or called, was that she had written how much she missed him and how she'd never gotten over him and how she regretted their breakup.

She'd stuffed the letter into the envelope addressed to him and, wiping her tears, had left it on her desk in her old room at the ranch as she climbed into bed. The next morning before daylight her mother had called up to her room to say that the mare had gone into labor. Forgetting all about the letter, she'd been so excited about the new foal that she'd put everything else out of her mind. By the time she remembered the letter, it was gone. Her aunt Stacy had seen it, put a stamp on the envelope and mailed it for her.

At first, Mary had been in a panic, expecting Chase to call as soon as he received the letter. She'd played the conversation in her head every way she thought possible, all but one of them humiliating. As days passed, she'd still held out hope. Now after more than two weeks and that horrible phone call, she knew it was really over and she had to accept it.

Still her heart ached. Chase had been her first love. Did anyone ever get over their first love? He had obviously moved on. Mary took another deep breath and tried to put it out of her mind. She loved summer here in the canyon. The temperature was perfect—never too cold or too hot. A warm breeze swayed the pine boughs and keeled over the tall grass in the pasture nearby. Closer a horse whinnied from the corral next to the barn as a hawk made a slow lazy circle in the clear blue overhead.

Days like this she couldn't imagine living anywhere else. She took another deep breath. She needed to get back to her office. She had work to do. Along with doing the ranch books for Cardwell Ranch, she had taken on work from other ranches in the canyon and built a lucrative business.

She would get over Chase or die trying, she told herself. As she straightened her back, her tears dried, and she walked toward her SUV. She'd give Deputy Dillon Ramsey a call. It was time she moved on. Like falling off a horse, she was ready to saddle up again. Forgetting Chase wouldn't be easy, but if anyone could help the process, she figured Dillon Ramsey was the man to do it.

Chapter Three

Chase was carrying the last of his things out to his pickup when he saw Fiona drive up. He swore under his breath. He'd hoped to leave without a scene. Actually, he'd been surprised that she hadn't come by sooner. As she was friends with Rick's wife, Patty, Chase was pretty sure she had intel into how the packing and leaving had been going.

He braced himself as he walked to his pickup and put the final box into the back. He heard Fiona get out of her car and walk toward him. He figured it could go several ways. She would try seduction or tears or raging fury, or a combination of all three.

Hands deep in the pockets of her jacket as she approached, she gave him a shy smile. It was that smile that had appealed to him that first night. He'd been vulnerable, and he suspected she'd known it. Did she think that smile would work again?

He felt guilty for even thinking that she was so calculating and yet he'd seen the way she'd worked him. "Fiona, I don't want any trouble."

"Trouble?" She chuckled. "I heard you were moving out today. I only wanted to come say goodbye."

Chase wished that was the extent of it, but he'd come

to know her better than that. "I think we covered good-bye the last time we saw each other."

She ignored that. "I know you're still angry with me—"

"Fiona—"

Tears welled in her green eyes as if she could call them up at a moment's notice. "Chase, at least give me a hug goodbye. Please." Before he could move, she closed the distance between them. As she did, her hands came out of her jacket pockets. The blade of the knife in her right hand caught the light as she started to put her arms around his neck.

As he jerked back, he grabbed her wrist. "What the—" He cursed as he tightened his grip on her wrist holding the knife. She was stronger than she looked. She struggled to stab him as she screamed obscenities at him.

The look in her eyes was almost more frightening than the knife clutched in her fist. He twisted her wrist until she cried out and dropped the weapon. The moment it hit the ground, he let go of her, realizing he was hurting her.

She dived for the knife, but he kicked it away, chasing after it before she could pick it up again. She leaped at him, pounding on his back as she tried to drag him to the ground.

He threw her off. She stumbled and fell to the grass and began to cry hysterically. He stared down at her. Had she really tried to kill him?

"Don't! Don't kill me!" she screamed, raising her hands as if she thought he was going to stab her. He'd forgotten that he'd picked up the knife, but he wasn't threatening her with it.

He didn't understand what was going on until he realized they were no longer alone. Fiona had an audience. Some of the apartment tenants had come out. One of them, an elderly woman, was fumbling with her phone as if to call the cops.

"Everything is all right," he quickly told the woman.

The older woman looked from Fiona to him and back. Her gaze caught on the knife he was holding at his side.

"There is no reason to call the police," Chase said calmly as he walked to the trash cans lined up along the street, opened one and dropped the knife into the bottom.

"That's my best knife!" Fiona yelled. "You owe me for that."

He saw that the tenant was now staring at Fiona, who was brushing off her jeans as she got to her feet.

"What are you staring at, you old crone? Go back inside before I take that phone away from you and stick it up your—"

"Fiona," Chase said as the woman hurriedly turned and rushed back inside. He shook his head as he gave Fiona a wide berth as he headed toward his apartment to lock up. "Go home before the police come."

"She won't call. She knows I'll come back here if she does."

He hoped Fiona was right about the woman not making the call. Otherwise, he'd be held up making a statement to the police—that's if he didn't end up behind bars. He didn't doubt that Fiona would lie through her teeth about the incident.

"She won't make you happy," Fiona screamed after him as he opened the door to his apartment, keeping an eye on her the whole time. The last thing he wanted was her getting inside. If she didn't have another weapon, he had no doubt she'd find one.

Stopping in the doorway, he looked back at her. Her makeup had run along with her nose. She hadn't bothered to wipe either. She looked small, and for a moment his heart went out to her. What had happened to that professional, together woman he'd met at the party?

"You need to get help, Fi."

She scoffed at that. "You're the one who needs help, Chase."

He stepped inside, closed and locked the door, before sliding the dead bolt. Who's to say she didn't have a half dozen spare keys made. She'd lied about the building manager opening the door for her. She'd lied about a lot of things. He had no idea who Fiona Barkley was. But soon she would be nothing more than a bad memory, he told himself as he finished checking to make sure he hadn't left anything. When he looked out, he saw her drive away.

Only then did he pick up his duffel bag, lock the apartment door behind him and head for his truck, anxious to get on the road to Montana. But as he neared his pickup, he saw what Fiona had left him. On the driver's-side window scrawled crudely in lipstick were the words *You'll regret it.*

That was certainly true. He regretted it already. He wondered what would happen to her and feared for the next man who caught her eye. Maybe the next man would handle it better, he told himself.

Tossing his duffel bag onto the passenger seat, he pulled an old rag from under the seat and wiped off what he could of the lipstick. Then, climbing into this truck, he pointed it toward Montana and Mary, putting Fiona out of his mind.

THERE WERE DAYS when Dana felt all sixty-two of her years. Often when she looked at her twenty-eight-year-old daughter, Mary, she wondered where the years had gone. She felt as if she'd merely blinked and her baby girl had grown into a woman.

Being her first and only daughter, Mary had a special place in her heart. So when Mary hurt, Dana did too. Ever since Chase and Mary had broken up and he'd left town, her daughter had been heartsick, and Dana had had no idea how to help her.

She knew that kind of pain. Hud had broken her heart years ago when they'd disagreed and he'd taken off. But he'd come back, and their love had overcome all the obstacles that had been thrown at them since. She'd hoped that Mary throwing herself into her accounting business would help. But as successful as Mary now was with her business, the building she'd bought, the apartments she'd remodeled and rented, there was a hole in her life—and her heart. A mother could see it.

"Sis, have you heard a word I've said?"

Dana looked from the window where she'd been watching Mary unsaddling her horse to where her brother sat at the kitchen table across from her. "Sorry. Did you just say *cattle thieves*?"

Jordan shook his head at her and smiled. There'd been a time when she and her brother had been at odds over the ranch. Fortunately, those days were long behind them. He'd often said that the smartest thing he'd ever done was to come back here, make peace and help Dana run Cardwell Ranch. She couldn't agree more.

"We lost another three head. Hud blames paleo diets," Jordan said, and picked up one of the chocolate chip cookies Dana had baked that morning.

"How many does this make?" she asked.

"There's at least a dozen gone," her brother said.

She looked to her husband who sat at the head of the table and had also been watching Mary out the window. Hud reached for another cookie. He came home every day for lunch and had for years. Today she'd made sandwiches and baked his favorite cookies.

"They're hitting at night, opening a gate, cutting out only a few at a time and herding them to the road where they have a truck waiting," the marshal said. "They never hit in the same part of any ranch twice, so unless we can predict where they're going to show up next... We aren't the only ones who've had losses."

"We could hire men to ride the fences at night," Jordan said.

"I'll put a deputy or two on the back roads for a couple of nights and see what we come up with," Hud said and, pushing away his plate and getting to his feet, shot Dana a questioning look.

Jordan, apparently recognizing the gesture, also got to his feet and excused himself. As he left, Hud said, "I know something is bothering you, and it isn't rustlers."

She smiled up at him. He knew her so well, her lover, her husband, her best friend. "It's Mary. Stacy told me earlier that she mailed a letter from Mary to Chase a few weeks ago. Mary hasn't heard back."

Hud groaned. "You have any idea what was in the letter?"

"No, but since she's been moping around I'd say she is still obviously in love with him." She shrugged. "I don't think she's ever gotten over him."

Her husband shook his head. "Why didn't we have all boys?"

"Our sons will fall in love one day and will probably have their heartbreaks as well." She had the feeling that Hud hadn't heard the latest. "She's going out with Deputy Dillon Ramsey tonight."

Hud swore and raked a hand through his graying hair.

"I shouldn't have mentioned that there was something about him that made me nervous."

She laughed. "If you're that worried about him, then why don't you talk to her?"

Her husband shot her a look that said he knew their stubborn daughter only too well. "Tell her not to do something and damned if she isn't even more bound and determined to do it."

Like he had to tell her that. Mary was just like her mother and grandmother. "It's just a date," Dana said, hoping there wasn't anything to worry about.

Hud grumbled under his breath as he reached for his Stetson. "I have to get back to work." His look softened. "You think she's all right?"

Dana wished she knew. "She will be, given time. I think she needs to get some closure from Chase. His not answering her letter could be what she needed to move on."

"I hope not with Dillon Ramsey."

"Seriously, what is it about him that worries you?" Dana asked.

He frowned. "I can't put my finger on it. I hired him as a favor to his uncle down in Wyoming. Dillon's cocky and opinionated."

Dana laughed. "I used to know a deputy like that."

Hud grinned. "Point taken. He's also still green."

"I don't think that's the part that caught Mary's attention."

Her husband groaned. "I'd like to see her with someone with both feet firmly planted on the ground."

"You mean someone who isn't in law enforcement. Chase Steele wasn't."

"I liked him well enough," Hud said grudgingly. "But

he hadn't sowed his wild oats yet. They were both too young, and he needed to get out of here and get some maturity under his belt, so to speak."

"She wanted him to stay and fight for her. Sound familiar?"

Hud's smile was sad. "Sometimes a man has to go out into the world, grow up, figure some things out." He reached for her hand. "That's what I did when I left. It made me realize what I wanted. You."

She stepped into his arms, leaning into his strength, thankful for the years they'd had together raising a family on this ranch. "Mary's strong."

"Like her mother."

"She'll be all right," Dana said, hoping it was true.

CHASE WAS DETERMINED to drive as far as he could the first day, needing to put miles behind him. He thought of Fiona and felt sick to his stomach. He kept going over it in his head, trying to understand if he'd done anything to lead her on beyond that one night. He was clear with her that he was not in the market for anything serious. His biggest mistake though was allowing himself a moment of weakness when he'd let himself be seduced.

But before that he'd explained to her that he was in love with someone else. She said she didn't care. That she wasn't looking for a relationship. She'd said that she needed him that night because she'd had a bad day.

Had he really fallen for that? He had. And when she became obsessed, he'd been shocked and felt sorry for her. Maybe he shouldn't have.

He felt awful, and not even the miles he put behind him made him feel better. He wished he'd never left Montana, but at the time, leaving seemed the only thing to do. He'd worked his way south, taking carpenter jobs, having no idea where he was headed.

When he'd gotten the call from his mother to say she was dying and that she'd needed to see him, he'd quit his job, packed up and headed for Quartsite, Arizona, in hopes that his mother would finally give him the name.

Chase had never known who his father was. It was a secret his mother refused to reveal for reasons of her own. Once in Arizona, though, he'd realized that she planned to take that secret to her grave. On her death bed, she'd begged him to do one thing for her. Would he take her ashes back to Montana and scatter them in the Gallatin Canyon near Big Sky?

"That's where I met your father," she said, her voice weak. "He was the love of my life."

She hadn't given him a name, but at least he knew now that the man had lived in Big Sky at the time of Chase's conception. It wasn't much, but it was better than nothing.

HE WAS IN the middle of nowhere just outside of Searchlight, Nevada, when smoke began to boil out from under the pickup's hood. He started to pull over when the engine made a loud sound and stopped dead. As he rolled to stop, his first thought was: could Fiona have done something to his pickup before he left?

Anger filled him to overflowing. But it was another emotion that scared him. He had a sudden awful feeling that something terrible was going to happen to Mary if he didn't get to Montana. Soon. The feeling was so strong that he thought about leaving his pickup beside the road and thumbing a ride the rest of the way.

Chase tried to tamp down the feeling, telling himself that it was because of Fiona and what she'd done before he'd left when she'd tried to kill him, not to mention what she'd done to his pickup. The engine was shot. He'd have to get a new one and that was going to take a while.

That bad feeling though wouldn't go away. After he called for a tow truck, he dialed the Jensen Ranch, the closest ranch to Mary's. He figured if anyone would know how Mary was doing, it would be Beth Anne Jensen. She answered on the third ring. "It's Chase." He heard the immediate change in her voice and realized she was probably the wrong person to call, but it was too late. Beth Anne had liked him a little too much when he'd worked for her family and it had caused a problem between him and Mary.

"Hey Chase. Are you back in town?"

"No, I was just calling to check on Mary. I was worried about her. I figured you'd know how she's doing. Is everything all right with her?"

Beth Anne's tone changed from sugar to vinegar. "As far as I know everything is just great with her. Is that all you wanted to know?"

This was definitely a mistake. "How are you?"

"I opened my own flower shop. I've been dating a rodeo cowboy. I'm just fine, as if you care." She sighed. "So if you're still hung up on Mary, why haven't you come back?"

Stubbornness. Stupidity. Pride. A combination of all three. "I just had a sudden bad feeling that she might be in trouble."

Beth Anne laughed. "Could be, now that you mention it. My brother saw her earlier out with some young deputy. Apparently, she's dating him."

"Sounds like she's doing fine then. Thanks. You take care." He swore as he disconnected and put his worry about Mary out of his mind. She should be plenty safe dating a deputy, right? He gave his front tire a kick, then paced as he waited for the tow truck.

IT HAD TAKEN hours before the tow truck had arrived. By then the auto shop was closed. He'd registered at a motel, taken a hot shower and sprawled on the bed, furious with Fiona, but even more so with himself.

He'd known he had a serious problem when he'd seen the smoke roiling out from under the hood. When the engine seized up, he'd known it was blown before he'd climbed out and lifted the hood.

At first, he couldn't understand what had happened. The pickup wasn't brand-new, but it had been in good shape. The first thing he'd checked was the oil. That's when he'd smelled it. Bleach.

The realization had come in a flash. He'd thrown a container of bleach away in his garbage just that morning, along with some other household cleaners that he didn't want to carry all the way back to Montana. He'd seen the bleach bottle when he'd tossed Fiona's knife into one of the trash cans at the curb.

Now, lying on the bed in the motel, Chase swore. He'd left Fiona out there alone with his pickup. He'd thought the only mischief she'd gotten up to was writing on his pickup window with lipstick. He'd underestimated her, and now it was going to cost him dearly. He'd have to have a new engine put in the truck, and that was going to take both money and time.

THREE DAYS LATER, while waiting in Henderson, Nevada for his new engine to be installed, he called Rick.

"Hey, Chase, great to hear from you. How far did you make it? I thought you might have decided to drive straight through all night."

"I broke down near Searchlight."

"Really? Is it serious?"

"I'm afraid so. The engine blew. I suspect Fiona put bleach in the oil."

Rick let out a curse. "That would seize up the engine."

"That's exactly what it did."

"Oh, man I am so sorry. Listen, I am beginning to feel like this is all my fault. Is there anything I can do? Where are you now? I could drive up there, maybe bring one of the big trailers. We could haul your pickup back down here. I know a mechanic—"

"I appreciate it, but I'm getting it fixed here in Henderson. That's not why I called."

"It's funny you should call," Rick said. "I was about to call you, but I kept putting it off hoping to have better news."

His heart began to pound. "What's wrong?"

His former boss let out a dry chuckle. "We're still friends, right?"

"Right. I forgave you for Fiona if that's what you're worried about."

"You might change your mind after you hear what I have to tell you," Rick said. "I didn't want you to hear this on the news." He felt his stomach drop as he waited for the bad news. "Fiona apparently hasn't been at work since before you left. Patty went over to her place. Her car was gone and there was no sign of her. But she'd called Patty the night you left from a bar and was pretty wasted and incoherent. When Patty wasn't able to reach her in the days that followed, she finally went over to her condo. It appeared she hadn't been back for a few days." Chase swore. She wouldn't hurt herself, would she? She'd said he would regret it. He felt a sliver of fear race up his spine. As delusional as the woman was—

Rick cleared his voice. "This morning a fisherman found her car in the Colorado River."

His breath caught in his throat. "Is she…?"

"They're dragging the river for her body, but it's hard to say how far her body might have gone downstream. The river was running pretty high after the big thunderstorm they had up in the mountains a few days ago."

Chase raked a hand through his hair as he paced the floor of his motel room as he'd been doing for days now. "She threatened to do all kinds of things, but I never thought she'd do something like this."

"Before you jump to conclusions, the police think it could have been an accident. Fiona was caught on video leaving the club that night and appeared to be quite inebriated," Rick said. "Look, this isn't your fault. I debated even telling you. Fiona was irrational. My wife said she's feared that the woman's been headed for a violent end for a long time, you know?"

He nodded to himself as he stopped to look out the motel room window at the heat waves rising off desert floor and yearned for Montana. "Still I hate to think she might have done this on purpose because of me."

"She wasn't right in the head. Anyway, it was probably an accident. I'm sorry to call with this kind of news, but I thought you'd want to know. Once your pickup's fixed you'll be heading out and putting all of this behind you. Still thinking about going to Colorado? You know I'd love to have you back."

No reason not to tell him now. "I'm headed home as soon as the pickup's fixed, but thanks again for the offer."

"Home to Montana? You really never got over this woman, huh."

"No, I never did." He realized that when he thought

of home, it was Mary he thought of. Her and the Gallatin Canyon. "It's where I grew up. Where I first fell in love."

"Well, I wish you luck. I hope it goes well."

"Thanks. If you hear anything else about Fiona—"

"I'll keep it to myself."

"No, call me. I really didn't know the woman. But I care about what happened to her." He thought of the first night he'd seen her, all dressed up in that dark suit and looking so strong and capable. And the other times when she'd stopped by his apartment looking as if she'd just come home from spring break and acting the part. "It was like she was always changing before my eyes. I never knew who she was. I'm not sure she did."

He and Rick said goodbye again. Disconnecting, he pocketed his phone. He couldn't help wondering about Fiona's last moments underwater inside her car. Did she know how to swim? He had no idea. Was it too deep for her to reach the surface? Or had she been swept away?

Chase felt sad, but he knew there was no way he could have helped her. She wanted a man committed to her, and she deserved it. But as he'd told her that first night, he wasn't that man.

If only he had known how broken and damaged she was. He would have given her a wide berth. He should have anyway, and now he blamed himself for his moment of weakness. That night he'd needed someone, but that someone had been Mary, not a woman he didn't know. Not Fiona.

"I'm so sorry," he whispered. "I'm so sorry." He hoped that maybe now Fiona would finally be at peace.

Looking toward the wide-open horizon, he turned his thoughts to Mary. He couldn't wait to look into her beautiful blue eyes and tell her that he'd never stopped

loving her. That thought made him even more anxious.
He couldn't wait to get home.

DILLON WALKED HER to her door and waited while Mary
pulled out her keys.

"I had a wonderful time," he said as he leaned casually against the side of her building as if waiting to see
if she was going to invite him up. Clouds scudded past
the full moon to disappear over the mountaintops surrounding the canyon. The cool night air smelled of pine
and clear blue trout stream water. This part of Montana
was a little bit of Heaven, her mother was fond of saying. Mary agreed.

She'd left a light on in her apartment on the top floor.
It glowed a warm inviting golden hue.

"I had fun too," she said, and considered asking him
up to see the view from what she jokingly called her penthouse. The balcony off the back would be especially nice
tonight. But her tongue seemed tied, and suddenly she
felt tired and close to tears.

"I should go," Dillon said, his gaze locking with hers.
He seemed about to take a step back, but changed his
mind and leaned toward her. His hand cupped her jaw
as he kissed her. Chastely at first, then with more ardor,
gently drawing her to him. The kiss took her by surprise.
Their first date he hadn't even tried.

His tongue probed her mouth for a moment before
he ended the kiss as abruptly as it had begun. Stepping
back, he seemed to study her in the moonlight for a moment before he said, "I really do have to go. Maybe we
could do something this weekend if you aren't busy?"

She nodded dumbly. She and Dillon were close to the
same age, both adults. She'd expected him to kiss her on
their first date. So her surprise tonight had nothing to

do with him kissing her, she thought as she entered her building, locking the door behind her and hurrying up to her apartment.

It had everything to do with the kiss.

Mary unlocked her apartment door with trembling fingers, stepped in and locked it behind her. She leaned against the door, hot tears filling her eyes as she told herself she shouldn't be disappointed. But she was.

The kiss had been fine, as far as kisses went. But even when Dillon had deepened the kiss, she had felt nothing but emptiness. The memory made her feel sick. Would she always compare every kiss with Chase's? Would every man she met come up lacking?

She didn't bother to turn on a lamp as she tossed her purse down and headed toward her bedroom, furious with herself. And even more furious with Chase. He'd left her and Montana as if what they had together meant nothing to him. Clearly it didn't. That's why he'd gotten engaged and wasn't man enough to call her himself and tell her.

Still mentally kicking herself for writing that letter to him, she changed into her favorite T-shirt and went into the bathroom to brush her teeth. Her image in the mirror startled her. She was no longer that young girl that Chase had fallen in love with. She was a woman in her own right. She dried her tears, the crying replaced with angry determination. If that was the way Chase wanted to be, then it was fine with her.

Her cell phone rang, startling her. She hurried to it, and for just a moment she thought it was going to be Chase. Her heart had soared, then come crashing down. Chase had moved on. When was she going to accept that?

"I couldn't quit thinking about you after I left," Dillon said. "I was wondering if you'd like to go to the movies tomorrow night?"

She didn't hesitate. "I'd love to." Maybe she just hadn't been ready for his kiss. Maybe next time…

"Great," Dillon said. "I'll pick you up at 5:30 if that's all right. We can grab something to eat before we go to the theater."

"Sounds perfect." If Chase could see her now, she thought as she hung up. Dillon was handsome, but less rugged looking than Chase. Taller though by a good inch or two, and he wanted to go out with her.

She disconnected, determined to put Chase Steele behind her. He had moved on and now she was too. Next time, she would invite Dillon up to her apartment. But even as she thought it, she imagined Chase and the woman he was engaged to. While she was busy comparing every man she met to him, he'd found someone and fallen in love. It made her question if what she and Chase once had was really that unique and special. Just because it had been for her…

Mary willed herself not to think about him. She touched her tongue to her lower lip. Dillon had made her laugh, and he'd certainly been attentive. While the kiss hadn't spurred a reaction in her, she was willing to give it another chance.

Her father didn't trust the man, so didn't that mean that there was more to Dillon than met the eye? Chase had always been a little wild growing up. Her father had been worried about her relationship with him. Maybe there was some wildness in Dillon that would make him more interesting.

As she fell asleep though, her thoughts returned to Chase until her heart was aching and tears were leaking onto her pillow.

Chapter Four

"How was your date?"

Mary looked up the next morning to find her mother standing in the doorway of her office holding two cups of coffee from the shop across the street. "Tell me that's an ultimate caramel frappaccino."

Dana laughed. "Do you mean layers of whipped cream infused with rich coffee, white chocolate and dark caramel? Each layer sitting on a dollop of dark caramel sauce?"

"Apparently I've mentioned why I love it," she said, smiling at her mother as Dana handed her the cup. She breathed in the sweet scent for a moment before she licked some of the whipped cream off the top. "I hope you got one of these for yourself."

"Not likely," her mother said as she sat down across the desk from her. "The calories alone scared me off. Anyway, you know I prefer my coffee to actually taste like coffee. That's why I drink it black."

Mary grimaced and shook her head, always amazed how much she looked like her mother but the similarities seemed to have stopped there. What they shared was their love of Montana and determination to keep Cardwell Ranch for future generations. At least for the ones who wanted to stay here. Her three brothers had left quickly enough, thrown to the far winds. She wondered about her own children—when she had them one day with the man she eventually married. Would they feel wanderlust like Chase had? She knew she wouldn't be able to make them stay nearby any more than she had him.

She took a sip of her coffee, hating that she'd let her thoughts wander down that particular path.

"I'm trying to tell if the date went well or not," her mother said, studying her openly. "When I walked in, I thought it had, but now you're frowning. Is your coffee all right?"

Mary replaced her frown with a smile as she turned her attention to her mother and away from Chase. "My coffee is amazing. Thank you so much. It was just what I needed. Normally I try to get over to Lone Peak Perk when it opens, but this morning I was anxious to get to work. I wish they delivered."

Her mother gave her a pointed look. "Are you purposely avoiding talking about your date, because I'm more interested in it than your coffee habit."

Laughing, she said, "The date was fine. Good. Fun, actually. We're going out again tonight."

Her mother raised a brow. "Again already? So he was a perfect gentleman?" Her mother took a sip of her coffee as if pretending she wasn't stepping over a line.

"You're welcome to tell Dad that he was," she said with a twinkle in her eye.

"Mary!" They both laughed. "So you like him?"

Mary nodded. *Like* was exactly the right word. She had hoped to feel more.

"You are impossible. You're determined to make me drag everything out of you, aren't you?"

"Not everything," she said coyly. Her mother seemed to like this game they played. Mostly Dana seemed relieved that Mary was moving on after Chase. She didn't like to see her daughter unhappy, Mary thought. It was time to quit moping over Chase, and they both knew it.

"So HOW DID we do?" Deputy Dillon Ramsey asked his friend as he closed the cabin door and headed for the refrigerator for a beer as if he lived there.

"Picked up another three head of prime beef," Grady Birch said, and quickly added, "They were patrolling the fences last night just like you said they would be. Smart to hit a ranch on the other side of the river. We got in and out. No sweat."

"It's nice that I know where the deputies will be watching." Dillon grinned as he popped the top on his beer can and took a long swig.

"Trouble is, I heard around town that ranchers are going to start riding their fences. Word's out."

Dillon swore. "It was such easy pickings for a while." He plopped down in one of the worn chairs in Grady's cabin, feeling more at home in this ratty-ass place than in his nice apartment in Big Sky. "So we'll cool it until the heat dies down."

"Back to easy pickings, how did your date go?"

He grinned. "A couple more dates and I'll have her eating out of my hand."

Grady looked worried. "You're playing with fire, you know. The marshal's daughter?" His friend shook his head. "You sure this game you're playing is worth it?"

Dillon laughed. "To be able to drive out to the Cardwell Ranch, sit on that big porch of theirs and drink the marshal's beer right under his nose? You damn betcha it's worth it."

"Maybe I don't understand the end game," Grady suggested.

"I need this job until I can get enough money together

to go somewhere warm, sit in the shade and drink fancy drinks with umbrellas in them for the rest of my life. I have plans for my future and they don't include a woman, especially Mary Savage. But in the meantime..." He smiled and took a slug of his beer. "She ain't half bad to look at. For her age, I get the feeling that she hasn't had much experience. I'd be happy to teach her a few things."

"Well, it still seems dangerous dating his daughter," Grady said. "Unless you're not telling me the truth and you're serious about her."

"I'm only serious about keeping the marshal from being suspicious of me. I told you, he almost caught me that one night after we hit the Cardwell Ranch. I had to do some fast talking, but I think I convinced him that I was patrolling the area on my night off."

"And dating his daughter will make him less suspicious of you?"

"It will give him something else to worry about," Dillon said with a grin. He knew he'd gotten the job only because of his uncle. He'd gone into law enforcement at his uncle's encouragement. Also, he'd seen it as a get-out-of-jail-free card. No one would suspect a cop, right?

Unfortunately, his uncle had been more than suspicious about what Dillon had been doing to make some extra money. So it had come down to him leaving Wyoming to take the deputy job in the Gallatin Canyon of Montana.

"Mary Savage is a good-looking woman, no doubt about that," Grady said as he got up to get them more beer.

Dillon watched him with narrowed eyes. "Don't get any ideas. I've been priming this pump for a while now. And believe me, with your record, you wouldn't want Marshal Hud Savage looking too closely at *you*. That's one reason we can't be seen together. As far as anyone knows, you and I aren't even friends."

MARSHAL HUD SAVAGE had been waiting patiently for the call since Deputy Dillon Ramsey had gone off duty. Still, when his phone rang, it made him jump. It wasn't like him to be nervous. Then again, this was about his daughter. He had every right given his feelings about Dillon Ramsey.

He picked up the phone, glad to hear the voice of Hayes Cardwell, Dana's cousin, on the other end of the line. It was nice to have several private investigators in the family. "Well?"

"You were right. He headed out of town the moment he changed out of his uniform," Hayes said. "He went to a cabin back in the hills outside Gallatin Gateway. You're probably more interested in who is renting the cabin than who owns it. Ever heard of a man named Grady Birch?"

The name didn't ring any bells. "Who is he?"

"He has an interesting rap sheet that includes theft and assault. He's done his share of cattle rustling."

"And Dillon went straight there."

"He did. In fact, he's still inside. I'm watching the place from down the road with binoculars."

"So it's away from other houses," Hud said. "Any chance there's a truck around with a large horse trailer?"

"The kind that could be used to steal cattle?"

"Exactly," the marshal said.

"There's an old one parked out back. If they both leave, I might get a chance to have a look inside."

"I doubt they're going to leave together," Hud said. "Thanks for doing this but I can take it from here."

"No problem. What's family for?"

"I'll expect a bill for your time," the marshal said. "Or I'll tell Dana on you."

Hayes laughed. "Don't want *her* mad at me."

"No one does. Also," Hud added, "let's keep this just between the two of us for now." He disconnected and called up Grady Birch's rap sheet. Hayes was right. Grady was trouble. So why wasn't he surprised that his new deputy was hanging out with a man like that?

He'd known it the moment he laid eyes on the handsome lawman. Actually, he'd suspected there would be a problem when Dillon's uncle called, asking for the favor. He'd wanted to turn the man down, but the uncle was a good cop who Hud had worked with on a case down in Jackson, Wyoming.

Hud rubbed a hand over his face. Dillon was everything he'd suspected he was, and now he was dating Mary. He swore. What was he going to do about it? In the first place, he had no proof. Yet. So warning Mary about him would be a waste of breath even if she *didn't* find something romantic about dating an outlaw. Some people still saw cattle rustling as part of an Old West tradition. Also, his daughter was too old to demand that she stop seeing Dillon.

No, he was going to have to handle this very delicately, and delicate wasn't in his repertoire. That didn't leave him many options. Catching Dillon red-handed wouldn't be easy because the deputy wasn't stupid. Arresting him without enough evidence to put him away was also a bad move.

Hud knew he had to bide his time. He told himself that maybe he'd get lucky, and Dillon or Grady would make a mistake. He just hoped it was soon, before Mary got any more involved with the man.

CHASE FINALLY GOT the call. His pickup engine was in and he could come by this afternoon to pick it up. He hadn't talked to Rick in a few days and feeling at loose ends, pulled out his cell phone and made the call, dreading the news. Rick answered on the second ring.

"Has there been any word on Fiona?" The silence on the other end of the line stretched out long enough that Chase knew what was coming.

"They gave up the search. The general consensus is that her body washed downstream and will be found once the water goes down more."

"I'm sorry to hear that. I'm sure Patty is upset."

"She is," Rick said. "She felt sorry for Fiona. That's why she didn't cut ties with her after high school. Patty's over at Fiona's condo now cleaning it out since she has no next of kin. She found out from a bank statement that Fiona had drained her bank account almost a week ago. Took all of it in cash. Who knows what she did with that much money. Hell, it could be in the river with her. Patty's going to try to organize some kind of service for her."

"She doesn't have any family?"

"I guess I didn't tell you. Her whole family died in a fire when Fiona was eleven. She would have perished with her parents and three older stepbrothers, but she'd stayed over at a friend's house that night."

"Oh man. That could explain a lot," he said more to himself. "I wish I'd known all of this. Maybe I could have handled things better."

"Trust me, it would take a psychiatrist years to sort that woman out. So stop blaming yourself. I'm the one who should have warned you. But it's over now."

The fact that he felt relieved made him feel even more guilty as he promised to stay in touch and hung up.

Chapter Five

"Just fill out this application and leave it," the barista said as she dropped the form on the table in front of the dark-haired woman with the pixie haircut and the kind of cute Southern accent and lisp because of the gap between her front teeth.

She'd introduced herself as Lucy Carson, as if Christy was supposed to recognize the name.

"You're sure there's no chance of an opening soon?" Lucy Carson asked now before glancing at her name tag and adding, "Christy."

Christy shook her head. "Like I said. I just got hired, so I really doubt there will be anything for the rest of the season unless someone quits and that's unlikely. Jobs aren't that easy to find in Big Sky. Your application will be on file with dozens of others, so if I were you, I'd keep looking."

She didn't mean to sound cruel or dismissive, but she'd told the woman there weren't any openings. Still, the woman had insisted on filling out an application. If she wanted to waste her time, then Christy wasn't going to stop her. She just thought it was stupid.

From behind the counter, she watched how neatly Lucy Carson filled in each blank space. Was it stubbornness or arrogance? The lady acted as if she thought the manager would let someone go to hire *her*. That sounded like arrogance to Christy.

"What about a place to live nearby?" the woman asked, looking up from the application.

Christy laughed. "You'll have even worse luck finding an apartment. I've been waiting for months to get into the one across the street, and it's just a small bedroom."

Lucy glanced in the direction she pointed. "There's rentals over there?"

"There *was*. I got the last one. I'm moving in tomorrow." This Lucy was starting to get on her nerves. She found herself wishing that some customers would come in just so she had something to do. Usually she loved the slow afternoons when she could look at magazines and do absolutely nothing, even though she was supposed to be cleaning on her downtime.

The woman studied her for a moment, then smiled and resumed filling out the application.

"You should go down to Bozeman," Christy told her. "More opportunities in a college town than here in the canyon." Jobs weren't easy to get in Big Sky especially during the busy times, summer, and winter. Not just that, this job didn't even pay that well. Too many young people would work for nothing just to get to spend their free time up on the mountain biking and kayaking in the summer, skiing and snowboarding in the winter.

The woman finished and brought her application over to the counter. Christy glanced at the name. "Is Lucy short for something?" she asked.

"My mother was a huge fan of *I Love Lucy* reruns."

She looked at the application, almost feeling sorry for the young woman. According to this, she had a lot of experience as a barista but then so did a whole lot of other people. "I see you didn't put down an address." She looked up at the woman who gave her a bright smile.

"Remember, I'm still looking for a place to stay, but once I start working I'm sure an apartment will open up."

Christy couldn't help but chuckle under her breath at the woman's naive optimism. "Most everyone who works in Big Sky ends up commuting at least forty miles a day. There just aren't any cheap rentals for minimum wage workers even if you should luck out and get a job."

Lucy smiled. "I'm not worried. Things just tend to work out for me. I'm lucky that way."

Whatever, Christy thought. "I'll give your application to Andrea but like I said, we don't have any openings."

"Not yet anyway," Lucy said. "So where do you go to have fun on a Saturday night?"

"Charley's if you like country. Otherwise—"

"I'm betting you like country music," Lucy said. "Your car with the George Strait bumper sticker gives you away."

"My car?" Christy frowned.

"Isn't that your SUV parked across the street?"

She looked out the window and laughed. "Not hardly. Mine is that little blue beat-up sedan with all the stuff in the back since I can't move into my apartment until tomorrow. I've been waiting for weeks, staying with my mother down in Bozeman and driving back and forth when I can't find someone to stay with here. Do you have any family you could stay with?"

Lucy shook her head. "No family. Just me. Maybe I'll check out Charley's tonight." She smiled her gap-toothed smile. "Hopefully I'll get lucky and some handsome cowboy will take me home with him. Or maybe it's not that kind of place."

"No, it is. There'll be cowboys and ski bums."

"I might see you there then?" Lucy said. "Don't worry. I won't intrude if you've found your own cowboy. I'm guessing there's one you're planning to meet tonight."

Christy felt herself flush. "Not exactly. I'm just hoping he'll be there."

Lucy laughed. "Hoping to get lucky, huh? Well, thanks again for your help." She left smiling, making Christy shake her head as she tossed Lucy's application on the desk in Andrea's office. She'd ended up almost liking the woman. Now if she could just get through the rest of the day. She was excited about tonight at Charley's. She did feel lucky. She had a job, an apartment to move into tomorrow and with even more luck, she would be going home with the man she had a crush on. Otherwise, she would be sleeping in her car on top of all her belongings.

Tomorrow though, she'd be moving into the apartment across the street that Mary Savage owned. How handy was that since she could sleep late and still get to work on time with her job just across the street?

Lucy Carson was also looking at the small apartment house across the street from Lone Peak Perk as she walked to her car. She had her heart set on a job at the coffee shop and an apartment across the street in Mary Cardwell Savage's building. Not that she always got what she set her heart on, she thought bitterly, but she would make this happen, whatever she had to do.

As she climbed into her new car, she breathed in the scent of soft leather. She really did like the smell of a new car. Her other one was at the bottom of the Colorado River—or at least it had been until a few weeks ago when it was discovered.

Her disappearing act had gone awry when she'd tried to get out of the car and couldn't before it plummeted toward the river that night. By the time she reached the bank way downriver, she'd wished she'd come up with a better plan. She'd almost died and she wanted to live. More than wanted to live. She'd wanted to kill someone. Especially the person responsible for making her have to go to such extremes: Chase Steele. As she'd sat on that riverbank in the dark, she knew exactly what she had to do. Fortunately, when she'd tried to bail out of the car, she'd grabbed her purse. She'd almost forgotten the money. Her plan really would have gone badly if she'd lost all this money. With it, she could do anything she wanted.

But as close a call as it had been, everything had worked out better than even she'd planned. The authorities thought she was dead, her body rotting downriver. Fiona Barkley was dead. She was free of her. Now she could become anyone she chose.

Since then she'd had to make a few changes, including her name. But she'd never liked the name Fiona anyway. She much preferred Lucy Carson. Getting an ID in that name had been easier than she imagined. It had been harder to give up her long blond hair. But the pixie cut, the dark brown contacts and the brunette hair color transformed her into a woman not even she recognized. She thought she looked good—just not so good that Chase would recognize her.

Her resulting car wreck had pretty much taken care of her change in appearance as well. She had unsnapped her seat belt to make her leap from the car before it hit the water. Had she not been drunk and partway out of the car, she wouldn't have smashed her face, broken her nose and knocked out her front teeth.

As it turned out, that too proved to be a stroke of luck. She'd lost weight because it had hurt to eat. When she looked in the mirror now, she felt she was too skinny, but she knew once she was happy again, she'd put some pounds back on. She still had curves. She always had.

It was her face that had changed the most. Her nose had healed but it had a slight lean to it. She liked the imperfection. Just as she liked the gap between her two new front teeth. It had taken going to a dentist in Mexico to get a rush job. She liked the gap. It had even changed the way she talked giving her a little lisp. She'd been able to pick up her former Southern accent without any trouble since it was the way she'd talked before college. It was enough of a change in her appearance and voice that she knew she could get away with it—as long as she never got too close to Chase.

In the meantime, she couldn't wait to meet Mary Cardwell Savage.

MARY STOOD ACROSS the street from Lone Peak Perk thinking about her date last night with Dillon. She'd seen the slim, dark-haired woman come out of the coffee shop and get into a gray SUV, but her mind had been elsewhere. As the SUV pulled away, she turned from the window, angry with herself.

She was still holding out hope that Chase would contact her. The very thought made her want to shake herself. It had been weeks. If he was going to answer, he would have a long time ago. So why did she keep thinking she'd hear from him? Hadn't his fiancée told him that she'd called? Maybe he thought that was sufficient. Not the man she'd known, she thought.

And that was what kept nagging at her. She'd known Chase since he was fifteen. He'd come to work for the Jensen Ranch next door. Mary's mom had pretty much adopted him after finding out the reason he'd been sent to live in the canyon was because his mother couldn't take care of him. Muriel was going through cancer treatment. He'd been honorable even at a young age. He wasn't the kind of man not to call and tell her about a fiancée.

So his not calling or writing felt…wrong. And it left her with nagging questions.

That was only part of the problem and she knew it. She'd hoped that Dillon Ramsey would take her mind off Chase. They'd been dating regularly, and most of the time she enjoyed herself. They'd kissed a few times but that was all. He hadn't even made a pass at her. She couldn't imagine what it was about Dillon that had worried her father. At one point, she'd wondered if her father the marshal had warned him to behave with her.

The thought made her cringe. He wouldn't do that, would he?

She'd asked Dillon last night how he liked working for her dad.

"I like it. He's an okay dude," he'd answered.

She'd laughed. No one called her father a dude.

Now, she had to admit that Dillon was a disappointment. Which made her question what it was she was looking for in a man. A sense of adventure along with a sense of humor. Dillon didn't seem to have either.

Was that why she felt so restless? She looked around her apartment, which she'd furnished with things she loved from the turquoise couch to the weathered log end tables and bright flowered rug. But the spectacular view was the best part. The famous Lone Peak, often snow-capped, was framed in her living room window. The mountain looked especially beautiful in the moonlight.

Which made her think of Chase and how much she would have liked to stand on her back deck in the moonlight and kiss him—instead of Dillon. She groaned, remembering her hesitation again last night to invite Dillon up to her apartment. He'd been hinting that he really wanted to see it. She could tell last night that he'd been hurt and a little angry that she hadn't invited him up.

Standing here in the life she'd built, all she could think about was what Chase's opinion would be of it. Would he be proud of her accomplishments? Would he regret ever leaving her?

She shook him from her head and hurried back downstairs. She still had work to do, and all she was doing right now was giving herself a headache.

BY THE NEXT MORNING, news of the hit and run death of Christy Shores had spread through most of Big Sky and the canyon.

As Marshal Hud Savage walked into Charley's, the last place Christy Shores had been seen alive, he saw the bartender from last night wasn't alone.

"Mike French, bartender, right?" Hud asked the younger of the two men standing nervously behind the bar. Twentysomething, Mike looked like a lot of the young people in Big Sky from his athletic build to the T-shirt and shorts over long underwear and sandals.

If Hud had to guess, he'd say Mike had at least one degree in something practical like engineering, but had gotten hooked on a lifestyle of snowboarding in the winter and mountain biking or kayaking in the summer. Which explained the bartending job.

He considered the handsome young man's deep tan from spending more hours outside than bartending. It made him wonder why a man like that had never appealed to his only daughter.

He suspected Mary was too much of a cowgirl to fall for a ski bum. Instead, she was now dating his deputy,

Dillon Ramsey. That thought made his stomach roil, considering what he suspected about the man.

The bartender stepped forward to shake his hand. "Bill said you had some questions about Christy?"

Hud nodded and looked to the bar owner, Bill Benson, before he turned back to Mike. "I understand she was one of the last people to leave the bar last night?"

Mike nodded as Hud pulled out his notebook and pen. "I was just about to lock up when she came out of the women's bathroom. She looked like she'd been crying. I hadn't realized she was in there since I had already locked the front door." He shot a guilty look at his boss. "I usually check to make sure everyone was gone, but last night…"

"What was different about last night?" Hud asked.

Mike shifted on his feet. "A fight had broken out earlier between a couple of guys." He shot another look at Bill and added, "Christy had gotten into the middle of it. Not sure what it was about. After I broke it up, I didn't see her. I thought she'd left."

"Christy's blood alcohol was three times the legal limit," Hud said.

Again Mike shot a look at his boss before holding up his hands and quickly defending himself. "I cut her off before the fight because she'd been hitting the booze pretty hard. But that doesn't mean she quit drinking. The place was packed last night. All I know is that I didn't serve her after that."

Hud glanced toward the front door. "Her car is still parked outside. You didn't happen to take her keys, did you?"

The young man grimaced. "I asked for her keys, but she swore to me that she was walking home." He shrugged. "I guess that part was true."

Hud had Christy's car keys in a plastic evidence bag in his patrol SUV. The keys had been found near her body next to the road after she was apparently struck by a vehicle and knocked into the ditch.

"I'm going to need the names of the two men who were involved in the fight," he said. He wrote them down, hiding his surprise when he wrote Grady Birch, but Chet Jensen was no surprise. Chet seemed to think of the local jail as his home away from home. "What about friends, girlfriends, anyone Christy was close to."

Mike shook his head. "She hadn't been working at Lone Peak Perk very long. I'm not sure she'd made any friends yet. When she came into the bar, she was always alone. I think someone said that she was driving back and forth for work from Bozeman where she was living with her mom."

"Did she always leave alone?" he asked.

With a shake of his head, the bartender said, "No." He motioned toward the names he'd given the marshal. "It was usually with one or the other of those two."

Hud thanked Mike and went outside to the car. He'd already run the plates. The vehicle was registered to Christy Shores. Bill came out and drove off, followed by Mike who hopped on his mountain bike.

Christy's older model sedan wasn't locked Hud noted as he pulled on latex gloves and tried the driver's-side door. It swung open with a groan. He looked inside. Neatness apparently wasn't one of the young woman's traits. The back seat was stuffed full of clothing and boxes. He'd been told that she was planning to move into an apartment on the second floor of Mary's building today. The front floorboard on the passenger side was knee-deep in fast-food wrappers and Lone Peak Perk go cups.

He leaned in and took a whiff, picking up the stale

scent of cigarettes and alcohol. All his instincts told him that after the apparent night Christy'd had, she would have driven home drunk rather than walk.

On impulse, he slid behind the wheel, inserted the key and turned it. There was only a click. He tried again. Same dull click. Reaching for the hood release, he pulled it and then climbed out to take a look at the engine, suspecting an old battery.

But he was in for a surprise. The battery appeared to be new. The reason the car hadn't started was because someone had purposely disabled it. He could see fresh screwdriver marks on the top of the battery.

Hud suspected that whoever had tampered with her battery was the same person who had wanted Christy to take off walking down this road late last night.

WHEN MARY WALKED across the street to the Lone Peak Perk the next morning, she was surprised to find her favorite coffee shop closed. There was a sign on the door announcing that there'd been a death.

She wondered who had died as she retraced her footsteps to climb into her pickup and head for the ranch. Cardwell Ranch was a half mile from Meadow Village on the opposite side of the Gallatin River. She always loved this drive because even though short, the landscape changed so drastically.

Mary left behind housing and business developments, traffic and noise. As she turned off Highway 191 onto the private bridge that crossed the river to the ranch the roar of the flowing river drowned out the busy resort town. Towering pines met her on the other side. She wound back into the mountains through them before the land opened again for her first glimpse that day of the ranch buildings.

Behind the huge barn and corrals, the mountains rose

all the way to Montana's Big Sky. She breathed it all in, always a little awed each time she saw it, knowing what it took to hang on to a ranch through hard times. Behind the barn and corrals were a series of small guest cabins set back against the mountainside. Her aunt Stacy lived in the larger one, the roof barely visible behind the dark green of the pines.

At the Y in the road, she turned left instead of continuing back into the mountains to where her Uncle Jordan and his wife, Liza, lived. The two-story log and stone ranch house where she'd been raised came into view moments later, the brick-red metal roof gleaming in the morning sun.

There were several vehicles parked out front, her father's patrol SUV one of them. When she pushed open the front door, she could hear the roar of voices coming from the kitchen and smiled. This had been the sound she'd come downstairs to every morning for years growing up here.

Mary knew how much her mother loved a full house. It had been hard on her when all of her children had grown up and moved out. But there were still plenty of relatives around. Mary had seven uncles and as many aunts, along with a few cousins who still lived in the area.

As she entered the kitchen, she saw that there was the usual group of family, friends and ranch hands sitting around the huge kitchen table. This morning was no exception. Her uncle Jordan signaled that it was time to get to work, giving her a peck on her cheek as he rose and headed out the door, a half dozen ranch hands following him like baby ducks.

Mary said hello to her aunt Stacy and kissed her mother on the cheek before going to the cupboard to pull down a mug and fill it with coffee. There was always a pot going at Cardwell Ranch. The kitchen had quieted down with Jordan and the ranch hands gone. Leaning against the kitchen counter, she asked, "So what's going on?" She saw her mother glance down the table at the marshal.

"Some poor young woman was run down in Meadow Village last night," Dana said, getting up from the table as the timer went off on the oven. "It was a hit and run," she added, shaking her head as if in disbelief.

Mary moved out of the way as her mother grabbed a hot pad and pulled a second batch of homemade cinnamon rolls from the oven.

"You might have known her," her mother said. "She worked at that coffee shop you like."

"Lone Peak Perk?" she asked in surprise as she took a vacated seat. "I stopped by there this morning and it was closed. There was a note on the door saying there'd been a death, but I never dreamed it was anything like that. What was the woman's name?"

"Christy Shores," her father said from the head of the large kitchen table.

"Christy." She felt sick to her stomach as she called up an image of the small fair-haired young woman. Tears filled her eyes. "Oh, no. I knew her."

"Honey, are you all right?" her mother asked.

"Christy was going to move into the apartment I had available today. She'd only been working at the coffee shop for a few weeks. I can't believe she's dead. A hit and run?" she asked her father.

He nodded and glanced at his watch. "The coroner should have something more for me by now," he said, getting to his feet.

"Do you have any idea who did it?" she asked her father.

Hud shook his head. "Not yet. Unfortunately, it happened after the bars closed, and she was apparently alone walking along the side of the road dressed in all black. It's possible that the driver didn't see her."

"But whoever hit her would have known that he or she struck something," Dana said.

"Could have thought it was a deer, and that's why the person didn't stop," Hud said. "It's possible."

"And then the driver didn't stop to see what it was? Probably drunk and didn't want to deal with the marshal," Aunt Stacy mocked. "I've heard he's a real—"

"I'd watch yourself," her father said, but smiled as he took his Stetson off the hook on the wall, kissed his wife and left.

Mary took a sip of her coffee, her hands trembling as she brought the mug to her lips. It always shocked her, death and violence. She'd never understood how her father could handle his job the way he did. While there wasn't a lot of crime in the canyon, there was always something. She remembered growing up, overhearing about murders but only occasionally. Now there'd been a hit and run. Poor Christy. She'd been so excited about renting Mary's apartment, which was so close to her work. It would save her the commute from her mother's house in Bozeman, she'd said.

As the patrol SUV left, another vehicle pulled in. "Well, I wonder who that is?" she heard her mother say as she shifted in her seat to peer out the window.

Mary did the same thing, blinking in the bright morning sun at the pickup that had pulled up in front of the house almost before the dust had settled from her father leaving.

She stared as the driver's-side door opened and Chase Steele stepped out of the vehicle.

Chapter Six

"It's Chase," Mary said as if she couldn't believe it. For weeks she had dreamed of him suddenly showing up at her door. She shot a look at her mother.

"Do you need my help?" Dana asked. "If you aren't ready to talk to him, I could tell him this isn't a good time."

She shook her head and turned back to watch Chase stretch as if it had been a long drive. He looked around for a moment, his gaze softening as he took in the ranch as though, like her, he still had special memories of the place. He appeared taller, more solid, she thought as she watched him head for the front porch. Was he remembering how it was with the two of them before he left?

"I can't imagine what he's doing here," Mary said, voicing her surprise along with her worry.

Her mother gave her a pitying look. "He's here to see you."

"But why?"

"Maybe because of the letter you sent," Dana suggested.

She couldn't believe how nervous she was. This was Chase. She'd known him since they were teens. Her heart bumped against her ribs as she heard him knock. "He could have just called."

"Maybe what he has to say needs to be said in person."

That thought scared her more than she wanted to admit. She hadn't told her mother about the call from Chase's fiancée. She'd been too embarrassed. It was enough that her aunt Stacy had told her mother about the letter she'd sent him.

"Do you want me to get that?" her mother asked when he knocked. "Or maybe you would like to answer it and let him tell you why he's here."

Another knock at the door finally made her move. Mind racing, she hurried to the door. Chase. After all this time. She had no idea what she was going to say. Worse, what *he* would say.

As she opened the door, she glanced past him to his pickup. At least he was alone. He hadn't brought the woman who'd called her, his fiancée who could by now be his wife.

"Mary."

The sound of his voice made her shift her gaze back to the handsome cowboy standing in her doorway. Her heart did a roller-coaster loop in her chest, taking all her air with it. He'd only gotten more handsome. The sleeves on the Western shirt he wore were rolled up to expose muscled tanned arms. The shirt stretched over his broad shoulders. He looked as solid as one of the large pines that stood sentinel on the mountainside overlooking the ranch.

He was staring at her as well. He seemed to catch himself and quickly removed his Stetson and smiled. "Gosh dang, you look good."

She couldn't help but smile. He'd picked up the expression "gosh dang" from her father after Hud had caught Chase cussing a blue streak at fifteen out by their barn. The words went straight to her heart, but when she opened her mouth, she said, "What are you doing here?"

"I had to see you." He glanced past her. "I'm sorry it took me so long. My pickup broke down and… Could we talk?"

She was still standing in the doorway. She thought of her mother in the next room. "Why don't we walk down to the creek?"

"Sure," he said, and stepped back to let her lead the way.

Neither of them spoke until they reached the edge of the creek. Mary stopped in the shade of the pines. Sunlight fingered warmth through the boughs, making the rippling clear water sparkle. She breathed in the sweet familiar scents, and felt as if she needed to pinch herself. Chase.

She was struck with how different Chase looked. Stubble darkened his chiseled jawline. He was definitely taller, broader across the shoulders. There were faint lines around his blue eyes as he squinted toward the house before settling his gaze on her.

She felt heat rush to her center. The cowboy standing in front of her set off all kinds of desires with only a look. And yet after all this time, did she know this man? He'd come back. But that didn't mean that he'd come back to *her*.

"I got your letter," he said as he took off his Stetson to turn the brim nervously in his fingers.

"You didn't call or write back," she said, wondering when he was going to get to the news about the fiancée.

His gaze locked with hers. "I'm sorry but what I wanted to say, I couldn't say over the phone let alone in a letter."

Her heart pounded as she thought, *Here it comes.*

There was pain in his gaze. "I've missed you so much. I know you never understood why I had to leave. I'm not sure I understood it myself. I had to go. Just as I had to come back. I'm so sorry I hurt you." His blue-eyed gaze locked with hers. "I love you. I never stopped loving you."

She stared at him. Wasn't this exactly what she'd dreamed of him saying to her before she'd gotten the call from his fiancée? Except in the dream she would have been in his arms by now.

"What about your fiancée, Chase?"

"*Fiancée?* What would make you think—"

"She called me after I sent the letter."

He stared at her for a moment before swearing under his breath. "You talked to a woman who said she was my fiancée?"

She nodded and crossed her arms protectively across her chest, her heart pounding like a drum beneath her ribs. "Wasn't she?"

He shook his head. "Look, I was never engaged, far from it. But there was this woman." He saw her expression. "It wasn't what you think."

"I think you were involved with her."

He closed his eyes and groaned again. When he opened them, he settled those blue eyes on her. "It was one night after a party at my boss's place. It was a barbecue that I didn't even want to go to and wish I hadn't. I'd had too much to drink." He shook his head. "After that she would break into my apartment and leave me presents, go through my things, ambush me when I came home. She found your letter, but I never dreamed that she'd call you." He raked a hand through his hair and looked down. "I'm so sorry. Fiona was…delusional. She was like this with anyone who showed her any attention, but I didn't know that. I told her that night I was in love with someone else." His gaze came up to meet hers. "You. But I didn't come here to talk about her."

Fiona? Of course he had dated while he was gone. So why did hearing him say the woman's name feel as if he'd ripped out another piece of her heart? She felt sick to her stomach. "Why *did* you come here?"

"That's what I've been trying to tell you. I hated the way we left things too," Chase said. "Mary, I love you. That's why I came back. Tell me that you'll give us another chance."

"Excuse me."

They both turned to see a man silhouetted against the skyline behind them. Mary blinked as she recognized the form. "Dillon?"

Chase's gaze sharpened. "Dillon?" he asked under his breath.

"What are you doing here?" she asked, and then realized that she'd agreed to a lunch date she'd completely forgotten about because of Chase's surprising return.

"Lunch. I know I'm early, but I thought we'd go on a hike and then have lunch at one of the cafés up at the mountain resort," he said as he came partway down the slope to the creek and into the shelter of the pines. "More fun than eating at a restaurant in the village." He shrugged. "When your pickup wasn't at your office, I figured you'd be here." Dillon's gaze narrowed. "Why do I feel like I'm interrupting something?"

"Because you are," Chase said, and looked to Mary. "A friend of yours?"

"Mary and I are dating," Dillon said before she could speak. "I'm Deputy Dillon Ramsey."

"The deputy, huh," Chase said, clearly unimpressed.

Dillon seemed to grind his teeth for a moment before saying, "And you are…"

"Chase Steele, Mary's…" His gaze shifted to her.

"Chase and I grew up together here in the canyon,"

she said quickly as she saw the two posturing as if this might end with them exchanging blows before thrashing in the mud next to the creek as they tried to kill each other. "I didn't know Chase was…in town."

"Passing through?" Dillon asked pointedly.

Chase grinned. "Sorry, but I'm here to stay. I'm not going anywhere." He said that last part to her.

His blue eyes held hers, making her squirm for no reason she could think of, which annoyed her. It wasn't like she was caught cheating on him. Far from it since he had apparently recently dated someone named Fiona.

"If you're through here," Dillon said to her, "we should get going before it gets too hot."

"Don't let me stop you," Chase said, his penetrating gaze on her. "But we aren't finished."

"You are now," Dillon said, reaching for Mary's hand as if to pull her back up the slope away from the creek.

Chase stepped between them. "Don't go grabbing her like you're going to drag her away. If she wants to go with you, she can go under her own steam."

Dillon took a step toward Chase. "Stop," Mary cried, sure that the two were going to get physical at any moment. She looked at Chase, still shocked by his return as well as his declaration of love. "I'll talk to you later."

He smiled again then, the smile that she'd fallen in love with at a very young age. "Count on it." He stepped back and tipped his Stetson to her, then to Dillon. "I'll be around." In a few long-legged strides, he climbed the slope away from the creek.

"You coming?" Dillon asked, sounding irritated.

She sighed and started up the slope away from the creek. As they topped the hill, she saw Chase had gone to the house and was now visiting with her mother on the front porch. She could hear laughter and felt Dillon's angry reaction to Chase and her mother appearing so friendly.

He seemed to be gritting his teeth as he asked, "What's his story, anyway? He's obviously more than a friend," Dillon said as he opened the passenger-side door of his pickup and glared in Chase and Dana's direction.

"I told you, we grew up together," she said as she slid in and he slammed the door.

Dillon joined her. He seemed out of breath. For a moment he just sat there before he turned toward her. "You were lovers." It wasn't a question.

"We were high school and college sweethearts," she said.

"He's still in love with you." He was looking at Chase and her mother on the porch.

She groaned inwardly and said nothing. Of course with Chase showing up it was only a matter of time before he and Dillon crossed paths in a place as small as Big Sky. But why today of all days?

"He acts like he owns you." Dillon still hadn't reached to start the truck. Nor did he look at her. "Did he think he could come back and take up where the two of you left off?"

She'd thought the same thing, but she found herself wanting to defend Chase. "We have a history—"

He swung his head toward her, his eyes narrow and hard. "Are you getting back together?"

For a moment she was too taken aback to speak. "I didn't even know he was back in town until a few minutes ago. I was as surprised as you were, but I don't like your tone. What I decide to do is really none of your business." Out of the corner of her eye, she saw Chase hug her mother, then head for his pickup.

"Is that right?" Dillon demanded. "Good to know where I stand."

"You know, I'm no longer in the mood for a hike or lunch," she said, and reached for the door handle as Chase headed out of the ranch.

Dillon grabbed her arm, his fingers biting into her tender flesh. "He comes back and you dump me?"

"Let go of me." She said it quietly, but firmly.

He quickly released her. "Sorry. I hope I didn't— It's just that I thought you and I… And then seeing him and hearing him tell you that he was still in love with you." He shook his head, the look on his face making her weaken.

"Look, I told you. It came as a shock for me too," she said. "I don't know what I'm going to do. I'm sorry if you feel—"

"Like I was just a stand-in until your old boyfriend got back?"

"That isn't what you were."

"No?" His voice softened. "Good, because I'm not ready to turn you over to him." As he said the words, he trailed his fingers from her bare shoulder slowly down to her wrist. Her skin rippled with goose bumps and she shivered. "I still want to see that penthouse view. Can I call you later?"

She felt confused. But she knew that she wasn't in any frame of mind to make a decision about Dillon right now. She felt herself nod. "We'll talk then," she said, and climbed out of the pickup, closing the door behind her. Still rattled by everything that had happened, she stood watching him drive away, as tears burned her eyes. Chase had come back. Chase still loved her.

But there was the threatening woman who'd called her saying she was his fiancée. Fiona. And no doubt others.

And there was Dillon. Chase had no right to come back here and make any demands on her. He'd let her go for weeks without a word after he'd gotten the letter.

Chase and Dillon had immediately disliked each other, which Mary knew shouldn't have surprised her. Dillon's reaction threw her the most. Did he really have feelings for her? She felt as if it was too early. They barely knew each other. Was it just a male thing?

Still, it worried her. The two men were bound to run into each other again. Next time she might not be around to keep them from trying to kill each other.

CHASE MENTALLY KICKED HIMSELF. He should have called, should have written. But even as he thought it, he knew he'd had to do this in person. If it hadn't been for Fiona and her dirty tricks… He shook his head. He was to blame for that too and he knew it.

Well, he was here now and damned if he was going to let some deputy steal the woman he loved, had always loved.

He let out a long breath as he drove toward the ranch where he would be working until he started his carpenter job. All the way to Montana he'd been so sure that by now he'd be holding Mary in his arms.

He should have known better. He'd hurt her. Had he really thought she'd still be waiting around for him? He thought of all the things he'd planned to tell her—before that deputy had interrupted them.

Assuring himself that he'd get another chance and soon, he smiled to himself. Mary was even more beautiful than she'd been when he left. But now there was a confidence about her. She'd come into her own. He felt a swell of pride. He'd never doubted that the woman could do anything she set her mind to.

Now all he had to do was convince her that this cowboy was worth giving a second chance.

HUD READ THROUGH the coroner's report a second time, then set it aside. Prints were still being lifted from Christy Shore's car, but the area around the battery where someone had disabled the engine had been wiped clean. Fibers had been found from what appeared to be a paper towel on the battery.

There was no doubt in his mind that Christy's death had been premeditated. Someone had tampered with her battery, needing her to walk home that night so she could be run down. Which meant that the killer must have been waiting outside the bar. Just her luck that she had stayed so late that there was no one around to give her a ride somewhere.

The killer wanted him to believe the hit and run had been an accident. He'd already heard rumors that she'd been hit by a motor home of some tourist passing through. He knew better. This was a homicide, and he'd bet his tin star that the killer was local and not just passing through.

Picking up his notebook, he shoved back his chair and stood. It was time to talk to the two men who'd fought over Christy earlier in the night. Only one name had surprised him—Grady Birch, Deputy Dillon Ramsey's friend—because the name had just come up in his cattle rustling investigation.

He decided to start with Grady, pay him a surprise visit, see how that went before he talked to the other man, Chet Jensen, the son of a neighboring rancher who'd been in trouble most of his life.

But when he reached the rented cabin outside Gallatin Gateway, Grady was nowhere around. Hud glanced in the windows but it was hard to tell if the man had skipped town or not.

MARY JOINED HER mother in a rocking chair on the front porch after Chase and Dillon had left. Dana had joked about feeling old lately, and had said maybe she was ready for a rocking chair. Mary had laughed.

But as she sat down in a chair next to her, she felt as if it was the first time she'd looked at her mother in a very long time. Dana had aged. She had wrinkles around her eyes and mouth, her hair was now more salt than pepper and there was a tiredness she'd seldom seen in her mother's bearing.

"Are you all right?" her mother asked her, stealing the exact words Mary had been about to say to her. Dana perked up a little when she smiled and reached over to take her daughter's hand.

"I saw you visiting with Chase," Mary said.

Her mother nodded. "It was good to see him. He left you his phone number." With her free hand she reached into her pocket and brought out a folded piece of notepaper and gave it to her.

She glanced at the number written on it below Chase's name. Seeing that there was nothing else, she tucked it into her pocket. "What did he tell you?"

"We only talked about the ranch, how much the town has grown, just that sort of thing."

"He says he came back because he loves me, never stopped loving me. But I never told you this…" She hesitated. There was little she kept from her mother. "I got a call from a woman who claimed to be his fiancée. She warned me about contacting him again."

Dana's eyes widened. "This woman threatened you?"

"Chase says it was a delusional woman he made the mistake of spending one night with. Fiona." Even saying the name hurt.

"I see. Well, now you know the truth."

Did she? "I haven't forgotten why we broke up." She'd caught Chase kissing Beth Anne Jensen. He'd sworn it was the first and only time, and that he hadn't initiated it. That he'd been caught off guard. She'd known Beth Anne had had a crush on Chase for years.

But instinctively she'd also known that her parents were right. She and Chase had been too young to be as serious as they'd been, especially since they'd never dated anyone else but each other. "You try to lasso him and tie him down now, and you'll regret it," her father had said. "If this love of yours is real, he'll come back."

She'd heard her parents love story since she was a child. Her father had left and broken her mother's heart. He'd come back though and won her heart all over again. "But what if he isn't you, Dad? What if he doesn't come back?"

"Then it wasn't meant to be, sweetheart, and there is nothing you can do about that."

"Will you call him?" her mother asked now.

"I feel like I need a little space without seeing either Dillon or Chase," she said. "I still love Chase, but I'm not sure I still know him."

"It might take some time."

"I guess we'll see if he sticks around long enough to find out." She pushed to her feet. "I need to get to my office."

"I'm glad he came back," her mother said. "I always liked Chase."

Mary smiled. "Me too."

But as she drove back to her office, she knew she wouldn't be able to work, not with everything on her mind. As she pulled into her parking spot next to her building, she changed her mind and left again to drive up into the mountains. She parked at the trailhead for one of her favorite trails and got out. Maybe she'd take a walk.

Hours later, ending up high on a mountain where she could see both the Gallatin Canyon and Madison Valley on the other side, she had to smile. She was tired, sweaty and dusty, and it was the best she'd felt all day.

The hike had cleared her mind some. She turned back toward the trailhead as the sun dipped low, ignoring calls on her cell phone from both men.

DOWN THE STREET from Mary's building, Lucy studied herself in the rearview mirror of her SUV, surprised that she now actually thought of herself as Lucy. It was her new look and her ability to become someone else. It had started in junior high when she'd been asked to audition for a part in a play.

She'd only done it for extra credit since she'd been failing science. Once she'd read the part though, she'd felt herself become that character, taking on the role, complete with the accent. She'd been good, so good that she'd hardly had to try out in high school to get the leading roles.

Now as she waited, she felt antsy. Mary had come home and then left again without even getting out of her car. Lucy had been so sure that Chase would have made it to Montana by now. Waiting for him, she'd had too much time to think. What if she was wrong? What if he hadn't been hightailing it back here to his sweet little cowgirl?

What if he'd left Arizona, then changed his mind, realizing that what he had with her was more powerful than some old feelings for Mary Cardwell Savage? What if he'd gone back for her only to find out that she'd drowned and that everyone was waiting for some poor soul to find her body along the edge of the river downstream?

The thought made her heart pound. Until she remembered what she'd done to his pickup engine. Who knew where he'd broken down and how long it would take for him to get the engine fixed. If it was fixable.

No, he'd made it clear that he didn't want her. Which meant he would show up here in Big Sky. She just had to be patient and not do anything stupid.

She'd realized that she should approach this the same way she'd gone after prospective buyers in real estate. The first step was to find out what she was up against. Lucy smiled. She would get to know her enemy. She would find her weakness. She already had a plan to gain Mary's trust.

Not that she was getting overconfident. Just as important was anticipating any problems—including getting caught. With each step toward her goal, she needed to consider every contingency.

Some precautions were just common sense. She'd purchased a burner phone. She hadn't told anyone she'd known that she was alive, not even Patty. She hadn't left a paper trail. Taking all her money out of the bank before what the authorities thought was an attempted suicide had been brilliant. Just as was wearing gloves when she tampered with Christy Shores' battery.

It had been pure hell living with three older stepbrothers. But they'd taught her a lot about cars, getting even and never leaving any evidence behind. She'd used everything they'd taught her the night she burned down her stepfather's house—with her stepfather, mother and stepbrothers inside.

But sometimes she got overzealous. Maybe she'd gone too far when she'd put the bleach into Chase's engine oil. She'd considered loosening the nuts on his tires, but she hadn't wanted him to die. *Not yet.* And definitely not where she wouldn't be there.

But what if he couldn't make it to Montana now? Shouldn't he have been here by now? If he was coming. She was beginning to worry a little when she saw him. As if she'd conjured him up, he drove past where she was parked to stop in front of Mary's building. Lucy watched him park and jump out. Her heart began to pound as he strode purposely toward Mary's building to knock on the door.

Her stomach curdled as she watched him try to see into the windows before he stepped back to stare up at the top floor. "Sorry, your little cowgirl isn't home," she said under her breath. There were no lights on nor was Mary's pickup where she always parked it. But it was clear that Chase was looking for her. What would he do when he found her? Profess his undying love? As jealousy's sharp teeth took a bite out of her, she was tempted to end this now.

She'd picked up a weapon at a gun show on her way to Big Sky. All she had to do was reach under her seat, take out the loaded handgun, get out and walk over to him. He wouldn't recognize her. Not at first.

He would though when she showed him the gun she would have had hidden behind her back. "This is just a little something from Fiona." She smiled as she imagined the bullet sinking into his black heart.

But what fun would that be? Her plan was to make him suffer. The best way to do that was through his precious Mary. She'd promised herself she wouldn't deviate from the plan. No more acting on impulse. This time, she wouldn't make the same mistakes she'd made in the past.

As she watched Chase climb back into his pickup and drive away, she was trembling with anticipation at just the thought of what she had in store for the cowboy and his cowgirl.

Chapter Seven

The next morning, Mary saw that Lone Peak Perk was open again. Just the thought of one of her ultimate caramel frappaccinos made her realize it was exactly what she needed right now.

Stepping through the door, she breathed in the rich scent of coffee and felt at home. The thought made her smile. She would be in a fog all day if she didn't have her coffee and after the restless night she'd had...

As she moved to the counter, she saw that there was a new young woman working. Had they already replaced Christy? The woman's dark hair was styled in a pixie cut that seemed to accent her dark eyes. She wore a temporary name tag that had LUCY printed neatly on it.

"So what can I get you?" Lucy asked with a slight lisp and a Southern accent as she flashed Mary a wide gap-toothed smile.

"One of your ultimate caramel frappaccinos to go."

The young woman laughed. "That one's my favorite."

"I was so sorry to hear about Christy," Mary said.

"I didn't really know her." Lucy stopped what she was doing for a moment to look over her shoulder at her. "I was shocked when I realized that Christy was the one who took my application. She was nice. I couldn't believe it when I got the call. I hate that her bad luck led to my good luck. My application was on the top of the pile."

"What brought you to Big Sky?" Mary asked, seeing that she'd made the young woman uncomfortable.

"Wanderlust. I had a job waiting for me in Spokane, but I found exactly what I was looking for right here in Big Sky, Montana. Is this the most beautiful place you've ever seen?"

Mary had to smile. "I've always thought so. Where are you from? I detect an accent."

Lucy laughed. "Texas. I can't seem to overcome my roots."

"I'd keep it if I were you."

"You think?" the woman asked as she set down the go cup on the counter in front of her.

Mary nodded. "I do. I hope you enjoy it here."

"Thanks. I know I will."

CHASE WAS RELIEVED when he got the call from Mary. He'd had a lot of time to think, and he didn't want to spend any more time away from her. He'd gone over to her place last night in the hopes that they could talk. But she hadn't been home. Was she out with the deputy? The thought made him crazy.

But he had only himself to blame. He'd broken her heart when he'd left Montana. Even now though, he knew that he'd had to go. He was definitely too young for marriage back then.

But he'd grown up in the years he'd been gone. He'd learned a trade he loved. He'd seen some of the world. He wasn't the kid Mary used to hang out with. He'd known for some time what he wanted. It wasn't until he'd gotten her letter that he'd realized there was still hope. He'd been afraid that Mary had moved on a long time ago. But like him, she hadn't found anyone who tempted her into a relationship. That was until the deputy came along.

"I'm sorry about the other day, surprising you like that. You were right. I should have called."

"That's behind us," she said in a tone that let him know there was a lot more than a simple phone call to be overcome between them. He'd hurt her. Had he really thought she'd forgive him that quickly? "Just understand, I wrote that letter to tell you about the package that came for you. The rest of it was just me caught in a weak moment."

"I didn't think you had weak moments," he joked.

"Chase—"

"All I'm asking is for a chance to prove myself to you." Silence. "There's something I didn't tell you. My mother contacted me. She'd been sick off and on for years, in and out of remission. This time she was dying and wanted to see me. That's why I went to Arizona. She recently died."

"Oh, Chase, I'm so sorry. I hadn't heard."

"She asked me to bring her ashes back here. To Big Sky." He could almost hear Mary's hesitation.

"Did she…?"

"Tell me who my father was? No. I was with her the night she died. She took it to her grave."

"I'm so sorry." Mary knew how not knowing had haunted him his whole life. It was a mystery, one that had weighed him down. He wanted to know who he was, who he came from, why his mother refused to tell him. Was his father that bad? He'd known there was much more to the story, and it was a story he needed to hear.

"She did tell me one thing. She'd met the man who fathered me here in Big Sky. It's why she wanted her ashes brought back here."

"But that's all you know."

"For now. Listen—"

"I called about the package," Mary said quickly. "If your mother met your father here, well that would explain why a woman saying she was once your mother's friend left you the package. If you'd like to stop by my office to pick it up—"

"I can't come by before tomorrow. I'm working on the Jensen Ranch to earn some extra money. I had pickup trouble on the way back to town. But I was hoping we could go out—"

"I need time. Also I'm really busy."

"Is this about that deputy?" he asked, then mentally kicked himself.

"I'm not seeing Dillon right now either, not that it is any of your business. You don't get to just come back and—"

"Whoa, you're right. Sorry. I'll back off. Just know that I'm here and that I'm not going anywhere. I want you back, Mary. I've never stopped loving you and never will."

As if Mary could forget that Chase was back in town. After the phone call, she threw herself into her work, determined not to think about the handsome cowboy who'd stolen her heart years ago. Dillon kept leaving her messages. She texted him that she had a lot of work to do, and would get back to him in a day or two.

That night, she lay in bed, thinking about Chase, her heart aching. He'd hurt her, and angry, she'd broken up with him only to have him leave. She'd lost her friend and her lover. After all the years they'd spent growing up together, Mary had always thought nothing could keep them apart. She'd been wrong, and now she was terrified that she'd never really known Chase.

In the morning, she went down to work early, thankful

for work to keep her mind off Chase even a little. Mid-morning she looked up to see the new barista from the Lone Peak Perk standing in her doorway.

"Don't shoot me," Lucy said. "I just had a feeling you might need this." She held out the ultimate caramel frappaccino.

Mary could have hugged her. "You must be a mind reader," she said as she rose from her desk to take the container of coffee from her. "I got so busy, I actually forgot. I had no idea it was so late. I can't tell you how much I need this."

"I don't want to interrupt. I can see that you're busy," Lucy said, taking a step toward the door. "But when I realized you hadn't been in…"

"Just a minute, let me pay you."

Lucy waved her off. "My treat. My good deed for the day." She smiled her gap-toothed smile and pushed out the door.

"Thank you so much!" Mary called after her, smiling as she watched the young woman run back across the street to the coffee shop.

HUD FOUND CHET JENSEN in the barn at his father's place just down the canyon a few miles. The tall skinny cowboy was shoveling manure from the stalls. He heard him gag, and suspected the man was hungover even before he saw his face.

"Rough night?" he asked, startling the cowboy.

Chet jumped, looking sicker from the scare. "You can't just walk up on someone like that," he snapped.

"I need to talk to you," Hud said. "About Christy Shores."

"I figured." Chet leaned his pitchfork against the side

of the stall. "I could use some fresh air." With that he stumbled out of the barn and into the morning sunshine.

Hud followed him to a spot behind the ranch house where a half dozen lawn chairs sat around a firepit. Chet dropped into one of the chairs. Hud took one opposite him, and pulled out his notebook and pen.

"You heard about the fight."

He nodded. "What was that about?"

"Christy." Chet scowled across at him. "You wouldn't be here unless you already knew that. Let's cut to the chase. I had nothing to do with her getting run over."

"Who did?"

He shrugged. "Not a clue. Beth Anne heard that a motor-home driver must have clipped her."

Hud shook his head. "I'm guessing it was someone local with a grudge. How long have you been involved with her?"

"It wasn't like that. I brought her back here a couple of times after we met a few weeks ago. I liked her."

"But?"

"But she liked Grady who was always throwing his money around, playing the big shot. I tried to warn her about him." He shook his head, then leaned over to take it in his hands.

"Are you saying you think Grady Birch might be responsible?"

"Beats me." Lifting his head, he said, "After we got thrown out of Charley's, I came home and went to bed."

"Did you see Grady leave?"

He nodded. "That doesn't mean he didn't come back."

"The same could be said about you."

Chet wagged his head. "Beth Anne was home. My sister knows I didn't leave. She was up until dawn making cookies for some special event she's throwing down at the flower shop. I couldn't have left without her seeing me."

"Christy have any enemies that you knew about?" he asked.

"I didn't think she'd been in town long enough to make enemies."

"But she'd been in town long enough to have the two of you fighting over her," he pointed out.

Chet met his gaze. "Grady and I would have been fighting over any woman we both thought the other wanted. It wasn't really even about her, you know what I mean?"

He did, he thought as he closed his notebook and got to his feet. "If you think of anyone who might have wanted her dead, call me."

Chapter Eight

Mary was just starting across the street the next morning to get her coffee when the delivery van from the local flower shop pulled up in front of her building. It had been three days since she'd seen Chase. Both men had finally gotten the message and given her space. Not that the space had helped much except that she'd gotten a lot of work done.

She groaned as she saw Beth Anne Jensen climb out of the flower shop van. "I have something for you," the buxom blonde called cheerily.

Mary couldn't remember the last time anyone had sent her flowers. Reluctantly, she went back across the street since she could already taste her ultimate caramel frappaccino. Also, the last person she wanted to see this morning was Beth Anne. The blonde had her head stuck in the back of the van as she approached.

As her former classmate came out, she shoved cellophone wrapped vase with a red rose in it at her. "I'm sure you've already heard. Chase is back."

"I know. He came by the ranch a couple of days ago." That took some of the glee out of Beth Anne's expression.

"He's gone to work for my daddy."

Mary tried not to groan at the old news or the woman's use of "daddy" at her age. Of course, Chase had gone to work for Sherman Jensen. The Jensen Ranch was just down the road from the Cardwell spread. No wonder Chase had said he would be seeing her soon. The Jensens would be rounding up their cattle from summer range— just like everyone on Cardwell Ranch.

"Chase looks like being gone didn't hurt him none," the blonde said.

She didn't want to talk about Chase with this woman. She hadn't forgotten catching Chase and Beth Anne lip-locked before he left. Mary didn't know if she was supposed to tip the owner of the flower store or not. But if it would get Beth Anne to leave... She pulled out a five and shoved it at her. "Thanks," she said, and started to turn away.

"That's not all," the blonde said as she pocketed the five and handed her a wrapped bouquet of daisies in a white vase. "Appears you've got more than one admirer." Beth Anne raised a brow.

Mary assumed that the woman knew who had sent both sets of flowers—and had probably read the notes inside the small envelopes attached to each. But then again seeing the distinct handwriting of two men on the outside of the envelopes, maybe Beth Anne was as in the dark as Mary herself. The thought improved her day.

"Have a nice day," she sang out to Beth Anne as she headed for her office. Opening the door, she took the flowers inside, anxious to see whom they were from. She didn't want to get her hopes up. They both could be from one of the ranchers she worked for as a thank-you for the work she'd done for them.

She set down the vases on the edge of her desk and pulled out the first small envelope. Opening it, she read: "I know how you like daisies. I'm not giving up on us. Chase."

It would take more than daisies, she told herself even as her heart did a little bump against her ribs.

Shaking her head, she pulled out the other small white envelope, opened it and read: "Just wanted you to know I'm thinking of you, Dillon."

"I don't believe this," she said, and heard the front door of her building opening behind her. Spinning around, she half expected to see one or both of the men.

"Lucy," she said on a relieved breath. As touched as she was by the flowers, she wasn't up to seeing either man right now.

"Did I catch you at a bad time?" the barista asked, stopping short.

"Not at all. Your timing is perfect."

"I saw you start across the street to get your coffee and then get called back, so I thought I'd run it over to you. Your usual." She held out the cup.

"Thank you so much. I do need this, but I insist on paying you." Mary looked around for her purse. "Let me get you—"

"I put it on your account."

She stopped digging for money to look at her. "Lucy, I don't have an account."

The woman smiled that gap-toothed smile of hers that was rather infectious. "You do now. I just thought it would be easier but if I've overstepped—"

"I don't know why I hadn't thought of it, as many of these as I drink," Mary said, and raised the cup.

"I hope you don't mind. But this way, if you get too busy, just call and if we aren't busy, one of us can bring your coffee right over."

"Lucy, that's so thoughtful, but—"

"It really isn't an inconvenience. We haven't been that busy and I could use the exercise. Also it looks like you're celebrating something." She motioned to the flower delivery.

Mary laughed. "It's a long story."

"Well, I won't keep you. I better get back. It wasn't busy but it could be any minute. My shift ends soon, and I have to get back on my search for a place to live." She started to open the front door to leave.

"Lucy, wait. I have an apartment open. I haven't put up a notice that it's available. Christy was going to move in."

"The girl who died." She grimaced. "The one I replaced at Lone Peak Perk."

"Is that too weird for you?" Mary asked.

"Let me give it some thought. But could you hold on to it until later today? Thanks." And she was gone.

Mary sipped her coffee, thinking she probably shouldn't have offered the apartment without checking the young woman's references. But it was Lucy, who'd just bought her a coffee and run it across the street to her.

She turned to look at her flowers, forgetting for the moment about anything else. What was she going to do about Chase? And Dillon?

Sitting down at her desk, she picked up her phone and called her best friend, Kara, who had moved to New York after college. But they'd managed to stay in touch by phone and Facetime. It was the kind of friendship that they could go without talking for weeks and pick up right where they'd left off.

"Chase is back," she said when her friend answered.

"In Big Sky?"

"He says he loves me and that he won't give up."

Kara took a breath and let it out slowly. "How do you feel about that?"

She sighed. "I still love him, but I've been seeing someone else. A deputy here. His name is Dillon. He's really good-looking in a kind of nothing-but-trouble kind of way."

Her friend was laughing. "When it rains it pours. Seriously? You have two handsome men who are crazy about you?"

She had to laugh. "Crazy might be the perfect word. They met the other day and sparks flew. I still love Chase, but when we broke up he didn't stay and fight for me. He just left. What's to keep him from doing it again?"

"And Dillon?"

"It's too new to say. They both sent me flowers today though."

"That's a good start," Kara said with a laugh.

"Chase sent daisies because he knows I love them."

"And Dillon?"

"A rose to let me know he was thinking about me."

"Mary! Who says you have to choose between them?"

"My father doesn't like me dating either one of them."

"Which makes you want to date them even more, knowing you."

"You *do* know me," she said, and laughed again. "How are you and your adorable husband and the kids?"

"I was going to call you. I'm pregnant again!"

"Congrats," she said, and meant it. Kara was made to be a mother.

"I have morning sickness, and I'm already starting to waddle."

Mary felt a stab of envy and said as much.

"Excuse me? If anyone is envious, it's me of you. You should see me right now. Sweats and a T-shirt with a vomit stain on it—my daughter's not mine."

She laughed. "And I'll bet you look beautiful as always."

A shriek and then loud crying could be heard in the background.

"I'll let you go," Mary said. "Congrats again."

"Same to you."

She sat for a moment, idly finishing her coffee and considering her flowers before going back to work. A while later, she picked up her phone and called Chase. "Thank you for the daisies. They're beautiful. If you have some time, I thought maybe you could stop by if you're free. Like I said, I have your package here at the office. I can tell you how to find the place."

Chase chuckled. "I know how to find you. I'll be right there."

LUCY LOOKED OUT the window of the coffee shop and with a start saw Chase's truck pull up across the street. Her heart squeezed as if crushed in a large fist. Had he seen Mary before this? Had they been meeting at night on the ranch? Jealousy made her stomach roil.

Chase had been hers. At least he had until Mary wrote him that letter. She was why he'd dumped her. To come back here to his precious cowgirl. She wasn't sure at that moment whom she hated more, him or Mary, as she watched him disappear into her office.

"Excuse me?" A woman stepped in front of her, blocking her view. It was all she could do not to reach across the counter and shove her out of the way. She wanted to see what was going on across the street. "I'd like to order."

Fortunately, she got control of herself. She needed this job to get closer to Mary and pull off her plan. If she hoped to pay back Chase, she couldn't lose her cool. She plastered a smile on her face.

"I'm sorry, what can I get you?" She hadn't even realized that her Texas accent had come back until that day when she'd finally met Mary Cardwell Savage. She'd thought she'd put Texas and her childhood behind her. But apparently all of this had brought it back—along with her accent.

As she made the woman a latte, she thought about spitting in her cup, but didn't. Instead, she let herself think about the apartment in Mary's building. Of course she was going to take it. She had already gained the woman's trust. It didn't matter that Chase was over there with Mary. Soon enough she would end their little romance.

She would just have to be careful to avoid Chase. The changes in her appearance were striking, but given what they'd shared, he would know her. He would sense her beneath her disguise. He'd feel the chemistry between them. So she needed to avoid him until she was ready to make her dramatic reveal.

Smiling to herself, she considered all the ways she could make their lives miserable, before she took care of both of them. As she'd told Christy Shores, she was lucky when it came to getting what she wanted. Hadn't she gotten this job and was about to get Christy's apartment, as well?

She wanted Chase and his precious Mary to suffer. She just had to be patient.

CHASE REMOVED HIS Stetson as he stepped into Mary's office. He couldn't help but admire the building and what she'd done with it. Hardwood floors shone beneath a large warm-colored rug. The walls were recycled brick, terra-cotta in color, with paintings and photographs of the area on the walls.

"Your office is beautiful," he said. "This place suits you."

Mary smiled at the compliment, but clearly she hadn't thawed much when it came to him.

"I heard you have a couple of apartments upstairs that you rent and live on the third floor," he said. "Wise investment."

That made her chuckle. "Thank you. I'm glad you approve."

"Mary, can we please stop this?" He took a step toward her, hating this impersonal wall between them. They knew each other. Intimately. They'd once been best friends—let alone lovers.

"Thank you again for the daisies." She picked up a package from her desk and held it out to him, blocking his advance. "This is what was dropped off for you."

He chewed at the side of his cheek, his gaze on her not on the package. "Okay, if this is the way you want it. I'll wait as long as it takes." He could see that she didn't believe that. She'd lost faith in him and he couldn't blame her. For a while, he'd lost faith in himself.

"So you're working for Beth Anne's father at their ranch."

So that was it. "It's temporary. I have a job as a finish carpenter for a company that builds houses like the upscale ones here in Big Sky. It's a good job, but since it doesn't start for a week, I took what I could get in the meantime." He didn't mention that buying a new engine for his pickup had set him back some.

His gaze went to the daisies he'd had sent to her, but quickly shifted to the vase with the rose in it. "Is that from your deputy?"

MARY RAISED HER CHIN. "Don't start, Chase." She was still holding the package out to him.

He took it without even bothering to look at it. He was so close now that she could smell his masculine scent mixed with the outdoors. "I can be patient, Mary," he said, his voice low, seductive. "Remember when we couldn't keep our hands off each other?" He took another step toward her, his voice dropping even more dangerously low. "I remember the taste of you, the feel of you, the way your breath quickens when you're naked in my arms and—"

His words sent an arrow of heat to her center. "Chase—"

He closed the distance, but she didn't step back as if under the cowboy's spell. With his free hand, he ran his fingertips leisurely down her cheek to the hollow of her throat toward the V of her blouse.

She shivered and instinctively she leaned her head back, remembering his lips making that same journey. Her nipples puckered, hard and aching against her bra. "Chase—" This time, she said his name more like a plea for him not to stop.

As he pulled his hand back, he smiled. "You and I will be together again come hell or high water because that's where we belong. Tell me I'm wrong."

When she said nothing, couldn't speak, he nodded, took the package and walked out, leaving her trembling with a need for him that seemed to have grown even more potent.

Chapter Nine

Chase still hadn't paid any attention to the package Mary had given him until he tossed it on the seat of his pickup. The lightweight contents made a soft rustling sound, drawing his attention from thoughts of Mary for a moment.

As he climbed behind the wheel of his pickup, he considered what might be inside. It appeared to be an old shoebox that had been tied up with string. Both the box and the string were discolored, giving the impression of age. Why would someone leave him this? Mary had said the woman claimed to be a friend of his mother's.

His thoughts quickly returned to Mary as he drove back to the Jensen Ranch. He remembered the way she'd trembled under his touch. The chemistry was still there between them, stronger than ever. He'd wanted desperately to take her in his arms, to kiss her, to make love to her. If only she could remember how good they were together.

At the ranch, he took the shoebox inside the bunkhouse, where he was staying, tossing it on his bed. He told himself that he didn't care what was inside. But he couldn't help being curious. He sat down on the edge of the bed and drew the box toward him. It wasn't until then that he saw the faded lettering on the top and recognized his mother's handwriting.

For Chase. Only after I'm gone.

His heart thumped hard against his ribs. This was from his mother?

He dug out his pocketknife from his jeans pocket and with trembling fingers cut the string. He hesitated, bracing himself for what he would find inside, and lifted the lid. A musty scent rose up as the papers inside rustled softly.

Chase wasn't sure what he'd expected. Old photos? Maybe his real birth certificate with his father's name on it? A letter to him telling him the things his mother couldn't or wouldn't while she was alive?

What he saw confused him. It appeared to be pages torn from a notebook. Most were yellowed and curled. His mother's handwriting was overly loopy, youthful. Nothing like her usual very small neat writing that had always been slow with painstaking precision.

He picked up one of the pages and began to read. A curse escaped his lips as he realized what he was reading. These were diary pages. His mother had left him her diary? He'd never known her to keep one.

His gaze shot to the date on the top page. It took him only a moment to do the math. This was written just weeks before he was conceived.

His pulse pounded. Finally he would know the truth about his father.

WHEN HER OFFICE door opened, Mary looked up, startled from her thoughts. Chase had left her shaken. She still wanted him desperately. But she was afraid, as much as she hated to admit it. She'd trusted her heart to Chase once. Did she dare do it again?

That's what she kept thinking even as she tried to get some work done. So when her door had opened, she was startled to realize how much time had gone by.

"Lucy." She'd forgotten all about her saying she might stop by later to discuss the apartment. Mary was glad for the distraction. "Come in."

The young woman took the chair she offered her on the other side of her desk. "Did you mean what you said earlier about renting me the apartment? It's just so convenient being right across the street, but I wanted to make sure you hadn't had second thoughts. After all, we just met."

Mary nodded since she'd *had* second thoughts. But as she looked into the young woman's eager face, she pushed them aside and reached into the drawer for the apartment key. "Why don't I show it to you." She rose from her desk. "We can either go up this way," she said, pointing to the back of her office, "or in from the outside entrance. Let's go this way." They went out of the back of her office to where a hallway wound around to the front stairs.

"The apartment is on the second floor," Mary told her as they climbed. "I live upstairs on the third floor. Some people don't want to live that close to their landlady," she said.

"I think I can handle it," Lucy said with a chuckle.

They stopped at the landing on the second floor, and Mary opened the door to the first apartment. "As you can see, it's pretty basic," she said as she pushed open the door. "Living room, kitchen, bedroom and bath." She watched Lucy take it in.

"It's perfect," the young woman said as she walked over to the window and looked out.

"There's a fire escape in the back, and a small balcony if you want to barbecue and not a bad view of Lone Peak." Mary walked to door and opened it so Lucy could see the view."

"That's perfect." She stepped past Mary out onto the small balcony to lean over the railing, before looking up. "So the fire escape goes on up to your apartment and balcony?"

"It does. I wouldn't use the fire escape except in an emergency so you will have privacy out here on your balcony."

Lucy stepped back in and closed the door. "I didn't even ask what the rent was." Mary told her. "That's really reasonable."

"I like providing housing for those working here in Big Sky. Most of the employees have to commute from the valley because there is so little affordable housing for them." She shrugged. "And it's nice to have someone else in the building at night. This area is isolated since it is mostly businesses that close by nine. The other apartment on this floor is rented to a man who travels a lot so I seldom see him."

Lucy ambled into the bedroom to pull down the Murphy bed. "This is great."

"You can use this room as an office as well as a bedroom. Since it has a closet, I call it a one bedroom."

"And it comes furnished?"

"Yes, but you can add anything you like to make it more yours."

Lucy turned to look at her. "I can really see myself living here. It's perfect. I would love it."

Mary smiled. "Then it's yours. You can move in right away if you want to."

"That's ideal because I've been staying in a motel

down in the valley just hoping something opened up before I went broke."

"I'll need first and last month's rent, and a security deposit. Is that going to be a problem?"

Lucy grinned. "Fortunately, I'm not that broke yet, so no problem at all. I promise to be the perfect tenant."

Mary laughed. "I've yet to have one of those."

Back downstairs, Lucy paid in cash. Seeing her surprise, the young woman explained that she'd had the cash ready should she find a place. "They go so fast. I didn't want to miss a good opportunity. I feel as if I've hit the lottery getting first the job and now this apartment."

Mary smiled as she handed over the key. "It's nice to have you here."

"I wouldn't want to be anywhere else."

After Lucy left, Mary went back down to her office and called her mother. "I have a new tenant. It's a bit strange, but she's the barista who took Christy's place."

"That is odd. What do you know about her?"

Mary thought about it for a moment. Nothing really. "She's nice." She told her how Lucy had run across the street to bring her coffee twice when Mary had gotten busy and forgotten.

"She sounds thoughtful."

"I like her so I hope it works out." Most of her tenants had, but there was always that one who caused problems.

"Guess who sent me flowers?" she said, changing the subject and putting her new tenant out of her mind.

LUCY COULDN'T BELIEVE how easy that had been. She smiled to herself as she drove back to her motel to get her things.

Mary would be living right upstairs. It would be like taking candy from a baby. She thought of the fire escape and balconies on the two levels behind the apartment. It would be so easy to climb up to Mary's on the third floor, anytime, day or night. While there was a railing around the stairs—and the balconies—still it could be dangerous, especially if Mary had been drinking.

Her thoughts turned sour though when she recalled the two sets of flowers that had been delivered this morning. Anger set off a blaze in her chest. They had to be from Chase, right? She would have loved to have seen what he'd written on the cards. Now that she would be living in the building, maybe she would get her chance.

She still felt surprised at just how easy it had been. Then again, Mary was just too sweet for words, she thought. Also too trusting. At first, she'd just wanted to meet the woman who'd taken Chase from her. At least that's what she'd told herself. Maybe she'd planned to kill her from the very beginning. Maybe it really had been in the back of her mind from the moment she decided to go to Montana and find her—find Chase.

Her feeling had been that if she couldn't have Chase, then no one else could. She'd had dreams of killing them both. Of killing Mary and making him watch, knowing there was nothing Chase could do to save her.

But in her heart of hearts, when she was being honest with herself, she knew what she wanted was for him to fall in love with her again. Otherwise, she would have no choice. It would be his own fault. He would have to die, but only after he mourned for the loss of his precious Mary. She would kill him only after she shattered his life like he'd done hers.

Living just one floor below the woman would provide the perfect opportunity to get closer to Mary—and Chase—until she was ready to end this.

It would be dangerous. She smiled to herself. There

was nothing wrong with a little danger. Eventually she and Chase would cross paths. Lucy smiled in anticipation. She couldn't wait to see the look on his face when he realized she wasn't dead. Far from it. She'd never been more alive.

Chapter Ten

After the first sentence, Chase couldn't believe it. The pages in the shoebox were from a diary. His mother's. His fingers trembled as he picked up another page. All these years he'd wanted answers. Was he finally going to get them?

He thumbed through the random pages, looking for names. There were none. But he did find initials. He scooped up the box and pages and sat down, leaning against the headboard as he read what was written before the initials. "I woke up this morning so excited. Today was going to be wonderful. I was going to see J.M. today. He told me to meet him in our secret spot. Maybe he's changed his mind. I can only hope."

Changed his mind about what?

Chase took out another page, but it was clear from reading it that the page wasn't the next day. He began to sort them by date. Some weren't marked except by the day of the week.

But he found one that began "Christmas Day." Whoever J.M. was, his mother had been in love with the man. And since his birthday was in September—nine months from Christmas...

The entry read: "Christmas Day! I thought I wouldn't

get to see him, but he surprised me with a present—a beautiful heart-shaped locket."

Chase felt his heart clench. His mother had worn such a locket. She never took it off. It was with the few things of hers that he'd kept. But he knew there was nothing but a photo of him in the locket. On the back were the words: *To my love always.*

He picked up the phone.

Mary answered on the second ring. "Chase?"

"I don't mean to bother you. But I had to tell you. It's my mother's diary."

"What's your mother's diary?"

"In the shoebox. It's pages from my mother's diary during the time that she got pregnant with me." Silence. "I really could use your help. I think the answer is somewhere in these pages but they're all mixed up. Some have dates, some don't and—"

"Bring them over. We can go through them in my apartment."

A short time later, Mary let him into the door on the side of the building, the shoebox tucked under his arm as they climbed to the third floor.

"Do you want something to drink?" she asked as he closed the door behind them.

The apartment was done in bright cheery colors that reminded him of Mary. "No, thanks." He felt nervous now that he was here.

She motioned to the dining-room table standing in a shaft of morning sun. Through the window, he could see Lone Peak. "Your apartment is wonderful," he said as he put the shoebox on the table and sat down.

"Thanks." Mary pulled out a chair opposite him. "May I?" she asked, and pulled the box toward her.

He nodded. "I looked at some of it, but truthfully, I didn't want to do this alone."

She took out the diary pages, treating them as if they were made of glass. "There had to be a reason her friend was told to give you this after she was gone." She picked up one page and read aloud, "'Friday, I saw him again at Buck's T-4. He didn't see me but I think he knew I was there. He kept looking around as if looking for me.'"

"She met him here in Big Sky!" Mary exclaimed as she flipped the page over. "'Saturday. I hate that we can't be together. He hates it too so that makes me feel a little better.'"

She looked up at Chase. "They were star-crossed lovers right here in Montana."

"Star-crossed lovers?" He scoffed. "From what I've read, it's clear that he was a married man." He raked a hand through his hair. "What if my father has been here in Big Sky all this time, and I never knew it?"

MARY COULD SEE how hard this was on him, just as she could tell that a part of him wasn't sure he wanted to know the truth. "Are you sure you want to find him?"

Chase had been fifteen when his mother had gotten sick the first time, and he'd come to the area to work on a neighboring ranch. Later, Mary's family had put him to work on their ranch, giving him a place to live while he and Mary finished school.

They'd both believed that he'd been sent to Montana because of one of Hud's law-enforcement connections. Her father had never spelled it out, but she now realized that both of her parents must have known Chase's mother back when she'd lived here. She must have been the one who'd asked them to look out for him.

Mary and Chase had been close from the very start.

From as far back as she could remember, he'd been haunted by the fact that he didn't know who his father was. He'd been born in Arizona. He'd just assumed that was where his mother met his father. He hadn't known that there was much more of a Montana connection than either he or Mary had known. Until now.

"Truthfully? I'm not sure of anything." His gaze met hers. "Except how I feel about you."

"Chase—"

He waved a hand through the air. "Sorry. As for my... father... I have to know who he is and why he did what he did."

She nodded. "So we'll find him," she said, and picked up another page of the diary. "There has to be some reason he couldn't marry your mother."

He swore under his breath. "I told you. He was already married. It's the only thing that's ever made sense. It's why my mother refused to tell me who he is."

"Maybe she mentions his name on one of the pages," Mary suggested. "If we put them in order." She went to work, sorting through them, but quickly realized that she never mentioned him by name, only J.M.

She stopped sorting to look at him. "J.M.? He shouldn't be hard to find if he still lives here." She got up and went to a desk, returning with a laptop. "Maybe we should read through them first though. It doesn't look as if she wrote something every day." She counted the diary sheets. "There are forty-two of them with days on both sides, so eight-four days."

"About three months," Chase said. "If we knew when the affair started..." They quickly began going through the pages. "This might help," he said as he held up one of the pages.

Something in his voice caught her attention more than his words. "What is it?"

"Christmas Eve." He read what his mother had written. "'It was so romantic. I never dreamed it could be like this. But he reminded me that I didn't have much to compare it with. He said it would get better. I can't imagine.'"

Chase looked up. "I was born nine months later."

"I'm sorry," she said.

He shrugged as if it didn't matter, but it was clear that it mattered a whole lot. "I have to know who he is."

She heard the fury in his voice as he told her about the heart-shaped necklace that his mother had never taken off. "Maybe he loved her."

He scoffed at that. "If he'd loved her, he wouldn't have abandoned her. She was alone, broke and struggling to raise his child."

"Maybe the answer is in these pages, and we just missed something," Mary said after they finished going through them.

He shook his head and scooped up the diary pages, stuffing them roughly back into the shoebox and slamming down the lid.

Mary wanted to know the whole story. She looked at the box longingly. It was clear that Chase had already made up his mind. Even after reading all the diary entries, she knew it was his mother's view of the relationship, and clearly Muriel's head had been in the stars.

"What are you going to do?" she asked, worried.

"Find him. J.M. The Big Sky area isn't that large." He stepped over to the laptop and called up local phone listings from the browser and started with the *M*s. "We can surmise from what she wrote that he's older, more experienced and married. The necklace he gave her wasn't some cheap dime-store one. He had money, probably owned a business in town."

She hesitated, worried now what he would do once he found the man in question. "I think you should let me go with you once we narrow down the list of men."

He looked at her, hope in his expression. "You would do that?"

"Of course." She picked up the phone to call her mother. Dana had known Chase's mother Muriel. That was clearly why Chase had come to live on the ranch at fifteen. "I need to know how Chase came to live with us."

She listened, and after a moment hung up and said to Chase, "Your mother worked in Meadow Village at the grocery store. She says she didn't know who Muriel was seeing, and I believe her. She would have told us if she'd known. She did say that your mother rented a place on the edge of town. So your mother could have met your father at the grocery store or on her way to work or just about anywhere around here."

Chase shook his head. "His wife probably did the grocery shopping."

"We don't know that he had a wife. We're just assuming…" But Chase wasn't listening. He was going through the phone listings.

GRADY BIRCH HAD been leaving when Hud pulled into the drive in front of the cabin. For just a moment, he thought the man might make a run for it. Grady's expression had been like a deer caught in his headlights. Hud suspected the man always looked like that when he saw the law—and for good reason.

It amused the marshal that Grady pretended nonchalance, leaning against the doorframe as if he had nothing to hide. As Hud exited his patrol SUV and moved toward the man, Grady's nerves got the better of him. His elbow slid off the doorframe, throwing the man off balance. He stumbled to catch himself, looking even more agitated.

"Marshal," he said, his voice high and strained before he cleared his throat. "What brings you out this way?"

"Why don't we step into your cabin and talk?" Hud suggested.

Grady shot a look behind him through the doorway as if he wasn't sure what evidence might be lying around in there. "I'd just as soon talk out here. Unless you have a warrant. I know my rights."

"Why would I have a warrant, Mr. Birch? I just drove out here to talk to you about Christy Shores."

Grady frowned. That hadn't been what he'd expected. The man's relief showed on his ferret-thin face. Grady's relief that this was about Christy told Hud that this had been a wasted trip. The man hadn't killed the barista. Grady was more worried about being arrested for cattle rustling.

"I just have a couple of quick questions," Hud said, hoping Grady gave him something to go on. "You dated Christy?"

"I wouldn't call it dating exactly."

"You were involved with her."

Grady shook his head. "I wouldn't say that either."

Hud sighed and shifted on his feet. "What would you say?"

"I knew who she was."

"You knew her well enough to get in a fight over her at Charley's the night she was killed."

"Let's say I had a good thing going with her, and Chet tried to horn in."

"What did Christy have to say about all this?"

Grady frowned as if he didn't understand the question. He was leaning against the doorframe again, only this time he looked a lot more comfortable.

Hud rephrased it. "What did she get out of this...relationship with you?"

"Other than the obvious?" Grady asked with a laugh. "It was a place to sleep so she didn't have to go back to her mother's in Bozeman."

"Is that where she was headed that night, to your cabin?"

Grady shook his head. "I told her it wasn't happening. I saw her making eyes at Chet. Let him put her up out at his place. I won't be used by any woman."

Hud had to bite his tongue. The way men like Grady treated women made his teeth ache. "When was the last time you saw her?"

"When Chet told her to scram and she ran into the bathroom crying."

"That was before the two of you got thrown out of the bar?" the marshal asked.

Grady nodded. "So have you found out who ran her down?"

"Not yet."

"Probably some tourist traveling through. I was in Yellowstone once, and there was this woman walking along the edge of the highway and this motor home came along. You know how those big old things have those huge side mirrors? One of them caught her in the back of the head." Grady made a disgusted sound. "Killed her deader than a doornail. Could have taken her head off if the driver had been going faster."

"Christy Shores wasn't killed by a motor home. She was murdered by someone locally."

Grady's eyes widened. "Seriously? You don't think Chet…"

"Chet has an alibi for the time of the murder. Can anyone verify that you came straight here to this cabin and didn't leave again?"

"I was alone, but I can assure you I didn't leave again."

Hud knew the value of an assurance by Grady Birch. "You wouldn't know anyone who might have wanted to harm her, do you?"

He wagged his head, still looking shocked. "Christy was all right, you know. She didn't deserve that." He sounded as if he'd just realized that if he'd brought her back to his cabin that night, she would still be alive.

DILLON WAS HEADED to Grady's when he saw the marshal's SUV coming out of the dirt road into the cabin. He waved and kept going as if headed to Bozeman, his pulse thundering in his ears. What had the marshal been doing out at the cabin? Was he investigating the cattle rustling?

He glanced in his rearview mirror. The marshal hadn't slowed or turned around as if headed back to Big Sky, and as far as Dillon could tell, Grady wasn't handcuffed in the back. He kept going until he couldn't see the patrol SUV in his rearview anymore before he pulled over, did a highway patrol turn and headed back toward the cabin.

His instincts told him not to. The marshal might circle back. Right now, he especially didn't want Hud knowing about his association with Grady Birch. But he had to find out what was going on. If he needed to skip the state, he wanted to at least get a running start.

He drove to the cabin, parking behind it. As he did, he saw Grady peer out the window. Had he thought the marshal had reason to return? The back door flew open. Grady looked pale and shaken. Dillon swore under his breath. It must be bad. But how bad?

"What—" He didn't get to finish his question before Grady began to talk, his words tumbling over each other. He caught enough of it to realize that the marshal's visit had nothing to do with cattle. Relief washed over him.

Pushing past Grady, he went into the cabin, opened the refrigerator and took the last beer. He guzzled it like a man dying of thirst. That had been too close of a call. He'd been so sure that Hud was on to them.

"Did you hear what I said?" Grady demanded. "She was *murdered*. Marshal said so himself."

Dillon couldn't care less about some girl Grady had been hanging with, and said as much.

"You really are a coldhearted bastard," Grady snapped. "And you drank the last beer," he said as he opened the refrigerator. "How about you bring a six-pack or two out for a change? I do all the heavy lifting and you—"

"Put a sock in it or I will." He wasn't in the mood for any whining. "I have my own problems."

"The marshal sniffing around you?"

He finished the beer and tossed the can into the corner with the others piled there. "It's the marshal's daughter. Things aren't progressing like I planned."

Grady let out a disgusting sound. "I really don't care about your love life. I've never understood why you were messing with her to start with."

"Because she could be valuable, but I don't have to explain myself to you."

His partner in crime bristled. "You know I'm getting

damned tired of you talking down to me. Why don't you rustle your own cattle? I'm finished."

"Where do you think you're going?" Dillon asked, noticing a flyer on the table that he hadn't seen before. With a shock, he saw that it advertised a reward from local ranchers for any information about the recent cattle rustling.

"I'm going into Charley's to have a few, maybe pick up some money shooting pool, might even find me a woman."

"You've already jeopardized the entire operation because of the last woman you brought out here."

Grady turned to look back at him. "What are you talking about?"

"Where'd you get that notice about the reward being offered by the ranchers?"

"They're all over town."

"So you just picked up one. Did the marshal see it?"

Grady colored. "No, I wouldn't let him in. I'm not a fool."

But Dillon realized that he *was* a fool, one that he could no longer afford. "I'm just saying that maybe you should lie low."

"I was headed into town when the marshal drove up. He doesn't suspect me of anything, all right? I've got cabin fever. You stay here and see how you like it." He turned to go out the door.

Dillon picked up the hatchet from the kindling pile next to the woodstove. He took two steps and hit Grady with the blunt end. The man went down like a felled pine, his face smashing into the back porch floor. When he didn't move, Dillon set about wiping any surface he had touched on his visits. He'd always been careful, he thought as he wiped the refrigerator door and the hatchet's handle.

His gaze went to the pile of beer cans in the corner and realized that his prints were all over those cans. Finding an old burlap bag, he began to pick up the cans when he saw an old fishing pole next to the door. Smiling, he knew how he could dispose of Grady's body.

Chapter Eleven

Dillon touched Mary's cheek, making her jump. "I didn't mean to startle you. It's just that you seemed a million miles away."

Actually only five miles away, on the ranch where Chase was working.

She couldn't quit thinking about him, which is why she hadn't wanted to go out with Dillon tonight, especially after she'd told him that she needed more time.

"I guess you forgot," he'd said. "The tickets to the concert I bought after the last time we went out? You said you loved that band, and I said I should try to get us some tickets. Well I did. For tonight."

She'd recalled the conversation. It hadn't been definite, but she hadn't been up to arguing about it. Anyway, she knew that if she stayed home, all she'd do was mope around and worry about Chase.

"You've been distracted this whole night."

"Sorry," she said. "But you're right. I have a lot on my mind. Which is why I need to call it a night."

"Anything I can help you with?" he asked.

She shook her head.

"It wouldn't be some blond cowboy named Chase Steele, would it?" There was an edge to his voice. She wasn't in the mood for his jealousy.

"Chase is a friend of mine."

"Is that all?"

She turned to look at him, not liking his tone. "I can go out with anyone I want to."

"Oh, it's like that, is it?"

She reached for her door handle, but he grabbed her arm before she could get out.

"Slow down," he said. "I was just asking." He quickly let go of her. "Like you said, you can date anyone you please. But then, so can I. What if I decided to ask out that barista friend of yours?"

"Lucy?" She was surprised he even knew about her.

"Yeah, Lucy."

If he was trying to make her jealous, he was failing badly. "Be my guest," she said, and opened her door and climbed out before he could stop her again.

She heard him get out the driver's side and come after her. "Good night Dillon," she said pointedly. But he didn't take the hint.

As she pulled out her keys to open her office door, he grabbed her and shoved her back, caging her against the side of the building.

"I won't put up with you giving me the runaround."

"Let me go," she said from between gritted teeth. Her voice sounded much stronger than she felt at that moment. Her heart was beating as if she'd just run a mile. Dillon was more than wild. She could see that he could be dangerous—more dangerous than she was interested in.

CHANCE HAD BEEN parked down the street, waiting for Mary to return home. He needed to talk to her about earlier. Since getting the box his mother had left for him, he'd been so focused on finding his father that he wanted to apologize. She'd offered to help. He wanted to get it over with as soon as possible since he'd managed to narrow it down to three names.

It wasn't until he saw the pickup stop in front of her building that he realized she had been on a date with that deputy.

He growled under his breath. There was something about that guy that he didn't like. And it wasn't just that he was going out with Mary, he told himself.

Now he mentally kicked himself for sitting down the street watching her place. If she saw him, she'd think he was spying on her. He reached to key the ignition and leave when he saw the passenger door of the deputy's rig open. From where he sat, he couldn't miss the deputy grabbing Mary as she tried to get out. What the hell?

He was already opening his door and heading toward her building when he saw Dillon get out and go after her. He could tell by her body language that she wasn't happy. What had the deputy done to upset her?

Chase saw that Dillon had pinned her against the side of her building. Mary appeared to be trying to get her keys out and go inside.

"Let her go!" he yelled as he advanced on the man.

Both Mary and Dillon turned at the sound of his voice. Both looked surprised, then angry.

"This is none of your business," the two almost said in unison.

"Let go of her," he said again to the deputy.

Mary pushed free of Dillon's arms and, keys palmed, turned to face Chase as he approached. "What are you doing here?"

"I needed to talk to you, but I'm glad I was here to run interference for you. If he's giving you trouble—"

"I can handle this," she said.

Chase could see how upset she was at Dillon and now him. "Date's over. You should go," he said to the deputy.

Dillon started to come at him. Chase was ready, knowing he could take him in a fair fight. He just doubted the man had ever fought fair. Dillon threw the first punch and charged. Chase took only a glancing blow before he slugged the deputy square in the face, driving him back, but only for a moment.

The man charged again, leading with a right and then a quick left that caught Chase on the cheek. He hit Dillon hard in the stomach, doubling him over before shoving him back. The deputy sprawled on the ground, but was scrambling to his feet reaching for something in his boot when Chase heard Mary screaming for them to stop.

"Stop it!" Mary cried. "Both of you need to leave. Now."

Dillon slowly slide the knife back into its scabbard, but not before Chase had seen it. He realized how quickly the fight could have gotten ugly if Mary hadn't stopped it when she did.

The deputy got up from the ground, cussing and spitting out blood. His lip was cut and bleeding. Chase's jaw and cheek were tender. He suspected he'd have a black eye by morning.

The look Dillon gave him made it clear that this wasn't over. The next time they saw each other, if Mary wasn't around, they would settle things. At least now Chase knew what he would be facing. A man who carried a blade in his boot.

"Leave now," Mary repeated.

"We'll finish our discussion some other time," Dillon said to her pointedly, making Chase wish he knew what had been said before Mary had gotten upset and tried to go inside. Now, she said nothing as Dillon started toward his pickup.

"That man is dangerous, Mary. If he—"

She spun on him. "Are you spying on me, Chase?"

"No, I needed to talk to you. I was just waiting…" He knew he sounded lame. It had been weak to wait down the street for her.

She didn't cut him any slack. "I'm sure whatever you need to talk to me about can wait until tomorrow." She turned to open her door.

"I'm sorry," he said behind her, glad he'd been here, even though he'd made her angry. He hated to think what could have happened if he hadn't intervened.

Mary didn't answer as she went inside and closed the door.

As he walked back to his pickup, he knew he had only himself to blame for all of this. He'd made so many mistakes, and he could add tonight's to the list.

Still, he worried. Mary thought she could handle Dillon. But the deputy didn't seem like a man who would take no for an answer.

TORN BETWEEN ANGER and fear, Mary closed and locked the door behind her with trembling fingers. What was wrong with her? Tears burned her eyes. She hadn't wanted to go out with Dillon tonight. So why had she let him persuade her into it?

And Chase. Parked down the street watching her, spying on her? She shook her head. If he thought he could come back after all this time and just walk in and start—

"Is everything okay?" asked a voice behind her, making her jump. "I didn't mean to startle you," Lucy said, coming up beside her in the hallway of her building.

Mary was actually glad to see Lucy. She'd had it with

men tonight. She wiped her eyes, angry at herself on so many levels, but especially for shedding more tears over Chase. Her life had felt empty without him, before Dillon, but now she missed that simple world.

Even as she told herself that, she knew she was lying. Chase was back. She loved him. She wanted him. So why did she keep pushing him away?

"What was that about?" Lucy asked, wide-eyed as they both watched the two men leave, Dillon in a hail of gravel as he spun out, and Chase limping a little as he headed for his truck.

"Nothing," she said, and took a deep breath before letting it out. She was glad to have Lucy in the building tonight.

Lucy laughed. "*Nothing?* They were fighting over you. Two men were just fighting over you." She was looking at her with awe.

Mary had to smile. "It had more to do with male ego than me, trust me." She thought about saying something to Lucy about Dillon's warning to Mary that he'd ask her out, but realized it was probably a hollow threat. Anyway, she was betting that Lucy could take care of herself.

LUCY TRIED TO keep the glee out of her voice. She'd witnessed the whole thing. Poor Chase. What struck her as ironic was that she'd had nothing to do with any of it. This was all Mary's own doing.

"Would you like to come up to my apartment for a drink? Sometimes I've found talking also helps." She shrugged.

Mary hesitated only a moment before she gave Lucy an embarrassed smile. "Do you have beer?"

Lucy laughed. "Beer, vodka, ice cream. I'm prepared for every heartbreak."

They climbed the stairs, Lucy opened the door and they entered her apartment. "I haven't done much with the space," Lucy said as she retrieved two beers from the refrigerator and handed one to Mary. "But I'm excited to pick up a few things to make it more mine. It really doesn't need anything. You've done such a good job of appointing it."

"Thank you," Mary said, taking the chair in the living room. "I'm just glad you're enjoying staying here. I'm happy to have you." Mary took a sip of her beer, looking a little uneasy now that she was here.

Lucy curled her legs under her on the couch, getting comfortable, and broke the ice, first talking about decorating and finally getting to the good part. "I had to laugh earlier. I once had two men fight over me. It was in high school at a dance. At the time I'd been mortified with embarrassment." She chuckled. "But my friends all thought it was cool."

"That was high school. It's different at this age," Mary said, and took another drink of her beer.

Lucy cocked her head at her as she licked beer foam from her lips and got up to get them another. "But I'm betting there was one of those men who you wanted to win the fight for you."

Mary looked surprised, then embarrassed.

"I wager it wasn't the deputy."

"You're right," her landlady admitted as she took the second beer. "Chase was my first love since the age of fifteen when he came to Montana to work on the ranch. We became best friends before…" Mary mugged a face. "Before we fell in love."

"So what happened to your happy ending?" Lucy asked as she took her beer back to the couch. She leaned toward Mary expectantly.

"I caught him kissing another woman. He swore the woman kissed him, but I guess I realized then that maybe what my parents had been saying was true. We were too young to be that in love. Only twenty-four. I let Chase go. He left Montana to…find himself," Mary said, and took another sip.

"*Find himself?* I'm guessing you didn't know he was lost."

Mary shook her head with a laugh. "We *were* too young to make any big decisions until we'd lived more. My father said that I had to let Chase sow some wild oats. But I didn't want him to leave."

Lucy groaned. "If he wanted to date other women, you didn't really want him to do it here, did you?"

"I wanted him to tell me that he didn't need to go see what else was out there. That all he wanted was me. But he didn't."

"And now it's too late?"

Mary shook her head. "I still love him."

Lucy traced her fingers around the top of her beer can for a moment. "Why do you think he came back now?"

Mary shook her head. "It's my fault." She sighed. "Have you ever had a weak moment when you did something stupid?"

She laughed. "Are you kidding? Especially when it comes to men."

"I found his address online since I didn't have his cell phone number or email, and he wasn't anywhere on social media. I wrote him a letter, late at night in a nostalgic mood." Mary shook her head. "Even as I wrote it, I knew I'd never mail it."

This was news. "You didn't mail it?"

"I did put it in an envelope with his address on it. I was staying out at the ranch because my horse was due to have her colt that night. I forgot about the letter—until I realized it was gone. My aunt Stacy saw it and thought I meant to mail it, so she did it for me."

Lucy leaned back, almost too surprised to speak. "So if your aunt hadn't done that…"

Mary nodded. "None of this would have probably happened, although Chase says he was planning to come back anyway. But who knows?"

The woman had no idea, Lucy thought. "So, he's back and he's ready to settle down finally?"

"I guess."

She sipped her beer for a moment. "Is that what you want?"

"Yes, I still love him. But…"

"But there is that adorable deputy," Lucy said with a laugh. "Sounds like a problem we should all have. And it's driving Chase crazy with jealousy."

"You're right about that. He can hardly be civil to Dillon when they cross paths. He says there's something about the guy that he doesn't trust."

"Obviously, he doesn't want you dating the guy."

"I'm not going out with Dillon again, and it has nothing to do with what Chase wants. I didn't date for a long time after Chase left. I was too heartbroken. I finally felt ready to move on, and I wrote that stupid letter." She drained her beer, and Lucy got up to get her another.

"What about you?" Mary asked, seeming more comfortable now that she'd gotten that off her chest and consumed two beers.

"Me?" Lucy curled up on the couch again. "There was someone. I thought we were perfect for each other. But in the end, I was more serious than he was." She shook her head. "You know what I think is wrong with men? They don't know what they want. They want you one day, especially if there is another guy in the picture, but ultimately how can you trust them when the next minute they're waffling again? Aren't you afraid that could happen if Dillon is out of the picture?"

Mary shook her head. "I'd rather find out now than later. Trust. That is what it comes down to. Chase broke my trust when he left, when he didn't answer my letter right away or even bother to call." She seemed to hesitate. "There was this woman he was seeing."

Her ears perked up. "He told you about her?"

"He had to after I told him that she'd called me. Apparently, she'd read my letter to him. She called to tell me to leave him alone because they were engaged."

"Were they?"

"No, he says that she's delusional."

"Wow, it does sound like she was emotionally involved in a big way. He must have cared about her a little for her to react that way."

Mary shrugged. "I know he feels guilty. He certainly didn't want her to die. He admitted that he slept with her one night. But that now just the sound of her name is like fingernails on a blackboard for me. *Fiona.*" She dragged out the pronunciation of the name.

Lucy laughed. "*He even told you her name? Men.* Sometimes they aren't very smart. Now you'll always wonder about her and if there is more to the story."

Chapter Twelve

Mary couldn't remember the last time she'd drunk three beers. But as she'd taken the stairs to her third-floor apartment, she'd been smiling. She'd enjoyed the girl-time with Lucy. It made her realize how cut off she'd been from her friends.

A lot of them had moved away after college, and not come back except for a week at Christmas or in the summer. They'd married, had children or careers that they had to get back to. Even though they often promised to stay in touch, they hadn't. Life went on. People changed.

Mary also knew that some of them thought staying in a place where they'd grown up had a stigma attached to it as if, like Chase, they thought the grass was greener away from Big Sky, away from Montana. They went to cities where there were more opportunities. They had wanted more. Just like Chase.

They had wanted something Mary had never yearned for. Everything she needed was right here, she told herself as she drove out to the ranch. She'd wandered past the state line enough during her college days that she knew there was nothing better out there than what she had right here.

So why hadn't she been able to understand Chase's need to leave? Why had she taken it so personally? He'd wanted her to go with him, she reminded herself. But she'd had no need to search for more, not realizing that losing Chase would make her question everything she held dear.

Mary found her mother in the kitchen alone. The moment Dana saw her she said, "What's wrong?"

She and her mother had always been close. While her male siblings had left Montana, she'd been the one to stay. Probably since she'd been the one most like her mother and grandmother.

"Nothing really," she said as she poured herself a cup of coffee and dropped into a chair at the large kitchen table. Sunshine streamed in the open window along with the scent of pine and the river. "Can't I just come by to see my mother?"

Dana cocked an eyebrow at her.

She sighed and said, "It's *everything*. Chase's mother left him this shoebox with diary pages from what appears to be the time she became pregnant with him."

"About his father? That's why you called me and asked me if I knew. Isn't his name in the diary pages?"

She shook her head. "Muriel didn't mention his name, just his initials, J.M. Does that ring any bells?"

"No, I'm sorry. I didn't know Muriel well. I'd see her at the grocery store. She came out to the ranch a couple of times. We went horseback riding. Then I heard that she'd left town. Fifteen years later, she contacted me, thanked me for my kindness back when she lived in Big Sky and asked for our help with Chase."

Mary nodded. "Well, we know why she left. It appears her lover might have been married or otherwise unavailable."

"That would explain a lot," Dana said. "How is Chase taking all of this?"

Mary shook her head. "Not well. He's determined to find him. But with only the man's initials…"

"That's not much help I wouldn't think."

"I'm afraid what he'll do when he finds him," Mary said. "He has such animosity toward him."

"It's understandable. If the man knew Muriel was pregnant and didn't step up, I can see how that has hurt Chase. But is that what happened?"

"That's just it. We don't know. Either she didn't include the diary pages at the end or she never wrote down what happened. The last page we found she was going to meet him at their special place and was very nervous about telling him the news. But that she believed their love could conquer anything."

Dana shook her head. "So Chase is assuming she told him and he turned her away."

Mary nodded. "It's the obvious assumption given that his mother refused to tell him anything about his father."

Dana got up to refill her cup. When she returned to the table, she asked, "How was your date with Dillon last night?"

Mary looked away. "I'm not going out with him again."

"Did something happen?" Dana sounded alarmed, and Mary knew if she didn't downplay it, her mother would tell her father, and who knew what he would do. He already didn't like Dillon.

"It was fine, but that's the problem. He's not Chase." Her mother was giving her the side-eye, clearly not believing any of it.

She realized that she had to give her more or her mother would worry. "Dillon doesn't like me seeing Chase."

"I see." She probably did. "So that's it?"

She nodded. "Chase isn't wild about me seeing Dillon, but he's smart enough not to try to stop me." Mary tried to laugh it all off as she got up to take her cup to the sink. "Kara says it's a terrible problem to have, two men who both want me."

"Yes," her mother said. "If Dillon gives you a hard time—"

"Do not say a word to Dad about this. You know how he is. I just don't want to go out with Dillon again. That should make Dad happy."

"Only if it is your choice."

"It is. I need to get to work."

Dana got up to hug her daughter before she left. "We just want you to be happy. Right now it doesn't sound like either man is making you so."

"His mother's diary has blindsided Chase, but it would anyone. This whole mystery about who his father is..." She glanced at the clock. "I have to get going. Remember, nothing about this to Dad."

Her mother nodded even though Mary knew there were few secrets between them.

LUCY COULDN'T HAVE been more pleased with the way things had gone last night. Mary had been furious with Chase. The cowboy had done it to himself. *Fiona* hadn't even had a hand in it.

She was still chuckling about it this morning when the bell over the coffee shop door jangled and she turned to see the deputy come in.

Dillon Ramsey. She immediately picked up a vibe from him that made her feel a kinship. They might have more in common than Mary.

"Good morning," she said, wondering what kind of night he'd had after everything that had happened. How serious was he about Mary? Not that much, she thought as he gave her the eye. He had a cut lip and bruise on his jaw, but he didn't seem any the worse for wear.

"What can I get you?" she asked, and he turned on a grin that told her he'd come in for more than coffee. What was this about?

"I'd take a coffee, your choice, surprise me."

Oh, she could surprise him in ways he never dreamed of. But she'd play along. "You got it," she said, and went to work on his coffee while he ambled over to the window to stare across the street at Mary's building.

She made him something strong enough to take paint off the walls, added a little sweetness and said, "I think I have just what you need this morning."

He chuckled as he turned back to her. "I think you're right about that." He blatantly looked her up and down. "Go out with me."

Okay, she hadn't been expecting that. But all things considered, the idea intrigued her. "I'm sorry, but aren't you dating my landlady?"

"Who says I can't date you too?"

She raised an eyebrow. Clearly, he wanted to use her to make Mary jealous. He could mess up her plans. She couldn't let him do that. Realizing he could be a problem, she recalled that Mary had plans tonight so she wouldn't be around.

"I'll tell you what. I'm working the late shift tonight. I wouldn't be free until midnight." She wrote down the number of her burner phone and handed him the slip of paper. "Why don't you give me a call sometime."

He grinned as he paid for his coffee. "I'll do that."

Lucy grinned back. "I'm looking forward to it," she said, meaning it. Dillon thought he could use her. The thought made her laugh. He seriously had no idea who he was dealing with.

MARY LOOKED UP as Chase came in the front door of her building.

He held up his hands in surrender. "I don't want to keep you from your work, but I thought maybe we could have lunch together if you don't have other plans. I really need to talk to you. Not about us. You asked for space, and I'm giving it to you. But I do need your help."

She glanced at her watch, surprised to see that it was almost noon. Which meant that all the restaurants would be packed. She said as much to him.

He grinned, which was always her undoing with him. "I packed us a picnic lunch. I know you're busy, so I thought we would just go down by the river. I'll have you back within the hour. If it won't work out, no sweat. I'll leave."

She hadn't been on a picnic in years. But more important, Chase wasn't pressuring her. There was a spot on the river on the ranch that used to be one of their favorite places. The memory of the two of them down by the river blew in like a warm summer breeze, a caress filled with an aching need.

"It's a beautiful day out. I thought you could use a little sunshine and fresh air," he said.

She glanced at the work on her desk. "It is tempting." *He* was tempting.

"I didn't just come here about lunch," he said as if confessing. "I've narrowed down the search for my father to three names." That caught her attention. "I was hoping—"

"Just give me a minute to change."

They drove the short distance to the Gallatin River and walked down to a spot with a sandy shore. A breeze whispered in the pines and off the water to keep the summer day cool.

Chase carried a picnic basket that Mary knew he'd gotten from her mother. "Was this my mother's idea?"

He laughed. "I do have a few ideas of my own." His blue gaze locked with hers, sending a delicious shiver through her. She remembered some of his ideas.

She sighed and took a step away from him. Being so close to Chase with him looking at her like that, she couldn't think straight. "It makes me nervous, the two of you with your heads together." When he said nothing, she'd looked over at him.

He grinned. She did love that grin. "Your mom and I have always gotten along great. I like her."

She eyed him for a moment and let it go. Did he think that getting closer to her mother was going to make her trust him again? "How is work going on the Jensen Ranch?"

"I've been helping with fencing so if you're asking about Beth Anne? I haven't even seen her." He shook his head. "Like I told you, it's temporary. I start as finish carpenter with Reclaimed Timber Construction next week. I'll also be moving into my own place in a few days. I was just helping out at the Jensens' ranch. Since I left, I've saved my money. I'm planning to build my own home here in the canyon." He shrugged and then must have seen her surprised expression. "Mary, I told you, I'm not leaving. I love you. I'm going to fight like hell to get you back. Whatever it takes. Even if I have to run off that deputy of yours."

"Don't talk crazy." She noticed the bruise on his cheek from last night reminding her of their fight.

"Seriously, there is something about him I don't like."

"That was obvious, but I don't want to talk about him. Especially with you."

"Not a problem," he said as he spread out a blanket in

the sand and opened the picnic basket "Fresh lemonade. I made it myself."

"With my mother's help," she said as he held up the jug. She could hear the ice cubes rattling.

"I know it's your favorite," he said as he produced a plastic glass and poured her some. As he handed it to her, he smiled. "You look beautiful today, by the way."

She took the glass, her fingers brushing against his. A tingle rushed through her arm to her center in a heart-beat. She took a sip of the lemonade. "It's wonderful. Thank you."

"That's not all." He brought out fried chicken, potato salad and deviled eggs.

"If I eat all this, I won't get any work done this after-noon," she said, laughing.

"Would that be so terrible?"

She smiled at him as she leaned back on the blanket. The tops of the dark pines swayed in the clear blue overhead. The sound of the flowing clear water of the Gallatin River next to them was like a lullaby. It really was an amazing day, and it had been so long since she'd been here with Chase.

"I haven't done this since…"

"I left. I'm sorry."

"Not sorry you left," she said, hating that she'd brought it up.

"Just sorry it wasn't with you."

She nodded and sat up as he handed her a plate. "I guess we'll never agree on that."

"Maybe not. But we agree on most everything else," he said. "We want the same things."

"Do we?" she asked, meeting his gaze. Those old feel-ings rushed at her, making her melt inside. She loved this cowboy.

"We do. Try the chicken. I fried it myself."

She took a bite and felt her eyes widen. "It's delicious." It wasn't her mother's. "There's a spice on it I'm having trouble placing."

"It's my own recipe."

"It really is good."

"I wish you didn't sound so surprised." But he grinned as he said, "Now the potato salad."

"Equally delicious. So you cook?"

His face broke in a wide smile. "You really underestimate me. Cooking isn't that tough."

They ate to the sound of the river, the occasional birdsong and the chatter of a distant squirrel. It was so enjoyable that she hated to bring up a subject that she knew concerned him. But he'd said he needed to talk to her about the names of men he thought might be his father.

"You said you've narrowed your search to three names?" she asked.

He nodded. "J.M. I've searched phone listings. Since it was someone in the Big Sky area that helps narrow the scope."

Unless the man had just been passing through. Or if he'd left. But she didn't voice her doubts. "What is your plan? Are you going to knock on the door of the men with the initials J.M.?"

He laughed. "You have a better suggestion?"

She studied him. "You're sure you want to do this?"

Chase looked away for a moment. "I wish I could let it go. But I have to know."

"What will you do when you find him?"

He chuckled. "I have no idea."

"I don't believe that."

Chase met her gaze. "This man used my mother and when she got pregnant, he dumped her."

"That isn't what she said in her diary."

"No, she didn't spell it out, if that's what you mean. But I know how it ended. With her being penniless trying to raise me on her own. It's what killed her, working like a dog all those years. I want to look him in the face and—" His voice broke.

She moved to him. As he drew her into his arms, she rested her head against the solid rock wall of his chest. She listened to the steady beat of his heart as tears burned her eyes. She knew how important family was. She'd always known hers. She could feel the hole in his heart, and wanted more than anything to fill it. "Then let's find him."

As they started to pack up the picnic supplies, Chase took her in his arms again. "You know I've never been that good with words."

"Oh, I think you're just fine with words," she said, and laughed.

"I love you," he said simply.

She met his gaze. Those blue eyes said so much that he didn't need words to convince her of that. "I love you."

"That's enough. For now," he said, and released her. The promise in his words sent a shiver of desire racing through her. Her skin tingled from his touch as well as his words. She'd wanted this cowboy more than she wanted her next breath.

Still, she let him finish picking up the picnic supplies. He smiled at her. "Ready?"

Just about, she thought.

LUCY HAD BEEN shocked when Chase had stopped by Mary's and the two had left together. She'd thought Mary was angry with him. Clearly, not enough.

Where had they been? Not far away because he'd brought her back so soon. But something was different. She could sense it, see it in the way they were with each other as he walked her to her door. They seemed closer. She tried to breathe. Her hands ached from being balled up into fists.

Watching from the window of the coffee shop, she saw Mary touch his hand. Chase immediately took hers in his large, sun-browned one. The two looked at each other as if… As if they shared a secret. Surely they weren't lovers again already. Then Chase kissed her.

Lucy brought her fist down on the counter. Cups rattled and Amy, who'd been cashing out for the day, looked over at her. "Sorry. I was trying to kill a pesky fly."

Amy didn't look convinced, but she did go back to what she was doing, leaving Lucy alone to stare out the window at the couple across the street. Chase had stepped closer. His hands were now on her shoulders. Lucy remembered his scent, his touch. He was hers. Not Mary's.

Chase leaned in and kissed her again before turning back to his pickup. It wasn't a lover's kiss. It was too quick for that. But there was no doubt that Mary was no longer angry with him. Something had changed.

She watched him drive away, telling herself to bide her time. She couldn't go off half-cocked like she had that night at the river. Timing was everything.

A customer came in. She unfisted her hands as she began to make the woman's coffee order and breathe. But she kept seeing the way Chase had kissed his cowgirl and how Mary had responded. It ate at her heart like acid, and she thought she might retch.

But she held it together as the coffee shop filled with a busload of tourists. Soon Mary would come over for her afternoon caffeine fix. Lucy touched the small white package of powder in her apron pocket. She was ready for her.

MARY TRIED TO concentrate on her work. She had to get this report done. But her mind kept going back to Chase and the picnic and the kisses.

She touched the tip of her tongue to her lower lip and couldn't help but smile. Some things didn't change. Being in Chase's arms again, feeling his lips on hers. The short kiss was a prelude to what could come.

"Don't get ahead of yourself," she said out loud. "You're only helping him look for his father." But even as she said it, she knew today they'd crossed one of the barriers she'd erected between them.

She shook her head and went back to work, losing herself in the report until she heard her front door open. Looking up, she saw Lucy holding a cup of coffee from Lone Peak Perk.

"I hope I'm not disturbing you," she said. "When it got late, I realized you might need this." She held out the cup.

"What time is it?"

"Five thirty. I'm sorry. You probably don't want it today." She started to back out.

"No, it's just what I need if I hope to get this finished today," Mary said, rising from her desk. "I lost track of time and I had a big lunch. It's a wonder I haven't already dozed off."

Lucy smiled as she handed her the coffee. "I saw your cowboy come by and pick you up. Fun lunch?"

Mary nodded, grinning in spite of herself. "Very fun." She reached for her purse.

"I put it on your account."

She smiled. "Thank you." She took a sip. "I probably

won't be able to sleep tonight from all this sugar and caffeine this late in the day, but at least I should be able to get this report done now. Thank you again. What would I do without you?"

Chapter Thirteen

Mary thought she was going to die. She'd retched until there was nothing more inside her, and yet her stomach continued to roil.

When it had first hit, she'd rushed to the restroom at the back of her office. She'd thought it might have been the potato salad, but Chased had ice packs around everything in the basket.

Still, she couldn't imagine what else it could have been. Flu? It seemed early in the season, but it was possible.

After retching a few times, she thought it had passed. The report was almost finished. She wasn't feeling great. Maybe she should go upstairs to her apartment and lie down for a while.

But it had hit again and again. Now she sat on the cool floor of the office bathroom, wet paper towels held to her forehead, as she waited for another stomach spasm. She couldn't remember ever feeling this sick, and it scared her. She felt so weak that she didn't have the strength to get up off this floor, let alone make it up to her third-floor apartment.

She closed her eyes, debating if she could reach her desk where she'd left her cell phone. If she could call her mother...

"Mary? Mary, are you here?"

Relieved and afraid Lucy would leave before she could call her, Mary crawled over to the door to the hallway and, reaching up, her arm trembling, opened it. "Lucy." Her throat hurt. When her voice came out, the words were barely audible. "Lucy!" she called again, straining to be heard since she knew she couldn't get to her feet as weak as she was.

For a moment it seemed that Lucy hadn't heard her. Tears burned her eyes, and she had to fight breaking down and sobbing.

"Mary?"

She heard footfalls and a moment later Lucy was standing over her, looking down at her with an expression of shock.

"I'm sick."

"I can see that." Lucy leaned down. "Do you want me to call you an ambulance?"

"No, if you could just help me up to my apartment. I think it must be food poisoning."

"Oh no. What did you have for lunch?" Lucy asked as she reached down to lift her into a standing position. "You're as weak as a kitten."

Mary leaned against the wall for a moment, feeling as if she needed to catch her breath. "Chase made us a picnic lunch. It must have been the chicken or the potato salad."

"That's awful. Here, put your arm around me. Do you think you can walk?"

They went out the back of the office and down the hallway to the stairs.

"Let me know if you need to rest," Lucy said as they started up the steps.

Her stomach empty, the spasms seemed to have stopped—at least for the moment. Having Lucy here made her feel less scared. She was sure that she'd be fine if she could just get to her apartment and lie down.

"I'm all right." But she was sweating profusely by the time they'd reached her door.

"I didn't think to ask," Lucy said. "Are your keys downstairs?"

Mary let out a groan of frustration. "On my desk."

"If you think you can stand while I run back down—"

"No, there's a spare key under the carpet on the last stair at the top," she said. "I sometimes forget when I just run up from the office for lunch."

"Smart."

She watched Lucy retrieve the key. "I can't tell you how glad I was to see you."

"I saw that your lights were still on in your office, but there was no sign of you. I thought I'd better check to make sure everything was all right. When I found your office door open and you weren't there…" She opened the door and helped her inside.

"I think I want to go straight to my bedroom. I need to lie down."

"Let me help you." Lucy got her to the bed. "Can you undress on your own?"

"If you would just help me with my boots, I think I can manage everything else."

Lucy knelt down and pulled off her Western boots. "Here, unbutton your jeans and let me pull them off. You'll be more comfortable without them."

Mary fumbled with the buttons, realizing the woman was right. She felt so helpless, and was grateful when Lucy pulled off her jeans and helped tuck her into bed. "Thank you so much."

"I'm just glad I could help. Would you like some ginger ale? My mother always gave me that when I had a stomachache."

Mary shook her head. "I think I just need to rest."

"Okay, I'll leave you to it. I don't see your phone."

"It's downstairs on my desk too."

"I'll get it so you can call if you need anything, and I mean anything, you call me, all right? I'll be just downstairs."

Mary nodded. Suddenly she felt exhausted and just wanted to close her eyes.

"Don't worry. I'll lock your apartment door, put the key back, lock up downstairs—after I get your phone. You just rest. You look like something the cat dragged in."

Even as sick as she was, Mary had to smile because she figured that was exactly what she looked like given the way she felt.

Lucy started to step away from the bed, when Mary grabbed her hand. "Thank you again. You're a lifesaver."

"Yep, that's me."

Unable to fight it any longer, Mary closed her eyes, dropping into oblivion.

LUCY HAD TAKEN her time earlier when she'd finished work. She'd casually crossed the street, whistling a tune to herself. There'd been no reason to hurry. She'd known exactly what she was going to find when she got to Mary's office.

Now as Mary closed her eyes, she stood over the woman, simply looking down into her angelic face. She didn't have to wonder what Chase saw in Mary. She was everything Lucy was not.

That was enough to make her want to take one of the

pillows, force it down on Mary's face and hold it there until the life ebbed out of her.

She listened to Mary's soft breaths thinking how Mary had it all. A business, a building in a town where she was liked and respected, not to mention rentals and Chase. Lucy reminded herself that she used to have a great profession, where she was respected, where she had friends. What was missing was a man in her life. Then along came Chase.

With a curse, she shook her head and looked around the room as she fought back tears. The bedroom was done in pastel colors and small floral prints, so like Mary. She wondered what Chase thought of this room—or if he'd seen it yet. Not very manly. Nor was it her style, she thought as she left, closing the bedroom door softly behind her, and checked out the rest of the place.

She'd been sincere about Mary's decorating abilities. The woman had talent when it came to design and colors. It made her jealous as she took in the living room with its overstuffed furniture in bright cheery colors. Like the bedroom, there was a soft comfort about the room that made her want to curl up in the chair by the window and put her feet up.

But with a silent curse, she realized that what she really wanted was to be Mary Savage for a little while. To try out her life. To have it all, including Chase.

Shaking herself out of such ridiculous thinking, she left the apartment, leaving the door unlocked. As she put the spare key back, she told herself that it would come in handy in the future.

Smiling at the thought, she headed downstairs to Mary's office. It looked like any other office except for the large oak desk. The brick walls had been exposed to give the place a rustic look. The floor was bamboo, a rich color that went perfectly with the brick and the simple but obviously expensive furnishings.

She would have liked an office like this, she thought as she found Mary's cell phone on her desk and quickly pocketed it before picking up the woman's purse. It felt heavy. She heard the jingle of keys inside. Slipping the strap over her shoulder, she went to the front door and locked it.

Across the street she saw that the coffee shop was still busy and the other baristas were clearly slammed with orders. She wondered if anyone had seen her and quickly left by the back way again, turning out the lights behind her after locking the door. That's when she realized that she couldn't kill Mary here. She would be the first suspect.

Once on the stairs, out of view of anyone outside or across the street, she sat down on a step and went through Mary's purse. She found a wallet with photos of people she assumed must be relatives. Brothers and sisters? Cousins? Her parents?

Friends? She realized how little she knew about the woman.

There was eighty-two dollars in cash in the wallet, a few credit cards, some coupons... Seriously? The woman clipped coupons? Other than mints, a small hairbrush, a paperback and miscellaneous cosmetics there was nothing of interest.

She turned to Mary's cell phone.

Password protected. Swearing softly, she tried various combinations of words, letters, numbers. Nothing worked.

A thought struck her like a brick. She tried Chase. When that didn't work, she tried Chase Steele. Nope.

She had another thought, and taking the keys to the

office, she went back inside. Turning on a small lamp on the desk, she quickly began a search. She found the list of passwords on a pull-out tray over the right-hand top drawer. The passwords were on an index card and taped down. Some had been scratched out and replaced.

Lucy ran her finger down until she found the word cell. Next to it was written Homeranch#1. She tried the password and the phone unlocked.

Quickly she scanned through contacts, emails and finally messages. She found a cell phone number for Chase and on impulse tried it, just needing to hear his voice.

It was no longer in service.

Surely he had a cell phone, not that she'd ever had his number. Wouldn't he have given it to Mary though?

She went through recent phone calls, and there it was. She touched the screen as she memorized the number. It began to ring. She held her breath. He would think it was Mary calling. He would call back.

Lucy quickly hit the hang-up button but not quick enough. "Hello, Mary, I was just thinking of you." She disconnected, wishing she hadn't done that. He'd sounded so happy that Mary was calling him that she felt sick to her stomach.

Just as she'd feared, he called right back. She blocked his call. He tried again. What if he decided to come check on Mary? This was the kind of mistake she couldn't make.

She answered the phone, swallowed and did her best imitation of Mary's voice, going with tired and busy. "Working. Didn't mean to call."

"Well, I'm glad you did. Don't work too late."

"Right. Talk tomorrow." She disconnected, pretty sure she'd pulled it off. He wouldn't question the difference in their voices since he'd called Mary's phone. At least she hoped she'd sounded enough like the woman. Sweet, quiet, tired, busy. When the phone didn't ring again, she told herself that she'd done it.

Hurrying back upstairs, she picked up Mary's purse from where she'd left it on the step on her way. Outside the third-floor apartment, she stopped to catch her breath. Putting Mary's cell on mute, she carefully opened the door, even though she didn't think Mary would be mobile for hours.

An eerie quiet hung in the air. She stepped in and headed for the bedroom. The door was still closed. She eased it open. The room had darkened to a shadowy black with the drapes closed. Mary lay exactly where she'd left her, breathing rhythmically.

Taking the cell phone, she stepped in just far enough to place the now turned off phone next to her bed. Then she left, easing the bedroom door closed behind her. The apartment was deathly quiet and growing darker. It no longer felt cozy and she no longer wanted to stay. Leaving Mary's purse on the table by the door, she left, locking it behind her.

It had been an emotional day, Lucy thought. She took the stairs down to her apartment, unlocked her door and, turning on a light, stepped in. The apartment was in stark contrast to Mary's. While everything was nice, it was stark. Cold.

"That's because you're cold," she whispered as she locked the door behind her. "Anyway, it's temporary." But even as she said it, she was thinking that she should at least buy a plant.

The apartment had come furnished right down to two sets of sheets and two throw pillows that matched the couch. Suddenly Lucy hated the pillows. She tossed them into the near empty closet and closed the door. Tomorrow was her day off. After she checked on Mary, she'd go into Bozeman and do some shopping.

She needed this apartment to feel a whole lot less like Mary Savage. Now that she had Chase's cell number, it was time for her to make him pay.

Chapter Fourteen

Lucy tapped lightly at Mary's door the next morning. Given how sick the woman had been the evening before, she thought she still might be in bed.

So she was a little surprised when Mary answered the door looking as if she'd already showered and dressed for the day.

"Oh good, you look like you're feeling better," she said.

"Much. Thank you again for yesterday."

"Just glad I could help." She started to turn away.

"Do you ride horses?" Mary asked.

Lucy stopped, taken aback by the question. She'd hoped to get close to Mary, befriend her, gain her trust and then finish this. She'd thought it would take more time. "I used to ride when I was younger."

"Would you like to come out to the ranch sometime, maybe on your day off, and go for ride?"

"I would love to." The moment she said it, she knew how dangerous it could be. Chase might show up. She'd managed not to come face-to-face with him. Even with the changes in her appearance, he could recognize her. They'd been lovers. Soul mates. He would sense who she was the moment they were in the same room.

"Good," Mary was saying. "Let's plan on it. Just let

me know what day you're free. And thank you again for yesterday. I don't know what I would have done without you."

Lucy nodded, still taken aback. "I'm glad I was here." She took a step toward the door, feeling strangely uncomfortable. "Off to work," she said as she walked backward for a few steps, smiling like a fool.

Could this really be going as well as she thought it was? She couldn't believe how far she'd come from that night in Arizona when she'd gone into the river. She had Mary Savage, the woman who'd stolen Chase from her, right where she'd wanted her. So why wasn't she more euphoric about it? Her plan was working. There was no reason to be feeling the way she was, which was almost…guilty.

The thought made her laugh as she crossed the street. Guilt wasn't something she normally felt. She was enjoying herself. Maybe too much. She'd thought it would take longer, and she'd been okay with that.

As she settled into work, she realized that she would have to move up her revenge schedule. She was starting to like Mary and that was dangerous. No way could she go on a horseback ride with her, and not just because she might run into Chase. She couldn't let herself start liking Mary. If she weakened… She told herself that wouldn't happen.

But realizing this was almost over, she felt a start. She hadn't given any thought as to what she would do after she was finished here. Where would she go? What would she do? She'd been so focused on destroying Chase and his cowgirl that she hadn't thought about what to do when it was over.

That thought was nagging at her when she looked up to find Chase standing in front of her counter. Panic made her limbs go weak. He wasn't looking at her, but at the board with the day's specials hanging over her head. Could she duck in the back before he saw her? Let the other barista wait on him?

But Amy was busy with another customer. Lucy knew she couldn't hide out in the back until Chase left. All her fears rushed through her, making her skin itch. She'd come so far. She was so close to finishing this. What would she do when he recognized her?

He'd know what she was up to. He'd tell Mary. All of this would have been for nothing. Mary's father was the marshal. It wouldn't take long before he'd know about what had happened in Texas, about the suspicions that had followed her from town to town and finally to Big Sky, Montana. Once he saw through her disguise, and he would. Just like that and it would be all over. She wanted to scream.

"Good morning," he said, and finally looked at her.

"Morning." She held her breath as she met his blue eyes and gave him an embarrassed gap-toothed smile.

He smiled back, his gaze intent on her, but she realized with a start that she saw no recognition in his face. *It's me*, she wanted to say. *The love of your life. Don't tell me you don't see me, don't sense me, don't feel me standing right here in front of you.*

"I hope you can help me. I want to buy my girlfriend the kind of coffee she loves, but I forgot what it's called. She lives right across the street. I thought you might know what she orders. It's for Mary Savage."

Girlfriend? "Sorry, I'm new."

"That's all right. It was a shot in the dark anyway. Then I guess I'll take one caramel latte and a plain black coffee please."

She stared at him for a moment in disbelief. She'd been

so sure he would know her—instinctively—even the way she looked now. But there was no recognition. *None*.

Fury shook her to her core. They'd made *love*. They had a connection. *How could he not know her?*

"You do have plain black coffee, don't you?" he asked when she didn't speak, didn't move.

She let out a sound that was supposed to be a chuckle and turned her back on him. Her insides trembled, a volcano of emotions bubbling up, ready to blow. She fisted her hands, wanting to launch herself across the counter and rip out his throat.

Instead, she thought of Mary and something much better. Ripping out Mary's heart, the heart he was so desperately trying to win back.

She made the latte and poured him a cup of plain black coffee. He handed her a ten and told her to keep the change.

Thanking him, she smiled at the thought of him standing over Mary Savage's grave. "You have a nice day now."

"You too," he said as he left.

She watched him go, still shocked and furious that the fool hadn't known her. She promised herself that his nice days were about to end, and very soon.

IT WASN'T UNTIL he was headed across the street to Mary's office that Chase looked back at the woman working in the Lone Peak Perk. What was it about her…? He frowned until it hit him. Her voice. Even with the slight lisp and Southern drawl, the cadence of her voice was enough like Fiona's to give him the creeps.

He shuddered, wondering if he would ever be able to put the Fiona nightmare behind him. Yesterday he'd called Rick, and Patty had answered.

"I'm so sorry about what happened with you and Fiona," she'd said. "I just feel so sorry for her. I know it's no excuse, but she had a really rough childhood. Her mother remarried a man who sexually abused her. When she told her mother, the woman didn't believe her. That had to break her heart."

"Did she have anyone else?"

"No siblings or relatives she could turn to. On top of that, her stepfather had three sons."

He had sworn under his breath "So they could have been abusing her too."

"Or Fiona could have lied about all of it. When her mother, stepfather and the three sons died in a fire, I had to wonder. Fiona could have been behind it. I wouldn't put anything past her, would you?"

"Or she could have lied about the sexual abuse and then been racked with guilt when they all died."

Patty had laughed. "You really do try to see the best in people, and even after the number she pulled on you. You're a good guy, Chase. You take care of yourself."

He didn't feel like a good guy. He'd made so many mistakes. Fiona for one. Mary for another. He couldn't do much about Fiona, but he still had a chance to right things with Mary.

Patty had put Rick on the phone. The news was the same. Fiona's body still hadn't turned up.

"Some fisherman will find her downstream. It will be gruesome. A body that's been in the water that long…"

Chase hadn't wanted to think about it.

Like now, he tried to put it behind him as he neared Mary's office door. He wanted to surprise her with coffee. He just wished the barista had known the kind of coffee she drank. Mary was helping him today with his search for a man with the initials J.M. She understood

his need to find his father even though there were days
when he didn't. Why couldn't he just let it go? His mother
apparently had forgiven the man if not forgotten him.

For all he knew, the man could have moved away by
now. Or his mother hadn't used his real initials. Or… He
shook off the negative thoughts. He would be spending
the day with the woman he loved. Did it really matter if
they found his father today?

As Chase came in the front door of her office, Mary saw
him look back toward the coffee shop and frown. "Is
something wrong?" she asked.

He started as if his thoughts had been miles away.
"There's a woman working over there. Lucy?"

"I know her." She took the coffee he handed her. Not
her usual, but definitely something she liked.

"She just reminded me of someone I used to know—
and not in a good way," he said.

"She just started working at Lone Peak Perk only a
week or two ago. Why?"

He shook his head. "Just a feeling I got." He seemed
to hesitate. "That dangerous woman, Fiona, who I told
you about from Arizona. Lucy doesn't look anything like
her, but she reminds me of her for some reason."

Mary shook her head. She really did not want to hear
anything more about Fiona. "You do realize how crazy
that sounds. I know Lucy. She's really sweet. I like her. I
rented one of my apartments to her. I'm sure she's nothing like *your*… Fiona."

"She wasn't *my* Fiona. Look, you've never asked, but I
didn't date for a long time after I left. I wasn't interested
in anyone else. That wasn't why I left and you know it. If I
hadn't been drinking, if I hadn't just picked up my mother's ashes the day of the barbecue at my boss's house…"

Mary stood up. "I don't need to hear this."

"Maybe you do," he said, and raked a hand through his hair as he met her gaze. "It was one drunken night. I regretted it right away. She became…obsessed, manufacturing a relationship that didn't exist. She must have stolen my extra house key and copied it. I came home several times to find her in my apartment. She knew I was in love with someone else. But that seemed to make her even more determined to change my mind." He shook his head. "She wouldn't stop. She tried to move some of her stuff into my apartment. Needless to say it got ugly. The last time I saw her…" He hesitated as if he'd never wanted to tell her the details about Fiona and she didn't want to hear them now.

But before she could stop him, he said, "She tried to kill me."

Mary gasped. "You can't be serious."

"She knew I was leaving. She said she wanted to give me a hug goodbye, but when she started to put her arms around me, I saw the knife she'd pulled from her pocket. I would have gotten to Montana weeks sooner, but she sabotaged my pickup. I had to have a new engine put in it." He shook his head. "What I'm saying is that I wouldn't put anything past her. She supposedly drowned in the Colorado River after driving her car into it. But her body was never found."

Mary couldn't believe what she was hearing.

"Lucy doesn't look anything like her except…" He glanced up at her and must have seen the shock and disbelief in her eyes. Couldn't he tell that she didn't want to know anything more about Fiona?

She shook her head, wished this wasn't making her so upset. He'd said Fiona was obsessed with him? It sounded like he was just as obsessed. "This woman really did a number on you, didn't she?"

He held up both hands in surrender. "Sorry. I thought you should know."

About a woman he'd made love to who was now dead? But certainly not forgotten. Even Lucy reminded him of her even though, as he said, she looked nothing like Fiona? Her heart pounded hard in her chest. She pushed her coffee away, feeling nauseous. "We should get going. I need to come back and work."

He nodded. She could tell that he regretted bringing up the subject. So why had he? She never wanted to hear the name Fiona again. Ever.

"I'm sorry. You're right. Forget I mentioned it. I promise not to say another word about her."

But she saw him steal a look toward the coffee shop as they were leaving. He might not mention Fiona's name again, but he was definitely still thinking about her.

Chapter Fifteen

With Mary's mother's help, Chase had narrowed down their search to three local men—Jack Martin, Jason Morrison and Jonathan Mason. Dana had helped him weed out the ones that she knew were too young, too old or hadn't been around at the time.

His mother had been eighteen when she'd given birth to him. If her lover had been older, say twenty-five or thirty as Chase suspected, then his father would now be in his fifties.

Jack Martin owned a variety of businesses in Big Sky, including the art shop where his wife sold her pottery. A bell tinkled over the door as Mary and Chase entered. A woman passed them holding a large box as if what was inside was breakable. Chase held the door for her, before he and Mary moved deeper in the shop.

The place smelled of mulberry candles, a sickeningly sweet fragrance that Mary had never liked. She tried not to breathe too deeply as they moved past displays of pottery toward the back counter.

Jack had begun helping out at the shop during the busiest time, summer, Mary knew. She spotted his gray head coming out of the back with a large pottery bowl, which he set on an open space on a display table. There was a young woman showing several ladies a set of pottery dishes in an adjoining room, and several visitors were looking at pottery lamps at the front of the shop.

As Mary approached, Jack turned and smiled broadly. "Afternoon, is there something I can help you with?"

Mary knew Jack from chamber of commerce meetings, but it took him a second before he said, "Mary Savage. I'm sorry, I didn't recognize you right away."

"This is my friend Chase Steele." She watched for a reaction. For all they knew, Chase's father could have kept track of his son all these years. But she saw no reaction. "Is there a private area where we could speak with you for a moment?"

Jack frowned, but nodded. "We could step into the back." He glanced around to see if there were customers who needed to be waited on. There didn't appear to be for the moment.

"We won't take much of your time," she promised.

Chase tensed next to her as if to say, if Jack Martin was his father, he'd damned sure take as much of his time as he wanted.

Mary was glad that she'd come along. She knew how important this was, and could feel how nervous Chase had become the moment they stepped into the shop.

In the back it was cool and smelled less like the burning candles. "Did you know a woman named Muriel Steele?" Chase asked the moment they reached a back storage and work area.

Jack blinked in surprised. "Who?"

"Muriel Steele," Mary said with less accusation. "It would have been close to thirty years ago."

Jack looked taken aback. "You expect me to remember that long ago? Who was this woman?"

"One you had an affair with," Chase said, making her

cringe. She'd hoped he would let her handle this since he was too emotionally involved.

"That I would remember," the man snapped. "I was married to Clara thirty years ago. We just celebrated our fortieth anniversary." Jack was shaking his head. "I'm not sure what this is about or what this Muriel woman told you, but I have never cheated on my wife."

Mary believed him. She looked to Chase, whom she could tell wasn't quite as convinced.

"Would you be willing to take a DNA test to prove it?" Chase demanded.

"A DNA test? How would that prove..." Realization crossed his face. "I see." His gaze softened. "I'm sorry young man, but I'm not related to you."

"But you'd take the test," Chase pressed.

Jack grew quiet for a moment, his expression sad. "If it would help you, yes, I would."

Mary saw all the tension leave Chase's body. He looked as if the strain had left him exhausted.

"Thank you," Mary said as she heard more customers coming into the shop. "We won't keep you any longer."

"IT'S NOT HIM," Chase said as he climbed behind the wheel and started the pickup's engine. A floodgate of emotions warred inside him. He wasn't sure what he'd hoped for. That he could find his father that quickly and it would be over? He'd wanted to hate the man. Worse, he'd wanted to punch him. But when realization had struck Jack Martin, Chase had seen the pity in the man's eyes.

"No, it wasn't Jack," she said. "Are you up to visiting the rest of them?"

He pulled off his Stetson and raked a hand through his hair. "I'm not sure I can do this. I thought I could but..." He glanced over at her.

"It's all right."

He shook his head. For a moment, they merely sat there, each lost in their own thoughts. Then Chase smiled over at her. "Could we drive up to Mountain Village and have an early lunch and forget all this for a while? Then I promise to take you back to work. I shouldn't have dragged you into this."

She reached over and placed a hand on his arm. He felt the heat of her fingers through his Western shirt. They warmed him straight to his heart and lower. What he wanted was this woman in his arms, in his bed, in his life. He felt as if he had made so many mistakes and was still making them.

"My stomach is still a little upset. I was really sick last night." He looked at her with concern. "I'm sure it was just some twenty-four-hour flu," she said quickly.

"I hope that's all it was," he said. "I was really careful with our picnic lunch."

"And you didn't get sick, so like I said, probably just a flu bug." He must not have looked convinced. "I was just going to eat some yogurt for lunch. Maybe some other time?"

He studied her for a moment, so filled with love for this woman. "You're the best friend I've ever had."

She laughed at that, and took her hand from his arm.

"Is it any wonder that I haven't been able to stop loving you?" he asked.

Their gazes met across the narrow space between them. He could feel the heat, the chemistry. He reached over and cupped the back of her neck, pulling her into the kiss. He heard her breath catch. His pulse quickened. A shaft of desire cut through him, molten hot.

Mary leaned into him and the kiss. It felt like coming home. Chase had always been a great kisser.

As he drew back, he looked into her eyes as if the kiss had also transported him back to when they were lovers.

"You're just full of surprises today, aren't you," she said, smiling at him as she tried to catch her breath. She loved seeing Chase like this, relaxed, content, happy, a man who knew who he was and what he wanted.

The cowboy who'd left her and Montana had been antsy, filled with a need she couldn't understand. Just like he'd been only minutes ago when they'd gone looking for his father.

He needed to find him. She would help him. And then what?

"You have work to do, and I'm keeping you from it," he said. "We can have lunch another day when you feel better and aren't as busy. I've already taken up too much of your morning."

She shook her head as she met his gaze. "If I didn't have this report due—"

"You don't have to explain. You took off this morning to help me. I appreciate that." His smile filled her with joy as much as his words. "We have a lot of lunches in our future. I hope you know how serious I am about us, about our future. I'll do whatever it takes because I know you, Mary Savage. I know your heart."

She felt her eyes burn with tears at the truth in his words. "Tomorrow. Let's go talk to the other two men tomorrow morning."

"Are you sure?" Chase asked. "I don't like keeping you from your work."

She managed to nod. "I'm sure." Swallowing the lump in her throat, she reached to open her door. If she stayed out here with him a minute longer, she feared what she might say. Worse, what she might do. It would have been too easy to fall into his arms and take up where they'd left off and forget all about the report that was due.

But she climbed out of the pickup, knowing it was too soon. She had to know for sure that Chase wouldn't hurt her again. Her heart couldn't take being broken by him again.

As Chase was leaving, he glanced toward the coffee shop. Was Lucy working? He swung his pickup around and parked in front of Lone Peak Perk. Getting out, he told himself to play it cool. He had to see her again. He had to know. But just the thought that he might be right…

As he walked in, Lucy looked up. Surprise registered in those dark eyes. Nothing like Fiona's big blue ones. Still, he walked to the counter. She looked nervous. "Is it possible to get a cup of coffee in a real cup?" he asked. "Just black."

She looked less nervous, but that too could have been his imagination. He wondered what he'd been thinking. The woman looked nothing like Fiona and yet… She was much skinnier, the gapped two front teeth, the short dark hair, the brown eyes. What was it about her that reminded him of Fiona? Mary was right. He was obsessed with the disturbed, irrational woman.

Lucy picked up a white porcelain coffee cup and took her time filling it with black coffee. "Can I get you anything else?" she said with that slight lisp, slight Southern accent. Nothing like Fiona. She flashed him a smile, clearly flirting.

He grinned. "Maybe later." He took the coffee cup by the handle over to an empty spot near the door. Sitting with his back to her, he took a sip. Coffee was the last thing he wanted right now. But he drank it as quickly as the hot beverage allowed.

Taking advantage of a rush of people coming in for their afternoon caffeine fix, he carefully slipped the now empty cup under his jacket and walked out. He'd expected to be stopped, but neither Lucy or the other barista noticed. When he reached his pickup, he carefully set the cup on the center console and headed to the marshal's office.

He would get Hud to run the prints because he had to know what it was about the woman that turned his stomach, and left him feeling like something evil had come to Big Sky.

LUCY COULDN'T BELIEVE that Chase had come back into the coffee shop. She smiled to herself as she whipped up one of the shop's special coffees for a good-tipping patron. As she finished the drink, she turned expecting to see Chase's strong back at the corner table. To her surprise, he'd left during the rush. He'd certainly finished his coffee quickly enough. She frowned as concern slithered slowly through her.

It took her a moment to realize why the hair was now standing up on the back of her neck. The table where Chase had been sitting. His empty porcelain cup wasn't where he should have left it.

She hurriedly glanced around, thinking he must have brought it back to the counter. Otherwise…

Her heart kicked up to double time. Otherwise… He wouldn't have tossed the cup in the trash and she could see from here that he hadn't put it in the tray with the few other dishes by the door.

Which left only one conclusion.

He'd taken the cup.

Why would he—

The reason struck her hard and fast. *He had recog-*

nized her. Warring emotions washed over her. Of course he'd sensed her behind the disguise. She hadn't been wrong about that. It was that unique chemistry that they shared. But at the same time, fear numbed her, left her dumbstruck. She could hear the patron asking her a question, but nothing was registering.

Chase would go to the marshal, Mary's father, have him run the prints. Once that happened… She told herself that there was time. And, there was Deputy Dillon Ramsey.

"Miss! I need a receipt, please."

Lucy shook her head and smiled. "Sorry," she said to the woman, printed out the receipt and handed it to her. "You have a nice day now."

AFTER HIS INITIAL surprise at seeing the cowboy, Hud waved Chase into a chair across from his desk. As the young man came in, he carefully set a white porcelain coffee cup on the edge of the desk. Hud eyed it, then Chase.

"I need you to run the fingerprints on this cup."

The marshal lifted a brow. "For any particular reason?"

"I really don't want to get into it. I'm hoping I'm wrong."

Hud leaned back in his chair. "That's not enough reason to waste the county's time running fingerprints."

"If I'm right, this person could be a danger to Mary. Isn't that enough?"

Rubbing his jaw, he studied the cowboy. "You do understand that unless this person has fingerprints on file—"

"They'll be on file if I'm right."

Intrigued, Hud sighed and said, "Okay. I'll let you know, but it might take a few days."

A deputy was walking past. Hud called to him as he bagged the cup Chase had brought in. "Dillon, run the fingerprints on this cup when you have a minute. Report back to me."

"WE'RE STILL ON for tonight, right?" Lucy asked when Dillon called. The last thing she wanted him to do was cancel.

"You know it."

"Then I have a small favor," she said. "It's one that only you can grant." She could almost hear the man's chest puff out. "And I'll make it worth your while."

"Really?" He sounded intrigued. She reminded herself that he was only doing this to get back at Mary. The thought did nothing for her disposition, but she kept the contempt out of her voice. She needed his help.

"Really. But then maybe you don't have access to what I need down there at the marshal's office."

"Name it. I have the run of the place."

"I believe Chase Steele might have brought in a cup and asked that fingerprints be run on it?"

Dillon chuckled. "The marshal asked me to do it when I had time and report back to him."

"Have you had time?" she asked, her heart in her throat.

"I like to do whatever the marshal asks right away."

She closed her eyes and tried to breathe. Her prints were on file. Chase must have suspected as much.

"I haven't seen him though to give him the report."

Lucy took a breath and let it out slowly. "Is there any way that the report could get lost?"

He snickered. "Now you've got me curious. Why would you care about prints run on a Fiona Barkley?"

So her prints had come back that quickly? "If that report gets lost, I'd be happy to tell you when I see you. Like I said, I'll make it worth your while."

"Are we talking money?" he asked quietly. "Or something else?"

"Or both," she said, her heart pounding. "I can be quite…creative."

He laughed. "What time shall I pick you up?"

"I have a better idea. Why don't I meet you later tonight after I get off my shift? I know just the spot." She told him how to get to the secluded area up in the mountains. She'd spent her free time checking out places for when it came time to end this little charade.

Dillon thought he was going to get lucky—and use her to bring Mary into line. She'd known men like him. He would blackmail her into the next century if she let him.

"I have to work late. Is midnight too late for you?" she asked sweetly.

"Midnight is perfect. I can't wait."

"Me either." The deputy had no idea that he'd walked right into her plot, and now he had a leading role.

Chapter Sixteen

Later that night, as Lucy prepared for her date with Dillon, she couldn't help being excited. She'd spent too much time waiting around, not rushing her plan, being patient and pretending to be someone she wasn't.

Tonight she could let Fiona out. The thought made her laugh. Wait until Dillon met her.

She had to work only until ten, but she needed time to prepare. She knew all about forensics. While she had little faith in the local law being able to solve its way out of a paper bag, she wasn't taking any chances. Amy, who worked at the coffee shop, had seen her talking to Dillon when he'd asked her out, but as far as the other barista knew, he was just another customer visiting after buying a coffee.

If Amy had heard anything, she would have thought he had been asking her for directions. There was no law in him flirting with her, Lucy thought with a grin. That exchange would be the only connection she had to Dillon Ramsey.

At least as far as anyone knew.

She didn't drive to the meeting spot. Instead, she came in the back way. It hadn't rained in weeks, but a thunderstorm was predicted for the next morning. Any tire or foot tracks she left would be altered if not destroyed. She had worn an old pair of shoes that would be going into the river tonight. Tucked under her arm was a blanket she'd pulled out of a commercial waste bin earlier today.

The hike itself wasn't long as the crow flew, but the route wound through trees and rocks. The waning moon and all the stars in the heavens did little to light her way. She'd never known such a blackness as there was under the dense pines. That's why she was almost on top of Dillon's pickup before she knew it.

As she approached the driver's-side door, she could hear tinny sounding country music coming from his pickup's stereo. He was drumming on his steering wheel and glancing at his watch. From his expression, she could tell that he was beginning to wonder if he'd been stood up.

When she tapped on his driver's-side window, he jumped. His expression changed from surprise to relief. He motioned for her to go around to the passenger side.

She shook her head and motioned for him to get out of the truck.

He put his window down partway, letting out a nose-wrinkling gust of cheap aftershave and male sweat. "It's warmer in here."

"I'm not going to let you get cold."

Dillon gave that a moment's thought before he whirred up the window, killed the engine and music, and climbed out.

Lucy had considered the best way to do this. He had his motivation for asking her out. She had hers for being here. Everyone knew about Dillon and Chase's fight. The two couldn't stand each other. So whom would the marshal's first suspect be if anything happened to Dillon?

She tossed down the blanket she'd brought onto the bed of dried pine needles. Dillon reached for her. He would be a poor lover, one who rushed. "Not yet, baby," she said, holding him at arm's length. "Why don't you strip down, have a seat and let me get ready for you. Turn your back. I want this to be a surprise."

It was like leading a bull to the slaughterhouse.

"Well hurry, because it's cold out tonight," he said as he began to undress. She'd brought her own knife, but when she'd seen his sticking out of his boot, she'd changed her plans.

The moment he sat down, his back to her, she came up behind him, grabbed a handful of his hair and his knife, and slit his throat from ear to ear. It happened so fast that he didn't put up a fight. He gurgled, his hand going to his throat before falling to one side.

She stared down at him, hoping he'd done what he promised and lost the report on her fingerprints. Her only regret was that she hadn't gotten to see the surprise and realization on his smug face. He'd gotten what was coming to him, but she doubted he would have seen it that way.

As she wiped her prints from the knife and stepped away, she kicked pine needles onto her tracks until she was in the woods and headed for the small creek she'd had to cross to get there. She washed her hands, rinsing away his blood. She'd worn a short-sleeved shirt, and with his back to her, she hadn't gotten any of his blood on anything but her hands and wrists.

She scrubbed though, up to her elbows, the ice-cold water making her hands ache. She let them air-dry as she walked the rest of the way back to her vehicle. Once she got rid of the shoes she had on, no one would be able to put her at the murder scene.

THE MOMENT MARY saw her father's face, she knew something horrible had happened. Was it her mother? One of her brothers or someone else in the family? Chase? She rose behind her desk as her father came into her office, his Stetson in hand, his marshal face on.

"Tell me," she said on a ragged breath, her chest aching with dread. She'd seen this look before. She knew when her father had bad news to impart.

"It's Dillon Ramsey."

She frowned, thinking she'd heard him wrong. "Dillon?"

"You weren't with him last night, were you?"

"No, why?"

"He was found dead this morning."

Her first thought was a car accident. The Gallatin Canyon two-lane highway was one of the most dangerous highways in the state with all its traffic and curves through the canyon along the river.

"He was found murdered next to his truck up by Goose Creek."

She stared at him, trying to make sense of this. "How?"

He hesitated but only a moment, as if he knew the details would get out soon enough and he wanted to be the one to tell her. "He was naked, lying on a blanket as if he'd been with someone before that. His throat had been cut."

Her stomach roiled. "Why would someone want to kill him?"

"That's what I'm trying to find out. I'm looking for a friend of his, Grady Birch. Do you know him?"

Mary shook her head. "I never met any of his friends."

Her father scratched the back of his neck for a moment. "I understand that Dillon and Chase got into a confrontation that turned physical."

"Chase? You can't think that Chase… You're wrong. Chase didn't trust him, but then neither did you."

"With good reason as it turns out. I believe that Dillon was involved in the cattle rustling along with his friend Grady Birch."

Mary had to sit back down. All of this was making her sick to her stomach. "I'd broken up with him. I had no plans to see him again. He'd threatened to ask out one of my tenants." She shook her head. "But Chase had nothing to do with this."

The marshal started for the door. "I just wanted you to hear about it from me rather than the Canyon grapevine."

She nodded and watched him leave. Dillon was dead. Murdered. She shuddered.

GRADY BIRCH'S BODY washed up on the rocks near Beckman's Flat later that morning. It was found by a fisherman. The body had been in the water for at least a few days. Even though the Gallatin River never got what anyone would call warm, it had been warm enough to do damage over that length of time.

Hud rubbed the back of his neck as he watched the coroner put the second body that day into a body bag. Dillon was dead; Grady had been dead even longer. What was going on?

He would have sworn that it was just the two of them in on the cattle rustling. But maybe there was someone else who didn't want to share the haul. He'd send a tech crew out to the cabin to see what prints they came up with. But something felt all wrong about this. Killers, he'd found, tended to stay with the same method and not improvise. A drowning was much different from cutting a person's throat. The drowning had been made to look like an accident. But Grady's body had been held down with rocks.

"I'll stop by later," he told the coroner as he walked to his patrol SUV. There was someone he needed to talk to.

Hud found Chase fixing fences on the Sherman Jensen ranch. He could understand why Sherman needed the help and why Chase had agreed to working for board. He was a good worker and Sherman's son was not.

Chase looked up as Hud drove in. He put down the tool he'd been using to stretch the barbed wire and took off his gloves as he walked over to the patrol SUV.

"Did you get the prints off the cup back?" Chase asked.

Hud shook his head. He'd been a little busy, but he'd check on them the first chance he got. He studied the man his daughter had been in love with as far back as he could remember. Out here in his element, Chase looked strong and capable. Hud had thought of him as a boy for so long. At twenty-four, he'd still been green behind the years. He could see something he hadn't noticed when he saw him at the marshal's office. Chase had grown into a man.

Still he found himself taking the man's measure.

"Marshal," Chase said. "If you've come out here to ask me what my intentions are toward your daughter…" He grinned.

"As a matter of fact, I would like to know, even though that's not why I'm here."

Chase pushed back his Stetson. "I'm going to marry her. With your permission, of course."

Hud chuckled. "Of course. Well, that's good to hear, as far as intentions go, but I'm here on another matter. When was the last time you saw Dillon Ramsey?"

Chase grimaced. "Did he think that's why I was in your office the other day?" He shook his head. "That I'd come there to report our fight? So he decided to tell you his side of it?"

"Actually no. But I heard about it. Heard that if Mary hadn't broken it up, it could have gotten lethal."

"Only because Dillon was going for a knife he had in his boot," Chase said.

Hud nodded. Chase had known about the man's knife. The knife Dillon had been killed with. "So the trouble between you was left unfinished." Chase didn't deny it. "That's the last time you saw him?"

Chase nodded and frowned. "Why? What did he say? I saw the way he was trying to intimidate Mary."

"Not much. Someone cut his throat last night." He saw the cowboy's shocked expression.

"What the hell?"

"Exactly. Where were you last night?"

"Here on the ranch."

"Can anyone verify that you were here the whole time?"

"You can't really believe that I—"

"Can anyone verify where you were?" Hud asked again.

Chase shook his head. "Can't you track my cell phone or something? Better yet, you know me. If I saw Dillon again, I might get in the first punch because I knew he'd fight dirty. But use a knife?" He shook his head. "Not me. That would be Dillon."

Hud tended to believe him. But he also knew about the knife Dillon kept in his boot, and he hadn't seen Chase in years. People change. "You aren't planning to leave town, are you?"

Chase groaned. "I have a carpenter job in Paradise Valley. I was leaving tomorrow to go to work. But I can give you the name of my employer. I really don't want to pass up this job."

Hud studied him for a moment. "Call me with your employer's name. I don't have to warn you not to take off, right?"

Chase smiled. "I'm not going anywhere. Like I told you, I'm marrying your daughter and staying right here."

Hud couldn't help but smile. "Does Mary know that?"

The cowboy laughed. "She knows. That doesn't mean she's said yes yet."

"ARE YOU ALL RIGHT? I just heard the news about the deputy," Chase asked when he called Mary after her father left. "I'm so sorry."

"Dillon and I had broken up, but I still can't believe it. Who would want to kill him?"

"Your father thought I might," he said. "I just had a visit from him."

"What? You can't be serious."

"He'd heard about the fight Dillon and I had in front of your building," Chase said. "I thought maybe you'd mentioned it to him."

"I didn't tell him, but he can't believe that you'd kill anyone."

Chase said nothing for a moment. "The word around town according to Beth Anne is that Dillon had been with someone in the woods. A woman. You have any idea who?"

She thought of Lucy, but quickly pushed the idea away. Dillon had said he was going to ask her out, but she doubted he'd even had time to do that—if he'd been serious. Clearly, he'd been seeing someone else while he was seeing her.

"I'll understand if you don't want to go with me late to see the next man on my list," Chase said.

"No, I'm going. I'm having trouble getting any work done. I'm still in shock. I know how much finding your father means to you. Pick me up?"

"You know it. I'm going to get cleaned up. Give me thirty minutes."

"You questioned Chase about Dillon's murder?" Mary cried when he father answered the phone.

He made an impatient sound. "I'm the marshal, and I'm investigating everyone with a grudge against Dillon Ramsey."

"Chase doesn't hold grudges," she said indignantly, making Hud laugh.

"He's a man, and the woman he's in love with was seeing another man who is now dead. Also, he was in an altercation with the dead man less that forty-eight hours ago."

"How did you know about the fi—"

"I got an anonymous call."

"I didn't think anyone but me…" She thought of Lucy. No, Lucy wouldn't do that. Someone else in the area that night must have witnessed it.

"You can't possibly think that Chase would…" She shook her head adamantly. "It wasn't Chase."

"Actually, I think you're right," her father said. "I just got the coroner's report. The killer was right-handed. I noticed Chase is left-handed."

Mary felt herself relax. Not that she'd ever let herself think Chase was capable of murder, but she'd been scared that he would be a suspect because of their altercation.

As she looked up, she saw Lucy on her way to work. The woman turned as if sensing she was being watched, and waved before coming back to the front door of the office to stick her head in.

"Mary, are you all right? I just heard the news on the radio about that deputy you were seeing, the one your cowboy got into a fight with the other night."

"I know, it's terrible, isn't it?"

"You don't think Chase—"

"No." She shook her head. "My dad already talked to him. It wasn't him."

Lucy lifted a brow. "Chase sure was angry the other night."

"Yes, but the forensics proved that Chase couldn't have done it." Mary waved a hand through the air as if she couldn't talk about it, which she couldn't. "Not that I ever thought Chase could kill someone."

Lucy still didn't look convinced. "I think everyone is capable. It just has to be the right circumstances."

"You mean the wrong ones," Mary said, the conversation making her uncomfortable. She no longer wanted to think about how Dillon had died or who might have killed him.

"Yes," Lucy said, and laughed.

"Did you ever go out with Dillon?" Mary asked, and wished she hadn't at Lucy's expression.

"Seriously?" The woman laughed. "Definitely not my type. Why would you ask me that?"

"He mentioned that he might ask you out. I thought maybe—"

Lucy sighed. "Clearly, he was just trying to make you jealous. I think he came into the coffee shop once that I can remember. You really thought I was the woman who had sex with him in the woods?"

"We don't know that's what happened."

"It's what everyone in town is saying. They all think

that the killer followed the deputy out to the spot where he was meeting some woman. That's why I asked about Chase. If your cowboy thought it was you on that blanket with him…"

"That's ridiculous. Anyway, it wasn't me."

"But maybe in the dark, Chase didn't know that."

"Seriously, Lucy, you don't know him. I do. Chase wouldn't hurt anyone."

"Sorry. Not something you want to dwell on at this time of the morning. I can't believe you thought I could be the woman with him."

And yet Lucy seemed determine to believe that Chase had been the killer.

"Coming over for your coffee?" Lucy asked. "I can have it ready for you as soon as I get in."

"No, actually. I have an errand to run this morning."

Lucy frowned but then brightened. "Well, have a nice day. Maybe I'll see you later."

From the window, Mary saw her hesitate as if she wanted to talk longer before she closed the door and started across the street. She seemed to quicken her pace as Chase drove up.

Mary hurried out, locking her office door behind her before climbing into his pickup. He smiled over at her. "You okay? I saw Lucy talking to you as I drove up."

"Nothing important."

"Then let's get it over with. I never realized how… draining this could be," Chase said.

"Who's next?"

"Jason Morrison."

Morrison was a local attorney. His office was only a few doors down from Mary's. They'd called to make an appointment and were shown in a little before time.

Jason was tall and slim with an athletic build. He spent

a lot of time on the slopes or mountain biking, and had stayed in good shape at fifty-five. He was a nice looking man with salt and pepper dark hair and blue eyes. When his secretary called back to say that his eleven o'clock was waiting, he said to send them on back.

Jason stood as they entered and came around his desk to shake Mary's hand and then Chase's.

Mary watched as he shook Chase's hand a little too long, his gaze locked on the younger man's.

Was it Chase's blue eyes, or did Jason see something in him he recognized?

"Please, have a seat," the attorney said, going behind his desk and sitting down. "What can I do for the two of you?"

"We're inquiring about a woman named Muriel Steele," Mary said. "We thought you might have known her twenty-seven years ago."

Jason leaned back in his chair and looked from Mary to Chase and back. "Muriel. Has it been that long ago?" He shook his head. "Yes, I knew her." He frowned. "Why are you asking?"

"I'm her son," Chase said.

Jason's gaze swung back to him. "I thought there was something about you that was familiar when we shook hands. Maybe it's the eyes. Your mother had the most lovely blue eyes."

As Chase started to rise, Mary put a hand on his thigh to keep him in his chair. "Chase is looking for his father."

"His father?" He glanced at Mary and back to Chase.

"When my mother left Big Sky, she was pregnant with me, but I suspect you already know that," Chase said through clenched teeth.

The attorney looked alarmed. "I had no idea. Wait a minute. You think I was the one who…" He held up his hands. "I knew your mother, but I was already married by then. Linda was pregnant with our daughter Becky." He was shaking his head.

"My mother left a diary," Chase said.

Jason went still. "If she said it was me…" He shook his head. "I'm sorry, but I'm not your father."

"She didn't name her married lover," Chase said. "Just his initials. J.M. Quite a coincidence you knew her and you have the exact initials."

A strange look crossed the man's face. "I'm sorry. Like I said, you have the wrong man."

"Then you wouldn't mind submitting to a DNA test," Mary said.

"I'm a lawyer. No good can come of submitting to a DNA test, not with the legal system like it is. No offense to your father the marshal, ma'am," he added quickly.

"So you're saying no?" Chase asked as he got to his feet.

Jason sighed. "I want to help you, all right? If it comes to that, I'd get a DNA test. I assume there are others you're talking to?"

"Actually, a friend of yours," Mary said. "Jonathan Mason."

Jason groaned. He looked as if he wanted to say more, but changed his mind. "My heart goes out to you. But maybe there was a reason your mother never told you who your father was."

"Other than she wanted to protect him?" Chase demanded.

Jason sighed again. "I wish I could help you. I really do. But after all this time…"

"You think I should let it go?" Chase leaned toward the man threateningly.

Jason held up his hands. "I can see your frustration."

"It's not frustration. It's anger. The man knocked up my mother, broke her heart and her spirit, and let her raise me alone. She was only seventeen when she became pregnant, had no education and no way to support herself but menial jobs. So, I'm furious with this man who fathered me."

"Then why find him? What good will it do?" the lawyer asked.

Chase leaned back some. "Because I want to look him in the eye and tell him what I think of him."

Mary rose and so did the attorney. "We'll probably be back about that DNA test," she said.

Jason nodded, but he didn't look happy about it. His gaze went to Chase and softened. "I cared about your mother, but I wasn't her lover."

"I guess we'll see," Chase said as they left.

"It's him," Chase said as they left the attorney's office. His heart was pounding. He thought about what the man had said. "It's him, I'm telling you."

"I don't know."

"He admitted knowing her. You saw the way he looked at me. He knew the moment he shook my hand. He practically admitted it."

"But he didn't admit it," Mary pointed out.

"He's a lawyer. He's too smart to admit anything."

"He admitted that he knew her, that he cared about her. Chase, I think he's telling the truth."

He stopped walking to sigh deeply. Taking off his Stetson, he raked a hand through his hair and tried to calm down. "I don't know why I'm putting myself through this. I'm twenty-eight years old. He's right. What do I hope to get out of this?"

"A father."

He let out a bark of a laugh. "That ship has sailed. I don't need a father."

"We all need family."

He shook his head. "When I find him, I want to tell him off—not bond with him. Hell, I want to punch him in his face."

At a sound behind them, they turned to see Jason hurrying toward his car.

"I think we should follow him," Mary said as they watched him speed away.

Chase nodded, his gaze and attention on the attorney. "I think you're right. He certainly took off fast enough right after we talked to him. Let's go."

They climbed into his pickup, turned around in the middle of the street and followed at a distance. "Where do you think he's going?"

"Good question. Maybe home to talk to his wife."

Mary shook her head. "He doesn't live in this direction."

"What if he is going to warn Jonathan Mason?"

"Maybe. But only if Jonathan is up at the mountain resort." Chase drove up the road toward Lone Peak.

"Maybe he's going to lunch," he suggested.

"Maybe." After a few miles, the lawyer turned into the Alpine Bar parking lot.

Jason parked, leaped out and went inside.

"He could have called someone to meet him," Chase said.

She nodded. "Let's give him a minute and go inside."

Chase pulled into the lot next to the attorney's car. It was early so there were only three cars out front. During ski season, the place would have been packed. "Recognize any of the rigs?"

She shook her head.

"Have I thanked you for doing this for me? I really do appreciate it."

She smiled over at him. "You have thanked me. I'm glad to help, you know that. But Chase—"

"I know. Try not to lose my temper."

"I don't want to have to bail you out of jail," she said, still smiling.

"But you would, wouldn't you?" He reached out and stroked her cheek, his gaze locking with hers. "I've never loved you more than I do right now, Mary Cardwell Savage." He drew back his hand. "Marry me when this is all over."

She laughed and shook her head.

"I'm serious. What is it going to take to make you realize that you're crazy about me? I want to make you Mrs. Chase Steele. We can have the big wedding I know your mother wants. But I was thinking—"

"You're stalling. Come on, let's go in," she said, and they climbed out. He caught up with her and, taking her arm, pulled her around to face him.

"For the record? I was serious about asking you to marry me. Soon." As he pushed open the door, country music from the jukebox spilled out. Chase heard a familiar song, and wished he and Mary were there to dance— not track down his no-count biological father.

He spotted Jason at the bar talking to the bartender, a gray-haired man with wire-rimmed glasses. As the door closed behind them, a man came through the back door. He caught a glimpse of a residence through the doorway and a ramp before the door closed.

The man motioned to Jason to join him at one of the tables in the back.

"Do you recognize him?" he asked Mary.

"It's Jim Harris," Mary said, and grabbed Chase's arm

to stop him. "What if the initials J.M. were short for Jim? Jim Harris owns this bar. He and his wife live in a house behind it."

Chase stared at the man the attorney had joined. Blond, blue-eyed, midfifties. The scary part was that as he watched the man, he saw himself in Jim Harris's expression, in the line of his nose, the way he stroked his jaw as he listened.

Chase didn't know that he'd stopped in the middle of the room and was still staring until the man looked up. Their gazes met across the expanse of the bar.

Jim Harris froze.

Chapter Seventeen

Chase felt as if he'd been punched in the stomach. He couldn't breathe, had no idea how he'd gotten out of the bar. He found himself standing outside, bent over, gasping for breath, Mary at his side.

The bar door opened behind him. Sucking in as much air as he could, he straightened and turned. He was a good two inches taller than his father, but the similarities were all too apparent. He stared at the man who was staring just as intensely back at him.

"I didn't know," Jim said, his voice breaking. "I had no idea."

"You didn't know my mother was pregnant? Or you didn't know you had a son?" Chase demanded, surprised he could speak.

"Neither." The man suddenly dropped to the front steps of the bar and put his head in his hands. "When Jason told me…" He lifted his head. "I didn't believe him until I saw you."

"How was it you didn't know?" Mary asked. For a moment, Chase had forgotten she was there.

"She never told me…" Jim moaned.

"You weren't at all curious why she left?" Chase said, his voice breaking. His strength was coming back. So was his anger.

"I knew why Muriel left," the man said, meeting his gaze. "I separated from my wife when I met your mother. We fell in love. I was in the process of filing for divorce to marry Muriel when…" His voice broke and he looked away. "My wife was in a car accident. She almost died."

"And you decided not to leave her," Chase said, nodding as if he could feel his mother's pain. She'd been young and foolish, fallen for a man who was taken only to realize all his promises had come to nothing—and she was pregnant with his child. So she hadn't told him. What would have been the point since by then she knew he was staying with his wife?

The door behind Jim opened. Chase heard a creak and looked up to see a woman in a wheelchair framed in the doorway. The woman had graying hair that hung limp around her face. She stared at him for a long moment before she wheeled back and let the door close behind her. He looked at his father, who was looking at him.

"She's been in a wheelchair since the accident," Jim said quietly as he got to his feet. "I blamed myself since she had her accident after an argument we had over the bar. The bar," he said with disgust. "We both wanted the divorce. That wasn't the problem. It was the bar. I wanted to keep it. She wanted it sold, and half the money. If only I'd let her have it…" His voice dropped off. "I wanted to be with your mother. Muriel was the love of my life. If I'd known she was pregnant…"

"But she didn't tell you after she heard about your wife's accident," Chase said more to himself than his father.

Jim nodded. "If I'd known where your mother had gone…" He didn't finish because it was clear he didn't know what he would have done.

Chase thought of how close his father had been in the

years from fifteen on that he'd lived and worked on the Cardwell Ranch. All that time, his father had been not that far away. But there was no reason for their paths to cross. His father's bar was up on the mountain at the resort and Chase had lived down in the canyon.

He looked at his father and could see that the man had paid the price for all these years, just as his mother had. Jim Harris stood for a moment, his hands hanging at his sides, a broken man. "I'm sorry you didn't find a better father than me." With that he turned and went back inside.

Chase felt Mary touch his arm. "I can drive," she said, and took his pickup keys from his hand.

HOURS LATER, SHE and Chase lay curled up in her apartment bed, his strong arms around her. They'd stayed up and talked until nearly daylight, and finally exhausted had climbed into her bed.

Chase had found his father. Not the man he'd thought he was going to find. Not a man he'd wanted to punch. A man who looked like him. A man who'd made mistakes, especially when it came to love.

Mary had told him what she knew about Jim and his wife, Cheryl. They'd gotten married young when Cheryl had been pregnant, but she'd lost the baby and couldn't have another. It had been a rocky marriage.

"Jim said they were separated when he met your mother, but they must have kept it quiet. She wandered down in Meadow Village and he lived up on the mountain behind the bar." She'd called her mother to ask her what she knew and Jim and Cheryl.

Dana had said she remembered that Cheryl had been staying with a sister down in Gateway near Bozeman when she'd had her accident.

"So no one knew about my mother and Jim," Chase had said.

"Apparently not. I guess they hadn't wanted it to be an issue in the divorce, especially since the bar was already one."

When it got late and they'd talked the subject nearly to death, she'd suggested they go to bed.

"Mary, I—"

"Not to make love. Sleep. I don't want you leaving after what you've been through. Also, it won't be long before morning. We both need sleep and you have to leave for you carpentry job tomorrow."

Now as they lay in bed, Chase said, "I don't want to be like him, a coward, a man who never followed his heart."

"You're not like him."

He made a groaning sound. "I have been. Out of fear. I should have stayed in Montana and fought for you. Instead, I left. I was miserable the whole time. I missed you and Montana so much. I didn't think I was good enough for you. I'm still not sure I am."

She touched her finger to his lips. "That's ridiculous and all behind us."

"Is it? Because I still feel like you don't trust me," Chase whispered in the dark room as he pulled her closer. "What is it going to take to make you trust me again?"

LUCY LAY IN BED listening to the noises coming from upstairs. She hadn't been able to sleep since she'd heard Mary come in with Chase. They'd gone right upstairs. She had heard them moving around and the low murmur of voices, but she hadn't been able to tell what was going on until minutes ago when they'd gone into the bedroom. It was right over her own.

Not that she could hear what they were doing. The

building was solid enough that she'd had to strain to hear anything at all. But she'd heard enough to know that they were still in the bedroom. Both of them. She knew exactly what they were doing, and it was driving her mad.

Getting up, she went into the living room, got herself a stiff drink and sprawled on the couch. She had hoped that Mary wouldn't fall for him again. What was wrong with the woman? How could she trust a man like that? Lucy fumed and consumed another couple of shots until she'd fallen asleep on the couch only to be awakened by movement upstairs later in the morning.

She sat up and listened. Chase's boots on the stairs. Mary's steps right behind him. Lucy listened to them descend the stairs as she fought the urge to charge out into the hall and attack them both with her bare hands. Mary was a fool.

She cracked her door open to listen and heard them talking about Chase leaving the area for a carpenter job he was taking. Leaving? She tiptoed to the top of the stairs, keeping to the shadows. They had stopped on the main floor landing.

"I don't like leaving you," he said. "But I'll be back every weekend. This job will only last about six weeks, and then my boss said we have work around Big Sky so I'll see you every night. That's if you want to see me."

Lucy couldn't hear what Mary said, but she could hear the rustle of clothing. Had Mary stepped into his arms? Were they kissing? She felt her blood boil.

"You'll be careful?" Chase said.

"Please, don't start that again."

Lucy heard the tension in her voice and moved down a few steps so she could hear better.

"I'm sorry, but there is still something about Lucy that

bothers me," Chase said. "Doesn't it seem strange that three people have died since she came to town?"

"You can't believe that she had anything to do with that."

"Lucy just walks into the job at the coffee shop after the last new hire gets run down on the road? Then she moves into the same apartment Christy Shores was going to rent before she was murdered? A coincidence?"

"Big Sky is a small place, so not that much of a coincidence since I live across the street from the coffee shop and had an apartment for rent."

"And didn't you tell me that Dillon was going to ask Lucy out?"

She rolled her eyes. "And that was reason enough to kill him? She said he hadn't and she wouldn't have gone out with him if he had."

Chase shrugged. "It's…creepy."

"What's creepy is that she reminds you of an old girlfriend."

"Fiona wasn't my girlfriend. But Lucy definitely reminds me of her. Fiona went after what she wanted at all costs and the consequences be damned."

"I really don't want to talk about this."

"I just want you to be careful, that's all. Don't put so much trust in her. Promise?"

"I promise. I don't want to argue with you right before you leave me."

Lucy could hear the two of them smooching again.

"I'll be back Friday night. I'd love to take you to dinner."

"I'd love that."

Lucy pressed herself against the wall as the door opened and light raced up the stairs toward her. She stayed where she was and tried to catch her breath. Chase suspected she was Fiona. So far he hadn't convinced Mary. Nor had the marshal gotten her prints off the cup and found out she was Fiona Barkley. The deputy had done his job. She almost felt bad about killing him.

But it was only a matter of time before Mary started getting suspicious.

After hearing her go into her office, Lucy inched her way back to her apartment. She wanted to scream, to destroy the apartment, anything to rid herself of the fury boiling up inside her. She'd tried to be patient, but the more she was around Mary, the more she hated seeing her with Chase.

She clenched her fists. Mary had said she wasn't sure about the two of them. Liar. But Lucy knew Chase was to blame. He'd somehow tricked his way into Mary's bed. Chase was the one chasing the cowgirl.

She'd come here planning to kill them both. It wasn't Mary's fault that Chase went around breaking women's hearts. But even as she thought it, she knew that Mary had disappointed her by falling for Chase all over again.

Not that it mattered, she thought as she calmly walked into the kitchen, opened the top drawer and took out the knife she'd planned to use on the deputy. She stared at it, telling herself it was time to end this and move on. And there was only one way to finish it.

"It's my day off," Lucy announced as she came out of her apartment as Mary was headed downstairs a few days later.

Mary couldn't help but look confused as she took in Lucy's Western attire and tried to make sense of the words. She knew that she'd been avoiding her tenant since their conversation about Dillon and Chase and felt guilty for it.

"Oh no, I'm sorry," Lucy said quickly. "You forgot. That's all right." She started to turn back toward her apartment.

"Horseback riding." Mary racked her brain, trying to remember if they'd made a definite date to go.

"You said on my day off. I thought I'd mentioned that I would be off today. Don't worry about it. I'm sure we can go some other time."

"No," Mary said quickly. "I did forget, but it will only take me a moment to change." She was thinking about what work she'd promised to do today, but she could get it done this afternoon or even work late if she had to. She didn't want to disappoint Lucy. The woman had looked so excited when she'd first mentioned it.

The more Chase had said Lucy reminded him of the woman he'd known in Arizona, the more Mary had defended her. If she never heard the name Fiona again, she'd be ecstatic.

And yet she found herself pulling away from Lucy, questioning the small things, like how close they'd become so quickly. Also she'd always tried to keep tenants as just that and not friends. More than anything, it was Chase's concern that had her trying to put distance between her and Lucy. Mary didn't want the woman always reminding him of Fiona.

So the last thing she wanted to do today was go horseback riding with the woman. But it had been her idea, and she had invited her. If anything, she prided herself on keeping her word. After this though, she would put more distance between them.

"I'll run across the street and get us some coffee," Lucy said, all smiles. "I'm so excited. It's been so long since I've been on a horse."

Mary hurried back upstairs to change. She missed

Chase. He called every night and they talked for hours. He never mentioned his father, and she didn't bring it up. But she'd felt a change in him since discovering that Jim Harris was his biological father. He seemed stronger, more confident, more sure of what he wanted. He said he didn't want to be like the man. She wasn't sure exactly what he'd meant. Jim Harris was an unhappy man who'd made bad decisions before finding himself between a rock and hard place. She wondered if Chase could ever forgive him. Or if he already had.

When she came back downstairs, dressed for horseback riding, she found Lucy sitting at her desk. Two coffees sat on the edge away from the paperwork. Mary stopped in the doorway and watched for a moment as Lucy glanced through the papers on her desk before taking the card with the daisies that Chase had sent her, reading it and putting it back. As she did, she caught one of the daisies in her fingers.

Mary watched her crush it in her hand before dropping it into the trash can. She felt a fissure of irritation that the woman had been so nosy as to read the card let alone destroy one of the daisies. It was clear that Lucy resented Chase. Was she jealous? Did she not want Mary to have any other relationships in her life?

She cleared her voice, and Lucy got up from her desk quickly.

"Sorry, I was just resting for a moment." Lucy flashed her a gap-toothed smile. "I'm on my feet all day. It will be nice to sit on the back of a horse for a while."

HUD HAD THREE unsolved murders within weeks of each other and no clues. He got up to get himself some coffee when he remembered the cup Chase had brought in to be fingerprinted.

With a curse, he recalled that he'd given the cup to Dillon. Back in his office, he called down to the lab. "Last week a cup was brought down to be fingerprinted. I haven't seen the results yet."

The lab tech asked him to hold for a moment. "I have the order right here. I did the test myself, but I don't see my report on file. You didn't get a copy?"

"No, who did you give it to?"

"Dillon Ramsey, the deputy who brought it down. He asked that I give it to him personally. I did."

Hud swore. "You don't happen to remember—"

"The prints *were* on file," the tech said. Just as Chase had thought they would be. "Give me a minute. It was an unusual name. Fiona. Fiona Barkley."

Hud wrote it down and quickly went online. Fiona Barkley had been fingerprinted several times when questioned by police, starting with a house fire when she was eleven. Her entire family died in the fire.

The marshal shook his head as he saw that she'd been questioned and fingerprinted in a half dozen other incidents involving males that she'd dated.

Where had Chase gotten this cup? He put in a call to the cowboy's number. It went straight to voice mail. He didn't leave a message. Mary had said that Chase would be home Friday night. Hud would ask him then.

As Chase took a break, he noticed that Rick had left several messages for him to call. Tired from a long day, he almost didn't call him back. He wasn't sure he could stay awake long enough to talk to both Mary and Rick, and he much preferred to talk to Mary before he fell asleep. But the last message Rick had left said it was important.

Chase figured that Fiona's body had been found, and Rick wanted him to know. So why hadn't he just left that message? The phone rang three times before Rick answered. Chase could hear a party going on in the background and almost hung up.

"Chase, I'm so glad you called back. Hold on." He waited and a few moments later, Rick came back on, the background noise much lower. "Hey, I hate to call you with bad news."

"They found her body?"

"Ah, no. Just the opposite. Some dentist down on the border recognized Fiona's photograph from a story in the newspaper about her disappearance. He contacted authorities. Chase, it looks like Fiona is alive. Not just that. She had the dentist change her appearance. Apparently, the Mexican dentist thought it was strange since she'd obviously been in some kind of accident. But he gave her a gap between her two front teeth."

Chase felt his heart stop dead. Lucy. The woman living on the floor below Mary. Lucy. The barista who Mary had befriended. He tried to take a breathe, his mind racing. Hadn't he known? He'd sensed it gut deep, as if the woman radiated evil. Why hadn't he listened to his intuition?

"I have to go." He disconnected and quickly dialed Mary's cell phone number. It went straight to voice mail. "When you get this, call me at once. It's urgent. Don't go near Lucy. I'll explain when I see you. I'm on my way to Big Sky now." He hung up and called the ranch. Mary's mother answered.

"Dana, it's Chase. Have you seen Mary?"

"No. Chase, what's wrong?"

"I'm on my way there. If you see or hear from Mary, keep her there. Don't let her near Lucy, the barista at Lone Peak Perk, okay? Tell Hud. She's not who she is pretending to be. She's come to Montana to hurt me. I'm terrified that she will hurt Mary." He hung up and ran out to his pickup. He could be home within the hour. But would that be soon enough?

Or was it already too late?

Chapter Eighteen

"You haven't touched your coffee," Lucy said, glancing over at her as Mary drove her pickup to the ranch. Lucy had wanted to see the place and asked if they could take the back roads—unless Mary was in a hurry.

She'd taken a sip of the coffee. It had tasted bitter. Or maybe the bitter taste in her mouth had nothing to do with the coffee and more to do with what she'd seen earlier in her office—Lucy going through her things.

Now she took another sip. It wasn't just bitter. It had a distinct chalky taste—one that she remembered only too well. Even as she thought it, though, she was arguing that she was only imagining it. Otherwise, it would mean that there'd been something in the coffee that Lucy had brought her that day that had made her deathly ill—and again today.

"My stomach is a little upset," she said, putting the coffee cup back into the pickup's beverage holder.

Lucy looked away, her feelings obviously hurt. "Maybe we should do this some other day. I feel like you're not really into it."

"No, I asked you and this is the first day you've had off," Mary said, hating that she'd apparently forgotten. Worse, hating that she'd let Chase's suspicions about Lucy get to her. Not that the woman hadn't raised more suspicions by her actions earlier.

Lucy turned away as if watching the scenery out the window. Mary pretended to take a sip of her coffee, telling herself that after today, she would distance herself from the woman and the coffee shop—at least for a while. It wasn't good to get too involved with a tenant, maybe especially this one.

Even the little bit of the coffee on the tip of her tongue had that chalky taste and made her want to gag. She looked over at Lucy as she settled her cup back into the pickup's beverage holder. She'd taken the long way to the ranch for Lucy but now she regretted it, just wanting to get this trip over with.

As she slowed for a gate blocking the road, she asked, "Lucy, would you mind getting the gate?"

Without a word, the woman climbed out as soon as Mary stopped the vehicle. Easing open her door, Mary poured half of the coffee onto the ground and quietly closed her door again. Lucy pushed the gate back and stepped aside as Mary drove through and then waited for her to close it.

Would she notice the spot on the ground where the coffee had been dumped? She hoped not. She also hoped that she was wrong about the chalky taste and what might have caused it. She didn't want to be wrong about Lucy, she thought as she watched the young woman close the gate and climb back in the truck.

Mary saw her glance at the half-empty coffee cup. Did she believe that Mary had drunk it?

Looking away again, Lucy asked, "How much farther to where you keep the horses?"

"Just over the next hill." Mary had called ahead and asked one of the wranglers to saddle up her horse and a gentle one for Lucy. As they topped the hill, she could see two horses waiting for them tied up next to the barn. She tried to breathe a sigh of relief. Maybe Lucy had gotten up on the wrong side of the bed this morning. Or maybe she had drugged Mary's coffee and was angry that she hadn't drunk it.

"Is everything all right?" Lucy asked. "You seem upset with me."

Mary shot her a look. "I'm sorry. I just feel bad that I forgot about our horseback ride today. That's all."

"Not just your upset stomach?" the woman asked pointedly.

"That too, but I'm feeling better. There is no place I like better than the back of a horse."

Lucy said no more as Mary parked behind the bar and they got out. She helped the woman into the saddle. After she swung up onto her mount, they headed off on a trail that would take them to the top of the mountain. Mary was already planning on cutting the horseback ride short as she led the way up the trail.

"I'm out of sorts this morning too," Lucy said behind her. "I haven't slept well worrying about you."

Mary turned in her saddle to look back at her. "Worrying about *me*?"

"I probably shouldn't say anything, but there is something about Chase that bothers me."

She wanted to laugh out loud. Or at least say, *There's something about you that bothers him*. Instead, she said, "There is nothing to worry about."

"You just seem to be falling back into his arms so quickly. I heard him up in your apartment. He didn't leave until the next morning."

Mary felt a sliver of anger ripple through her. Chase

was right about one thing. Lucy had become too involved in her life. "Lucy, that is none of your business."

"I'm sorry, I thought we were friends. You told me that night in my apartment all about him and the deputy."

"Yes." That, she saw now had been a mistake. "Then you know I never stopped loving him."

"But he stopped loving you."

She brought her horse up short as the trail widened, and Lucy rode up beside her. "Lucy—"

"You're the one who told me about this Fiona woman he had the affair with," she said, cutting Mary off.

"It was *one* night."

Lucy shrugged. "Or so he says. You said this woman called you. Said they were engaged. Why would she do that if they'd only had one date?"

Had Mary told her about that? She couldn't remember.

Lucy must have seen the steam coming out of her ears. "Don't get angry. I'm only saying this because you need someone who doesn't have a dog in the fight to tell you the truth."

She had to bite her tongue not to say that they didn't have that kind of friendship. "I appreciate your concern. But I know what I'm doing."

"It's just that he hurt you. I don't want to see him do it again."

"We probably shouldn't talk about this," Mary said, and spurred her horse forward. The sooner they got to the top of the mountain and finished this ride, the better. Chase was right. Somehow Lucy had wormed her way deep into Mary's life. Too deep for the short time they had known each other.

Lucy was jealous of her being with Chase, she realized. Had he sensed that? Is that why he didn't like Lucy? Why she reminded him of Fiona?

They rode in silence as the trail narrowed again, and Lucy was forced to fall in behind her. When they finally reached the top of the mountain, Mary felt as if she could breathe again. She blamed herself. Lucy had been kind to her. Lucy had managed to somehow always be there when needed. Mary had let her get too close, and now it was going to be awkward having her for a tenant directly below her apartment.

She just had to make it clear that her love life was none of Lucy's business. When they rode back to town, she'd talk to her.

HUD LISTENED TO his wife's frantic call. He thought of the cup that Chase had brought him wanting the fingerprints checked. "Lucy? You're sure that's what he said?"

"She's a barista at a coffee shop across the street from Mary's building and one of her tenants." He thought of the plain white cup.

"Chase sounded terrified. He's on his way here. I tried to call Mary before I called you. Her phone went straight to voice mail. I'm scared."

"Okay, don't worry," Hud said. "I'll find this Lucy woman and see what's going on. If you see Mary, call me. Keep her there until I get to the bottom of this."

He disconnected, fear making his heart pound, and headed for his patrol SUV. The town of Big Sky had spread out some since the early days when few would have called it a real town. Still, it didn't take him but a few minutes to get to the coffee shop. As he walked in, he looked about for a barista with the name tag Lucy. There was an Amy and a Faith, but no Lucy.

"Excuse me," he said to the one called Amy. "Is Lucy working today?"

"Day off," she called over her shoulder as she contin-ued to make a coffee that required a lot of noise.

"Do you know where she might have gone?" A head-shake. He looked to the other barista. Faith shook her head as well and shrugged.

Dana had said that Lucy rented an apartment across the street. He headed over to Mary's building. With his master key, he opened the door and started up the stairs. An eerie quiet settled over him as he reached the second floor. He knocked at the first door. No answer. He tried the other one. No answer.

He was thinking about busting down the doors when the second one opened. A young man peered out. "I was looking for Lucy," he said.

"Lucy? The woman who is renting the apartment next door? I haven't met her but I overheard her and Mary talking about going horseback riding."

"Do you know where?"

"On Mary's family ranch, I would assume."

Lucy had gone horseback riding with Mary? He quickly called the ranch as he took the stairs three at a time down to his patrol SUV. "Dana," he said when she answered, "a tenant in the building said that Lucy and Mary went horseback riding. You're sure they aren't there?"

"I don't see her rig parked by the barn unless…" He could hear Dana leaving the house and running toward the barn. "She parked in back. They must have come in the back way," she said, out of breath. "Oh, Hud, they're up in the mountains somewhere alone." He heard the sound of a vehicle come roaring up.

"Who is that?" he demanded.

"Chase."

The marshal swore. "Tell him to wait until I get there.

Don't let him go off half-cocked." But even as he said the words, he knew nothing was going to stop Chase. "I'm on my way." The moment he disconnected, he raced toward his patrol SUV.

Hud swore as he climbed behind the wheel, started the engine and headed for the ranch. It didn't take much to put the coffee cup and the barista named Lucy together with an apparently disturbed woman named Fiona Barkley who had a lot of priors in her past. His dead deputy had seen the report and kept the results to himself. He had the tie-in with Dillon and the barista, he thought his stomach roiling. His daughter was on a horseback ride with a killer.

LUCY GRITTED HER teeth as she watched Mary ride to the edge of the mountain and dismount. As she stared at her back, there was nothing more Lucy could say. She could tell that Mary was angry with her. Angry at a friend who was just trying to help her. Mary thought she knew Chase better than her.

Lucy wanted to laugh at that. She knew the cowboy better than Mary assumed. Maybe it was time to enlighten her. Look how easily Chase had cast her aside. How he'd gotten that irritated look whenever he saw her after that first night. He'd wanted her to go away. He'd gotten what he wanted from her and no longer needed her.

Instead, he thought he needed Mary. Sweet, precious Mary. She glared at the woman's back as she rode toward her, reined in and dismounted. She told herself that she'd tried to save Mary. It was Mary's own fault if she wouldn't listen. Now the cowgirl would need to die. It would have to look like an accident. Earlier, she'd thought about pulling the pocketknife she'd brought and jamming it into the side of her horse.

But she'd realized that Mary had been raised on horses. She probably wouldn't get bucked off when the horse reared or even when it galloped down the narrow trail in pain.

No, it had been a chance she couldn't take. But one way or another Mary wasn't getting off this mountain alive, she thought as she stepped over to stand beside her.

The view was just as Mary had said it was. They stood on a precipice overlooking a dozen mountains that stretched far into the horizon.

Below them was the canyon with its green-tone river snaking through the pines and canyon walls. It would have been so easy to push Mary off and watch her tumble down the mountain. But there was always the chance that the fall wouldn't kill her.

Lucy reached into her pocket and fingered the gun as she said, "I slept with Chase in Arizona."

Chapter Nineteen

Chase roared up in his pickup and leaped out as Dana ran toward him.

"The wrangler had horses saddled for them. He said they headed up the road into the mountains," she told him as he rushed toward her. He could see that she'd been saddling horses. "Hud wants you to wait for him. If this woman is as dangerous as you say she is—"

"I'm the one she wants. Not Mary. If I wait, it might be too late." He swung up into the horse she'd finished saddling and spurred it forward. Dana grabbed the reins to stop him.

"I know I can't talk you out of going. Here, take this." She handed him the pistol he knew she kept in the barn. "It's loaded and ready to fire. Be careful." Her voice broke. "Help Mary."

He rode off up the road headed for the mountaintop. He knew where Mary would take Lucy. It was her favorite spot—and the most dangerous.

As he rode at a full-out gallop, he thought of his misgivings about Lucy. Fiona must have loved the fact that she'd fooled him. That she'd fooled them all, especially trusting Mary. The woman had known exactly how to worm her way into Mary's life, how to get her claws into her and make her believe that she was her friend.

What Fiona didn't know how to do was let go.

He took the trail, riding fast and hard, staying low in the saddle to avoid the pine tree limbs. His heart was in his throat, his fear for Mary a thunderous beat in his chest and his abhorrence for Fiona a bitter taste in his mouth. He prayed as he rode that he would reach them in time. That the woman Fiona had become would spare Mary who'd done nothing to her.

But he had little hope. He knew Fiona. She had come all the way to Montana to extract her vengeance. She'd become another person, Lucy, taking her time, playing Mary. Did she know that they were on to her? That's what frightened him the most. If she thought that Mary was turning against her or that the authorities knew...

MARY TURNED TO the woman in surprise, telling herself she must have heard wrong. "What did you just say?"

"I slept with Chase before you sent the letter."

She stared at the woman even as her heart began to pound. "What are you talking about?"

"I'm Fiona."

Mary took a step back as the woman she'd known as Lucy pulled a gun and pointed it at her heart.

Lucy laughed. "Surprise! I read your pathetic letter, and I hated you for taking him from me. You're the reason Chase broke up with me. Instead, the accident helped me become Lucy. You liked Lucy, didn't you? We could have been such good friends. But then Chase showed up—just as I knew he would."

Mary's mind was reeling. This was Lucy. And yet as she stared at her, she knew this was the woman who Chase said had tried to kill him before he left Arizona. The woman he'd said was delusional.

"You think you know him so well." Lucy shook her

head. "I was in love with him. He and I were so good together. You don't want to believe that, do you? Well, it's true. There was something between us, something real and amazing, but then you wrote that letter." Lucy's face twisted in disgust. "You ruined my life. You ruined Chase's."

Mary was shaking her head, still having trouble believing this was happening. Chase had tried to warn her, but she'd thought she knew Lucy. She'd really thought she was a friend.

Until she'd taken a sip of the coffee this morning and tasted that horribly familiar chalky taste. "You drugged me."

Lucy shrugged. "You shouldn't have poured out your coffee this morning. That was really rude. I was nice enough to get it for you."

"You wanted to make me sick again?"

"I was being kind," Lucy said, looking confused. "This would have been so much easier if you'd been sick. Now, it's going to get messy." She jabbed the gun at her. "If you had just stayed mad at Chase, this wouldn't be happening either."

Mary didn't know what to say or do. She'd never dealt with someone this unbalanced. "You want to make him suffer. Is that what this is about?"

Lucy smiled her gap-toothed smile. "For starters."

"You want him to fall in love with you again." She saw at once that was exactly what Lucy wanted. "But if you hurt me, that won't happen."

"It won't happen anyway and we both know it. Because of you." The woman sounded close to tears. "I could have made him happy. Before the letter came from you, he needed me. I could tell. He would have fallen in love with me."

Mary doubted that, but she kept the thought to herself. "If you hurt me, you will lose any chance you have for happiness."

Lucy laughed, sounding more like the woman she'd thought she knew. "Women like me don't find happiness. That's what my mother used to say. But then she let my stepfather and brothers physically and sexually abuse me."

Mary felt her heart go out to the woman despite the situation. "I'm so sorry. That's horrible. You deserved so much better."

Lucy laughed. "I took care of all of them, sending them to hell on earth, and for a while, I was happy, now that I think about it."

"Lucy—"

"Call me Fiona. I know how much you hate hearing that name. Fiona. Fiona. Fiona." She let out a high-pitched laugh that drowned out birdsong but not the thunder of hooves as a horse and rider came barreling across the mountaintop.

CHASE REINED IN his horse as all his fears were realized. The women had been standing at the edge of the mountaintop, Fiona holding a gun pointed at Mary's heart. But when they'd heard him coming, Fiona had grabbed Mary and pressed the muzzle of the weapon to her rival's throat.

"Nice you could join us," Fiona said as he slowly dismounted. "I wondered how long it would take before you realized who I was."

"I sensed it the first time I saw you," he said as he walked toward the pair, his gaze on Fiona and the gun. He couldn't bear to look into Mary's eyes. Fear and disgust. This was all his fault. He'd brought Fiona into their lives. Whatever happened, it was on him.

"I knew it was you," he said, and she smiled.

"It's the chemistry between us. When you pretended not to know me, well, that hurt, Chase. After everything we meant to each other…"

"Exactly," he said. "That's why you need to let Mary go. This is between you and me, Fiona."

Her face clouded. "Please, you think I don't know that you came riding up like that to save her?"

"Maybe I came to save you."

Fiona laughed, a harsh bitter sound. "Save me from what?"

"Yourself. Have any of the men you've known tried to save you, Fiona?" The question seemed to catch her off guard. "Did any of them care what happened to you?"

She met his gaze. "Don't pretend you care."

"I'm not pretending. I never wanted to hurt you. When I heard they found your car in the river, I was devastated. I didn't want things to end that way for you." He saw her weaken a little and took a step toward her and Mary.

"But you don't love me."

That was true and he knew better than to lie. "No. I'd already given away my heart when I met you. It wasn't fair, but it's the truth."

"But you picked me up at that party and brought me back to your place."

He shook his head as he took another step closer. "Rick asked you to drive me home because I'd had too much to drink."

She stared at him as if she'd told herself the story so many times, she didn't remember the truth. "But we made love."

"Did we? I remember you pulling off my boots and jeans right before I passed out."

Fiona let out a nervous laugh. "We woke up in the same bed."

"We did," he agreed as he stepped even closer. "But I suspect that's all that happened that night."

She swallowed and shook her head, tears welling in her eyes. "I liked you. I thought you and I—"

"But you knew better once I told you that I was in love with someone else."

"Still, if you had given us a chance." Fiona made a pleading sound.

"Let Mary go. She had nothing to do with what happened between us."

Fiona seemed to realize how close he was to the two of them. She started to take a step back, dragging Mary along with her. The earth crumbled under her feet and she began to fall.

Chase could see that she planned to take Mary with her. He dived for the gun, for Mary, praying Fiona didn't pull the trigger as she fell. He caught Mary with one hand and reached for the gun barrel with the other. The report of the handgun filled the air as he yanked Mary forward, breaking Fiona's hold on her. But Mary still teetered on the sheer edge of the cliff as he felt a searing pain in his shoulder. His momentum had carried him forward. He shoved Mary toward the safety of the mountain top as was propelled over the edge of the drop-off.

He felt a hand grab his sleeve. He looked up to see Mary, clinging to him, determined not to let him fall.

Below him, he saw Fiona tumbling down the mountainside over boulders. Her body crashed into a tree trunk, but kept falling until it finally landed in a pile of huge rocks at the bottom.

As Mary helped pull him back up to safety, he saw that Fiona wasn't moving, her body a rag doll finally at rest. Behind them he heard horses. Pulling Mary to him, he buried his face in her neck, ignoring the pain in his shoulder as he breathed in the scent of her.

"He's shot," Chase heard Dana cry before everything went black.

Chapter Twenty

Chase opened his eyes to see Mary sitting next to his hospital bed as the horror of what had happened came racing back. "Are you—"

"I'm fine," she said quickly, and rose to reach for his hand. "How are you?"

He glanced down at the bandage on his shoulder. "Apparently, I'm going to live. How long have I been out?"

"Not long. You were rushed into surgery to remove the bullet. Fortunately, it didn't hit anything vital."

He stared into her beautiful blue eyes. "I was so worried about you. I'm so sorry."

She shook her head. "I should have listened to you."

Chase laughed. "I wouldn't make a habit of that."

"I'm serious. You tried to warn me."

He sobered. "This is all my fault."

"You didn't make her do the things she did." Her voice broke. Tears filled her eyes. "I thought we were both going to die. You saved my life."

"You saved mine," he said, and squeezed her hand. "Once I'm out of this bed—"

"Slow down, cowboy," the doctor said as he came into the room. "It will be a while before you get out of that bed."

"I need to get well soon, Doc. I'm going to marry this woman."

Mary laughed. "I think he's delirious," she joked, her cheeks flushed.

"I've never been more serious," he called after her as the doctor shooed her from the room. "I love that woman. I've always loved Mary Cardwell Savage," he called before the door closed. He was smiling as he lay back, even though the effort of sitting up had left him in pain. "I need to get well, Doc. I have to buy a ring."

HUD LEANED BACK in his office chair and read the note Fiona-Lucy had left in her apartment. That the woman had lived just a floor below his daughter still made his heart race with terror.

By the time, you find this, I will probably be dead. Or with luck, long gone. Probably dead because I'm tired of living this life. Anyway, I have nowhere to go. I came here to make Chase Steele pay for breaking my heart. Sometimes I can see that it wasn't him that made me do the things I've done. That it started long before him. It's the story of my life. It's the people who have hurt me. It's the desperation I feel to be like other people, happy, content, loved.

But there is an anger in me that takes over the rest of the time. I want to hurt people the way I've been hurt and much worse. I killed my mother, stepfather and stepbrothers in a fire. Since then, I've hurt other people who hurt me—and some who didn't. Some, like Deputy Dillon Ramsey, deserved to die. Christy Shores, not so much.

Today, I will kill a woman who doesn't deserve it in order to hurt a man who I could have loved if only he had loved me. He will die too. If not today, then soon. And then... I have no idea. I just know that I'm tired. I can't keep doing this.

Then again, I might feel differently tomorrow.

Hud carefully put the letter back into the evidence bag and sealed it. Fiona was gone. She'd died of her injuries after falling off the mountain. Because she had no family, her body would be cremated. Chase had suggested that her ashes be sent back to Arizona to her friend, Patty, the one person who'd stuck by her.

Two of his murders had been solved by the letter. The third, Grady Birch, was also about to be put to rest. A witness with a cabin not far from where Grady's body was found had come forward. He'd seen a man dragging what he now suspected was a body down to the river. That man had been Deputy Dillon Ramsey, who the witness identified after Dillon's photo had run in the newspaper following his murder.

According to the law, everything would soon be neatly tied up, Hud thought as he put away the evidence bag. But crimes left scars. He could only hope that his daughter would be able to overcome hers. He had a feeling that Chase would be able to help her move on. He wouldn't mind a wedding out at the ranch. It had been a while, and he was thinking how much his wife loved weddings—and family—when his phone rang. It was Dana.

"I just got the oddest call from our son Hank," his wife said without preamble. "He says he's coming home for a visit and that he's bringing someone with him. A woman."

Hud could hear the joy in Dana's voice. "I told you that it would just take time, didn't I? This is great news."

"I never thought he'd get over Naomi," she said, but

quickly brightened again. "I can't wait to meet this woman and see our son. It's been too long."

He couldn't have agreed more. "How's Mary?"

"She's picking up Chase at the hospital. Given the big smile on her face when she left the ranch, I'd say she's going to be just fine. How do you feel about a wedding or two in our future?"

He chuckled. "You just read my mind, but don't go counting your chickens before they hatch. Let's take it one at a time." But he found himself smiling as he hung up. Hank was coming home. He'd missed his son more than he could even tell Dana. He just hoped Hank really was moving on.

CHASE COULDN'T WAIT to see Mary. He was champing at the bit to get out of the hospital. He'd called a local jewelry store and had someone bring up a tray of engagement rings for him to choose one. He refused to put it off until he was released. The velvet box was in his pocket. Now he was only waiting for the nurse to wheel him down to the first floor—and Mary—since it was hospital policy, he'd been told.

Earlier, his father had stopped by. Chase had been glad to see him. Like his father, he'd made mistakes. They were both human. He'd been angry with a man who hadn't even known he existed. But he could understand why his mother had kept the truth from not only him, but also Jim Harris.

He didn't know what kind of relationship they could have, but he no longer felt as if there was a hole in his heart where a father should have been. Everyone said Jim was a good man who'd had some bad luck in his life. Chase couldn't hold that against him.

When his hospital room door opened, he heard the

creak of the wheelchair and practically leaped off the bed in his excitement. He and Mary had been apart for far too long. He didn't want to spend another minute away from her. What they had was too special to let it go. He would never take their love for each for granted again.

To his surprise, it wasn't the nurse who brought in the wheelchair. "Mary?"

She looked different today. He was trying to put his finger on what it was when she grinned and shoved the wheelchair to one side as she approached.

MARY COULDN'T EXPLAIN the way she felt. But she was emboldened by everything that had happened. When Chase had first come back, she'd told herself that she couldn't trust him after he'd left Montana. But in her heart, she'd known better. Still, she'd pushed him away, letting her pride keep her from the man she loved.

Instead, she'd trusted Lucy. The red flags had been there, but she'd ignored them because she'd wanted to like her. She'd missed her friends who had moved away. She'd been vulnerable, and she'd let a psychopath into her life.

But now she was tired of being a victim, of not going after what she wanted. What she wanted was Chase.

She stepped to him, grabbed the collar of his Western shirt and pulled him into a searing kiss. She heard his intake of breath. The kiss had taken him by surprise. But also his shoulder was still healing.

"Oh, I'm so sorry," she said, drawing back, her face heating with embarrassment.

"I'm not," he said as he pulled her to him with his good arm and kissed her. When she drew back he started to say something, but she hushed him with a finger across his lips. "I have to know, Chase Steele. Are you going to be mine or not?"

He let out a bark of a laugh. "I've always been yours, Mary Savage."

She sighed and said, "Right answer."

His grin went straight to her heart. He pulled her close again and this time his kiss was fireworks. She melted into his arms. "Welcome home, Chase."

* * * * *

CALCULATED RISK

JANIE CROUCH

To the Chamblee High School Class of 1965
(and thereabouts)— my mother's graduating class.
Thank you for letting me borrow your names.

Chapter One

Bree Daniels froze, fork halfway to her mouth, at the sound of the knock at her apartment door. She forced herself to put the fork down slowly and remain calm.

A knock on the door wasn't a cause for panic for most people. But from the time Bree was twelve, she'd been taught that danger of the most deadly kind could wait on the other side of any door.

She took a deep breath and let it out.

It wasn't that no one ever knocked on her door. She regularly ordered things that had to be delivered. As a matter of fact, most of her shopping was done online. Everything from clothing to groceries. Buying what she needed on the internet meant less interaction with people and no need to leave her downtown Kansas City apartment.

But Bree always knew exactly—usually to the hour—when the items would arrive. When a knock would come on her door.

This was not one of those times.

She waited, hoping it was just some kid or lost person who would go away, tensing when a second knock came. She stood, moving toward the emergency bug-out bag she kept packed in the coat closet. It contained everything she needed for a quick getaway: clothing, a wad of cash, a few items that could be used to change her appearance and a fake ID she'd never used.

She hadn't needed the bag since arriving here three years ago on her twenty-first birthday. She didn't want to use it now unless she absolutely had to. Despite the wisdom of it, she loved this little apartment. It had become home. She didn't want to leave.

A woman's voice came from the other side of the door. "Bethany?"

Now Bree ran for the closet. It was definitely time for the bug-out bag.

Nobody knew her by the name Bethany. At least, no one who wanted her alive.

Another soft knock. Another whisper at the door. "Please, Bethany. I don't have anywhere else to go."

Bree didn't stop, just grabbed the bag and ran toward the window in the living room. The fire escape outside her second-floor apartment was the reason she had chosen this unit in the first place.

Always have multiple exits. Always have a plan.

And she did. To get the hell out. She was climbing through the window when she heard the words from the door.

"Crisscross, applesauce."

Bree froze. No, it couldn't be. She hadn't heard those words, the code she'd shared with her cousin when they were younger, in more than a decade.

Melissa had been the only person Bree had ever truly opened up to, the only person who'd taken the time to try to understand the socially awkward Bethany. Their upbringing had been isolated and cold—before Bree's had turned into a total nightmare—but together it had been bearable.

Crisscross, applesauce.

That phrase had been their agreed-upon code, hidden

from the Organization, to let each other know if they were truly in need.

They were quite possibly the only words in the world that could've stopped Bree from crawling out that window and leaving here forever.

Was it a trap?

If Bree's mother was still alive, she would've definitely said yes. They would've already been out the window and moving to separate locations to meet up later if it was safe. That had always been their agreed-upon plan, even when it meant Bree had to spend a week living by herself when she was fourteen. Whatever kept them alive.

Knowing she might be making the worst mistake of her life, that her mother was probably rolling over in her grave, Bree stopped and turned back toward her front door.

Saying a quick prayer and calling herself all sorts of stupid, she cracked open the door.

She knew immediately it was Melissa. She was more than a decade older than when Bree had last seen her at thirteen, but her features and long blond hair were still the same. Bree had been so jealous of Mel's beautiful curls when they were kids. Her own straight brown hair had seemed so boring in comparison.

She'd made a mistake by opening the door. Even if Melissa wasn't here because she meant to kill her—and Bree still wasn't sure of that—Melissa was part of a life Bree wanted nothing to do with.

"I'm sorry, you've got the wrong place. There's nobody by that name here." Bree quickly shut the door.

"Bethany, I know it's you. Please, it's Melissa. I'm not going to hurt you, and I haven't told anybody in the Organization where you are. But I need your help."

Bree rested her forehead against the door. It had been so long since…everything. Since seeing Melissa. Since hearing anyone call her by her real name.

Since talking to anyone person to person at all.

"Crisscross, applesauce. Crisscross, applesauce." Melissa kept softly saying it over and over against the door.

Shaking her head, Bree opened it again.

"Oh, God, thank you," Melissa said before Bree yanked her inside. Immediately Bree started patting down her cousin, looking for a weapon. Not finding one didn't make her feel any better. If the other woman was here to betray Bree, she wouldn't be here alone.

"I don't have any guns," Melissa said as Bree finished the pat down. "And I don't have very much time."

"Why are you here, Mel?"

Bree stood stiff as her cousin threw her arms around Bree's torso. She couldn't remember the last time someone had hugged her. Her mom had stopped long before she died.

"Why are you here?" she asked again. "How did you find me?"

Melissa stepped back. "I discovered you were in Kansas City a few months ago. But only recently did I find this place."

Bree tried to focus on what Melissa was saying and not on the fear coursing through her system. If Melissa could find her, so could the rest of the Organization.

Melissa grabbed her hands. "Nobody knows but me. I promise. I need your help, Bethany."

"Bree," she said automatically. "I go by Bree now."

"Bree. It suits you." Melissa gave her a small smile, her hands wringing. "I don't have much time. It won't take them long to figure out I'm gone. They're suspicious already."

Bree watched her closely, still ready to run if needed. "What do you need?"

"I found out the truth about the Organization. I want

to get out. I've wanted to for a long time, but now I think I have the means."

Bree shut her eyes and shook her head. "I—"

"Things are so much worse now than when you were there. The things they can do now…"

Bree didn't want to get drawn back into this. She was already going to have to run again. The thought of leaving this place hurt. "I can't help you. Honestly, I'm not in any position to help *anyone*. And if you know I'm here, the Organization does, too."

Melissa grabbed Bree's hand, and she fought not to flinch away. "No, they don't know. They may know I'm here, but they don't know it's *you*. And I have a couple of allies on the inside now. People who can be trusted."

The only person Bree trusted was herself. When it came to the Organization, the price on her head was too high to trust anybody.

The phone in Melissa's hand pinged, and she let out a curse.

"I'm out of time." Her features became more pinched. "There's so much I need to tell you. Please, Bethany— *Bree*—please meet me tonight so I can explain everything. There's so much more at stake than you could ever dream, than *I* could've ever dreamed. I have to make my move now or I'll lose everything." Desperation dripped from every word.

"Mel, I just don't think—"

"Just meet me tonight," Melissa cut her off. "At the downtown train station at midnight. I'll bring the hard drive. It has everything we need to truly get our freedom. I'll show you why it's critical I make my move now."

When the phone in her hand beeped again, Melissa bolted to the door. She turned, eyes entreating. "Crisscross, applesauce, Bethany. Please."

All Bree could do was watch her go.

TWELVE HOURS LATER, at almost midnight, Bree sat in her car in a location giving her good visual access to the train station.

She was making a mistake. She *knew* she was making a mistake, that this was all going to end badly…yet here she was.

She'd been watching the station for the past two hours, looking for any sign that Melissa had set her up, that this was a trap and the Organization would be moving in to capture Bree.

She'd found no indication at all that that was the case.

Just like she'd found no indication of betrayal after she'd immediately vacated her apartment this afternoon when Melissa left. As far as Bree could tell—and she'd become very proficient at the tactical skill of observation—no one had been watching or following her all day.

It disturbed her slightly how much she wanted to believe her cousin's intentions were good. Even if it went against the idea her mother had spent so many years instilling: *no one* could be trusted.

In the end, her mother hadn't even trusted Bree. She rubbed the raised flesh of the knife scar on her shoulder under her shirt. Her mother's parting gift, before taking her own life, thinking Bree was about to do it.

But Bree had seen nothing suspicious or out of the ordinary here for hours. So she was fairly certain she was going to do the stupid thing and get out of this car to help Melissa.

Even if she knew the smart thing would've been to already be two hundred miles outside Kansas City. That's why she'd chosen the city right smack in the middle of America—she could travel in any direction if she needed to get out quick.

But the fact of the matter, and the reason Bree was sitting here right now, was that if Melissa had intended to turn over Bree to the Organization, her best bet would've been to do it earlier today when she had the element of surprise. Melissa had known her apartment number, so all she'd really needed to do was have someone guarding the fire escape and ready to catch Bree when she ran.

But Mel hadn't.

Crisscross, applesauce.

Shaking her head, Bree got out of the car and headed toward the designated parking lot to meet Melissa.

The choice of locations was a good one. Trains were accessible, of course, and the bus depot was only two blocks away. In a personal vehicle someone could be on three different major interstates in less than five minutes.

Bree kept to the shadows, circling the area and waiting for Melissa. When by fifteen minutes past their scheduled meeting time Melissa hadn't arrived, Bree began to get worried. She gave her ten more minutes after that, then knew it wasn't safe to stay in one place any longer.

Something had changed—planned or unplanned. Either way, Bree couldn't stay here. All she could do was pray her mother's voice screaming in her head hadn't been right and this was all a setup.

She had her answer a few moments later as she approached her car and felt the cold metal of a gun muzzle against the back of her neck.

Sorry, Mom, I guess you were right.

"Would've probably been less conspicuous to take me out at my apartment. Nobody knew me there anyway," she said, raising her hands to shoulder level, as if she had no plans to fight.

There weren't too many self-defense moves she could do if the shooter was going to assassinate her with a slug to the back of the head. But if he or she had instructions to bring Bree back alive, Bree would have opportunities to make her own attack. Better to make the person think she was compliant.

Bree very definitely wasn't compliant, and there was no way in hell someone was taking her back to the Organization alive.

"Melissa sent me." A man's voice.

"Well, tell her I said she played me just right. I honestly believed she needed my help right up until the second I felt your gun at my neck."

"She does need your help. I'm not here to hurt you. Melissa was being watched, so she couldn't come herself." And then, amazingly, the cold metal eased back from her skin.

Bree turned around slowly, then blanched as she found herself looking into cold eyes she hadn't seen in over ten years.

It took every ounce of self control she had not to scurry away or whimper.

Everyone had called him Smith, although that certainly wasn't his real name. He'd been in charge of discipline. He'd been old even then. He looked ancient now.

"You know who I am?" he asked.

"Yes." How could she possibly forget the man who had broken more than one of her bones? "What I don't know is why I'm alive and still conscious."

Smith shook his head. "As I said, I'm not here to harm you. Melissa needed me to deliver important…items that are required in order for her to escape the Organization."

"You're helping her?"

"They've gone too far, even for me." He gave the smallest shrug with his shoulder. "And maybe what I'm doing here today will help make up for the sins of my past. But we don't have much time. I'll lead them away from your direction, but that's all I can do."

He pushed an old flip phone into her hand. "You hold

the future now. Melissa will be in touch as soon as she can. I placed the items in the back seat of your car. Be careful. They are everything."

Bree turned toward her car. *They* were everything? She turned back toward the caretaker. "What are you talking about—"

He was gone, disappeared into the darkness.

She shook her head and turned back toward her car—a nondescript late-model Honda most people wouldn't pay attention to—cautiously, even knowing she could've been killed multiple times over by now if that was someone's intent.

She heard yelling on the other side of the parking lot and picked up her pace. Maybe it was just the normal type of trouble that could be found in an empty downtown parking lot in the middle of the night, but maybe it was trouble coming specifically for her. She paused again as she came up on her car, seeing two large, odd-shaped boxes in the back seat.

She'd been expecting some files, but electronic ones on a hard drive. Definitely not anything that size.

After another couple steps, Bree realized those weren't file boxes at all. She ran the last few feet to her car, pushing her face up against the window.

"Oh, my God, Mel, what have you done?"

Chapter Two

Bree stared, rubbed her eyes just to make sure she hadn't been affected by some sort of airborne hallucinogen, then stared some more.

Not file boxes at all. Strapped into the back seat of her car were two separate baby carriers. Inside each of them was a tiny sleeping infant. Bree didn't know anything about babies, but those were definitely fresh ones. New. Couldn't be more than five minutes old, right?

A note was taped to the top of one of the carriers, so she carefully opened the door and grabbed it.

> I couldn't get out. But you see now why I have to. Their names are Christian and Beth, and they're two months old. The Organization doesn't know about them. I will keep it that way and hope you will keep them safe until I can escape.
>
> Crisscross, applesauce, Bree. You hold my heart in your hands every time you pull the twins close. I never knew what true family was until I had them.

Bree removed the small hard drive attached to the paper then crumpled it, bringing her fist down softly on the roof of the car. She didn't know the first thing about babies. Had never held one in her life. What was she going to do now?

She quietly shut the back door—heaven forbid she wake one of them up—and got into the driver's side. Staying here wasn't safe. Her fingers wrapped around the steering wheel in a death grip as she pulled the car out of the parking lot.

She'd known it was going to be hard. But this was so much worse than she thought.

There were babies in the back seat.

Not just one. *Two. Babies.* One of them even named after her. *Oh, Mellie.*

This changed every possible plan that had been stirring around in Bree's head since Melissa showed up this afternoon. All the routes she and Melissa could choose, modes of transportation they could take. She'd had multiple possible plans.

Prepare for the unexpected and you're much more likely to get out of a situation alive. She could almost hear her mother's voice.

But of all the scenarios Bree had run in her head, none of them had involved the particular variables she was dealing with right now. All her options were now defunct.

Because *babies.*

She glanced down at the phone Smith had given her. It wasn't a high-tech smartphone; it was a low-tech flip phone that could barely be used to make a call.

A safe phone, so low-tech that it would be difficult for the Organization to use it to find someone.

She quickly scrolled through the call history to see if she could find any information, a way to get in touch with Melissa, let her know what a terrible plan this was, but there was nothing. Until Melissa called Bree, the phone was basically useless.

How long before Melissa could get away from the Organization? Hours? Days?

Years?

When one of the babies let out a soft gurgle from the back seat, Bree put the phone down and focused on figuring out where to go. Maybe the best plan was to go back to her apartment. Obviously, Melissa didn't intend her any harm, so Bree's home was probably safe.

At least it would allow her a chance to regroup. Figure out what she was going to do.

She knew something was wrong as soon as she drove up to her block. Her apartment was in a busy, but not dangerous, part of the city, something she'd been specifically looking for when she'd chosen the place. She'd wanted to be able to slip in and out, day or night, without people paying much attention to her. To be able to blend into a crowd instantly if needed.

There were enough units in the building that people were constantly coming and going, and it was urban enough that nobody thought much of it if you didn't stop and talk to them.

But right now it looked like every single person in the building was out on the street surrounding it. At one o'clock in the morning.

Bree parked the car on a side street. She left the twins sleeping inside, tucked most of her long brown hair up into a ball cap so it looked much shorter and then jogged over to the people at the edge of the crowd. She kept an eye on the car as she spoke to an older couple she'd seen around but had never talked to.

"Hi, I live in 4A. I just got home. What's going on? Is it a fire?"

The old man kept his arm around his wife while he shook his head at Bree. "Gas leak. They came door to door about an hour ago. Told us it would be at least five or six hours before we could get back in."

"Where's the fire department?"

The older woman shrugged. "I guess the rest of them

are on their way. We only saw one. It was the gas company employees knocking on doors and checking people off their list."

Bree knew if it was dangerous enough to be taking people out of their homes in the middle of the night, it was dangerous enough to have a full firefighting crew here. This definitely wasn't right.

"So everyone just has to stand out here for five or six more hours?"

"No," the man said. "They said they'd provide rooms at a local hotel down the block for free. All you needed to do was show them your ID and let them run a credit card for any incidentals."

Bree grimaced. More likely a convenient place to herd everyone from the building and double-check their identification.

She glanced over at the car. Nobody was near it, but she needed to get the twins out of here. This had the Organization written all over it.

The older woman gave out a weary sigh. "Harold just walked down to use the ATM and couldn't get it to work. It said our account was temporarily on hold. I don't want to go to some strange hotel in my pajamas with no money."

A younger woman turned to them from a few yards away. "Did you guys say your bank account is on hold? Mine told me the same thing a few minutes ago when I went to grab some cash."

Harold let out another frustrated sigh. "Unbelievable. At First National Trust?"

The woman shook her head. "No, Bank United. Everybody's system must be down."

Or somebody was making sure that everybody in the building ended up where they were subtly being directed.

The Organization was casting a net. They didn't know

what their fish looked like, so they were going to dredge everything, then sort it out.

Bree pulled her hat farther down on her head. Everything happening on the street right now—all the people gathered here—was being recorded, she was sure of it.

After all, hadn't the Organization started teaching her how to use her computer skills for surveillance when she was only ten years old? They'd taught her how to target, how to track, how to incapacitate an enemy virtually. Then used her natural abilities to further develop methods of spying and tracking.

Until her mother had realized the prestigious computer school that was supposed to be providing a young Bethany a leg up in coding and systems was actually using her abilities to further their own nefarious purposes. And had no plan to ever let her leave.

Bree spoke to Harold and the others for just a few more moments before easing herself away and walking nonchalantly back to her car and slipping inside. She started the car and pulled away slowly despite every instinct that screamed to drive as fast as she could. That would do nothing but draw attention to her. Attention she desperately could not afford.

As she passed Harold and his wife, she noticed that a man wearing a Central Gas jacket was now talking to the older couple, clipboard in hand. When Harold pointed in her direction, she dipped lower in her seat, gritting her teeth, forcing herself to hold her speed consistent.

She could feel computerized eyes on her everywhere. Every phone in this vicinity was recording—whether the owners knew it or not—and sending information back to the Organization.

If Bree made one wrong move, did anything that drew unwanted attention to herself, they would be on her in a heartbeat.

She could feel the phantom pain of her leg being broken by the Organization. Hear her own screams. Her mother's sobs.

She couldn't let them take her again. So she forced herself to remain calm, to keep her car steady and slow, even though her eyes were almost glued to the rearview mirror expecting vehicles to be chasing her any moment.

But none came.

The gas man would be asking who she was. Hopefully the couple would remember Bree said 4A. The real person from 4A was the one in the building who looked most similar to Bree. Caucasian female. Brown hair. Average height and weight. Mid-to late-twenties.

Side by side it would be obvious Bree and 4A's occupant weren't the same person, but in general description they were similar enough to buy Bree some time as they searched for the wrong person.

She was going to need every extra minute she could get. She had no doubt her accounts, like everyone else's, had been frozen. They would be unfrozen as soon as she stepped foot in a bank and showed ID. But then the Organization would have a record of her, photographs.

They would figure out she was alive, and the hunt would truly begin.

So she was trapped with just the cash she had on her. Alone, that would've lasted her six months or more. More than enough time to get established somewhere and get a new job.

As if on cue one baby began crying in the back. It wasn't long before the other was joining its sibling.

Bree definitely wasn't alone anymore.

Chapter Three

Tanner Dempsey didn't spend a lot of his time in the baby aisle of Risk Peak's lone drugstore. His sister had made him an uncle three times over in the last decade, but when he was shopping for his niece and nephews, it was in the toy department.

He didn't spend a lot of time at the drugstore at all. He was only here now at 7:00 p.m., after working a twelve-hour shift, because if he showed up at his mother's house tomorrow without shaving, he'd never hear the end of it from his siblings.

Since Tanner tended to have a five o'clock shadow about two hours after he shaved, Gary, the manager here, kept a couple packages of the special razor refill brand Tanner liked. Gary stuffed them in the back aisle so no one else would buy them.

Tanner meant to just grab the pack and run, but his attention was caught by a young mother—one crying baby in her arms, another in a car seat carrier on the ground—moving in odd, jerky movements in the baby aisle.

Tanner immediately knew the woman wasn't from around here. He'd lived in Risk Peak, Colorado, his entire life, except for the four years he'd gone to college about an hour east in Denver. Risk Peak definitely wasn't so large that he wouldn't know an attractive brunette in her twenties who'd recently had twins.

And man, that one kid had a set of lungs on him. The fact that the mother was moving so awkwardly wasn't helping calm the baby.

Tiredness pushed aside, Tanner stayed at the end of the aisle out of the woman's sight, picking up a random package and pretending to read the back of it in case she looked at him. His subterfuge probably wasn't even necessary. She was so busy with her odd movements and the crying baby, she definitely wasn't looking his way.

It didn't take him long to figure out what was going on. The woman was taking individual packets of formula out of a larger box and stuffing them wherever she could manage. In her own pockets, in the diaper bag and even inside the onesie of the crying child.

No wonder the kid was bawling.

Tanner had seen a lot in his thirty-three years, but a mother stealing formula by stuffing it in the baby's clothes? That was a first. Now he'd seen it all.

Then she opened a package of diapers and started stuffing those in with the second baby in the carrier, hidden under the blanket.

Correction. *Now* he'd seen it all.

She was watching the other end of the aisle, toward the front of the store, to make sure no one caught her. But evidently she thought the back of the store was empty, which it normally would be.

He watched her for a few more moments to make sure he understood what was going on. When she dropped the half-empty pack of diapers and was struggling to pick them up, Tanner decided he had seen enough.

"Let me get those for you." He moved quickly toward her, ignoring her startled little shriek, and grabbed the half-open package of diapers from the floor and offered them to her.

And was met by the most brilliant green eyes he'd ever seen.

It took him a second to recover enough to even take in the rest of her features. Long brown hair pulled back in a low ponytail, pert nose covered in freckles that also covered her cheeks and full sensual lips.

Kissable lips.

This was definitely a woman he would know if she lived here, whether she'd just had twins or not. Not that anyone in Risk Peak would allow a young mother to become so desperate that she had to shoplift formula and diapers.

She didn't show any sign of drug use or intoxication, as he'd half feared she would. Her eyes were clear, not at all bloodshot, and her skin, although pale since he'd just startled her, lacked the sunken pallor that so often accompanied substance abuse.

She was beautiful.

But surrounding her beauty was an air of desperation and weariness—much more than just a new mother's exhaustion. This was almost like a tangible fear.

But maybe it was because she'd just gotten busted shoplifting.

"Thank you," she muttered in a husky voice, taking the diaper package. "I was just about to pay for them, and then the package ripped open."

Tanner gave her a nod, ignoring the lie. "I'm sure handling everything with two little ones is a hardship. Is their dad around? Your husband? Someone who can help you?"

"No. No, it's just me. I don't have a husband." She looked so overwhelmed and breakable, all big eyes and crying baby. It made Tanner want to forget everything that he was, the vows he had made, and help her.

More than just help her—fight against whatever it was

that was putting such fear in those green eyes. Even if that was her own bad choices.

Which was absurd, considering he'd met her thirty seconds ago and didn't even know her name.

"Maybe I can help you." He took a step forward but paused when she jerked back.

She began looking around frantically. "I just realized I don't have my purse. I—I better go get that. I'll leave the diapers here and come back for them."

She shifted the crying baby, a boy by the look of the blue outfit, into her other arm, shushing him softly and kissing his forehead. Then hefted up the baby in the carrier with her free arm. Without another word to him, she turned and walked toward the door.

Tanner was only a step behind her as she walked toward the front of the store. He wasn't sure what he was going to do. He should've made his official position known from the beginning. Mentioning it now was going to throw her into an even bigger panic.

But he wanted to help. Every instinct screamed that this was a woman at the end of her rope. He might have just caught her in the act of breaking the law, but that didn't necessarily mean she was the villain in this story.

Sometimes justice and the law weren't the same thing. Even a lawman sometimes had to break the rules if it was the right thing to do. His father had taught him that.

Of course, his father had also been killed in the line of duty.

Tanner would follow her out and make sure she made it to her car all right and wasn't in so much a hurry that she got in an accident. Then he could come back and pay for what she'd taken, and nobody had to be wiser about any of it. Gary would understand.

They were walking past the front counter, the woman throwing a worried glance at him over her shoulder every few seconds, when Gary decided to be friendly. The way he always was.

"Officer Dempsey," Gary called out. "Did you find your razor refill?"

Tanner could see every muscle in the small woman's body tense as she spun around and looked at him. "Officer?"

The baby finally stopped crying. The woman looked like she wanted to bolt but knew she wouldn't make it very far with her cargo in tow.

Tanner tilted his head toward Gary but kept his eyes on the woman. "Technically, it's captain of the southeast department of the Grand County Sheriff's Office. And yeah, Gary, I did find what I was looking for, but this lovely young mother—what's your name again?"

"Bree," she murmured.

He turned back to Gary. "Bree seems to have forgotten her wallet, and I thought I would show her a little Risk Peak hospitality and pay for the diapers and formula she needs."

She didn't say anything, just looked at him like she expected him to start reading her her rights any second.

"Here's the diaper and formula package." Tanner placed the tattered packaging on the counter. "They both…somehow ripped."

"Are you serious? I'm so sorry," Gary muttered. "If you wait just a second, miss, I'll go get you packages that aren't ripped."

She finally broke eye contact with Tanner to look at Gary. "There's no need to do that. I think half of it fell out in the baby carrier anyway."

Gary smiled and looked at the baby in her arms. "Yep, look, there's a formula packet right there in this little guy's outfit." He reached over and grabbed the small packet of formula from near the baby's neck. Bree flushed and looked away.

They stood there awkwardly as Gary rang up the items, chatting the entire time about the weather, Tanner's upcoming fly-fishing trip and the decline of the quality of plastic as evidenced by the ripped diaper and formula packages, before finally putting the items in a bag.

Bree murmured her thanks and then moved with the babies out the door.

Tanner was right behind her.

He followed her out to her gray Honda, which at least didn't look like it was going to fall apart on the side of the road. She immediately began buckling the car seats into the car.

"Were you waiting until we got out here to arrest me?" she asked when she saw he had followed her.

He leaned against her hood. "No laws were broken. Everything was paid for before anyone exited the store. So, no need for an arrest."

She let out a sigh. "Thank you. It's very kind of you to help me. Can I pay you back?"

The tightness in her features screamed that she didn't have the money to pay him back. He was almost tempted to say yes just to see what she would do.

But his mother hadn't raised him that way. "No, there's no need."

Some of the tension faded. "Well, thanks again. I've got to get going."

He kept his posture as relaxed as possible. "There are government assistance measures in place if you can't afford what you need. If you come down to my office, we could help get you set up."

She stiffened, then shook her head. "No, it's not like that. My wallet got stolen, but I'll be fine."

Her wallet may have gotten stolen, but he had a feeling

there was a lot more to it than that. "If you're in some sort of trouble, I can help."

She shook her head before walking around to the driver's side. "No, I'm fine. I just need to get to where I'm going."

"And where is that?" He hefted himself from the hood and walked toward her. She immediately took the long way around the car, keeping distance between them. She opened the driver's-side door.

"Thank you for your help," she said, not answering the question.

He sighed. "I'd like to do more."

"Well, I appreciate it, but I don't need more." She gave him a smile, but it didn't come anywhere close to meeting her eyes. All the desperation and fear he'd sensed earlier was back again. "We'll be fine and out of your hair in no time, Sheriff."

"Just captain of the department. Sheriff Duggan is my boss, although she's at the office about forty miles north of here," he corrected with a smile.

She nodded but didn't say anything further.

She was slipping through his fingers, and there wasn't a damned thing he could do about it. But since he wasn't going to arrest her and couldn't force her to come in and get help, he had to let her go.

He gripped the roof of her car and leaned toward her. "The Sunrise Diner is down the street on the way out of town. At least stop by there and grab yourself something to eat before you head out. Tell them to put in on my tab. Believe me, they'll get a hoot out of it."

Cheryl and Dan Andrews ran the place together. They'd known Tanner since he was born and would be more than thrilled to provide a meal for Bree and coo over the babies. They probably wouldn't even let him pay them back.

"Yeah, okay. Maybe."

She looked so fragile. He wanted to do more. But sometimes pushing did more harm than good.

"Good luck to you, Bree, and your babies. I hope you get to where you're going before you run out again." He wasn't just talking about running out of baby supplies.

"Me, too," she whispered. Then she got in the car and drove away.

BREE'S WHOLE BODY was shaking so badly she could barely make it out of the parking lot. If the cop hadn't been there, she wouldn't even have tried. But there was no way she could stay there and continue to talk to him.

Talking to anyone was almost impossible for her. But then to have been caught red-handed and almost been arrested? She couldn't believe she'd been so stupid.

If law enforcement got her name and ran a background check on her, the name Bree Daniels would be fine and shouldn't alert anyone in the Organization. But if they took her fingerprints and ran her through any database?

She was as good as dead.

But shoplifting had been her only option. Six weeks on the run with two newborns had depleted nearly everything of Bree's. Almost all her money. Then all her energy and stamina. And maybe now her sanity.

She felt one breath away from a breakdown.

She didn't know what to do. They'd burned through her saved money much faster than she'd anticipated. Who knew that tiny little humans could need so much *stuff*?

She'd stayed near Kansas City the first few days after the twins had been left in her care. It was a little risky, but Bree was familiar with the city and had been praying the phone Melissa had provided would ring. But it didn't.

Bree could write elaborate computer code, had an innate ability at developing software and could hack into some of the most secure databases on the planet if she wanted to.

But babies? Bree had no idea.

She wasn't good with people on any day. She definitely wasn't equipped to provide 24/7 care for two beings whose only method of communicating was screaming their heads off when they weren't happy.

Diaper changing, feeding schedules, holding, swaddling, sleeping on their back, buckling in car seats, burping…

She'd rather try to hack Department of Defense nuclear codes. It would take less time and energy.

From a purely intellectual level, Bree could understand why Melissa had chosen her to care for the babies. Bree was quite possibly the only person in the world who was living completely free of the Organization but still knew how dangerous they were. How important it was to keep away from them.

But just because she knew that didn't mean she wasn't ruining these children's lives. For six weeks Bree had barely kept the three of them above water. And things were just getting worse.

If Melissa could see them all now, both kids starting to wail from the back seat, Bree barely able to make it out of a parking lot after almost being arrested—Melissa would know she'd made the wrong choice by asking Bree to help.

She'd stayed at hotels at first, paying with cash, not realizing how much the babies would need and how much it would cost.

In the third week, low on cash, she'd made the biggest mistake of all. She'd decided to use her credit card. It wasn't under the name Bree Daniels—it wasn't under a name associated with her at all.

But in her exhaustion she forgot it had been linked to her address in Kansas City.

If they hadn't run out of diapers, forcing an emergency trip to the local supercenter in the middle of the night, she would've been there when the Organization's hired thugs came crashing into the hotel room.

As it was, she'd narrowly escaped. The number of sedans in the hotel parking lot—and the fact that her mother, in all her paranoia, had taught Bree to notice these types of things—had tipped her off.

Once again she'd forced herself to drive sedately by as the most hideous type of danger surrounded her.

Then they'd left town. It didn't matter if Melissa might call or not, they couldn't stay in Kansas City.

She drove west, since it was in the opposite direction from the Northeast, where the Organization's main office was located. Or, at least the main office where they showed their *public* face.

It wouldn't have mattered which direction she drove. The days wore on her. Lack of finances wore on her.

Why were baby formula and diapers so damn expensive?

Even only eating one meal a day herself and spending every night they possibly could in the car, she was still down to her last twenty dollars just outside Denver.

Desperate, she'd taken to shoplifting the stuff she could for the babies, using all her spare cash for gas, and had been successful a few times.

But it looked like her luck had run out today here in the tiny town of Risk Peak.

At least she wasn't in jail waiting for someone from the Organization to come kill her—or worse, take her back into captivity with them—so maybe her luck wasn't completely gone.

Not that the screaming in the back seat was any indication of that. Bree gripped the steering wheel tighter, feeling pressure sitting like a hundred-pound weight on her chest. Breathing was becoming harder.

She tried to think rationally. She couldn't go any farther

right now. Christian and Beth were hungry and needed to be changed. And she couldn't drive in this condition. She was too strung out, her body crashing now that the adrenaline wasn't coursing through her system.

When she saw the diner the cop had mentioned, she pulled in. Might as well take him up on his offer of a free meal. For the past week she'd been living off a loaf of bread, a jar of peanut butter and what food she could steal from sneaking into the lobbies of hotels that offered free breakfasts.

God, she was so tired. When was the last time she got more than two hours of sleep in a row? Maybe food would help. It couldn't possibly hurt.

She grabbed the diaper bag filled with the shoplifted formula packets. If she'd known someone was going to buy her formula, she would've gotten the cans of the powder. Those were so much more economical.

Bree was now an expert on finding the cheapest possible formula.

She got out and hefted Beth in her carrier up with one arm, then walked around to get Christian with the other. She only made it a couple of steps before she had to stop, dizziness assailing her. She took deep breaths, trying to force strength into her limbs. She could not pass out here, leaving the babies defenseless. The door got more blurry as she moved toward it, but she forced herself to take the steps. She just needed to get inside and sit down. Then she would be okay.

She had to be okay. She didn't have any other option.

The bell that clanked against the door as she opened it seemed almost at a distance. Bree walked as straight as she could, trying not to stumble, toward the first booth she saw.

She almost cried in relief when she put the carriers down on the booth with a thump. Neither twin liked being set down so hard, and they began crying harder.

"Shh, it's okay," she whispered, the words sounding garbled to her own ears.

She half sat, half fell into the booth next to one of the babies. At this point she couldn't even tell which one it was.

"Good thing one of you is a boy and one is a girl, or I would never know who was who," she whispered.

They both just kept screaming.

For the life of her, Bree couldn't remember how to get them to stop crying. She just wished everything would stop spinning before she got sick.

When an older lady wearing a bright yellow apron walked up to the table, Bree wondered if they were going to get kicked out. And what in the world she was going to do if they did.

"Can I help you, sweetie?" the woman said.

Bree just stared at the woman for a few moments. "I never planned on being a mother. This is too hard. I was the wrong choice."

She was saying too much, maybe putting them all in danger. But the older woman just smiled and sat down across from Bree. "I think all mothers feel like that sometimes. How about if I help you? It looks like these little guys need to be fed."

Bree tried to study the woman's face, but it was going in and out of focus. "Yes, they need their bottle. I need to give them their bottle."

"When was the last time you got a decent night's sleep, honey?"

Hadn't she just been asking herself that question?

"When I was ten." Before she'd realized what the Organization really was capable of.

The older woman chuckled and patted Bree's hand. She wasn't used to touch, but this felt warm, comforting. "I'm sure it feels like it. I'm Cheryl Andrews. Me and my husband, Dan, own the Sunrise Diner. We raised three kids of our own, so if you don't mind, I'd like to help you out and make a bottle for your little ones. Give you a chance to rest."

Could she trust this woman?

Did she have a choice?

"Why don't you just let me get the bottles ready for you. Is it okay if I go into the diaper bag?"

Bree just nodded, everything still fuzzy as she watched the woman walk. Bree was still staring at the doorway when the woman came back out a few moments later, an older man behind her.

She'd made the bottles.

"Thank you," she whispered. She felt like crying she was so thankful for the kindness.

"This is my Dan. He and I are just going to feed your babies. Is that okay? You just sit there and rest, okay?"

"Okay." She leaned her head against the back of the booth and watched as the older couple spoke soothingly to both children before putting the bottles up to their tiny faces.

Then there was blessed silence.

Then there was nothing at all.

THE FIRST THING that penetrated Bree's consciousness as she awoke was the silence. Followed by liquid under her cheek. It took her a moment to realize she'd been sleeping with her arms folded on a table.

Where were Christian and Beth?

She jackknifed upright, looking around. The carriers were still in the booth, but neither baby was there.

Terror slammed into her like a sledgehammer. How long had she been asleep? How could she have let this happen? She bolted out of the booth, looking around frantically, then came to an abrupt halt.

There at a corner table, the old couple—what were their

names? Dan and Sherri? No, Cheryl—were holding the babies, cooing and smiling at them.

A half dozen other people of varying ages were standing around, too, talking, smiling, reaching over Dan and Cheryl to make funny faces at the twins.

It was like something out of a television show. Not even a show from this decade. Something from forty years ago.

It definitely wasn't something she'd ever been a part of herself. Emotions weren't easy for her on any given day. But this? She had no idea how to react to this scenario.

"Hey, honey." Cheryl smiled up at her, a noncrying Christian in her arms. "Are you feeling better? We weren't sure if you needed a doctor but finally figured maybe you just needed a little break from these two. Babies can be so exhausting."

"Um, yes. I guess I did."

Dan smiled at her, standing and handing Beth over. "Thanks for letting us hold your young'uns." His Southern accent was more pronounced than Cheryl's. "We haven't had babies to hold in a long time. Hope you don't mind."

Bree just shook her head, still feeling like she was in some black-and-white television show. As if someone would tell John Boy good-night at any moment.

"No, I don't mind. Thank you. I'm not sure what happened, but I feel a lot better."

Dan patted her shoulder. "Why don't you sit down with everyone and I'll go make you something to eat in the back."

Bree looked at the group, teeth grinding. She didn't have anything against people sitting around chatting, she just didn't think she was capable of joining them. Didn't know *how*.

Dan smiled gently at her. "Or, if gabbing like a bunch of squawking ducks doesn't suit your fancy, you're welcome to come in the back with me. Bring the baby, or I'm positive they'll all fight to the death for the chance to hold her."

Bree wasn't quite sure what to do, so she kept Beth in her arms as she followed Dan into the kitchen, using the baby almost as a shield. Not that she thought the older man would do her any physical harm, but from all the questions she knew would have to be coming.

But the only question Dan asked was if she would prefer the breakfast sampler or Cheryl's famous meat loaf.

Bree would much rather have the breakfast food, but she didn't want to make a social faux pas by insulting the famous meat loaf in this sitcom she was currently starring in.

"The breakfast sampler does come with pancakes, so I can't blame you if that's the route you'd rather go." Dan winked at her.

"I do like pancakes," she whispered, pulling Beth a little closer.

"Then pancakes it is."

She offered to help, but Dan would hear nothing of it as he made her food. When Cheryl stuck her head through the window and told him someone wanted the daily, Dan didn't even bat an eye, just immediately started fixing the meat loaf platter.

He never asked Bree any questions about where she was from, what she was doing or why she'd fallen asleep in the middle of his restaurant. Just whistled, working contentedly in a kitchen he obviously was very familiar with. He passed the daily special order out to Cheryl, then added a couple more pancakes to the griddle, putting them on Bree's plate as soon as she'd finished the first ones.

"Oh, I don't know if I should…" She trailed off. It wasn't that she wasn't hungry enough to eat them, she just didn't want to be completely greedy.

"Might as well finish them now," he said. "I hate to waste food if I don't need to."

That was all the invitation she needed. He even reached out and took Beth from her so she could more easily cut and engulf the pancakes.

She took Beth back when she was finished. She was pretty amazed how a couple hours of sleep and a full meal made her almost feel like she could handle the situation she found herself in.

Although that was just as much fiction as any sitcom. Except not as funny.

Because what was she going to do once she left here?

"Thank you." She took the plate back to the dishwashing sink and began washing it off.

"It's my pleasure. I enjoy seeing someone partaking in my food with such exuberance—"

Cheryl came rushing back through the kitchen door, Christian sleeping in one carrier, the empty one in her other hand. "We just had a bus full of tourists pull up. I sent Judy home an hour ago because her husband's been so sick. I didn't think we'd have much business tonight."

Dan began setting out items of food he'd need for the group. "By the time you call her and she gets back here, it'll be too late."

"I can help." The words were out of her mouth before Bree knew they would come—a common problem for her—but it was still true. It was the least she could do given that they'd basically allowed her to set up camp here. Tanner had told her to put it on his tab, but there was no way she was doing that. "The kids have been fed, and if you've got an office or somewhere we can sit them, I'll keep an eye on them while I wait or bus tables or whatever you need. Consider it payment for today's room and board."

Both Dan and Cheryl were shaking their heads no, communicating silently with each other, and she thought they weren't going to let her. She didn't blame them—they didn't know her at all. But Cheryl opened the door off the back of the kitchen to a small office. "If you don't mind, we can definitely use your help. Dan and I are getting too old for rushes like this alone. But you're definitely going to get paid. That's not negotiable."

"I sort of lost my purse. I don't really have stuff for tax purposes." She didn't like lying to them, but the less they knew about her, the better.

Dan tossed her an apron. "We'll worry about Uncle Sam later. Right now, get those young'uns stashed away and let's get these tourists fed."

Chapter Four

Eight days after watching Bree drive away, Tanner walked from the department's office over to the Sunrise Diner. His body nearly dragged with exhaustion. He wanted a good meal and fifteen hours of sleep in his own bed, as soon as possible.

He'd spent the last eight days working almost nonstop on an interstate task force a couple hours away, in a town only slightly larger than Risk Peak, combating a rising gang problem plaguing Colorado more and more. Tanner didn't mind helping out, even though he'd never be able to put in for all the overtime hours he'd worked.

The way he saw it, stopping these types of criminal situations before they made it to Risk Peak was worth the extra hours.

And the hours had been hell. As he and his fellow law enforcement officers had moved in for arrests after days and multiple sleepless nights of undercover work and observation, one of the suspects had grabbed a preteen boy—skinny and terrified—as a human shield. Before Tanner could even talk the perp down, he'd stabbed the kid and run.

They'd caught the guy, but someone way too young and completely innocent had paid the price.

The overall outcome had been heralded a success. The

gang had been broken up before it could take root in the community. But none of the men and women working the case had felt like celebrating. They'd driven out a criminal element, but not in time to save the life of that one boy.

Tanner knew it could happen in any town at any time. He was willing to volunteer hours to keep the front lines away from Risk Peak. Because if he didn't fight it when he could, it might end up being some kid from here in the morgue.

He walked down the streets he'd been walking his whole life. These people were his to protect, and he took that very seriously, just like his father had.

He was looking forward to a meal with friendly faces and people dropping by his table just to say hello. Today he would not be taking for granted that there was always tomorrow to chat.

But inside the Sunrise, everybody seemed too busy to pay him much attention. The diner wasn't particularly full even though it was nearly dinner, but everyone seemed preoccupied.

A couple of people gave him a little wave, but nobody came over to talk to him. He rubbed his fingers against his tired eyes, then down his cheeks that definitely needed a shave again. He was being too sensitive. Exhaustion could blow a lot of things out of proportion.

But why the hell were five people huddled around the back corner booth—including Mrs. Andrews? He couldn't recall her sitting down during a dinner shift his entire life.

Judy Marshall, who'd gone to school with Tanner's younger sister, brought his normal cup of coffee over to his table. "Haven't seen you around for a while."

"Yeah, I've been working over in Pueblo County helping out with a gang issue. I'm ready to sleep for a week. I'll just have whatever's on special."

"Sounds good. I'll get Mr. A started on it for you."

"Is Mrs. A feeling all right? Why is she sitting in the booth rather than working? That's not like her."

Judy rolled her eyes. "She finally found something she loves more than Mr. Andrews and the Sunrise. Not that I can blame her."

Tanner raised an eyebrow. The older woman might have found someone she loved more than her husband, but more than this diner? No way.

Whatever was causing the commotion over in the corner, it definitely had everyone's attention. He was too tired to worry about it. Nobody was hurt or breaking the law, so he was just going to sit and enjoy his meal and get home.

That resolution lasted about two minutes.

He grabbed his coffee and started making his way toward the corner booth, to see for himself what the fuss was about. He wasn't quite there when he heard a baby's muffled cry. That would explain it.

And it immediately made him think of Bree. She hadn't been far from his mind all week. Was she all right? Had she and the babies made it safely to wherever they were going?

The chances of him ever knowing were slim to none.

He caught Mrs. A's gaze and gave her a little salute with his coffee cup. Then the woman uncharacteristically shifted her eyes to the side and down. If Tanner had been interrogating a suspect, he would've taken it as an indication that the perp was hiding something. Acting suspiciously.

Exhaustion was definitely clouding his judgment. The Andrewses were as straightforward and honest as people came. And Mrs. Andrews wasn't someone who hid her actions from anyone. Other people's opinions had never concerned her.

He shrugged it off and was turning back to the table when a second cry joined the first. Even louder.

That set of pipes Tanner recognized. He immediately

spun back toward the booth, marching all the way to the edge. Sure enough, there they were. Twins.

He didn't know a lot about babies, but he was willing to bet these were Bree's. He looked around but didn't see her anywhere.

He crossed his arms over his chest. "What's going on, Mrs. A?"

The older woman raised a single eyebrow. "I've got a couple of infants here crying. It happens. You cried quite a bit too when you were this age, if I recall."

Tanner just studied her. Overfamiliarity was an issue from time to time, since he'd known most of the people in Risk Peak his entire life. Generally, Tanner used it to his advantage.

But today it wasn't going to be so easy.

"I have no problem with babies crying," he finally answered evenly. "I'm fairly certain they're not doing anything against the law. Where is their mother?"

Because she, he wasn't so certain about.

"To be honest, I'm not entirely sure right at this moment." Mrs. A shifted the baby in her arms and wiggled a pacifier in its mouth until it latched on and stopped crying. Across from her, Glenda Manning, who had a couple of teenage children of her own, cooed at the baby she was bouncing.

"Whose children are these, Cheryl?" He didn't take the use of her first name lightly.

Neither did she. "Why do you care, *Tanner*?"

One of the women sitting across from Mrs. Andrews looked like she might speak up, but was given the stink eye so quickly she abruptly looked away.

Why would Mrs. A be making such a big deal out of this if Bree wasn't in more trouble? Why wouldn't the older woman just say they were holding the babies while the mom was in the bathroom or at the gas station or wherever she was? Tanner would've believed that with no suspicion at all. The fact that Mrs. A refused to give any information was what made it suspicious.

A husky feminine voice spoke behind him. "I'm through for the day, Cheryl. Thank you again so much for watch—"

Tanner spun around to see the woman who hadn't been far out of his thoughts since he'd watched her drive away over a week ago. His breath almost whistled through his teeth. She was definitely as beautiful as he remembered. The long brown hair falling around her shoulders made him want to reach out and touch it to see if it was as soft as it was in his dreams.

"You." Her big green eyes widened, and the small smile faded from her face. Tension instantly ratcheted through her slim body.

He tilted his head to the side and raised an eyebrow. "Me."

"You two know each other?" Mrs. Andrews asked.

Tanner nodded then looked back at Bree. "We met at the drugstore a few days ago, although I don't think you got my name. Tanner Dempsey."

"Bree," she whispered.

"I remember. I was under the impression that you were in a hurry to get out of Risk Peak."

"I, um…" She looked over at Mrs. A. "I, um…"

Mrs. Andrews stood with the now-quiet baby and walked over to stand beside her. "Bree was kind enough to come work for Dan and me. We needed some help around here."

There was definitely more to this story than was being given, evidenced by the silence surrounding them. But no one seemed to want to provide any details.

"Tanner, got your dinner here," Judy called out from behind him. "Mr. Andrews made country-fried steak just for you."

The Andrewses never let anyone forget that they'd lived in Georgia before moving to Colorado. This was probably the only place in the whole state where you could find genuine Southern cooking.

Tanner studied the two women in front of him. Bree was reaching over to get the baby Mrs. Andrews was holding. This one was in pink.

"Thanks for watching them, Mrs. Andrews," she whispered before kissing the child's fuzzy head.

"Call me, Cheryl, sweetheart. We've already talked about that."

He crossed his arms over his chest. "Why does she get to call you Cheryl and I have to call you Mrs. Andrews?"

She narrowed her eyes at him. "Because I haven't known her since she was in diapers. And I didn't have to take her out of a Sunday School class one time and swat her butt because she put a frog down Linda Dugas's dress."

Tanner chuckled with everyone else. It wasn't the only time he'd been dragged out of Sunday School class.

And he was smart enough to know when a battle wasn't going to be won head-on. He gave them both a nod. "Fine. I'll go eat. There will be plenty of time to talk later."

Because he sure as hell wasn't going anywhere. The exhaustion that had plagued him was gone. He ate his food, watching Bree pack up the babies and get ready to leave. The other women tried to get her to sit down and talk, but she didn't seem interested. And she was very careful not to look over in his direction.

This woman had *trouble* written all over her. Whether she was chasing it or it was chasing her remained to be seen.

He grabbed Judy as she drifted by with a coffee cup, watching Bree walk out the door without once looking his way. "Is the new girl with the babies staying at one of the hotels?"

Judy looked uncomfortable. "Actually, I'm not exactly sure where Bree is staying."

"It's okay, Judy. I'll talk to the *officer*." Mrs. Andrews put her hand on Judy's shoulder before sitting down across from Tanner.

Tanner took another bite of his steak. "You going to threaten to snatch me out of Sunday School again? My mom might be a little shocked to get the call."

"I just don't want Judy stuck in the middle of anything. You seem pretty interested in our new employee."

"My interest became piqued because you were dodging my questions." He chewed his food. "That's not something I've ever known you to do."

Mrs. Andrews let out a little sigh. "That girl wandered in here last week half a minute from a complete breakdown. She needed help, so we offered her a job. Nothing wrong with that."

Tanner took a sip of his coffee. "No, nothing wrong with that. Did she mention she and I met last week also, probably right before she came over here?"

This was obviously news to Mrs. A. The older woman bent her head to study her nails. "No, she didn't."

"I caught her shoplifting. Stuff for the babies, but Bree very definitely had no plans—and probably no means— of paying for it."

Mrs. A straightened in her seat, eyes narrowing. "Well, you just tell how much it was and Dan and I will pay for it ourselves. I'll go over and talk to Gary, and we can get it worked out."

"There's no need. It was handled before she even got out of the store. So technically, no laws were broken. But the point is, she's *trouble*. I'm not sure what kind yet, but I know we don't have all the facts when it comes to that woman. Has she told you anything about herself?"

"No. She keeps quiet. Does any work we ask her to and

either keeps the babies with her or lets us hold them out front. She's got quite a fan club now. Everybody wants to hold them. But Bree never really talks much to anyone."

All Tanner's exhaustion was back. He rubbed a hand over his eyes. "And none of this seems unusual to you?"

"She's not a bad person, Tanner."

He gritted his teeth. "Let's not forget that my father once felt that way about someone. That kid seemed young and innocent and helpless, too. Ended up costing Dad his life."

Mrs. Andrews reached out and took his hand on the table. "It's not the same. That gang situation was trouble from the first moment he got involved. The people were bad seeds. That's not what this is."

Wasn't it? Not gang related, but definitely trouble.

"No offense, but we don't know what this is. Maybe Bree isn't a criminal outside of an occasional shoplifting charge—"

"She did that because she was desperate!"

Tanner let out a sigh. "Fine, let's say I agree with you, which I actually do. Let's say she's not a criminal, only desperate. Desperate people do some pretty dangerous stuff, too. It's my responsibility to look out for the well-being of the town."

"So what do you want us to do? Just kick her out? Send her on her way?"

"How about if you just give me her full name and Social Security number from her tax stuff, and I'll run her through the system. See if anything comes up. At least that way we'll know."

"I'm afraid we can't do that."

Tanner raised an eyebrow. "Can't or won't?"

Mrs. Andrews let out a sigh. "Can't."

He muttered a curse under his breath. "You're paying her under the table."

Her lips tightened. "We are allotted a certain amount

of labor wages every year without having to claim it on our taxes."

He rubbed a hand across his face. "I'm not going to turn you into the IRS, Mrs. A. I'm concerned for your *safety*. You don't even know this woman's Social Security number."

"Actually, we don't even know her last name. She didn't want to give it, so we just let it go."

Tanner swallowed a curse that would definitely get him snatched out of the Sunday School class. "I can't just let it go."

She nodded. "I understand, but she's not the bad guy."

Tanner thought of those big green eyes and the exhaustion and desperation that seemed to hang over her like a cloud even now. "Maybe not. But I'd still like to talk to her further. Which hotel is she staying at?"

"Neither. She's staying at the apartment just outside town Dan and I spruced up last year for when the kids come to visit. We're letting her have it for free for right now, until she gets back on her feet. And don't you try to talk us out of it, Tanner Dempsey. Both Dan and I agree it's the right thing to do."

He took the last sip of his coffee. "I'm not going to try to talk you out of it. But I'm not going to ignore that she could be a threat to this town. That woman has secrets, and I intend to find out what they are."

Chapter Five

Bree waited for the knock at her door she'd known would be coming from the moment she saw Tanner Dempsey in the diner. She'd done her best to avoid eye contact with the sexy officer but had no doubt he'd be showing up here soon.

He wanted answers. And he didn't strike her as someone who would stop until he got them.

Should she run? Try to get out before he arrived?

She looked around the small one-bedroom apartment that Dan and Cheryl were letting them stay at as part of her "salary." The last eight nights had been the closest Bree had come to a full night's sleep in the six weeks since her life had been thrown into total upheaval with the care of the twins.

Those babies were a piece of her now. She would do anything to protect them, even what was almost impossible for her: trusting other people.

She didn't know exactly why the Andrewses were helping her, just knew right now she didn't have any other options, so she would accept it. She had a door that locked, a general feeling of security and their basic needs were being met.

Maybe she wasn't exactly doing a great job with the twins' care—Christian still cried all the time, obviously subconsciously aware in his little baby brain that Bree wasn't a qualified caretaker—but hopefully if Melissa could see them now she wouldn't completely regret her decision to trust Bree.

And being safe here had allowed Bree to start looking into the data on the hard drive Melissa had sent with the twins.

Very, very carefully.

The data on it could only be accessed by pinging off the Organization's own servers. Bree was an expert at covering her tracks, but nobody could completely hide from them while simultaneously attempting to access their own network. The best she could do was make them think she was harmless.

And that she definitely wasn't Bethany Malone, the hacker genius they'd helped create, forging her in brutality.

But coming at the data this way was slow, especially when Bree wasn't sure what exactly she was accessing and how it might help Melissa. She just knew she had to take some time to try while she was relatively safe, even if it meant working for hours at night after already putting in long shifts during the day.

Christian began to cry, so she picked him up, walking back and forth while rubbing his back. "Come on now, kiddo. I've had a full day on my feet. How about if you settle down so I can worry myself sick before the big bad cop arrives."

Beth, unlike her cranky brother, stayed asleep, as she tended to do. Even when she was awake, she was all smiles and big eyes. But both of them were growing more every day. Staying awake a little longer. Showing just a little more personality.

Soon they wouldn't be content to stay in their carriers most of the time. They'd want to sit up and look around more. Not long after that, they'd begin crawling.

That was beyond scary to think about.

"I know your mama misses you, buddy. She wouldn't believe how big you've gotten in the weeks since she's seen you. I'm going to try to get you back to her real soon."

As if those were the words Christian had been waiting to hear, he snuggled into her shoulder and closed his eyes.

Bree had only known these beautiful babies for a few weeks, and she already knew it was going to tear a hole in her when she had to give them back to Melissa.

But that was stupid. Bree had been completely alone for the past three years since her mom died, and really even before that, when her mom had started to deteriorate. She was used to being alone. *Loved* being alone. A few weeks couldn't change her entire outlook on life.

But she was already afraid it had.

The knock she'd been expecting finally came. Now she was about to find out whether the choice to stay here was taken out of her hands. She opened the door.

"Officer." She gave a nod of greeting.

"Looks like you were expecting me."

God, he was still as sexy as she'd remembered. Half a foot taller than her with thick black hair and warm brown eyes, before she quickly looked away from them. He was dressed in jeans and a beige Henley that molded over his chest.

Studying his shoulders and biceps, Bree let herself imagine what it would be like to be in the arms of a man. Not any man, *this* man. Being on the run most of her life hadn't left time for any sort of relationships. Not friendships and definitely not romantic entanglements. She'd never wanted to.

But, now…

She finally looked up and found him staring down at her. He was waiting for her to speak. "Um, yeah, I realized you would probably have some questions about why I was still in town."

He gave a nod. "Can I come in?"

"If I say no, are you going to arrest me?"

"Have you done anything for me to arrest you for?" One dark brow raised.

"Not today." She meant it as a joke, but he was obviously taking her seriously.

"Then I guess I won't be arresting you today. And if you tell me I can't come in then I'll leave. But I'll take Mrs. A's lemon pie with me." He held up a paper bag.

Her mouth immediately watered. "That's not fair, it's my favorite. How did you know?"

"You're breathing, aren't you? Of course it's your favorite. It's everybody's favorite. If it wasn't your favorite then I *would* have to arrest you."

She gestured for him to enter. "Since you have pie."

"I also have a chicken sandwich from Mrs. A. She said you left without getting your normal meal and that you weren't allowed to have the pie until you ate it."

She took the bag and turned back toward the small kitchen table in the corner. He followed her in, closing the door behind him.

"Cheryl says I don't eat enough." Bree put the chicken sandwich on a plate. "She makes me eat at least one meal at the diner every day."

He chuckled, a casually confident sound that mesmerized her. Bree couldn't remember ever chuckling like that in her life. And if she had, it definitely wouldn't have sounded that sexy.

"Mrs. Andrews says *everyone* doesn't eat enough. I would find it less suspicious if she wasn't the owner of a restaurant. But in your case, I think she might be right. Between being a new mother and working every day, you're probably burning a lot of calories."

"Do you want any of this sandwich?" She gestured for him to sit with her, but he shook his head.

"No, thanks. I already ate plenty."

She nodded. "So, Dempsey. Is that the same Dempsey as the teenager that comes in a couple times a week to help out at the diner?"

"That would probably be my cousin Robbie. My father's brother's son. I've got a lot of family that lives around here. How about you, got any family?"

She took another bite of her chicken sandwich. "None here in Risk Peak."

He leaned against the wall, stretching his long legs out in front of him. "Oh, I'm damn sure I would know it if you lived around here, believe me. Got any family anywhere else?"

She took another bite of chicken and chewed it slowly, more to give her time to decide what to say. She had a driver's license that said Bree Daniels. If he checked that out, it wouldn't bring the whole world crashing down. So she was probably best off sticking with it.

"No, no family. Just me."

He tilted his head to the side, eyes narrowing. "And the babies."

"Of course." Damn it. She was so used to thinking of herself as alone. "Christian and Beth."

"And their father? He's family, too, in a way. He around anywhere?"

She stuffed more food in her mouth. "He's not in the picture."

She didn't know if the twins' father was friend or foe. There were so many things she needed to ask Melissa. Every day she waited for that phone to ring, but it never did.

He let her finish eating without any more questions, but she didn't deceive herself into thinking he was done.

She immediately unwrapped the pie when she finished her sandwich. Partially to hold off more questions, but she hadn't been lying when she said it was her favorite.

"It looks like Cheryl put two slices in here. Do you want one?"

He nodded and sat down with her at the table. She got him a fork, and they both began to eat. She was only on her third bite when she looked over and found him finishing his.

"That's good pie," he said, shoveling the last bite into his mouth.

Bree watched with wide eyes, scooting her plate closer to her protectively. "You're not one for savoring, are you?"

He leaned back in his chair and smiled.

Good God, that smile was lethal.

She sat frozen as he reached across the table and wiped a little piece of pie that had gotten caught on the corner of her mouth.

He brought the crumb up to his lips and licked it off. "Oh, I'm definitely for savoring when the time is right. For savoring every little bit as long as possible."

She had the distinct feeling they weren't talking about pie anymore.

But then he straightened in his chair, breaking the spell. "But when it comes to one of the Sunrise lemon pies, I had two siblings and a mother and father all vying for as much of one pie as possible every Saturday evening when I was growing up. Whoever finished first generally got to eat whatever bits had been left in the tray. I learned how to eat my slice in three bites when it counted."

She put another bite in her mouth and chewed slowly. Except for the meals she'd eaten at the Sunrise Diner over the last week, she'd never really eaten with anyone else. Even her mother hadn't been interested in family meals at the table. She'd been too paranoid.

"Wow." She took another bite quickly, not completely sure he wouldn't try to make a grab for hers. "I guess you can buy your own pie now."

"Yeah, but sometimes my brother, sister and I still take a turn at it when we're together for a meal. My mom gets in on the action, too."

She could almost imagine it. A table full of grown people eating the delicious dessert as fast as they could to fight for leftovers.

It seemed…nice.

"Did your dad wise up? Does he stay out of the fray now?"

She peeked over at Tanner just in time to see the smile completely fade from his face. "No. My dad's dead."

She threw her gaze down to her pie again. "Oh. I'm sorry for your loss."

Mentioning his dad had completely broken the mood. Tanner stiffened in his chair. "What kind of trouble are you in, Bree?"

"What makes you think I'm in any trouble at all?"

"You've got *trouble* all but tattooed on your forehead. It was one thing when you were just passing through. But now you've stuck around, so whatever trouble you're in becomes my problem, too. I don't want to see the Andrewses get hurt."

"I'm not going to hurt them. I'm not going to hurt anyone." She just needed to stay under the radar.

He ran his fingers through that thick dark hair. "The babies' dad… Did he hurt you, maybe? I can help if that's the case."

She shook her head. "No, it's nothing like that."

"Are you in trouble with the law? On the run? You may not believe me, but I can help with that, too. Almost always, things go more leniently with a judge when a person turns herself in of her own accord."

She let out a sigh. "I'm not wanted by the law, either. I just…needed some changes in my life. Then before I knew it, I was broke, but the babies still needed all their baby stuff."

That was as close to the truth as she could come without bringing down the type of danger even the police weren't equipped to deal with.

Tanner studied her with those deep brown eyes that missed nothing. She forced herself to meet his gaze, to remain calm.

To not act guilty.

"So, if you told me your last name, and I run it right now in our system, there's not going to be some husband who has reported a kidnapping of his children by his wife? There's not going to be an APB out for your arrest somewhere?"

She stood and walked over to the diaper bag and got out her driver's license. She walked back to him and handed over the license. "Bree Daniels."

She'd surprised him. He'd thought she was just going to tell him a name. A lie.

But he recovered quickly. "You won't mind if I call this in and have them run it real quickly at the office?"

She crossed her arms over her chest. "Not at all."

He stood and pulled out his phone, an old flip version like the one she had. That reassured her. The Organization couldn't steal the info from that phone. Although if they figured out she was here, there weren't many places to hide in a town this size.

Tanner turned away from her to talk to someone in his office, reading her name and driver's license number.

Bree Daniels would look real in any system. She had a Social Security number, work history, even had a library card if someone searched that far.

Bree had built the identity herself after her mother died.

Had thought she would use this identity for a much longer time. Had hoped to be Bree Daniels forever.

That might not be possible soon.

He hung up and sat back down at the table with her. "They'll call me back in a few minutes. Shouldn't take long."

She stood and began clearing the dishes off the table.

"So you're from Missouri. Were the babies born in Kansas City?"

Damn it. She hadn't thought about Beth and Christian. Would he try to track down more information about them from hospitals? How many twins could possibly have been born there in the last few months?

She rinsed the plate off in the sink. "No, I was actually out of town when they were born."

When she turned, she found him studying her. "Were they premature?"

The more information she gave, the more easily she could get caught in a lie. "Not by much, a little early, I guess. Not unusual with twins."

He was still studying her too closely. "You look like you're in amazing shape."

She turned to wipe down the counter.

Keep calm.

He didn't know anything. He was fishing.

After she finished wiping, she turned and gave him the biggest smile she could muster. "Well, Mrs. Andrews's lemon pie certainly is not helping."

He was going to push the issue, she could tell. But his phone buzzed in his hand. He kept his eyes pinned on her as he lifted it to his ear.

He listened to the report without saying much of anything. At the end, he thanked whoever was on the line and hung up. He stood.

"It seems I owe you an apology. Bree Daniels has no

APBs out for her arrest, and no one has reported you either as a missing person or as someone of interest in any cases."

"Glad to hear it."

He wanted to say more. She could tell he wanted to say so much more, but one of the babies started to fuss from over in the playpen where they slept.

Tanner nodded. "You've had a full day of work, and I'm sure those kiddos don't sleep very long. I'll get out of your hair."

She was surprised at the disappointment that washed over her. She wanted him gone, right? She didn't long for a normal conversation with him, because that wasn't very smart.

Smart is how you stay alive.

"Thank you for bringing dinner," she whispered.

He nodded then walked to the door and opened it, looking back at her. "Bree?"

"Yes?"

Those brown eyes pinned her. "I'll see you around. *Soon.*"

It was both a threat and a promise.

Chapter Six

When Bree's name had come back clean in the report, Tanner immediately went to the station and ran it again himself.

It had been clean again.

After going home and sleeping for twelve hours, he'd come back to the station and run it again.

And yet again, *nothing*.

Bree Daniels was a law-abiding citizen with no criminal record and nothing to make anyone wary. Everything about her seemed legitimate. She was twenty-four years old, a little younger than he would've thought, but being a mother of two probably made someone grow up quickly. She'd never been married and, as she'd said, had no run-ins with the law, barring the shoplifting incident.

There was no reason to think she was anything other than what she said she was: someone making changes in her life that hadn't worked out the way she thought they would.

But Tanner couldn't shake the feeling that there was a lot more trouble surrounding her than that. Every instinct he had—honed by his ten years of law enforcement—told him there was more to Bree Daniels than met the eye.

A battle waged inside him between his sworn duty to protect Risk Peak and all of Grand County, and this unfamiliar need to help Bree with whatever danger was at her heels.

Because no clean record was going to convince him that she wasn't frightened of *something*.

So here he was a week later, having his second cup of coffee at the Sunrise, just like the last seven mornings. Mr. and Mrs. Andrews had taken to just ignoring him, since they knew he was there in a half-official capacity. In the unspoken battle between team Bree and team Tanner, they'd obviously chosen her side.

Tanner wasn't surprised. It was hard for anyone not to be protective of the quiet woman. Not to mention Bree could've been Jack the Ripper and the Andrewses would've loved her because of the babies.

Tanner sipped and watched the woman in question. One thing was for sure: she was becoming *more* fragile, not less so. In the week since he'd talked to her at her apartment, she'd lost weight, despite Mrs. Andrews's insistence that she eat, and the circles under her eyes had become more pronounced. Maybe the babies kept her up all night. It couldn't be easy having infant twins, even though they seemed pretty manageable during the day.

Mrs. A walked up beside him and refilled his coffee cup, both of them watching Bree clear off the table that had just been vacated.

"You're worried about her," she said.

Tanner turned slightly toward the older woman but kept his attention on Bree. "I thought you weren't talking to me."

Mrs. A shrugged. "Only if you're going to spend your time trying to convince me Bree is dangerous. You watch her like she's a suspect."

"It's my job to keep the people of Risk Peak safe."

And while he couldn't deny his attraction to Bree, he definitely didn't trust her.

Mrs. Andrews's lips tightened. "I'll be sure to let you know if she, or her two obviously trained miniature assassins, show any sign of evildoings."

Mrs. A was about to revert to the silent treatment. Tanner touched her arm. "Bree looks more tired, don't you think?"

She let out a sigh. "Like the weight of the world is on her shoulders."

"Is that normal for a new mother, do you think? Maybe it's postpartum depression or something. Or maybe the babies don't let her get sleep at night."

"Well, she's going to get sleep tonight. I already told her Dan and I are going to keep those babies so she could get a full night's rest."

"She agreed to that?"

Mrs. Andrews nodded. "Shows you how desperate she is, doesn't it? But I told her how the whole world would look different if she just got some good sleep." She shrugged. "Then I threatened to fire her if she didn't take us up on the offer, although I don't think she believed me."

Mrs. A left, and Tanner continued to observe Bree from his stool. She studiously ignored him, sweeping up the restaurant, pausing every once in a while to kiss or coo at the babies, who sat with Mr. Andrews and some of the couple's friends who were stopping by more often.

Having adorable twin babies that needed to be cuddled was good for diner business.

And Bree was a hard worker. Nobody minded helping her, since she was working so hard.

And just like that, he was back to that battle within himself again. On one hand, she was exactly what she seemed to be: a down-on-her-luck single mother.

On the other hand…

What the hell was up with that piece-of-junk flip phone of hers? He had one because that was the choice the department had made concerning official phones. No smartphones.

But why would Bree have one so basic? Hers looked like it would barely even call or text. He'd never seen her use it even once, but she always wanted it in her possession. He'd seen panic fall over her features a couple of days ago when she realized she'd left it in the back. She'd rushed to the kitchen and came back out clutching it to her.

It was like she was waiting for a call that never came.

But from whom? And about what? Was that what was causing her to look more weary and fragile with each passing day?

Or was that all in Tanner's head?

All his colleagues at the sheriff's office teased him about how much time he spent studying Bree. He took the good-natured ribbing with a smile. They thought he had a crush on her and joked about him being obsessed.

They weren't wrong.

But he couldn't let it go.

Tanner took his last sip of coffee, put some money on the counter and left. He wasn't surprised when Bree didn't acknowledge him.

What was he expecting? That she would run over to him and spill all the secrets she was keeping?

Tanner needed to pull his head out of his ass. The sheriff had entrusted him and made him the captain of the entire southeastern section of Grand County three years ago. There was a whole office full of people who looked up to and expected leadership from him.

So he damn well better start acting like the seasoned law enforcement agent he was, rather than a high schooler with a crush.

He headed to the office and found the rest of his day taken up with the mundane tasks of keeping his section of the county running smoothly.

But Bree was never far from his mind.

Later that night when Ronnie Kitchens, one of Tanner's deputies, called in sick, Tanner agreed to take his shift even though it meant working a double. Anything was better than sitting at home with his own thoughts, knowing Bree was alone in her little apartment tonight.

His thoughts about her were inappropriate enough without the temptation of potentially acting on them. Focusing on work was much better.

He was out doing a normal town drive-through, proud of himself for keeping well away from Bree's apartment, when he glanced over at the library parking lot as he drove past.

Then did an immediate double take, letting out a string of curses inside his Bronco.

What the hell was Bree's car doing in the small, secluded parking lot of the Risk Peak's library?

His immediate inclination was to swerve in there and confront her, but he forced himself to keep driving so she wouldn't notice him. His Bronco was an official vehicle, but unmarked. Anybody around town would know it was him immediately, but maybe not her.

Was she meeting someone?

He circled around the back of the library, turning off his lights and killing the engine in the grocery store parking lot across the street. She wouldn't spot him unless she turned around and really looked.

He grabbed the binoculars in the back seat and looked through them to get a better view. It was definitely Bree in the car, and no one was with her.

Yet.

She was working on a laptop. Why the hell would she be sitting in her car outside the damn library at one o'clock in the morning working on a computer?

He stayed in his car, watching and waiting, for hours.

She never got out, and nobody ever came to her. Just stared at the computer.

Finally, around 4:00 a.m., she turned her car back on and drove off. Tanner followed from behind, lights still off in his own vehicle, thankful he knew the roads well enough to drive this way.

But all she did was go back to her apartment.

Tanner stayed in his vehicle, lights still off, as she went inside. He was tempted to confront her right at this second, but he knew she wouldn't tell him anything.

She hadn't broken any laws, so he had no grounds to officially question her anyway. The best he would have was loitering.

He wanted to pull on his hair. Why, on the one night in particular when she was supposed to get as much sleep as possible, would she spend half the night sitting in her car outside the library working on a computer?

Not meeting anyone. Not talking on that phone of hers.

There were too many things about her that didn't make sense.

Was this what his father had felt before the teenager he'd been trying to help fifteen years ago had ultimately turned on him and killed him? Dad had gone to pick up the kid in Denver, trying to get him out of a dire situation. Tanner's parents had sat Tanner and his siblings down the day before and told them the kid might be staying with them for a while. That sometimes helping a stranger was the right thing to do.

Then the kid had shot his dad, point-blank, when Dad showed up to help him. Trying to gain a foothold into the local gang.

The kid himself had been killed two days later in a shootout with the police when they'd come to arrest him.

Had Dad had any inclination that the kid was going to turn on him? Had he felt the storm brewing but decided to ignore it? Up until the second a Glock 17 was pressed against his forehead, had Dad thought everything was going to work out?

Tanner wasn't going to need a Glock against his own skin before he recognized the danger in front of him. He already saw it.

Bree Daniels might be spotless on paper, but she was damn well trouble in flesh and blood. Deadly, wrapped in big green eyes and a fragile appearance.

One Dempsey man had died because he'd refused to see the truth.

Tanner wouldn't be the second.

Chapter Seven

Bree knew Cheryl and Dan were disappointed in her the next morning when she arrived for work, eyes gritty with exhaustion like they'd been every day before.

She'd hoped to be able to get so much more accomplished last night while the twins had been with Cheryl and Dan. But she'd just been so tired.

She should've known better. The Organization discovered many years ago that sleep deprivation didn't work on her. It affected her mental facilities too much for her to be able to do delicate hacking work.

Ten years later it was still the same, even if she was the one depriving herself.

"Oh, honey," Cheryl crooned. Bree stood stiffly as the older woman hugged her. "What happened? You still look so tired. Maybe you should take the day off."

Dan patted her back, not nearly as outwardly affectionate as his wife, although Bree knew he also cared. "Could you still not sleep?" he asked.

Bree pulled back from Cheryl, unable to bear her touch. Not with the way she was feeling right now. "I guess it was just hard for me, being without the kids. I was worried."

That was true, but it wasn't the whole truth. She'd been glad Christian and Beth were with the Andrewses so she didn't have to drag them out in the middle of the night.

But she'd desperately wanted to make more forward progress than she had.

The Wi-Fi at her apartment wasn't safe to use because her activities would lead the Organization directly to her. So she'd chosen the library, since the internet was hooked up through a government-issued router that she'd been able to hack in under two minutes, and the signal reached out to the parking lot. Using their system would keep her digital fingerprint from being traced back to any single computer—it would all just get hidden within the state of Colorado's virtual information flow.

But she hadn't been able to make any forward progress. She was too tired, or maybe she'd just lost her edge after being out of the hacking game for so long. Every day her skin itched and her mind burned with the knowledge of her failure.

It was just like being back inside the Organization all those years ago. When nothing she'd done had been good enough. When failure had meant pain and that people she'd cared about would suffer.

Was Melissa suffering?

Compounding all Bree's desperation was the knowledge that she was running out of time here. She felt eyes on her all the time.

Sometimes it was Tanner. She'd gotten used to his deep brown eyes watching her every time he was in here. Trying to figure out exactly what sort of threat she was to the people he was responsible for.

If he knew what sort of hell she could rain down on Risk Peak, he would've already escorted her to the county line.

But he didn't, so he watched and bided his time, piecing together what he could from what he observed. Determined to figure out her secrets.

She sensed other eyes on her, too. She could feel them day by day. And they didn't bring her a sense of comfort like Tanner's eyes did. They made her feel like she was being smothered.

But that didn't make sense. Why would anyone else be watching her? If it was the Organization, they would've made their move already. Killed her in her sleep if she was lucky. Dragged her back into hell if she wasn't.

So it wasn't the Organization. Bree drew in a shaky breath. That only left one option.

That she was following the same path of paranoia her mother had taken. That her mind was beginning to crumble in on itself the way Mom's had. She rubbed her shoulder again, at the wound her mother had given her the day her mind had snapped.

Maybe Bree's mind was snapping in the same way. Maybe somewhere down the road she was going to hurt the Andrewses or, worse, the twins, because her mind was convinced they were a threat.

She blinked rapidly and realized the older couple were both studying her now with abject concern. "I'm sorry, what?"

Cheryl gave Dan a worried look. "We're just wondering if you should take the day off, too. I'm sure we can manage."

She took a deep breath. "No, I'm fine." She was going to need the money if she had to leave suddenly. "I hope Christian and Beth were okay for you."

Cheryl smiled. "They were angels, as I knew they would be. Got up once during the night, but heck, Dan gets up more than that."

Bree was surprised how much she'd missed the kids, even though it had only been ten hours since she'd seen them last. Beth smiled sweetly like she always did, and even Christian was content in his carrier. Bree began rolling silverware in napkins while sitting at the corner "baby booth," but was soon scooted out of the way when some of Cheryl and Dan's friends came in and wanted to hold the babies.

The people in this town were so good. Bree didn't want to bring the Organization down on them. She had to be careful with her hacking. She was up against some of the most brilliant people on the planet, whose consciences were nonfunctional. They wouldn't hesitate to slaughter the people here if it would stop Bree.

She wasn't surprised when Tanner showed up a few minutes after she started her shift, looking just as haggard as she did. He didn't try to talk to her, like he usually did, just ordered breakfast and sat at his normal bar perch.

When she did catch sight of his brown eyes, they were hard. Cold, almost. No sign of the subtle invitation to reach out to him that she'd seen for the past week.

Or was that just her paranoia talking?

He ate his breakfast but then surprised her by not leaving afterward. He stayed put, pulling out a computer and starting to do some sort of work.

Bree ignored him, as always—a little easier today because of the frigid air that seemed to surround him. She did her duties in the back kitchen and helped out at lunch when a group of half a dozen construction workers came in.

Her paranoia ramped up once again with their arrival. She felt eyes on her all the time. But the only one she ever saw looking in her direction was Tanner.

She forced herself to shake off the feeling through the lunch rush and was clearing off the tables once the diner had nearly emptied when a buzzing noise caught her attention. She looked around, trying to figure out where it was coming from.

Then she realized it was coming from the phone in her apron.

She slammed the tray full of dishes down on the nearest table, wincing at the noise, thankful when nobody else seemed to notice. She started to hide the fact that she was looking at a message on her phone but realized that was absurd. People used phones all the time. No one would think twice about her getting a text. She flipped it open.

Come to Denver. Downtown Orthodox Church. 3:00. Crisscross, applesauce.

Bree stared at the message before snapping the phone closed. She couldn't even be sure it was from Melissa. Someone could've gotten hold of the phone and was trying to draw Bree out. Or maybe someone in the Organization was forcing Melissa to send the message.

No, Mellie wouldn't do that. She would die rather than risk the twins.

Right?

Bree stared at the phone again. She had to try. If this was Melissa's chance to get out, Bree couldn't let her down.

She couldn't take the twins with her into an unknown situation; if she had to run, it would be too hard with them in tow. Hopefully Dan and Cheryl would watch them again. She'd say she wasn't feeling well and needed to rest. She hated that they would so readily believe her just because they were honest people.

But Bree had to. She wouldn't let her paranoia suffocate her. And she at least knew the older couple would do whatever it took to keep Christian and Beth safe if Bree didn't come back.

She put the phone back in her apron and turned toward the kitchen, stopping in her tracks when she found Tanner studying her with hooded eyes.

"Everything okay?" he asked.

A bolt of panic jolted down her spine. Had he seen her get the message on her phone?

She forced air into her lungs and tried to relax her features. There was nothing suspicious about getting a text message. The only thing that would make it seem suspicious was her actions.

"Yes." She forced more air into her lungs so her voice didn't sound so weak. "Everything's fine."

"Get some news on your phone?" Tanner leaned back casually against the bar as he said it, but there was nothing casual about the way he studied her, reading every move she made.

She shrugged. "No. Just a junk sales message."

"Yeah, I hate those." He crossed his arms over his chest. "You look a little tired. I thought Mr. and Mrs. A were watching the babies for you last night so you could get some rest."

She fought the urge to shift back and forth on her feet. "I guess I just couldn't sleep anyway. You know how it is."

He cocked his head to the side. "I don't, actually. Why don't you tell me how it is? Did you go out?"

"Oh, no. I'm not big on nightlife stuff." She wasn't even sure if Risk Peak had any. "I just stayed home."

"But couldn't sleep, huh?"

Why was he so interested in her sleep habits? She didn't have time to talk to him about this. She needed to get to Denver, scope out as much as she could to make sure it was really Melissa who had contacted her.

"Yeah, just couldn't sleep. That's all. Do you need anything else, Officer?"

"Tanner." He reached over and touched her arm, just below her elbow. "Do *you* need anything, Bree? Tell me what's going on. I can help."

She looked into his eyes and almost believed him. Was tempted, maybe, because of the exhaustion, to tell him at least *something*. Not everything, of course, but enough to get his help.

He looked so strong. So capable. Like he could handle

anything. While she woke every day not sure how she was going to make it, each day worse than the one before.

He waited silently, not pushing, not demanding. Which just made her want to lean on him more.

But she couldn't. Melissa might be getting out today, and they would have to run. She couldn't depend on anyone but herself.

"I'm fine," she finally said. "But thank you for asking."

Tanner didn't say anything, but his finger stroked lightly across the bend of her elbow. Once again her resolve almost faltered.

"Who was that message from, Bree?"

She didn't look him in the eye while shaking her head. "It was nobody."

She moved from his soft grip and walked back to the kitchen. She had to get the sexy deputy out of her mind. She needed to ask Dan and Cheryl to watch the kids, then get to Denver and meet her cousin.

And pray it wasn't a trap.

Chapter Eight

An hour and a half later, dressed in as much of a disguise as she could manage, which basically consisted of stuffing her long brown hair in a ball cap and sunglasses that covered a lot of her face, Bree sat in a bookstore across from the church where she was supposed to meet Melissa. She'd already been in the highest floors of the surrounding buildings that she could get to without raising suspicion, trying to do as much short-term recon as she could manage.

Everything about the city made her want to panic. Denver, for all the natural beauty of the surrounding mountains, was also a hub for technology. The public face of the Organization had an office here.

And the message from Melissa—the more Bree considered it, the worse it seemed. No doubt the phone was being tracked. Otherwise, how would Melissa know Bree could even make it to Denver in two hours?

If it was Melissa at all.

Hopefully, the Organization still thought she was dead and completely off their radar. Because the Organization's radar was a deadly place to be—particularly for her.

But Bree saw no sign of them now. Even after searching for over thirty minutes, Bree found no evidence of a trap. She stayed where she was at the bookstore until she finally spotted Melissa going into the church right on time for their meeting. Her cousin didn't look around, didn't draw attention to herself in any way. Just did the smart thing and went straight in.

Bree stood at the window, coffee cup in hand, waiting to see if there would be further movement. She watched for light reflecting from the roofs of the surrounding buildings, a sign of a sniper. She looked for any hint that someone was surveilling the scene rather than performing their task at hand: turning pages too slowly or too quickly, or staring at a display stand for too long.

But…nothing. Nothing suspicious or out of place.

Bree finally went around to the alley so she could enter through the side door of the church. Still keeping an eye out for any problems, she moved silently through it, finding Melissa sitting in an empty, darkened corner near two possible exits. It was exactly where Bree would've chosen if she had gotten here first.

Since she was already in a church, Bree sent up a prayer that this wasn't a trap and walked up to her cousin.

"Hi, Mellie."

Melissa spun toward her, pure joy on her face. But it quickly faded. "You didn't bring them."

The twins. Of course she would want to see them. "It wasn't safe. I wasn't sure of the situation. I can't move quickly enough with the two of them."

Melissa wiped quickly at her eyes. "I know. That was smart, and the right thing to do. I'm just being emotional. But, God, Bree, I miss them so much."

Bree could definitely understand that. Those two little humans had a way of entrenching themselves into anybody's life. "They're getting so big. They're beautiful." Bree winced when Melissa's face fell even more—Bree was just making things worse. Meeting other people's emotional needs wasn't her forte. She tried to think of what might make her cousin feel better. "They're healthy, Mel. Happy."

"They're safe?"

Safe was definitely a relative term. She thought of the eyes she'd felt on her in Risk Peak. And the possibility that the Organization could be ready to move in on them even now.

Bree shrugged. "As safe as they can possibly be, given how you and I live. The older couple watching Beth and Christian love them. If something happened to me, they would take care of them to the best of their ability."

If Bree was better at personal stuff, she would probably pull her cousin in for a hug. But it would just be awkward for them both, so Bree quelled the urge.

Melissa wiped at tears again. "Thank you for taking them. I never planned to leave them alone with you—I thought I would be coming, too. I hope you've been all right."

She thought of all the sleepless nights. The running out of money. The sheer exhaustion and despair that had seemed like a constant companion for the past two months. Telling Melissa about how hard it had been wouldn't change anything. "We've managed."

"I just wish I could see pictures of them, you know? That you and I could be like any two other relatives in the world, where you pull out your phone and show me pictures of the kids."

They both knew that looking at pictures snapped on a smartphone would've been the worst possible thing they could do. It would lead the Organization right to them.

"Don't worry, I know it's impossible," Melissa continued. "I would never want you to put them in danger like that. To put yourself in danger like that."

"Is the Organization still capable of doing everything

they were before?" It had been bad enough ten years ago when she'd escaped.

Melissa rubbed her forehead. "Worse and growing. They now have unfettered access to the pictures and sounds recorded on millions of phones. They've gotten smarter in the last ten years. Nobody suspects software that seems to make phones *better*."

Most people accepted that Big Brother might possibly be listening when they called or video chatted with someone. But they never considered that their phone's cameras and audio could still be transmitting even when they were in off mode.

That's what the Organization had spent all their energy developing. Ways of using people's phones when they weren't aware of it. Basically creating a worldwide information network that they controlled and no one knew about.

Melissa grabbed Bree's hand. "They finally figured out what they need to hack every phone on the planet. It's software that on the surface will look like it enhances video and audio quality of all phones. No one will be able to hide once it goes into operation on the phones."

This was worse than Bree thought. "But how are they gaining access to all the major phone manufacturers? They'll have to do it at once, or the companies will start to ferret out what they're doing."

Melissa shook her head, looking at Bree with wonder. "I should've known you would grasp the ramifications from the beginning. The Organization was so mad when they lost you, Bree. You set them back years by not having your genius around anymore. They knew that."

Bree just shook her head. If they'd had Bree around— controlled her and forced her to cooperate—the technological advances would've been astounding.

And all used for evil.

"The Organization doesn't need to get to all the cellular manufacturers. They are all coming here," Melissa continued. "To Denver."

"The International Tech Symposium."

"Yep. And guess who the sponsor is."

"Communication for All," Bree whispered.

The Organization was so much more insidious because of who the world thought they were—Communication for All, a charity focused on using technology to improve education and living conditions all over the world. And they did help millions of people.

But for a small core group of the charity, the endgame was far more nefarious than improving lives. They wanted to be able to control information. The charity front allowed them access and a lack of scrutiny that private companies would never be able to obtain.

Melissa shrugged. "Tech companies are so busy looking for malicious software, they just tend to overlook systems and software that makes their product better, especially when it comes from a world-renowned charity group. Plus, Communication for All is providing the new technology for free."

Bree muttered a curse. "And being hailed as heroes."

Melissa nodded. "All over the world. What's worse is that the new software also serves as a virus. Once it's uploaded to the manufacturers at the symposium, it will spread and download to every phone, regardless if people refuse to accept the update or not."

Bree sucked in a breath. "They finally figured out the way to use people's personal passwords to access their phones." It had been something they were trying to force her to help do years ago.

Melissa nodded. "Once they've done it, no one will be able to hide from their networks unless they pay to do so.

They'll shelter whoever will pay their exorbitant fee and will be able to hunt whoever they desire."

Bree rubbed her eyes. "Now that sounds more like the Organization we know and hate."

They stared at each other for a few moments, both caught in a wave of despair.

"How did you keep them from finding out about the babies?" Bree finally asked.

"I was really sick early on in my pregnancy and didn't start gaining much weight until my fifth month."

"Then what did you do?"

"I followed your example. I got off the electronic grid completely. The Organization is convinced you're dead, Bree. For years they searched for you, even though you wiped all the pictures of you and your mom from the system before you ran. Only in the last couple of years did they give up."

"Why did they give up?"

Melissa shrugged. "I think they figured nobody living in this millennium could have resisted the lure of a smartphone or social media for that long. All they needed was one single picture on a smartphone, or even in the background of someone else's social media, and that would've been it. They would've known you were alive and they would've never stopped hunting you."

So her mother's paranoia had kept them alive after all.

"What you did was brilliant," Melissa continued.

Bree shrugged. "I'm not sure *brilliant* was the word for it." Lonely. Nerve-racking. So damn hard.

"Whatever it was, it worked for you, so I decided to try it." A sadness fell across Melissa's face. "The Organization killed the twins' father before I knew I was pregnant. I think they suspected I was going to make a move against them, and this was their way of letting me know they weren't afraid to play hardball." She swallowed rapidly.

"I'm so sorry, Mellie."

"Me, too. I never got to say goodbye to him. They ran his car off the road and tried to act like they had nothing to do with it. They sent me an obnoxiously large bouquet of flowers. That's how I knew they were behind it. But you know what? It was the best thing they could've done. Because it reminded me that I could play hardball, too."

There was a fire in her cousin's eyes.

"The loss of my fiancé, Christian, ended up giving me the excuse I needed to take a few months off and get away from them."

"Christian." Bree couldn't help but smile at the name.

Melissa's smile was tinged with sadness. "Yes, he went by Chris, but his full name was Christian. I named the twins after the two people I love most in the world."

Bree reached out and touched Melissa's arm. It felt stiff and unnatural, but Melissa didn't seem to mind.

"The Organization just let you go?"

"No, of course not. I kept working. But I did it from a remote location. They were tracking me to see if I would do something to hurt the company, not for anything as mundane as pregnancy. And that's going to be their downfall—the fact that they're so narrow and conceited in their focus."

"They don't understand the concept of family." Neither did Bree, if she was honest.

Melissa nodded. "I used their information system against them. I didn't have the babies in the hospital, and I made sure all social media and pictures from my phones created the narrative I wanted. One that gave no suggestion of their birth, just that I was grieving the death of my lover."

"You outstrategized them." Bree smiled and nodded. "Good for you."

Melissa smiled. "I was never what you were. Never a

prodigy. They tried to make me into you, but I was never good enough. You think like a computer, Bethany. I never did. My emotions got in my way."

Bree knew her cousin meant the words as a compliment. But the knowledge that she was colder, harder, more machinelike tore at her, at a level she wasn't really aware had existed before the babies came into her life.

She had feelings, too. They weren't easy to process or express, but she had them.

"Once the Organization's new system takes hold, it will be nearly impossible for you to hide," Melissa said. "You've been so careful, but rumors are flying again that you're still alive. You're the ghost in their machine."

Bree sighed. "I've been trying to poke at their system through a back door with the files you gave me. They shouldn't have been able to tell it was me."

"I've been covering for you as much as possible. Anything that looked like it was coming from Colorado, I rerouted, but I think they're onto you, or me. I'm not sure which."

Bree looked around at a phantom sound. She didn't see anyone, but that didn't mean no one was there. "Do you think someone followed you here?"

Melissa nodded. "I'm sure they did, but I bought us enough time to meet. I've made it common practice to duck into churches—it's part of the narrative I've set up to help deceive the Organization. So they won't find it uncommon for a while."

Bree shook her head in wonder. Melissa might not have had the natural programming and coding skills Bree possessed, but the woman was brilliant in her own right, evident by the way she'd fooled the Organization these last few months.

"But that's why I wanted to meet," Melissa continued.

"You haven't been able to make much progress with the files, have you?"

"Unfortunately, taking care of two infants and working full-time has been taking up a lot of my attention."

Melissa grabbed Bree's hand and squeezed it, tears in her eyes once again. "Thank you, for all you're doing. I wish it was me up all night with them. But you have to stop digging into the files. The Organization is too suspicious."

"I'm trying to be as secretive as I can. I don't think I've left any footprints that could be traced back to Risk Peak."

Melissa squeezed her hand again. "That's part of the problem. You're too good. They know someone is attempting access but aren't sure who or where. There aren't many people in the world who can breeze in and out undetected the way you can."

Bree was about to protest when Melissa's next words stopped her. "Michael Jeter came to see me last week."

Bree's entire body stiffened at the mention of the head of Communication for All. He had been the one who had recruited Bree when she was a child, and he had made her life a living hell when she'd refused to cooperate.

"He came to see you personally?" That was never good.

Melissa rolled her eyes. "The official reason he gave was to offer condolences about Chris's death, even though it was a year later. He wanted to make sure I was doing all right, since he knew I didn't have any family."

"But you didn't buy it?"

"Not even for a second. He was there to fish out whether I was in touch with you. And then, as a 'gift'—" Melissa put the word in air quotes "—they were giving me one of the first completely upgraded computer systems. They took mine without a word. If I'd had anything on there…"

She didn't finish, but she didn't have to. They hadn't given Melissa any warning or time to erase anything on her hard drive. If her computer had contained any trace of communication with Bree, they would've known about it.

Michael Jeter showing up himself just confirmed how suspicious they really were.

"There was nothing on there that could've led them to me and the kids?"

"Nothing. This is the only thing I use to communicate with your phone." She held out a phone that looked similar to Bree's—old with no camera. "I tracked you using a public system outside the Organization. But once this new system goes live, they'll find you, Bree. It will only be a matter of time."

"Okay, I'll work harder on the files you gave me." She didn't know how she would find the time and energy, but she would make it happen.

"No. That's the opposite of what needs to happen. I'll focus on the Organization files. You just keep off the grid and keep the kids safe."

"But—"

Melissa's phone buzzed in her hand.

"We're out of time," she said. "You need to get out right away. I'll go out the front and draw them away. You go out the side."

Bree grabbed Melissa's hand. "Are you going to be able to decode the files before the summit? Especially with them watching you?"

"I have to. That's all there is to it. Your job is to keep yourself and the babies safe. That's the most important thing. Nobody knows about Risk Peak, so just stay there and stay out of it."

Before Bree knew what was happening, Melissa pulled her in for a hug. Bree stiffened before forcing herself to relax into it. This was her cousin. They'd hugged each other as children. Melissa had been the only person who'd ever really befriended the stiff, difficult Bree.

"You're doing a great job with the kids," Melissa whispered in her ear. "Thank you."

They pulled away from each other as a door slammed in the back.

"Mellie, be careful."

"The twins are the only thing that matters. If something happens to me…"

Bree wasn't going to offer useless platitudes. She nodded. "The twins are the only thing that matters," she repeated. "I'll make sure they're safe, first and foremost."

They squeezed each other's hand, then Melissa's phone buzzed again and she rushed toward the front door.

Bree kept to the shadows, moving faster when she heard a man's voice talking on the phone in the hallway behind her, a priest saying something about communion for the next Mass. She crouched behind a pew and waited for the voice to move past, relieved when he didn't seem to slow at all near her. She made her way to the side door she'd come in through.

She slid the door open quietly and stepped back into the alley. Glancing both ways, she turned and walked rapidly in the opposite direction from the way she'd come.

It looked like she was going to make it out of the city alive after all.

She was about to round the corner into the larger avenue when a hand reached out from the shadows, covered her mouth and yanked her hard against the wall.

Chapter Nine

Tanner kept his hand tightly over Bree's mouth and pushed her harder against the wall. Her back went ramrod straight, and he knew it would only be a split second before she panicked and started fighting him.

Which was definitely going to draw the attention of the three armed men less than twenty feet away. Bree had been about to walk into them.

"Bree." His voice was so low it was almost silent. It was only because his mouth was right against her ear that she'd be able to hear him. "It's Tanner."

Her body relaxed enough that he at least knew she understood him and didn't think of him as a threat.

He couldn't help but be aware of all the feminine curves pushed up against him, but he forced those thoughts from his mind.

He loosened his hand on her mouth just the slightest bit. "We've got trouble. Do you understand?"

She nodded.

He heard footsteps and pushed up against her more tightly, making sure he was between her and the guys he'd seen carrying weapons at their waists a few minutes ago.

She pulled at his hand. He let her mouth go, and she immediately began wiggling around, shifting her small body until they were front to front.

Perfect—if ignoring the sexy back curves of this beautiful woman wasn't hard enough, now he had to ignore sexy front curves also.

He brought his finger up to his lips, and she nodded once more. He tucked her more firmly up into the doorway corner, drawing his own weapon from its holster.

It wasn't the best odds against three armed men, but it was better than nothing.

"Where is she?" one voice said from about ten feet away now. If the men shifted much closer, they would practically fall over him and Bree.

"She didn't come down my way. We had both exits covered," another voice said. "Did you see her inside?"

Bree stiffened as the third man responded. "I just got in there, since we were given the wrong info. I had to take care of the priest so he didn't wander out and see anything."

"Dead?"

"No. Seemed unnecessary. Unconscious. Weathers was talking to someone, but I didn't get there in time to see who."

All three men got quiet as a phone rang.

"Hello, Mr. Jeter," guy number one said.

Bree began breathing rapidly and was all but trembling in Tanner's arms now. What the hell was going on?

"We followed Ms. Weathers to a church in Denver. It looks like she was talking to someone, but we're not sure who."

Tension continued to rocket through Bree's slender body as the person on the other end spoke.

"No, sir," the first man finally replied. "No positive ID or pictures. We're working on that now."

Another pause.

"No, I don't think coming here yourself is a good option."

The trembling in Bree's limbs became more pronounced.

"By the time you got here, the scene would be cold.

Let us continue to search. It might have been a random stranger. Ms. Weathers has been known to stop and talk to people since the accident." He paused.

"Yes, sir. We'll keep looking and keep you posted." He obviously disconnected the call. "If we don't want the boss here trying to do our job for us and handing us our asses, let's find out who Weathers was talking to."

"Maybe she's still in the church. Whoever it was couldn't have gotten far," the third voice said.

The men's voices began to fade as they walked back toward the church door.

"The third one was inside the church," Bree whispered. "He was on the phone, talking about communion. He walked not five feet away from me."

"And if he had found you?" Tanner whispered in her ear.

She didn't say anything. Had he really expected her to? At least she wasn't shaking anymore.

He was going to have answers, but first they needed to get out of here.

A few moments later, he stepped back from her and took her hand, and they moved quickly together down the alley. As soon as they were at an open corner, relatively safe since people were around everywhere, he grabbed his phone.

"I've got to call this in."

He wasn't prepared for the utter panic that blanketed her features. She grabbed his wrist with both of her hands.

"No. Tanner, please."

He shook his head. "Those men were armed. You heard them. One said he hurt the priest. Were they going to hurt you if they had found you?"

She nodded slowly.

"Then I need to call this in," he continued. "I don't know why you're protecting them, but it ends now."

"I'm not protecting them. I'm protecting *me*. If you call this in, I'm as good as dead."

"Because you're on the run."

Her face was ashen, huge green eyes dwarfing the rest of her features. "Yes, but not from the law."

It was the first time she'd admitted there was something bad going on with her.

He shook his head. "I can't do nothing."

She rubbed her fingers over her eyes. "I know this is going to sound crazy, but can you drive to the nearest police station and tell them in person rather than call?"

He shook his head. "That will take too long. The priest might need medical attention. What if I call anonymously? I can even call the police department directly, so they won't trace the call like they do 911 calls. I won't give them my name."

He would do it, even though it went against his code as a law enforcement officer.

"No, they'll still be able to link it back to your phone. And it will draw even more attention because you didn't do what was expected." She began to look around frantically. "Plus, being here in Denver at the exact same time. They'd be stupid not to put that together."

"Exact same time as what? And who is *they*?"

"You're only going to believe me if I show you."

Tanner wanted to throw up his hands in frustration. "Bree." He put his hands on both her arms. "Show me *what*?"

"Do you trust me?"

He rolled his eyes. "About as far as I can throw you."

"Well, do you think you could throw me across that street?" She pointed at a man who was talking on his phone, standing at a coffee shop kitty-corner from the church.

"What do you want me to do?"

"Go to that man. Get him to call 911 and tell them the priest is in trouble. But as soon as he does it, you've got to get out of sight. They're in the area, so it won't take them long to pinpoint the location of the call. So have the guy make the call, then get back over here quickly."

This was a lot of cloak-and-dagger stuff even for a cop. But he had no doubt Bree's fear was real.

"You stay right here." He pointed to the ground. He wanted her where he could see her.

She shook her head. "I can't be out here. I can't be around anybody else when this happens. They'll immediately utilize every cell phone in a half-mile grid."

Tanner gritted his teeth. Before this day was over, he was going to understand what the hell she was talking about. "Remember that part about not as far as I can throw you?"

"If you don't trust me, can you at least trust that I want to get back to the twins without leading any sort of danger to them?"

He grimaced, but he had to agree. Bree wouldn't do anything to hurt the babies. They were wasting time. He nodded at her, and she took off to a little park with no people around.

Tanner jogged over to the man still glancing at his phone in front of the church. He pulled out his badge. This would be the easiest way.

"Excuse me." He flashed his badge in front of the guy. "My phone just broke and I need you to call 911. We've got a priest inside who passed out and injured himself."

The guy's eyes got big. "Are you serious, man? Sure, no problem."

Tanner stayed long enough to make sure the guy was really calling, then slipped away toward the park.

And didn't see Bree there.

Damn it, had she run? He was on his way to getting well

and truly angry when she stuck her head out from behind
a large tree and gestured frantically for him to come over.
He just made it to her, and was about to read her the riot
act, when a car—*multiple* cars—came screeching up behind him, pulling right up on the guy who had called 911.

"What the hell?" Bree's slender arm grabbed his shirt
and yanked him behind the tree with her.

There was no way emergency response could've gotten
there that fast, less than a minute after the call. And even
if they had, they wouldn't have wasted their time going to
the guy on the phone when there was a possibly injured
man inside the church.

Tanner peeked out to see the men in suits questioning
the 911 caller. Bree was between him and the tree, her
back to him, but she wasn't looking. She already knew
who was there.

"Those are the same guys from the alley, right?"

She nodded.

"How did they get there so fast?" Tanner asked. "Are
they tracing 911 calls or something?"

"No, it wouldn't have mattered what number he called.
He was flagged because he mentioned the priest in the
church. Only a witness would've known about the priest."

Tanner looked again before pulling his head back.
"Those men are dangerous. Are they going to hurt that
guy?" He couldn't sit by and let an innocent bystander
get hurt.

She shook her head. "Not when they find out someone
else asked him to make the call. It won't take them long
to figure out he's not who they want. You are."

"Fine. They can have me. I'm law enforcement. I can
call in Denver PD backup and we can arrest them. We'll
end this right now."

She let out a small laugh that held no humor whatsoever.

"Those guys are nothing more than hired guns. Arresting them wouldn't accomplish anything."

"It would be a start. I've got at least one admitting to hurting the priest."

"If you arrest them, you'll be bringing danger right to my doorstep. To Christian and Beth's doorstep."

He snatched his head back behind the tree as the 911 caller pointed in their general direction. The men in the suits evidently wanted to know who had asked him to make the call.

"We've got trouble," he said. "We're going to have to run."

She nodded. "I can keep up."

She wasn't lying. They moved from tree to tree, using the natural park coverage for as long as they could. And then they bolted. He heard a shout from behind them, and they pushed faster.

Tanner was in good shape, kept himself physically fit for the job and because it was how he liked to feel. Even with Bree's assurances, he thought he would have to slow down significantly for her to be able to keep up with him.

He was wrong.

Bree was with him almost step for step. Was actually running faster because her shorter gait meant more steps. She was definitely very much in shape.

They circled back around on the outside of the park, cutting sharply to the left down a crowded avenue.

"If anyone has their phone out, try to keep your face averted," she panted. "It's important that they don't catch your picture."

"If we don't want anyone getting us on picture or video, we're much better off blending in rather than bolting through."

She stopped running almost immediately. "You're right. Damn it, you're right."

It was like she was mad at herself for breaking a rule she knew about.

They kept moving quickly, but not fast enough to be interesting to any passersby. Tanner glanced over his shoulder and saw two of the men in suits turning down the avenue. They obviously weren't sure exactly who they were looking for, and their progress was slower because they had to look more closely at everyone.

"We should split up," Bree said.

"No way in hell." He reached down and wrapped her hand in his, a little afraid she might bolt.

"They're looking for a couple. Separating is logical. We could meet up later when it's safe."

"But it also makes us more vulnerable." He wasn't worried about himself, he was worried about her. "What would happen if they caught you?" He held her hand more tightly in his, ignoring the relief he felt when she didn't try to pull away.

"I'd probably be dead before my body hit the ground," she murmured.

Damn it. "Then we definitely stay together."

They ducked around a family, and Bree turned more fully to him, putting her hand on his forearm and squeezing. "It's me they want, not you. You don't have to be in danger. This isn't your fight."

He shook his head. "We stay together."

She looked like she wanted to argue further, but there was no time.

When Tanner saw a suit enter the crowded street from the other direction, conspicuous because of his obvious observation of everyone, he wrapped an arm around Bree and pulled her into the nearest shop.

"Someone just entered the street from the other end. Waiting them out is probably our best bet."

She nodded. "We need to find somewhere away from people. They'll start scanning phones soon."

He didn't know exactly what that meant, but it didn't sound good. "Mine, too?"

"No, your flip phone is too old. It's safe."

Thank God Grand County was behind the times when it came to updating communication devices.

Bree looked around the general discount store they'd entered and began pulling him toward the back and the restrooms, then into the separate handicapped bathroom that would give them full privacy. Tanner grabbed an out-of-order sign resting under the water fountain and hung it on the door's hook as they went inside before shutting and locking the door behind him.

Bree closed the toilet seat lid and sat down wearily. "This is one of the best places we could've probably picked to hide. But we'll have to stay here probably an hour to make sure they've given up. Hopefully by then they'll just assume they lost us."

Tanner leaned back against the sink. "Good. That should give us enough time for you to tell me exactly what's going on. Starting with who those babies belong to. Because you're sure as hell not their biological mother."

Chapter Ten

Bree stared at Tanner as he leaned up against the sink, his long legs stretched out in front of him and strong arms crossed over his chest.

How much could she tell him? Definitely not the whole truth. First of all, he was law enforcement. Under oath to fight bad guys or whatever. Knowing Tanner and his sense of justice, he would want to take on the Organization all by himself. The only thing that would succeed in doing was getting him killed.

If he even believed her at all. Why would anybody believe that a charity organization that had helped millions of underprivileged and impoverished people gain access to education and technology was actually housing a terrorist group buying and selling privacy and information?

Communication for All was the perfect front. They seemed so pure and altruistic in their motives.

No, she definitely couldn't tell him everything she knew. But she had to tell him something.

"Christian and Beth aren't my children. You're right. They belong to my cousin, Melissa."

"Melissa Weathers. The woman you met today at the church, and who the suits were talking about on the phone."

"How did you know I met her? How are you here at all?"

"I've been watching you carry around that phone every

day since you got to town like it held the secrets to the known universe, but you never actually talk or text anyone on it. Then today you get a text and ten minutes later you're bolting out the door. So I followed you."

He was a cop. A damn good one, she knew that. She shouldn't be surprised. "Ok, fine. The text was from Melissa, telling me to meet her."

"But you still scoped out the place. I watched you do that, too. Quite proficiently, I might add. Do you not trust her?"

This was where it got tricky. How to give Tanner enough info that he would be satisfied, but not so much that he felt like he needed to step in and save the world. "No, I trust her. But she's gotten in with some bad people. She didn't want the twins around them, so she asked me if I could take care of them for a while."

"And those are the same people we're hiding from now? The ones in the alley, who also hurt the priest? I thought those were just the hired muscle. They work for the Mr. Jeter on the phone. Is that the person who was able to get the cars to the 911 call so quickly?"

He was studying her too closely and had way too many details. She had to derail him. "Yes, the group Melissa is trying to get away from is really good with technology and has found a way to triangulate cell phone signals to locate people. Something to do with multilateration and hybrid positioning systems."

Most people's eyes started to glaze over any time technical terms came into play. But Tanner's didn't. He might not have understood what she was saying, but she had no doubt he would be further researching it.

Fine. Everything she was telling him was vague enough that he wouldn't draw attention from the Organization if he started searching the terms. And when the terms didn't really lead him anywhere useful, he wouldn't blame her. After all, why would she know specifics about triangulation?

It wasn't like she had helped design the technology when she was thirteen years old or anything.

"And that's it? It's some sort of technologically savvy group of general bad guys she's in trouble with?"

Yeah, it sounded ridiculous when he said it like that. But Bree nodded. "Pretty much."

"So you agreed to watch the twins to help her out?"

"Yes, she was afraid if they knew where the twins were, they would take them and force her to do more work for them."

At least that much was true.

Tanner's eyes narrowed. "If this group is so technologically advanced and wants your cousin, wouldn't they know to come after you first?"

Damn it, this man was too intelligent for his own good.

"We had a falling-out years ago and hadn't talked to each other in a decade. That's why she came to me, because there were no ties to be found."

Mostly because the Organization thought she was dead.

He was studying her with those brown eyes that never seemed to miss anything. She couldn't tell how much he was believing and how much he wasn't. There wasn't much more she could tell him.

She just needed him to let her lie low while Melissa tried to figure it out.

She ignored the voice in her head that told her that was never going to happen. That there was no way Melissa was a match for the Organization and would be able to crack the files she'd stolen, not when they were already a little suspicious of her.

Bree's heart hurt for her cousin. Hurt for the fact that she lost Christian—another victim of the Organization, just like her mother. Hurt that Melissa was missing seeing her babies get bigger day by day. Hurt that if Melissa didn't stop the Organization in time, all of this would be for naught anyway.

"What? What is it you're thinking right now?" She blinked rapidly as Tanner's thumb trailed gently down her cheek. She hadn't even realized he'd moved, but he was crouching beside her.

She couldn't tell him any of this. She wanted to—so desperately she wanted to share this burden, but she couldn't. Risk Peak needed him. He was a good man, and she refused to sign his death warrant.

But she couldn't seem to quite make herself pull away from his touch, either.

"I just want everything to be okay, but I don't see any way that that's going to happen."

"I can help. I might not be able to do anything as law enforcement in Risk Peak, but I've got contacts. Federal law enforcement. Colorado Springs is the headquarters for Omega Sector, a specialized task force equipped to handle this sort of thing. I know people there. I can help you and your cousin."

He said it with such conviction that she couldn't help but believe him. For just a moment, she almost caved. But she had no proof. Nobody would believe the word of a woman who was a ghost over that of a charity that had helped thousands and thousands of people.

"I have to give Melissa time. She's the only one who knows all the details of what's going on." She looked away as she told the lie, but his thumb was still gentle against her cheek.

"There's more, Bree. I know there's more you're not telling me."

She'd never had anyone be this gentle with her before. Not just the touch, but the patience. The concern.

Her mom, before the paranoia had completely taken her

mind, had loved Bree—loved her enough to risk her own life. But she'd always been gruff, worried, scared.

Tanner Dempsey was none of those things.

His fingers seemed to burn against her skin. She had to pull away.

But there was more truth she could give him.

"I'm afraid I'm ruining those kids. I'm not good with people, anyone can see that." It was one of the things she liked about computers. With technology there was no emotional subtext. Coding was straightforward, logical, decisive. She didn't have to worry about nuances and emotional harm. "If Melissa had any other choice, she wouldn't have chosen me to care for Christian and Beth, believe me."

He shook his head. "Anyone can tell that you love those children, Bree. They are not missing out on anything, especially not affection."

"Then how come Christian cries all the time?"

She meant it as a distraction, but as the words came out, she realized it was a true fear. Why would Christian cry all the time if he was getting what he needed?

"Some babies just cry more than others."

"Maybe he's smart enough to subconsciously realize I'm not as good as his mother and that his developmental needs aren't being met because his caretaker is emotionally stunted."

Tanner chuckled before his hands cupped her face and his lips touched hers briefly, lightly, before pulling away. "Or maybe the kid is just colicky."

He stood, backing away. Bree's fingers touched her lips where his had just been. He'd meant it as a kiss of camaraderie, encouragement. A show of support.

What would he think if he knew that was the first time she'd ever been kissed by a man in her entire life?

Then maybe he'd be more likely to agree with her about the emotional stuntedness.

"I want to help your cousin, Bree," he said. "And you. Because as long as they're willing to hurt other people to force her to do what they want, you're not safe. I can't turn a blind eye to that."

She couldn't let him start digging into it. "Just give her more time. She's gathering the evidence she needs, and when she has it, she'll go to the police."

Or they would run. Either way, it wouldn't be his problem anymore.

His dark brows furrowed together. "Doing nothing, knowing there's danger out there, doesn't sit well with me."

Now she stood and grabbed his hand. "I just need somewhere to lie low and keep the babies safe. Risk Peak is a good place to do that. No one is looking for me there."

She thought about her paranoia and the eyes she always felt on her there. But that couldn't be the Organization, so she would just have to keep it under control.

"Fine." Tanner nodded. "I'll let it go for now. But you can bet that I'm going to be sticking to you like glue, Bree Daniels. If someone is coming for you or those babies, they'll have to go through me first."

She didn't know if the fluttering in her chest was relief or panic.

Chapter Eleven

Over the next two weeks, Bree learned what normal life was supposed to be like.

She felt like she was back in the sitcom again, except this time she had a little more understanding of her role. She worked, played with the babies and got a good night's sleep each night.

But she had to keep reminding herself that this was just pretend. None of it—not the job, not the kids, not the man who came and walked her home from work every night—was real.

Eventually the season would be over and she would go back to what she had been before.

Alone.

"You've got an order up, Bree," Dan called out from the kitchen. Bree had moved up from jack-of-all-trades to regular lunch shift waitress. It was better for everyone. The Andrewses didn't have to pay her so much under the table, and she was able to make more money overall. Although now that she wasn't preparing to leave town as soon as possible, money wasn't so much of an issue.

But she wondered daily how it was going for Melissa. The phone had remained steadily silent in the two weeks since she'd last seen her cousin. Bree still had no way of getting in touch with her and no idea how the plan was going.

Not being an active part of the plan was difficult. Bree had always been someone who had plans, backup plans and backups to her backup plans. Ironically, it had been Michael Jeter who had first recognized that her mind worked like a flowchart. He'd been the one to help her develop that part of her brain, so that she was now able to see multiple scenarios at any given time.

She could see multiple scenarios for this situation also, but few of them ended well for Melissa, the twins or herself.

"Thanks, Dan." She grabbed the plate and took it out to the diners, glancing over where Judy sat with the babies.

They'd worked out a sort of schedule where someone could be keeping an eye on the twins whenever they were awake. Sometimes it was the other waitress, Judy, sometimes Dan or Cheryl, depending on the needs of the diner at the time.

Tanner had sat beside her as she'd told Dan and Cheryl that the babies weren't actually hers. Surprisingly, they hadn't seemed to care at all. The kids hadn't been kidnapped, and they still needed to be held and cared for. That was all that mattered to the older couple.

Bree forced a smile onto her face as she delivered the plates up for order. It was the construction crew again. More specifically, the skinny man with dark hair and dark eyes. She'd finally pinpointed him as the one who'd been watching her.

He never talked to her, never tried to get her to engage in conversation like some of the other workers did. Just watched her silently.

Everything about him made her want to take the babies and run. But she was determined not to let the paranoia take over her mind. This man could not be in the Organization. He would've already made his move.

She almost believed that, except for when all the doubts crept in.

Maybe the Organization was just biding its time.

Maybe they were waiting for Melissa to contact her so they could catch them both.

Maybe they had something so nefarious planned that Bree couldn't possibly imagine it.

She closed her eyes and shook the thoughts away. Maybe the guy was just awkward and rude and his parents had never taught him it was impolite to stare.

She had to let it go. She had real battles to fight. She didn't need to make up pretend ones in her head.

But as she delivered his food, she could swear the guy was planning to lock her in his basement to be his forever bride. She nodded at him and his buddies and backed away.

She took another order then walked back to the kitchen.

"Your creepy guy give you any problems?" Cheryl asked.

Bree shrugged. "Studied me with his creepy eyes and gave his creepy nod when I handed him his food."

"So basically acted the way he always does." Dan flipped a burger as he talked.

"Listen, buddy." Bree pointed at him after hanging her order on the spinning wheel. "Don't be bringing logic where it doesn't belong. Leave me and my paranoia alone."

Dan chuckled, and Cheryl rubbed Bree's shoulder. Two weeks ago Bree would've shifted away from the touch. But she was learning. Learning that touching could be normal. That it was okay to joke with people.

"I think he's just a strange guy," Cheryl said.

"That's for sure," Bree muttered. But they were right. Just because he was strange didn't mean he was dangerous.

If she wanted to be able to live any sort of normal life, she was going to have to accept that. Not every strange stranger was dangerous. Not every stranger was from the Organization.

Bree grabbed the pitcher of water and walked back into the dining room to refill empty glasses. The front doorbell rang as someone came in, and a few moments later Bree felt eyes on her again.

But these she knew. And they belonged to someone who was very definitely not a creepy, thin man.

A smile rose to her lips unbidden.

She should not be smiling when it came to Tanner. Should not be thinking about him as much as she was. Should definitely not be dreaming about him at night, wondering what a real kiss from him might feel like.

She was doing her best to keep her distance, but Tanner made it so damn difficult. He just had something about him that drew people in. People trusted him, knew he would look out for them. The entire town of Risk Peak depended on him.

Bree had met his mother, sister and something ridiculous like eighty-seven cousins. Tanner had more family in a quarter-block radius from the diner than Bree had known her whole life.

He was smart, focused and determined to help her out of this mess.

He was everything she should run from. He already knew too much about her and the situation.

Yet she counted the minutes every day until he would be back and she could see him again.

He was here for at least one meal every day. Today it was lunch. At first she'd tried letting Judy or one of the other waitresses take his table, but he'd shut that down immediately. Now everyone knew he only wanted her.

His words, not hers.

And they did funny things to her insides.

He had another police officer with him today—not Ronnie Kitchens, the deputy who sometimes came in with Tanner. This guy was younger, a little chubby, wearing his brown sheriff's uniform like he wasn't quite comfortable with the fit.

Probably because the guy looked like he couldn't be but half a day out of police officer school, or whatever it was called.

Bree grabbed a couple of glasses of water and brought them out to Tanner's table.

"Hi." She set the glasses down and looked everywhere but at Tanner's face. She knew darn well what he looked like. Those brown eyes had been starring front and center in her dreams for the last two weeks.

"Hey. How's your day going? Twins sleep all right last night?"

She felt his fingers against her hand where it was still wrapped around his glass of water. "Yeah. Even Christian slept five hours in one stretch."

She slipped her hand away from his and stuck both of them in the back pockets of her jeans, still staring down at the glasses.

Her withdrawal didn't seem to faze Tanner at all. "Five hours. That's a record for that little guy, isn't it?"

Now she looked him in the face, drawn in immediately by those deep brown eyes like she'd known she would be.

The moment stretched out between them.

"Hey there," he whispered, smiling, just like he had every day when she finally broke down and met his eyes. He was always patient, never frustrated that she found it hard to interact with him.

"You have twins? Holy cow!" Baby-face cop's booming question broke the moment. She looked away from Tanner and over at him. "I couldn't imagine having one baby, much less two. I'm Scott Watson. Nice to meet you."

She shook his outstretched hand as he grinned at her. "I'm Bree."

"Scott is on an intercounty task force. He's been traveling around to different departments, helping to regulate social media, reports, general communication with the public. He'll be here a week or so."

"I volunteered." Scott grinned. "Gives me a chance to meet people from all over Colorado. See towns and counties I might not get regular interaction with otherwise."

"No offense," Bree said, "but you almost don't seem old enough to be traveling around by yourself."

Scott chuckled, and the sound was so contagious Bree had to smile, too. "I know! I get that all the time. I wanted to do undercover work, but I was told they didn't get much call for chubby middle school kids undercover." He patted his smooth, round cheeks.

"I'll admit, I was a little irritated when I got the email about your arrival yesterday," Tanner said.

"Yesterday?" Scott's smile turned into a scowl. "You should've received the memo from the task force at least a month ago."

"Ends up I did, almost five weeks ago. Somehow it ended up in my junk mail."

"I'm still sorry. This sort of miscommunication is one of the things I'm trying to help eliminate. And I promise I won't be in your way. Just stuff me in an office under the stairs. Of course, if you have any action going on, I'd love to be a part of that, too."

Tanner just smiled. "We'll see."

Bree took their orders—Scott's choice of the pancake stack was not going to help his chubby middle school kid persona—when Tanner grabbed her hand again.

"I see who's back." He gestured toward the creepy,

thin guy's table with his head. "You have any problems with him?"

She shook her head. "No. Nothing concrete, as usual."

Tanner stood. "I'm just gonna go chat with them."

Bree grabbed Tanner's hand. "He didn't say or do anything. Really."

His thumb trailed across her wrist. "I'm not going to make a big deal. It never hurts for a deputy to say hello to people who work in town."

Tanner walked over to their table while Bree headed to the server station to get some coffee. When she brought the two mugs back, Tanner was still over talking to the construction guys.

"This is some really pretty country," Scott said. "Some of my favorite so far. Are you like Tanner—lived here all your life?"

Bree wasn't sure how much of her story he'd told Scott. Probably not much, if anything. They'd agreed to stick with a cover story of a violent ex-boyfriend if anyone ever really needed information.

"No, I've just moved here recently. Needed to get out of the situation I was in."

She looked over at Tanner. What was he saying to the men? She didn't trust the creepy guy, but neither was she trying to disrupt the whole town.

A few seconds later, Tanner turned and walked back to his table.

"Don't worry, I didn't say anything about you. Just chatting with them about the building progress. Normal Risk Peak stuff."

"Okay." She let out a sigh. "I'm probably being paranoid."

"I know I don't know what's going on," Scott said. "But sometimes it's good to be a little paranoid in this world. Even chubby middle schoolers know that."

Scott's rueful smile had her feeling better. She walked back to the kitchen to place their order.

But when she looked over her shoulder, creepy guy was staring at her again.

"ARE THE CONSTRUCTION workers giving your lady friend a hard time?"

Tanner watched as Bree walked back into the kitchen then glanced over to find that the man in question was indeed watching her.

He'd told her the truth about the talk he'd had with the guys—it had been friendly, neutral. No threats, veiled or otherwise.

But it had been a reminder that Tanner was here. Was always around. That anything that happened in this town was going to go through him. And he especially wasn't going to let anything happen to Bree.

He didn't think the creepy, thin guy had any dubious intent toward her, but he made Bree uncomfortable, which was enough for Tanner to make his presence known. Since there weren't any laws he was breaking just by looking at her, there wasn't much more Tanner could do other than that.

Sticking close to her hadn't been a problem. True to his word in that bathroom two weeks ago, Tanner had made sure he was around.

He knew she hadn't told him the full truth that day. There were still huge chunks of info about her situation he didn't have. But trying to force or bully the truth out of her would just cause her to shut down and withdraw. She would revert into that thick shell of hers.

So for the past two weeks he'd been trying to *gentle* the truth out of her.

This prickly woman had plenty of defenses against someone trying to force her to do something, but she seemed clueless when it came to someone being kind to her.

Of course, he should probably put her in protective custody. That would be the safest thing for both her and the babies. And he still might have to do that.

He grimaced at the thought. Bree would hate it. Would hate him.

But at least she would be safe.

"Tanner?"

Tanner brought his attention back to Scott. The younger man looked concerned. Having anybody shadowing the department was an annoyance, but at least Scott was easygoing and likable so far.

Tanner shook his head. "The construction guys aren't going to be a problem. Bree is just a little skittish."

Scott took a sip of his coffee. "She said she just moved here a few weeks ago. She running from something?"

Tanner sipped his own. "What makes you say that?"

"I may have only been on the force for eight months, but my deductive reasoning works just fine. A new mother, a little shaky. Maybe an abusive situation she got out of when the twins were born?"

"Bree pretty much keeps to herself. I don't know that much about her."

That was both true and not true. For someone who was so amazingly gentle and tender with the babies, she seemed to have no idea whatsoever how to interact on an emotional level with other adults.

Every time he came in here and got those green eyes of hers to finally meet his, he counted it a win.

"Oh." Scott took another sip of his coffee. "I thought you two were an item. My bad."

"No, not an item. She's a friend."

And if Tanner could figure out how to get through to her, maybe so much more than that.

*** *** *** *** *** *** ***
*** *** *** *** *** *** ***
*** *** *** *** *** *** ***
*** *** *** *** *** *** ***
*** *** *** *** *** *** ***
*** *** *** *** *** *** ***

Chapter Twelve

When Bree stepped out the back door of the Sunrise later that evening, Tanner was waiting. He took Beth's carrier from her, leaving her with only Christian. They were almost getting too heavy for her to carry both of them in their carriers. Soon she'd need to purchase a double stroller.

There were a lot of things she'd put off purchasing, not knowing how long the twins would be hers. If Melissa was successful, it would only be a couple more weeks.

If Melissa wasn't successful… Bree had no idea what was in store for any of them.

"Thank you," she whispered to Tanner.

As they walked toward her apartment on the outskirts of town, Tanner told her about his day. Then another funny story about his family—this time about how he broke a window in his parents' house while competing with his brother, Noah, for who could twirl the baseball bat around the most times.

Tanner had won. But they'd both spent their entire spring break doing chores to pay for the window.

"How about you?" he asked. "Got any brothers or sisters?"

"No, no siblings for me. My cousin, Melissa, was the closest thing I had to a sibling."

"Did you two ever do anything stupid to get in trouble?"

Yeah, right now. The kind where they'd both be dead if the Organization found out Melissa was trying to shut them down, and Bree was not only alive, but doing whatever she could to assist Melissa.

But she just shook her head. "No, I moved away before either of us got to the rebellious age. And I've always been more of a keep-your-head-down kind of girl."

"Ah, smart. If I'd been like you, I would've gotten into a lot less trouble."

"Seems like you've done okay."

His gorgeous grin had her almost forgetting how to walk. "Depends on who you ask. Linda Dugas might say otherwise."

"Linda Dugas from the Sunday School frog incident?"

He threw back his head and laughed. "I should've known you were too smart not to remember. Yes, Linda eventually forgave me for said frog incident. She and I even dated for a few months in high school."

"It didn't work out between you two?" The thought of him with someone else shouldn't bother her at all. Who he dated in the past or might date in the future was none of her business. She refused to even acknowledge her clenching stomach.

"No. We both went off to college. She met some accountant or something, fell madly in love and moved to somewhere completely insane like Philadelphia."

She couldn't stop her own chuckle. "Philly. Yeah, man, some people just go hog wild."

"Yes! See? I knew you would understand. Why would anyone ever want to leave Colorado?"

"Why indeed?"

He nudged her with his shoulder. "How about you, anybody special in high school or college?"

She wondered what he would say if he knew she'd never finished high school, much less gone to college, but that she had an IQ higher than ninety-nine percent of the world's population.

Yet another thing that made her abnormal.

"No, I pretty much kept to myself."

Fortunately, before he could dig into that information, they arrived at the apartment. Risk Peak wasn't that big, even walking.

"Thanks for your help. You know you don't have to do this every day, right? I mean, what are the chances of something happening between here and the diner? It's probably not necessary."

She took Beth's carrier and handed him the key, as had become their habit, and waited as he checked out the tiny apartment for possible intruders. A moment later he was back. Her apartment wasn't that big.

"All clear?" she asked.

"Yep." He took Christian's carrier this time, the baby thankfully asleep, and followed her inside.

"I just feel like I'm wasting your time. I know you have a lot of responsibilities, and walking me from one safe place to another safe place down a perfectly safe street seems like a waste of taxpayers' money."

Tanner set Christian's carrier down on the table and gently unbuckled him. "Playpen?"

"Yes, please." So far, Tanner had been the only one who had the magic touch with Christian, able to soothe him and, more importantly, move him from the carrier to the playpen that served as his crib without waking him up.

Watching Tanner's big hands carry the baby so tenderly and securely, his attention entirely focused on the tiny body in his care...

Her breath caught. If Bree had ever let herself dream about what the perfect future would look like, this would've been it. A strong, gorgeous man, holding a child with such care and concern.

But these weren't her children. And he definitely wasn't her man.

And letting herself dream was only going to make all of this so much worse when she finally woke up.

Bree moved Beth into the playpen next to her brother. That little angel never made a peep, even though her big eyes blinked open once before closing again.

She closed the door to the bedroom and walked with him toward the kitchen.

"Like I was saying, it's not a good idea for you to walk me home."

He raised an eyebrow. "We've gone from 'probably not necessary' to 'not a good idea' in under a minute."

"I just…" She let out a sigh. "You've just got to have better things to do than to walk here with me every day. Dan could do it, or that other deputy…"

"Ronnie."

"Yeah, Ronnie. He could make sure I was okay." Her voice was getting a little loud and higher pitched, so she forced herself to rein it in. Why was she getting upset when making this simple request?

Tanner leaned against the wall with one shoulder and crossed his arms over his chest. His head tilted to the side as he studied her. "Do you lie when we talk, Bree?"

"What?"

He shrugged with one shoulder. "Just wondering if you tell me the truth when we talk. I know there's stuff you don't tell me, and while I don't like it, I do understand. Like today, when I asked if you have brothers or sisters and you said no, was that the truth?"

"Yes."

"So you tell me the truth when you can?"

Her eyes narrowed. "Yes. But I don't understand what you're getting at."

"Twenty-four. Teal. Strawberry. Venice. *A Wrinkle in Time*. Security gate guard. *The Matrix*."

"What?" Was he having some sort of nervous breakdown or something?

Tanner pushed off from the wall and took a step closer. "Ballerina. Dogs. And, quite unfortunately, in my opinion, pop."

She stared at him, brows furrowed. "I don't understand." It was like some sort of code that seemed familiar, but that she couldn't decipher.

"Your age. Favorite color. Favorite flavor ice cream. The city in Europe you'd most like to visit. Your favorite book as a child. The worst job ever. Best movie."

"I—"

He took another couple of steps until he was standing right in front of her. "What you wanted to be when you grew up. Which is better, dogs or cats. And favorite genre of music. Sadly."

These were the things they'd talked about on the way home from the diner each night.

"Every day I can get the answer to one question out of you. Sometimes one and a half." He reached out and tucked a strand of hair behind her ear. "I walk you here because, yes, I want to make sure you're safe. But also because each day I get to learn something about you I didn't know the day before. And that is very definitely not a waste of my time."

"Oh."

His fingers trailed down her cheek. "I know all those little things don't make up the whole of who you are. But I still want to know them. And hopefully you're learning about me as well…although not all involving frogs and Linda Dugas."

He bent down until his lips were hovering just over hers, his other hand coming up to cup her other cheek. "Walking you home is the highlight of my day. So don't try to give my job to someone else."

She was completely lost in those brown eyes. "Okay."

And then he kissed her.

His lips were soft against hers. Light, feathery brushes, but definitely different than the brief kiss of camaraderie he'd given her when they'd been hiding out in the bathroom in Denver.

When he began to nibble her lips gently, her eyes slid closed with a sigh. Her hands came up and wrapped around his wrists at her face, and she leaned into him.

But all too soon, it was over and he was pulling back, giving her a moment to regain her bearings.

"Thank you for allowing me to walk you home, Bree Daniels. I'll see you tomorrow."

And without another word, he was gone.

Chapter Thirteen

Bree wasn't even going to be able to blame the babies for her lack of sleep tomorrow. That dubious honor fell directly on Captain Tanner Dempsey's wide shoulders.

And lips.

She'd stood staring at the door for a good five minutes after he'd left, just trying to process what had happened.

Now here it was, after two o'clock in the morning, and she still was trying to understand it all. And stop replaying the feel of his lips on hers.

She'd fed the babies when they'd woken up around midnight and normally would've been fast asleep, getting as much rest as she could before they woke up again between four thirty and five.

But she wasn't. And whose fault was that?

Captain hot lips, that's who.

Why did he remember all that stuff they'd talked about over the last couple of weeks as he walked her home?

And why did that make her feel all soft and gooey in the middle?

She rolled over on her double bed and punched the pillow next to her. When she heard something rattle against her nightstand, she thought it was from her anger management session. But then it happened again.

The phone Melissa had given her was vibrating.

Bree shot up in bed and grabbed it, opening it when she realized it was a call.

"Hello?" Her voice was tentative. She didn't want to give away any information before knowing who it was.

"Bree? Get out now!"

"Mel?"

"They found you." It was definitely Melissa. "Get the kids and get out of wherever you are. Destroy the phone. Hurry!"

"Mellie, are you safe?"

"Yes, they don't know it's me who gave you the phone, but they know it's someone from inside the Organization. I didn't realize they were tracking you already. Go now!"

Bree jumped up and pulled on her jeans and shoes. "But how will we get in touch if we don't have the phone?"

She took Beth out of the crib and rushed her to the carrier.

"I don't know. I'll be at the symposium. We'll have to find a way to get a message to each other there. We'll worry about that later. They're going to be there soon. I love you. Kiss them for me."

The phone went dead.

Bree threw the phone on the ground and stomped on it until it broke into pieces.

They had to get out now. Get to her car and leave town immediately. She refused to even think about having to leave without any sort of word to Tanner. What would he think, especially after that kiss? She forced those thoughts away or she would never make it through this.

Grabbing Beth's car seat carrier, she brought it over to the front door and set it down on the ground. Careful not to be noticed, she moved to the window and slid the curtain over just slightly so she could peek out. Her blood turned cold when she saw not one but two men walking toward her apartment in the darkness.

She darted to the back door and was pretty sure she could see someone in the darkness there.

Either door was going to spit her directly into their hands.

The only possibility would be climbing out the low kitchen window out the side of the building—maybe none of them would notice that. But the car seat carriers definitely wouldn't be an option that way.

She darted over to the bed and grabbed the baby carrier one of the ladies at the diner had lent her a couple days ago. She'd said it might help with Christian's fussiness. Bree prayed that would be the case now, because if he started howling before she made it to her car, the men would immediately be able to pinpoint her location.

She slipped the straps over her shoulder, wishing she'd paid more attention when the lady had shown her how to use it, and when it felt secure enough, she darted over to the crib and picked up Christian.

"Hey, sweet baby boy. Bree needs you to be nice and quiet, okay?"

Christian, of course, immediately began to fuss as she lifted him, but thankfully he settled back down when he was tucked up warm against her with the carrier.

"That a boy," she murmured kissing the top of his head.

She ran over to Beth and unhooked her from the car seat. "I'm counting on you to be your normal sweet self, baby."

Bree didn't know what she was going to do when she got them to the car without their car seats, but that was the least of her worries.

Taking Beth in one arm, she pried the window open as quietly as possible. When she heard someone try the doorknob on her front door, she knew she was out of time. Abandoning all attempts at quiet, she began trying to fit herself through the large window while carrying two babies.

Getting through from the inside was easy, but there were bushes on the outside. As she heard the doorknob rattle again, she propelled herself through the window, twisting to land on her back in the bushes, protecting Beth and Christian. She swallowed a cry of pain as something sharp ripped into her shoulder, but immediately got up as best she could with arms full of babies. She heard the men, now inside her apartment, say something to each other and knew it was just a matter of seconds before they figured out where she'd gone.

She sprinted toward her car, wincing at the pain in her shoulder, afraid she might run into the third man at any moment. Deciding on stealth rather than speed, she slowed down and tucked herself into the shadows. She sucked in her breath silently when the third man passed by not ten feet away from her. He was watching the streets, obviously the lookout guy.

His phone rang, and he answered it, turning his back to her.

"What?"

She was too far away to hear what the other person said, but whatever it was, this guy wasn't happy about it.

"Well, she damn well didn't come through here. Are we sure she was even in the house in the first place?" He muttered a curse and began walking away from her, toward the front of her apartment.

It was the break Bree needed. As soon as he was far enough that it was relatively safe, she began jogging toward the car. If she could just make it there, they would be okay.

But that was when sweet, angelic Beth decided she wasn't happy with all the sleep interruptions and let out a wail.

"Oh, no, sweetie," Bree crooned, slowing to bring Beth up to her shoulder and pat her.

But that just caused Christian to start crying.

There was no way the guy on the phone didn't hear them. Forgetting about stealth, Bree bolted into a sprint, grimacing when she realized the third man was between her and her car. For the first time, Bree wished her apartment wasn't on the outskirts of town, away from everything else. Even if she started yelling, no one would hear her.

Why hadn't she called for help rather than destroy her phone? Not that anyone could've gotten here in time.

Both babies were crying now, and she was way too slow to get away with the added weight. She glanced behind her and saw the third man was just a few feet away.

He was going to catch her. She wasn't going to make it. She pushed for one last burst of speed, but it wasn't enough.

When she felt fingers grasp at her shoulders and slip away, she started yelling. She was still too far out for anyone to hear her, but she had to try.

"Help me! Somebody help me!"

Both babies startled at her yell and wailed louder. Hard fingers gripped her shoulder, this time not letting go. Bree cried out as he jerked her back, fear coursing through her system.

The voice came heavy and dark in her ear. "You're going to regret making me chase you."

She pulled away from him, but he grabbed her hair, yanking her back. Bree struggled to hold on to the twins. And knew she couldn't allow herself to pitch forward—she might crush them.

Beth gripped firmly with one arm, Bree swung around, keeping her elbow out to use her momentum and catch the man off guard. But he was too quick and stopped her elbow before it could do any damage. He twisted her arm in a painful grip.

She got her first look at her attacker. He didn't look like a criminal. His face was nondescript, friendly even. Bree had no doubt he was from the Organization. They would send people who blended in.

His features might be neutral, but the menace in his eyes was obvious. "I'm going to enjoy teaching you some manners. And I know I'm not the only one. You've been making us look bad."

His hand raised in a fist, and she braced herself to take the punch without dropping the babies, but before he could connect, the guy went flying onto the ground.

Someone had tackled him.

Bree didn't know who it was, whether it was friend or foe or if karma had just chosen that moment to show up. She wasn't going to wait around to find out.

She took off toward the main part of town. If she could just make it another couple of blocks, she'd be able to yell for help. When someone rushed out from between two parked cars, she screamed and twisted away, trying to head in the other direction, but arms wrapped around her and held her firm.

"Bree! Bree, it's me." Tanner's voice finally got through to her. And she stopped trying to fight him.

"T-Tanner?"

"Yeah, sweetheart, it's me. Are you okay? I got a call that you were in trouble." He pulled her sideways against him, mindful of the babies, then took a crying Beth out of her arms.

"Somebody broke into my apartment. Three guys."

Tanner muttered a curse under his breath. Keeping Beth secure in one arm, he reached down and grabbed the police walkie-talkie at his belt.

"Ronnie, we've got a 10-64 off Lincoln Street. Three guys broke into Bree's apartment."

The other deputy responded, but Bree couldn't hear over the sound of her own labored breathing and the cries of the babies. When Tanner wrapped his arm back around her and began leading her somewhere, she just went.

"They found us," she said, almost on autopilot. "I've got to leave. We're not safe. They found us. They found us."

Bree could feel the panic welling up inside her. She had nothing she needed for the babies, no way of knowing if she could even get back to her car safely, and she still didn't have enough money to survive long on her own. How was she going to make it?

The world was starting to spin, the dark sky closing in on her. How was she going to do this? How would she keep the twins fed if she was on the run? Where else was going to allow her to work while good people helped look after them?

It would never happen. She wouldn't make it. What was she going to do?

Her throat was closing up, and she couldn't breathe. She began to scratch at it frantically, trying to get oxygen into her system.

Then suddenly Tanner's face was right in front of hers. His hand wrapped around the back of her head, his fingers digging into her hair. It wasn't painful, but there was definitely no ignoring it.

"Bree. Listen to me. I am not going to let anything happen to you. Not to you or the kids." As she stared into his brown eyes, so serious and authoritative, she couldn't help but believe him. Her throat loosened enough to let in some air.

"You're not in this alone anymore." His fingers rubbed at the back of her neck. "*Not alone.* Got it?"

She could only stare, couldn't quite formulate words. So Tanner moved her head in a nodding motion.

"You're going to stay here at the diner with Dan and Cheryl until I get back."

She realized she could see him so well because they'd made it back to the Sunrise. A few moments later, Cheryl and Dan pulled up in their car. Cheryl took Beth from Tanner, and Dan wrapped an arm around Bree.

Tanner reached over and kissed her forehead. "Not. Alone. Okay?"

He waited until she nodded, this time of her own accord, then took off running into the night.

Chapter Fourteen

Making sure Bree and the kids were safe had been the right priority, but damn if Tanner hadn't wanted to go straight to her apartment. Find those bastards who had put the normally reserved Bree into such a panic.

Even worse, if he hadn't received a message on his personal phone from an unknown number about the situation, he never would've been there to help her in the first place.

A three-man team? It definitely wasn't a burglary. There was nothing worth taking in an apartment that size.

When Tanner arrived back near the outside of Bree's place, Ronnie was cuffing a man.

Bree's creepy, thin guy. He was bleeding from a wound near his mouth and looked like the sleeve of his shirt had been torn.

"You read him his rights?" he asked Ronnie.

"Yep. Guy hasn't said a word."

Tanner got up in his face. "Where are your other two friends? Are they still around?"

The man just stared. "I'm not the person you're looking for. But yes, I would assume those three men are still nearby. Although what they're looking for isn't in reach, so they probably won't make themselves known."

"Oh, yeah?" Ronnie pushed the guy a little forward toward the police vehicle. "What exactly are they looking for? Bree doesn't have much cash or anything of value."

Tanner already knew what the men had been looking for. They'd been here to take Bree and the kids.

"Do you work for the people after her?" Tanner asked.

The guy looked surprised for a split second before covering it. "Believe me, I hate them more than anyone."

"What are we talking about?" Ronnie asked.

Tanner ignored his colleague. "Are you the one who sent me the message?"

"What message?" Ronnie asked, louder this time. But the man didn't respond.

Tanner turned to Ronnie. "Take him to holding then meet me back here to process the scene."

Tanner waited to see if the guy would protest his innocence or demand to be set free, but he didn't. Just silently watched what was happening around him, taking in everything.

The same way he'd been watching Bree.

Ronnie took him to the squad car, and Tanner walked the rest of the way inside the apartment, weapon drawn. He looked around her living room. Nothing seemed out of place or broken, except Bree's phone in pieces on the floor.

Once Tanner checked any place someone might be hiding and confirmed the apartment was empty, he put away his weapon. The broken phone caught his attention again. Had the burglars done that? Bree wouldn't have. She still carried that thing around with her faithfully every day.

A tap on the door had him looking up and his hand moving toward his weapon again. But it was only Scott, looking flushed and out of breath. He'd definitely been running.

"You okay?" Tanner asked.

Scott nodded. "I heard about the break-in over the walkie. Since I was awake, I thought I would come on over from the hotel, and saw a couple of guys running off one of the side streets. I followed but I wasn't able to catch them."

"Were you able to catch any sort of identifying features?"

The younger man grimaced. "No, nothing. I'm sorry."

Tanner nodded, but that wasn't the most important thing. "Next time you see something like that, be sure to call it in. You're not here to work active cases, Watson. I don't want you to get hurt."

"Will do. And maybe this is the motivation I need to get myself in better shape." Scott gave a half smile and hiked up his jeans.

It wasn't that he was really so heavy—it was more that he was cumbersome and bulky. Definitely not light or quick on his feet.

"I see you're carrying," Tanner said when he saw the holster at Scott's waist. "That's good."

The younger man touched his weapon softly. "Yeah. Always."

Tanner nodded. Maybe there was hope for this kid to be more than just a paper pusher, if he really wanted to improve his skill sets.

"Can I help since I'm here?"

"Sure." Tanner gestured for him to come in.

Scott entered the rest of the way. "This is Bree's apartment, right? Is it a burglary?"

"If they were looking for anything valuable, she certainly doesn't have much outside of baby equipment."

Scott glanced around. "Where is she now? Is she all right?"

"Shaken up, but she's all right. She's with some friends."

And as soon as Tanner was finished here, he was going to make sure Bree and the kids went someplace safe.

Scott looked around more. "I see that kitchen window

open. Did she have to climb out that? And why is her phone in pieces on the floor?"

Tanner went over to check out the open window. "Bree said there were three guys. Maybe they'd had both the front and back door covered and this was her only way out."

Fury pooled in his gut at the thought of her trying to make it out this window with both babies. She would've had to land hard and was probably more hurt than he thought. Might need medical attention. "Damn it."

Scott studied the window. "She had to have been pretty scared to go out that way with both kids in tow. Do you think the burglars made it all the way into the house?"

Tanner shook his head. "I don't think this was a burglary at all. I think it was an attempted abduction, and Bree foiled their plans by escaping."

Scott whistled through his teeth. "Abduction? To what end? Human trafficking? Selling her and the kids on the black market or something?"

Tanner wasn't going to drag Scott into the situation with Bree. Not until he had all the details. "Maybe. I plan to dig deeper into it."

"Look, man, I've got nothing but respect for you and your department here. But it's obvious you care about this woman, despite what you said earlier."

"Yeah, so?"

Scott shrugged. "Don't kill the messenger here, okay? I'm just saying if it was anyone else that maybe you weren't so attracted to, might you be considering some other... possibilities?"

"Other possibilities like what? That she's making this up?"

"No, not necessarily that. But you're right." Scott gestured around the apartment. "Nobody would break into this tiny little apartment to steal. And my kidnapping theory is pretty far-fetched, too. But what if she knew the guys who were after her?"

"Like the mob." Tanner had to admit, it did make sense. Who were these people after Bree and her cousin?

"She's new in town, right? She shows up here with her babies, needing help." Scott gave a one-shouldered shrug with a grimace. "And look, I'm not saying she doesn't need help. I'm not saying she's a criminal. But maybe these three guys who showed up tonight are people she owes money to or something. Maybe she's not completely innocent, and you should bring her in and question her officially."

Ronnie's voice spoke up from the door. "Okay, got our guy back to the station."

Scott looked surprised. "You caught one of the people who broke in?"

Tanner shook his head. "No. Just someone who happened to be out for a walk and heard some ruckus. Came to investigate. We brought him in for questioning."

Until Tanner had a chance to talk to creepy guy and ask him how the hell he knew those men were about to hit Bree's house, he didn't want to share too much information with anyone.

"He finally admitted the bumps and bruises on him were because he jumped on one of the men involved." Ronnie looked around. "Said the guy was about to hurt Bree and he couldn't let that happen."

"Lucky he was wandering around," Scott murmured.

Tanner didn't respond. It was both lucky and highly suspicious. Maybe he was the one who had been about to hurt Bree.

Bree had always seemed so skittish of the man. Was it possible she knew him and had been lying all this time? And if creepy man knew her and wanted to warn her trouble was coming, why message Tanner? Why not just contact Bree himself? He'd obviously been close by.

Too many questions. Not enough answers.

Tanner crouched down to look at the broken phone again. He was missing something big here.

"Look at it," Scott said. "That's more damage than just happens from a phone falling from your hand. Somebody stomped on it."

Scott was right. That was what Tanner had missed. The phone wasn't just broken, it was *destroyed*.

Why? And by whom?

Ronnie was still at the door. "This jamb was shimmied, but it probably wouldn't have been very loud, Tanner. How would Bree have gotten up and gotten both babies out a window in the time it took someone to break the lock and get in here? Seems impossible."

He had to agree. "Someone called and warned her."

Again, too many questions. Not enough answers.

Ronnie tilted his head and studied the pieces of the phone. "If so, it certainly seemed to make Bree mad."

"She thought someone was using the phone to trace her whereabouts," Tanner said. It made sense, given her paranoia about phones in Denver.

"This definitely goes back to her being involved with something bigger. Something she may not be admitting to," Scott said. "You really might want to question her and find out what she's been hiding. And if she's innocent, protective custody may be the safest place for her and the kids if someone from the mob is after her."

Maybe that was true, but Tanner wasn't bringing her into the station until they figured out exactly how creepy guy fit into this.

But he would send Ronnie over to the Sunrise, not only to make sure Bree was safe, but also to make sure she didn't make a run for it. Scott's comments had Tanner wondering if maybe he'd let himself be blinded to the truth. Maybe Bree wasn't a completely innocent party in all this. Maybe he'd only been seeing what he wanted to see.

Chapter Fifteen

Creepy, thin guy's name was Bill Steele.

Two hours after leaving Bree's apartment, Tanner stared at the printout of the man's background check. Nothing unusual. An out-of-state permanent address, tax filings for the last five years and a normal employment history.

There was no indication of any criminal wrongdoing whatsoever. No warrants out for his arrest or anything suspicious. In other words, he was clean. The last time Tanner had seen a record this clean was when he'd run Bree.

An interesting coincidence.

Tanner opened the door to the interrogation room. He wanted answers.

"Mr. Steele." He took a seat across from the man. "I understand you've refused your right to counsel." Tanner hated to remind him that he could call for a lawyer, but Miranda rights weren't something to be messed with.

Steele was sitting straight in the chair, with no signs of fatigue even though it was now dawn and he'd been here for hours. He nodded briefly at Tanner's statement but didn't respond.

He obviously wasn't going to be like some suspects who immediately spilled their guts when questioned.

"Your record shows you're from Texas. That you've

worked multiple construction jobs over the years. Why don't we start with how you ended up in Risk Peak?"

Steele shrugged. "I go where the work is."

"You're a long way from home. It's hard to believe there weren't any other jobs between here and Texas."

Steele's eyes were steady. "I like the mountains."

"So do I. But I have to say, if I hadn't been born and raised in Risk Peak, I'm not sure I ever would've found myself here." He leaned his forearms on the table. "According to Denny Hyde, the construction foreman, you've been here for exactly twenty-nine days."

"That sounds about right."

"Me and Denny's brother went to high school together, so we know each other pretty well. Denny was a little miffed at me because I had to wake him up in the middle of the night to ask him questions about you."

Steele crossed his arms over his chest. "And what did your good buddy Denny have to say about me?"

Tanner straightened in his chair, cocking his head to the side. "Said you show up for work every day, do your job and haven't given him a bit of trouble."

The other man raised an eyebrow. "Then there you go."

"You know what I find interesting? The fact that Denny started hiring for this project twelve weeks ago, but you didn't come on then. You came on exactly twenty-nine days ago."

"And why is that a problem?"

Now Tanner crossed his arms over his chest. He was larger than this man. Definitely heavier. But Steele wasn't intimidated by him. Tanner had sat across the interrogation table from a number of suspects who weren't intimidated by him. Some of them because of their own shape or size, some of them because they underestimated Tanner's good-naturedness and took it for weakness, and some because they were just flat-out braggarts.

But Bill Steele's lack of intimidation was something different. Like the man had already seen hell and knew there was nothing Tanner was going to do to him that could be as bad as what he'd already been through.

Steele might be a creepy, thin man, but that didn't mean he wasn't dangerous. Deadly, even.

Maybe Tanner had even underestimated *him*. He'd assumed that because of the man's gaunt face and slender build maybe he was a drug user.

But the eyes looking across from him now were not those of a man who would let narcotics control him. The thinness of his frame didn't seem to rest naturally on him. It was more like he was in recovery. But recovering from what?

"It's a problem because it was exactly one day after Bree and the twins got here."

Steele's eyes shifted away for just a second. "Coincidence."

Tanner leaned back a little farther in his chair. "You know, I might have believed that if I hadn't gotten the message from you tonight letting me know that Bree was in trouble. How did you know that?"

Steele shrugged. "I saw the guys headed toward her apartment. It's sort of isolated. I knew she was there alone with those kids and thought the guys might be looking for trouble. Ends up I was right."

"How do you know they were going to *her* apartment? If you called me when they were at her front door, there's no way I would've gotten there in time."

Steele's jaw stiffened. "Look, Dempsey, I don't sleep well. I was out for a walk, saw some guys who looked like trouble and did my civic duty. Nothing more or less than that."

"Any reason why you didn't just call 911?"

Steele's eyes shifted away again. "I guess I just had your number for some reason."

"It is public, so I guess that's a possibility." Tanner took out his phone—his piece-of-junk flip phone—and laid it on the table. "It wouldn't have anything to do with the fact that I carry this type of phone, would it?"

Steele's lips pursed and eyes narrowed. "What do you know?"

"What do *you* know?"

They stared each other down.

Steele finally shook his head, withdrawing into himself. "Nothing. I'm just a construction worker who gets to work outside with a hell of a view every day. Just counting my blessings."

Tanner didn't buy that horse manure for a second. "How did you know those men were coming for Bree?" he asked again.

But Steele wasn't budging. "Like I said, I saw them, and they gave me a hinky feeling."

Tanner decided to try a new line of questioning. "Deputy Kitchens said you tackled one of them? That's how you got banged up."

He shrugged. "Yeah, the guy was running after Bree. Least I could do was help out."

"How do I know *you* weren't the one chasing after Bree? You've certainly been making her uncomfortable for the last couple weeks. She says you're watching her all the time."

Steele sat up straighter. "If I was trying to hurt her, there were other times that would've been a damn sight more convenient than right after I just messaged you and told you she needed help."

That, Tanner believed. He didn't think Steele had been one of the guys after Bree. But he did think the man wanted something from her. Maybe Scott was right. Maybe Bree owed somebody money and this was about collecting.

"Did you know Bree before you came here, Steele?"

"I can promise you I had never heard of Bree Daniels before I set foot in Risk Peak." Frustration grew inside Tanner. He didn't think Steele was actually lying to him, he just wasn't telling the whole truth.

Exactly how he often felt about Bree.

It was like the answers were right there in front of him, if he just knew what questions to ask.

"Are you or Bree involved with the mob? Does she owe someone money? Does it have something to do with the same people her cousin is mixed up with?" Tanner felt like he was throwing spaghetti against the wall, hoping something would stick.

"Mob? No. Money? I don't think so. And I have no idea who Bree is, truly, so I don't know who her cousin or any other family is."

"Melissa Weathers."

If he hadn't been watching Steele so closely, he never would've seen it. Hell, he was looking directly at the man and almost didn't see it. Steele didn't startle, didn't stiffen, but the air around him changed.

He knew Melissa.

Tanner leaned forward until he was nearly halfway over the narrow table. "You know Melissa, don't you? Do you work for the people Melissa works for? Do you know what they're up to? How to stop them?"

Whatever Steele had been feeling, he swallowed it fast. "I don't work for anybody but Denny Hyde. And you know what? I'm tired. Either charge me and I'll call an attorney, or I'm ready to go. You can't hold me."

It was true. And although they could hold him for a few more hours, if he was requesting counsel, he would be out of here in no time.

"We're not going to charge you." Tanner made one last appeal. "But tell me what's going on so I can help. I can't protect Bree if I don't know what I'm up against."

Steele stood, and Tanner thought he would leave without saying anything else, but when he got to the door, he turned back. "Get her—get *them*—out of here. Out of this town, where no one can find them. Do it right now. Don't wait."

That was exactly what he'd planned on doing.

"Why? Who's coming, Steele?"

"Someone way too big for you to fight. Just get them out while you can."

He was gone without another word.

Chapter Sixteen

Bree had to get out. Out of Risk Peak, out of the entire state of Colorado.

She was currently inside Cheryl and Dan's office. Both babies were asleep—completely unharmed, thank God—in the playpen Cheryl and Dan had set up weeks ago.

Bree tried to think through the panic that seemed to surround her like a haze. The Organization had found her. If she stayed here any longer, she'd be putting everyone in danger. Herself. The babies. The Andrewses. Tanner.

Tanner. He'd gone running back toward the danger hours ago, and she hadn't heard from him. He'd thought he was dealing with a run-of-the-mill break-in, when the Organization was so much more dangerous than that. They wouldn't hesitate to kill him if it suited their purposes.

She paced back and forth across the office like she had dozens of times already tonight.

Was Tanner hurt? She should've told him more, done what she could to prepare him for what he would be up against, rather than send him in blind thinking he was just dealing with some burglars. She opened the door to the office, even knowing she would be too late to help him. She had to try.

Cheryl and Dan were sitting, bleary-eyed, at the booth closest to the kitchen, sipping coffee. Deputy Ronnie was at the counter, pouring himself a cup. She hadn't even realized he was here.

"I need to go help Tanner. He might be in danger."

Ronnie shook his head. "Nobody was at your place by the time we got there. They must've gotten spooked."

"And nobody was hurt? Tanner is all right?"

Ronnie nodded. "Yep. He's at the station now questioning a suspect. He wanted me to stay here and make sure you…" He trailed off.

"Make sure Bree and the kids were safe?" Cheryl finished for him.

Ronnie looked a little sheepish. "Yeah. Make sure they were safe."

But that was obviously not what he'd intended to say.

"Who's the suspect Tanner is questioning?" Dan asked.

Ronnie took a sip of his coffee and rubbed the back of his neck. "Come on now, Mr. A. You know I can't talk about that sort of stuff."

"Is it somebody from around here? It must be someone we know if you're keeping his identity a secret," Cheryl argued. "We just want to make sure Bree is safe. Why don't you just give us a little information while I make you some breakfast, Ronnie. You look hungry."

Watching the middle-aged man be so skillfully manipulated would've been entertaining to Bree if she wasn't so desperate to hear who was being questioned.

"I definitely wouldn't say no to some of your pancakes, Mrs. A. And honestly, I don't know the guy's name. Truly." He raised an eyebrow. "Although I will say he could definitely use some of your cooking."

Dan's and Cheryl's eyes flew to Bree's.

Creepy, thin man.

Damn it, she'd known he was watching her. She didn't know why he'd waited so long to make his move—maybe he'd been trying to confirm her identity before he did anything. It didn't matter, and it didn't matter that Tanner had arrested him. The Organization would get him out almost immediately, or they would just send someone else to come after her.

Bree had to leave *now*.

Without another word, she spun back toward the kitchen and the office.

She was grabbing everything that had accumulated in here over the past few weeks. The room looked less like an office and more like a day care. Bree's heart clenched. Cheryl and Dan had changed so much of their lives to make room for her and the babies. And now Bree had to run.

She was stuffing diapers everywhere she could—not unlike what she'd been doing when she first showed up in Risk Peak—when Cheryl appeared in the doorway. "I've tried my best not to ask you questions you might not want to answer. I know those children aren't yours, but I know you love them and want what's best for them."

Bree tried to swallow past the lump in her throat. She knew she wouldn't be able to get words out, so she just nodded.

"I know you think you need to run, but why don't you stay? Let us help. Me, Dan, Tanner—hell, most of Risk Peak would fight for you and them kids. Whoever your creepy guy is, or whoever decides to come after you, we can face them together."

Now Bree couldn't stop the tears from overflowing. "I can't stay."

She could elaborate more, spin up some tale of partial truths, but the fact was the Organization knew she was here. If she stayed, the town might fight for her, but the Organization would win and take Bree and the babies anyway. The best she could do for these people she'd started to care about—the first community she'd ever known—was to get out.

She started packing stuff up again.

"We don't want you to go." The voice from the door this time was Dan's.

A little sob escaped Bree before she could swallow it. She took a couple of deep breaths to get herself under control.

Where was all the training her mother had spent years instilling in her? Now Bree understood why the no-friendship rule had been so important. Because leaving friends without a backward glance was not an easy thing to do.

"Just for a few days until things calm down, then I'll be back," Bree finally said. That was a lie. She would never be coming back to Risk Peak again.

She heard Dan and Cheryl whispering to each other in the doorway. Were they going to try to talk her out of this? She couldn't let them. She just needed to get out while she still had the resolve to do so.

Once she had everything she could fit into the large diaper bag, she reached down to grab the babies.

She was putting Christian inside the baby carrier when Dan walked back into the room. She hadn't even realized he left. He set two baby car seat carriers on the ground. "We bought those a couple of days ago thinking it might be easier to have two sets than to have to lug them back and forth all the time."

Bree had no idea what to say. "I—I…"

Cheryl walked over and took Christian from her, kissing him on the head. "If you've got to go, then you've got to go. Your apartment might still be closed off as a crime scene. But at least you'll have car seats."

"Thank you." The simple thanks was so completely inadequate, but it was all Bree could think of. The older couple fastened the babies inside the car seats with the utmost care. Bree gathered the rest of the stuff.

"We want you to have this." Dan pressed something

into her hand, and when she looked down she realized it was a wad of cash.

She shook her head vehemently. "No. I can't take this."

Dan closed one of his hands over hers with the cash. "You can, and you will. Cheryl and I both agree there's nothing more important to us—nothing we could spend this money on—that would make us more happy than knowing that you and those children are safe. So you take it and maybe that will give you even more reason to come back around when you can."

She had to get out of here. Her mom had been right. No closeness was worth the agony she was feeling now. And Dan and Cheryl weren't even Tanner. Thank God she didn't have to say goodbye to him. She didn't think she would survive it.

But when they walked out to the front of the restaurant, there Tanner was standing in the doorway.

Staring at him, his dark hair tousled and brown eyes tired, she knew she didn't have the strength to fight him if he asked her to stay. Not even if it was what was best for him or her.

But those words weren't what came out of his mouth.

"You running?" Those strong arms crossed over his massive chest.

"I… Yes. It's what's best."

He nodded and definitely didn't look surprised. "Fine. I'll give you a police escort to the county line."

Almost from a distance, she heard Cheryl gasp and Dan say Tanner's name sharply, but he didn't respond and she found she couldn't look away from his brown eyes.

Eyes that had been so warm earlier tonight when he'd walked her home but were coldly focused now.

He'd finally realized what she'd known all along. She was trouble for this town, and having her here was a mistake.

THE WALK TO her car was made in silence. What could be said anyway? This was what she wanted, right?

He took the babies in their new carriers. "I'll put them in the car. Get whatever else you need from your apartment. It doesn't look like there was any damage to anything."

Was that what this was about? Did he think she'd made the whole thing up or something?

It didn't matter. It didn't matter that her legs were as heavy as her heart as she walked through her apartment door. It didn't matter that she had no plan. Had let herself become complacent and now would be paying the price.

It didn't matter that she was so weary that she just wanted to lie down on the floor and cry.

Not an option.

She looked over to the spot where she'd crushed the phone. It was gone now. She didn't know if Tanner had taken it for evidence or if the men who broke in had picked up the pieces.

She gathered the twins' items and anything she would be able to fit in her car, and made her way back outside.

Tanner was crouched down by the back seat, murmuring something to one of the babies, but he straightened when she came back out. He took the stuff from her and placed it in her trunk without saying a word.

"I'm sorry I brought trouble into your town," she finally said as she got behind the wheel. She was just trying to hold it together until she got away from him. There would be nothing but time to fall apart once she was on the go.

"I'm sorry this happened, too, Bree. Don't stop driving until you're completely out of town. Straight out Highway 70. Good luck."

Without another word, he shut her door and turned away.

And that was it. She started the car and pulled away

from the curb. By the time she'd made it out of Risk Peak, tears were stinging her eyes. She kept driving out Highway 70 like Tanner had told her. Why not? She didn't have any better plan.

A few miles out of town, there was some sort of detour, and she had to turn off on a side road. She thought nothing about it until she'd gone a half mile and there was a large car parked horizontally, blocking the road in front of her and forcing her to slow.

Fear trickled down her spine. Had she literally just driven into a trap set by the Organization? She'd been so caught up in her own personal drama she hadn't been paying attention. Maybe they'd been counting on that.

When two men got out of the car in front of her, she slammed on the brakes. She was just about to throw her car in Reverse when an SUV pulled up behind her, boxing her in.

Even though the temperature in the car was comfortable, sweat coated her body. With her own stupidity, she'd gotten them caught not even two miles out of town. Frantically, she tried to think of what she could do. If she ran, would they follow her? Leave the babies alone? But then what if nobody found them in time?

Her stomach was cramping in panic. She tried to think of what her mother would've done in the same situation.

Her mother never would've gotten herself in this situation. She would've left the babies at the first homeless shelter she could find an hour after they'd shown up in her car.

A tap on the window startled a scream out of Bree. She looked out the windshield first and saw two large men moving toward her, then looked out her window to see who had knocked, fearing the worst.

Chapter Seventeen

Tanner felt like a complete heel as he knocked on Bree's window. She had no color left in her face and was looking like she might vomit at any second. He hated that he had put her through this, but there'd been no other way. Her car had the tracking device and a transmitter.

She was looking at him, sucking in deep breaths, confusion clear on her face. Tanner put his finger up to his lips in a motion to be quiet and then gestured for her to open the door.

As soon as she did, he put two fingers over her lips, then reached over and cranked up the radio. As he helped Bree out of the car, he nodded to the two men who were assisting him—Zac Mackay and Gavin Zimmerman, friends of Tanner's brother—two men who had no tie whatsoever to Risk Peak. They went around to either side of the car and gently picked up the car seat carriers with the kids inside.

"I—" Bree started, but Tanner shook his head.

"There's both a tracking device and a recording device in your car," he whispered close to her ear. "The radio will drown out most of what we say, but not all."

If anything, her face got even paler. She nodded, and he led her over to his mother's car, a late-model Honda CR-V. They all got inside, a tight fit with four adults and two baby carriers.

"I don't understand what's happening," Bree said as soon as the doors closed.

Tanner gave her the most reassuring smile he could. "This is Gavin and Zac. They both served in the army with my brother, Noah. They live a couple hours from here in Wyoming. Gavin is going to take your car back in that direction and hopefully lead the people searching for you on a wild goose chase."

Zac gave her his charming grin that made Tanner itch to punch his friend in the face. "I'm just here as taxi service before going directly back home."

Bree looked at Gavin and Zac before returning her eyes to Tanner. "But I thought you wanted me out of Risk Peak."

"When I found the tracker and the bug, I knew you weren't safe in town anymore. But I needed to make it look like I thought it was better if you were gone. That you weren't my problem anymore and I had no idea of your whereabouts."

And he was going to catch hell for it. His phone was already ringing off the hook—friends, family, damn near everyone—and it would just continue to get worse as word spread.

"Oh. I didn't understand," Bree whispered.

As if he hadn't known that from the moment he'd mentioned leaving at the Sunrise. She was terrified and thought he'd just kicked her out on her own without so much as a goodbye.

That, they would be talking about later. Right now they had bigger problems.

"How did you know to get out of your apartment?"

"Melissa called me. They were tracking the phone. She told me to destroy it and get out."

He wanted more details, but they didn't have time.

Tanner reached over and covered Bree's hand that was clenched around the car seat. "I'm going to help hide you.

But Gavin has to take your car, and you might never see it again."

"That's fine," she whispered.

"I'll get all the twins' stuff out of it first. Stay here, okay?"

She nodded, exhaustion bracketing her mouth.

Tanner got out of the car with Zac and Gavin.

"I owe you guys one." He was careful to keep his volume low enough for the transmitter not to pick it up over the radio.

Zac shook his head. "Your brother is like family to us, so that means you are, too. But those tracking and transmitting devices are high-end. She's got some big-name trouble after her, I'm afraid."

Tanner was afraid of that, too.

Gavin slapped him on the shoulder. "We'll get them off your tail for as long as possible. You're going to have your hands full. Have Noah give a shout in our direction if you need the sort of help that doesn't involve government red tape, and we'll be there."

Tanner was hoping it wouldn't come to that.

He got the rest of Bree's belongings from her car and transferred them to his. A few moments later, Bree's car was pulling away, Gavin behind the wheel, Zac following in the second car.

He didn't have to worry about Zac and Gavin—they were both former Special Forces. They knew how to surveil, mislead and adapt to changing circumstances. If anyone could trick the people after Bree, it was them.

He made his way back to the car. Bree had fastened the babies' car seats in the back seat and climbed in the front.

Fear and exhaustion still pulled at her pale skin.

"I'm sorry I had to be a jerk back in town."

She gave a nod. "It's okay. I understand."

He wasn't exactly sure what she understood. "I thought

maybe you would see that I was trying to let you know something was wrong."

She shrugged. "I thought you finally wanted what was best for Risk Peak—me gone."

"Even after what happened yesterday afternoon?" He started the car.

"It was a kiss. It happens all the time."

He raised an eyebrow. "Does it happen all the time to you, Bree?"

She turned and looked out the window as he turned the SUV in the direction they needed to go. "Does it matter?"

In the greater scheme of things, with all his questions... no, it didn't really matter. But he wanted her to admit it meant something.

"Even if I had wanted you gone, I wouldn't have done it like that, Bree. Wouldn't have just told you to hit the road."

"Sometimes to do the smart thing you have to make a hard decision. I didn't blame you for that. You have a town you're responsible for. I'm not what's important."

"How can you say that? Everybody in Risk Peak loves you."

She shrugged. "They love Christian and Beth. I'm just part of that package. If I was here by myself, no one would care as much. I wouldn't be a big deal."

"That's not true."

And she was a big deal to him. But he wasn't sure if saying so would make things better or worse.

Like some of the horses he helped Noah raise, Bree needed time and gentling. He would try to give as much as he could of both.

She didn't say anything as time ticked by, just continued to stare out the window.

"Where are we going?" she finally asked.

"My house."

"In Risk Peak? Is that a good idea?"

He took a turn that led them in the opposite direction of the way they'd ultimately be going. Probably an unnecessary step, but one he was willing to take to ensure Bree's safety.

"I have a small apartment in Risk Peak, since it's more convenient for the hours I sometimes have to keep with the job. But that's not my actual house. I own a horse ranch with my brother, Noah, about twenty miles outside town."

"Horses?" She sounded like she couldn't quite understand it.

"Yes. Noah's house is on one end of our acreage, and he does most of the daily ranch work. But that ranch is home for me. Has been for nearly ten years."

"I didn't know that."

He shrugged. "I didn't tell you. I was just going to surprise you by taking you there one day. Guess that's today. Surprise."

"Do you think anyone will try to look for us there? Maybe Cheryl and Dan?"

He grimaced. "After what I just said at the Sunrise, I don't think anyone will be searching my property for you."

Her eyes closed. "Yeah." She paused for a few moments. "Are you sure, Tanner? Are you sure you want us there? It's one thing not to run us out of town and help us. But to bring us into your home? Are you sure that's what you want?"

All her words came out in a rush, as if she was afraid she was pointing out something he hadn't considered.

No other woman had ever lived with him there. Definitely no babies. He wouldn't have made this offer to just anyone. The ranch was important to him. Sacred, even. Not something he shared lightly.

He was surprised at how much he wanted Bree there.

He glanced at her for a second before turning his eyes back to the road. "I want you there. It's the safest place for you. I'll be there to make sure everything is secure, and when I'm not, I know Noah will have an eye on you and the kids. Family are the only ones I can completely trust in a situation like this."

A situation like what? Where a woman he barely knew, but who blew his focus straight to hell every time she was around, was coming to live with him? One where he wasn't certain of the exact danger, but suspected it was way more complicated than the mob? One where protocol said he should be taking her into protective custody right now, not taking her to his own damn house?

But thankfully she didn't ask what he meant by *situation*. She was stuck on another word.

"Family," she muttered, as if the concept was foreign to her.

"They're the only ones you can ultimately trust, right?"

She began rubbing at a spot on her shoulder. "I guess."

"You'll like Noah. He's quiet, keeps to himself. Since he got out of the Special Forces, he hasn't really wanted to be around people much."

She leaned the side of her face against the headrest and stared at eyes shadowed with exhaustion. "Sounds like a male version of me, minus the military background."

He smiled gently at her. "There's some similarities. Noah would definitely rather be around horses than people. Do you like horses?"

"I've never been around a horse before."

That didn't surprise him at all.

"But I've always wanted to be around animals or have a pet," she continued, her voice getting softer, eyes drooping. "But we never could."

"Who never could, Freckles?" He felt a little bad for fishing for info while her defenses were down and she was so exhausted. But there was one thing he was sure of: he had to solve the puzzle of Bree Daniels in order to be able to protect her.

"Me and Mom. We couldn't have pets because they would hamper us every time we had to leave suddenly."

"And how often was that?"

Bree let out a yawn. "Three or four times."

That wasn't as bad as he thought. "It must have been hard moving around three or four times in your life. Maybe a pet would've helped with your transition."

"No."

"No, it wouldn't have helped?"

Another yawn. "No, we moved three or four times a year. I never knew when. That's why I could never have a pet or friends. It was better that way for when we had to leave."

He gripped the steering wheel tighter. "Why would you need to leave so suddenly that many times?"

"If they found us, or sometimes if Mom even thought they might be close, we had to leave."

"If who found you?"

"Them. The Organization."

He glanced at her again, and her eyes were still closed. "Who is the Organization, sweetie?"

"They're the people who are going to kill us all."

He waited for her to say more, gritting his teeth when she didn't. He was about to probe her for more info when he realized she was asleep.

"Aw, hell, sweetheart."

He let her sleep. She needed rest.

A little over forty-five minutes later, sure no one was following them, Tanner pulled off onto the long driveway leading up to his house on the ranch.

He carried the twins inside. They would need a bottle soon, but hopefully he could at least move Bree inside first. Leaving the babies in his office with the door closed in case they started crying, he went back out to get Bree. The fact that she had fallen asleep at all was surprising.

The fact that she kept sleeping as he slipped his arms around her and picked her up was a testament to her exhaustion.

He'd just gotten in the door when she stirred.

"Tanner?"

"Shh," he said, easing the door closed behind him with his foot.

"The kids…" she murmured before a huge yawn overtook her.

"How about just for today you let someone take care of you. I can handle Christian and Beth."

He halfway expected an argument. But instead she snuggled into him.

Tanner pulled her closer, willing to accept her trust as what it was: a treasure.

Chapter Eighteen

Bree sat straight up in the bed, looking around. Something was wrong.

It was way too quiet, and the sun was high in the sky—probably midafternoon. When was the last time she'd woken up based on her body telling her it was time rather than because one of the twins needed something?

It took her a moment to get her bearings. She was in a giant king-size bed.

Tanner's bed.

She had no idea how to process that, so she threw off the blanket and jumped down. She was still fully dressed, except for her shoes, which sat neatly by the door. She rushed into the living room but heard no sound of either child crying.

Beth could possibly go this long without fussing. But Christian?

The house wasn't that big. She dashed into a room that seemed to be an office/library but found no signs of life. A blanket was dropped haphazardly on the sofa in the living room, but it was empty, as well were the back porch and large eat-in kitchen.

Panic truly struck at Bree. Where were the babies? How could she have just *slept* like this?

She'd worked herself into such a state that she almost

missed them as she walked by the window and came to an abrupt halt, unable to believe her eyes.

Actually, she could. And that was the problem.

Tanner stood outside in the sunshine, a baby in each arm. He was bouncing them both gently, talking to them in words Bree couldn't hear and showing them the horses in the corralled area in front of them.

Beth and Christian were too young to process anything they were seeing, which Tanner had to have known, but they were looking out at the animals like they were listening intently to whatever it was Tanner was telling them.

Bree's heart gave a little flutter.

Then she realized Tanner was wearing a cowboy hat. One obviously well-worn and loved.

Then her heart gave a big flutter.

She had to remind herself that Michael Jeter and the Organization would scour the earth to find her if he knew she was alive. No ranch would save her, no matter how remote or what type of Special Forces soldier Tanner's brother had been.

She could not think of this place—think of this *man*—as permanent. Bree would only be here for a few days.

As soon as she opened the door, Tanner turned toward her and gave her a smile that stole her breath.

A few days. A few days.

"Morning." His voice was husky, soft. "Well, afternoon, actually."

"Hi," she replied, taking Christian from him.

He half turned back toward the horses. "We were talking about all the animals' names and how long they've lived here."

"Thank you for letting me sleep. Have they been fed?"

"Yep, and are dry and happy. We were outside enjoying the sunshine and meeting the animals."

Bree held her face up to the sun. When was the last

time she'd just enjoyed being outside without worrying about being spotted by someone or accidentally captured on their cell phone?

Never, except for the rarest of occasions.

They walked around, Tanner pointing out different horses. A few minutes later, a large Labrador retriever came out of the tree line and began sniffing Bree.

"That's Corfu."

Bree reached down and rubbed the dog's head affectionately. "Corfu?"

"Yeah, it's a Greek isle. One of the places my brother visited when he was stationed overseas. I've always wanted to go."

She smiled. "Okay, I guess Corfu works for a pretty dog like him."

"Actually her. And she's pregnant. It won't be long until we have a slew of puppies around here." Tanner crouched down so the dog could lick his face, carefully keeping Beth to the side so the dog didn't frighten her.

Bree stared at the dog, wide-eyed. "Puppies," she murmured. "How many?"

"Usually between three and five. We'll give most of them away to people in town. Definitely keep one around here."

Bree just nodded. No sense thinking about cute little puppies that weren't hers. Or the babies that weren't hers. Or the home that wasn't hers.

Or the man that wasn't hers.

"If Corfu is around, that means Noah will be showing up any second also."

Sure enough, a few moments later a man came riding out of the trees from the opposite direction than she'd been expecting him.

Tanner rolled his eyes. "Surveilling?" he asked his brother.

Noah shrugged and slipped from the saddle. "Can't

be too careful." He turned toward her but didn't move closer. "Ma'am."

It was plain these two were definitely brothers. Both tall, broad shouldered. Same dark coloring and good looks. But where Tanner was approachable and trustworthy, Noah was closed off, wary, defensive.

She wasn't drawn to Noah at all like she was Tanner, but she definitely understood him.

"Nice to meet you," she murmured, taking a slight step back.

He gave her a brief nod before turning back to Tanner. "I've already gotten three calls from Cassandra, since you're not answering your phone, and one from Mom. Gotten quite an earful about how you ran a young mother and her twin babies out of town." He raised an eyebrow. "Doesn't look like they got far. These yours?" he asked his brother, gesturing to the babies.

"No," Tanner said, rolling his eyes.

"They're not even mine," Bree put in.

Noah tilted his head to the side and gave something that looked like a rusty smile. "You always did know how to complicate things, bro."

Tanner chuckled, but it faded quickly. "They need to lie low here for a while. Completely off the grid. No phones anywhere around."

That request didn't seem to faze Noah at all. He just nodded. "Trouble?"

Tanner nodded. "Of a big kind."

"How big?"

Tanner turned to her. "You want to provide details?"

She balanced Christian on her hip and turned to the side. "I can't. Not right now. I'm sorry, but I can't give you details." If anything went wrong, it would be signing their death warrants. Although she might have done that even if she didn't tell them.

"Makes it harder to protect you that way," Tanner said.

She swallowed the panic building up in her. "I know. Maybe I should leave. If you could lend me a car or—"

"No." Both Dempsey brothers said it at the same time.

"But I—"

Tanner moved closer until he was right in front of her. She had to crane her neck back to see him. "You're not leaving here on your own. Nobody knows you're here. You lie low like you said you needed to. We'll figure out the rest."

"Okay. But if—"

Tanner's phone beeping in his pocket cut her off. He cursed under his breath when he looked at the screen. "I've got to get into town if we have any hope of keeping your location here a secret. Evidently I'm not very popular right now."

Bree bit her lip. "Are you going to get in trouble?"

He winked at her. "I'm sure Mrs. A is ready to snatch me out of Sunday School class again. But in the end, all that matters is your safety. They'll all forgive me after this blows over."

She grabbed his arm. "And if it's not something that ever blows over?"

"Then we take it one day at a time."

"How long do Zac and Gavin think they can buy you?" Noah asked.

Tanner shifted Beth to his other arm. "Two or three days max. Then Gavin will make it look like Bree ditched the car." He turned to her. "But if this Organization is as proficient as you say at utilizing electronics for their purposes, it won't take them long to figure out they were tricked."

She looked over at Noah. "I'm not trying to lead danger to your friends."

Noah shrugged. "They can take care of themselves."

Tanner looked over at his brother. "Call Cassandra and get her to come out here, then once she is, figure out a way for her to get whatever baby supplies the kids will need. But don't mention it over the phone."

"Will do."

"And you'll probably want to carry." Both men nodded at each other in clear understanding.

"Carry what?" Bree asked.

"His weapon. We're not going to take any chances with your life. Everybody in town knows not to come around here—Noah doesn't like company. Anybody else coming around is just looking for trouble. Cassandra, our sister, will get you anything you need."

Before Tanner could say anything else, Noah whistled at Corfu then swung up onto his horse and headed out without a word. They both watched him go.

"He doesn't talk a lot."

"I know," Tanner said. "He has his own personal demons. But he'll keep you safe. Even if you can't see him, know that if I'm not here, he's got an eye on you and the kids. Nothing's going to happen."

Someone else she was dragging into danger. The list got longer and longer. "Tanner, I—"

He put a finger over her lips. "Don't say it again. You're not leaving. I want you here. Noah wants you here, even if he can't formulate the words. You're not going off on your own."

He led her inside and gave her a brief tour of the small, charming house that was obviously dear to him. Tanner handed her Beth then reached over and kissed her forehead. "I'll be home as soon as I can. It might be a while."

A few moments later, he was walking out the door. She just stared at the door he'd shut behind him.

Home.

For the first time in her adult life she would be waiting for someone at *home*.

Chapter Nineteen

Gayle Little didn't say a word to Tanner as he walked into the department office. Gayle had been a staple in the department before Tanner's dad had been sheriff. She'd been welcoming Tanner into the building since he was about ten years old.

But not today.

Today the coffeepot was cold. It was midafternoon, so not prime coffee-drinking hours, and Tanner had never demanded or expected Gayle to make it, she just always had.

There was no fresh coffee today.

And her glare was even colder than the coffeepot.

Evidently word about him running Bree out of town had spread, which was exactly what he wanted, but it was still a little painful.

He spent the next couple of hours going through the forty-nine voice mail messages, an untold number of emails and a dozen handwritten notes telling him—some more politely than others—what they thought of his actions with Bree. He didn't dare set foot inside the Sunrise for a while. Mr. and Mrs. A were likely to poison him.

Nobody was happy.

Bree wouldn't believe it if she could see it. Wouldn't believe so many people would care about her.

That was a misconception he planned to rectify once

the danger had passed, no matter how long it took. And she could just keep sleeping in his bed while they worked on it. He would take the couch as long as he needed to.

Or maybe, if he was the luckiest bastard on the planet, she might invite him to join her.

He shut down the emails and deleted the voice mails. There was nothing he could do about them right now. His office phone rang, and he cringed when he saw who it was. This call he couldn't ignore.

"What can I do for you, Sheriff Duggan?"

Blaine Duggan had been his boss since day one. She'd worked with Tanner's dad and had promoted Tanner steadily over the years. She was his mom's good friend, and he had nothing but respect for the older woman.

"You're quite the talk of the town today, Dempsey. My office is getting calls."

"Sorry, Sheriff. Guess I made an unpopular decision."

He didn't want to lie to his boss, but he wasn't sure if this call was being monitored.

"Anything I should know about?"

"Not at this time. I believe it was the right decision for my department and Risk Peak in general, and the people contacting you don't necessarily have all the facts."

"Which is exactly what I told them."

"I appreciate your trust, ma'am."

He was about to say his goodbyes when she spoke again. "But I buried your father because he got in over his head and didn't ask for help. I don't want you making the same mistakes. Take care of yourself, Tanner."

The call clicked off before he could say anything else. He stared at the phone receiver in his hand.

Was Tanner being just as blind as his father had been? He didn't think Bree would put a gun to his head, but he couldn't deny that he was courting danger by bringing her into his house.

But he still meant what he'd told her. He wasn't leaving her to deal with this alone.

He spent the next hour fielding calls he wished he could send straight to voice mail and looking over the report from the break-in to make sure there was nothing he'd missed.

Nobody in the office was talking to him. Gayle still wouldn't even look at him, so that at least allowed him to get a little more work done. He sent Ronnie to pick up Bill Steele from the construction site.

Tanner wanted to talk to him again. Maybe the man would refuse to come in. He certainly had that right. But Tanner wanted to see the man's face when he mentioned the *Organization*. The term was vague and obviously an inside reference, but Tanner was willing to bet Steele was familiar with it.

Tanner wanted a name. A real name. He didn't think Steele was working for said Organization, but maybe he had some details that would help Tanner better protect Bree and the kids.

And like it or not, she was going to have to tell him everything she knew.

Because there were puzzle pieces that didn't fit. Like if the Organization was the current threat, the people *who were going to kill them all*, according to her, then why had she and her mother been running from them when Bree was a child?

And if she hadn't seen her cousin in a decade, why were the same people who'd been after Bree's mom now after her cousin?

First he would find out what Steele knew, then he would use it to frame all the questions he had for Bree.

A tap on his door a few minutes later had Tanner looking up from his desk with a cringe. Was someone else here to tell him what a terrible person he was?

Scott stuck his head in. "Hey, boss. I brought you a sandwich from the Sunrise."

"Did you tell them it was for me?"

"No. Should I have? Do they do something special for your sandwiches?"

Tanner let out a sigh. "No. They just probably would've spit in it—or worse—if they'd known it was for me."

"Because of the whole Bree situation?"

He scrubbed a hand across his jaw. He needed a shave. "I guess you heard?"

Scott's baby face scrunched up. "The way the people around here are telling it, you lit her on fire before escorting her out of town."

Tanner rolled his eyes and took the sandwich Scott offered. "Got to love small-town drama. Bree told me she was leaving, and I didn't try to stop her. Like you said, I think she might be caught up with the mob or a gang or something. While I feel bad for her, really, my overall priority has to be to the town."

"So you're just going to leave the whole break-in alone? That doesn't seem right."

Good for you, kid. Hold the line. "No, you're right. I don't care who it is, someone breaking into a house isn't okay here. We've got forensics seeing if they can pick up any prints, but it doesn't look hopeful."

"Didn't Ronnie say you had a suspect? Anything come of that?"

"It was Bill Steele, that guy who was making Bree nervous. But we didn't have enough to charge him." Tanner gestured to the chair in front of his desk. "Want to come in?"

"Do you think Steele is one of the men who broke into her apartment?" Scott sat down as Tanner began unwrapping the sandwich.

"Maybe. I've got some more questions I'd like to ask

him. Ronnie has gone to bring him back. Hopefully he'll come voluntarily, because we definitely don't have enough to charge him."

But maybe he would want to go. Maybe, like Bree, Steele was concerned about phones tracking his location.

Fine. If he wouldn't—or felt like he couldn't—come to the department, Tanner would go out and find him. Steele didn't have to give him answers in an official setting, but he had to give Tanner some answers. It could be in the middle of a field as far as Tanner was concerned.

"Would you mind if I sat in on the questioning? See if I can learn something?"

"Yeah, we'll see." On one hand, the kid was pretty observant and might see or hear things Tanner missed. On the other hand, Steele was already pretty closed off. Having other people around wasn't going to help the man feel free to speak.

Tanner was one bite into his sandwich when his office phone rang.

"Tanner Dempsey."

"It's Ronnie. We've got a problem. Steele didn't show up for work today."

"Did he call in sick? We know for a fact he was up all night."

"Nope," Ronnie said. "Just didn't show up at all. I got his address from Denny Hyde and went over to the place he's renting. He's gone, Tanner."

"What?" Tanner stood, sandwich forgotten.

"Yep. He was renting Sue Ragan's place that she made out of her barn. And by the looks of it, he lit out of here in a hurry. You need to get here right away."

"Why?"

"We definitely should've arrested Steele while we had the chance."

Chapter Twenty

Mrs. Ragan's house was a couple of miles outside town, so Tanner drove, Scott riding with him, since the younger man looked so crestfallen at being left behind.

As soon as Tanner walked into the room where Steele had been staying, he let out a string of curses that would've made a seasoned sailor proud.

Steele had played him.

The walls were covered in photos of Bree and the babies. Dozens of them. He'd definitely been watching her— *stalking her*—since the day he arrived.

There were pictures of her at work, her walking home, her with Tanner, her taking a break at the back of the Sunrise. Worse, there were just as many pictures of the babies as there were of Bree.

"Nobody touch anything," Tanner said as he donned a pair of gloves and walked inside. "Ronnie, get the crime lab over here ASAP."

Ronnie was already calling it in when Tanner found a handwritten note listing Bree and the kids' schedule and habits.

Bree had been right to be wary of the creepy, thin man. This was nothing less than obsession.

And Tanner had had the man in custody and chose to let him go. He'd clung to a more complicated scenario—that

Steele had known or been a part of some sort of hidden nefarious organization—rather than the simple one that was
undoubtedly true: Steele was fixated on Bree and the kids.

And now wished he could kick his own ass.

Had everything Steele said this morning been a lie?
And why had he called Tanner last night when Bree had
been in trouble? *Before* Bree had really been in trouble?

"County forensics team is on their way, Tanner." Ronnie came back in the room. "I spoke to Mrs. Ragan—she
said Steele is paid up through the end of the month and
she's never had a problem with him. She heard him squeal
out of here early this morning."

"Did she notice which direction he was going?"

"Away from town. North up Highway 70."

So the same direction Gavin was driving Bree's car. Was
Steele the one who had put the tracker on it? Had the whole
break-in at her house been a setup to get her to run scared?

"Wow." Scott whistled through his teeth. "This is some
pretty advanced-level stalker stuff. Are we sure he isn't
Bree's baby daddy?"

"No, he wasn't. She would've mentioned that immediately. Wouldn't have been so creeped out by him." Tanner couldn't tear his eyes away from all the pictures of
Bree. Pictures of her with people. Without them. Some
with the babies.

But no matter what the scene or the situation, she always
had that stiff, pinched look on her face. In not one single
picture was she smiling, even the ones with the babies.

She always looked scared.

He'd gotten so used to that look on her face that he
didn't even notice it anymore.

Bree lived in terror.

He walked over to study one, obviously shot from a
small camera at a low angle. Bree was standing with Mr.
and Mrs. A, the babies and Judy. A couple of other peo-

ple, features not seen in the shot, were loitering around, too. A crowd.

Despite all the people around her, Bree looked completely alone. A misfit among laughing, content people. Like she didn't know how to feel what they were feeling and didn't even want to try in case she failed.

Damn it. Tanner wanted to teach this woman how to smile. Wanted to provide her a safe place where she could learn to find the smile he knew was inside her.

Ronnie cleared his throat. "This guy is a psycho. Maybe we shouldn't have sent Bree off on her own if he's now following her."

"Wasn't she afraid she was going to end up in his basement? I thought she was being melodramatic when she said it yesterday, but now…" Scott held his hand out toward the pictures. "Maybe not. Are you sure we have no way of getting in touch with her? No phone number?"

Tanner shook his head. He wanted to tell Ronnie and Scott what was going on but couldn't. "Her phone was last seen in multiple pieces in her apartment. And she didn't give any forwarding address. So, as far as we're concerned, she's gone."

Ronnie and Scott were both staring at him like he'd just kicked a puppy into oncoming traffic. He couldn't blame them; just the thought of Bree being out there alone with someone this crazy after her made him sick.

"Look," he continued, "the best thing we can do for Bree is get an APB out for Steele and make sure all our contacts in other counties know he could be dangerous. Bree wanted out of this town. She's an adult, hasn't broken the law and we couldn't keep her here against her will. Maybe she was going to family or something."

"What do we know about Steele?" Scott asked. "Any record?"

Tanner shook his head. "Completely clean. After seeing

this, I'm thinking probably a fake ID. Hopefully, the crime lab can get some prints and we can run them."

Scott looked around at the pictures again. "I just hope law enforcement finds him before he finds Bree. Because this is a man obsessed. And obsession is dangerous."

IT WAS NEARLY four in the morning before Tanner made it back out to the ranch.

Processing Steele's apartment had taken hours, and Tanner had stayed to make sure the crime lab didn't miss anything. He didn't normally micromanage the department like this, but when it came to Steele, he couldn't afford any more slipups.

When the head lab technician told Tanner that they didn't get a single fingerprint from the entire place, he was angry but not surprised. Steele had wiped the place down before he left.

Back at the office, Scott had assisted in digging further into Bill Steele's identity. It hadn't taken long to discover the ID was fake.

Again, angry but not surprised.

When they'd gotten a call of a possible sighting of Steele in Jackson County, again in the direction Gavin had taken Bree's car, Tanner had driven there himself. If they caught Steele, he wanted to be the first to question him, before any other county decided they had dibs if his real identity came back as someone more dangerous.

But it had been a false alarm, costing Tanner three hours of his time. Time he couldn't afford when there was both a psycho and some sinister technology organization out to harm the woman he couldn't get off his mind.

He shouldn't have come at all, should've just stayed at his place in town. But despite trusting his brother implicitly, he needed to see with his own eyes that Bree was okay.

He rubbed the back of his neck as he got to the door,

then held his hand up in a wave to Noah. He didn't bother looking around. He didn't know where his brother was, but Tanner had no doubt he was close.

Tanner let himself in the house, closing the door behind him, and just listened. Quiet.

But not the utter stillness that normally permeated his house when he arrived. There were signs of life everywhere. A bib resting on the kitchen table. One of the car seat carriers sitting on his couch. Bree's sweater hanging off the back of a chair.

He'd always purposely lived a solitary life. He'd known since he was ten he wanted to go into law enforcement, then had seen what it had done to his mother when his father died in the line of duty. And even before that, the long, odd hours—sometimes being called away in the middle of the night—and the general stress of this job had often placed a heavier burden on his parents' marriage.

So Tanner had always kept his relationships casual and simple, never planning to drag a woman into this life with him.

But nothing about Bree was casual.

And very definitely not simple.

He took off his holster and out of habit—niece and nephews—set it in the small gun safe next to the door. He kicked off his shoes and planned to grab a blanket out of the linen closet and immediately lie down on the couch.

He found himself walking into his bedroom instead.

Found himself stopping and staring at Bree lying curled in his king-size bed.

Found his breath stolen at the way moonlight shined through the window, casting an otherworldly glow on her long brown hair and delicate features.

At least in sleep she didn't have the same pinched and uncomfortable expression she'd had in all the photos he'd studied of her today. Like she would never know what it meant to fit in with other people.

Like she would always be alone.

He wanted to go to her and pull her up against him, tell her she didn't have to look like that anymore.

He took a step closer before he could stop himself then breathed out a curse as her eyes fluttered open, afraid he'd frightened her.

"Tanner?"

"Yeah, it's just me. Go back to sleep. I didn't mean to wake you up."

"Are you okay?" She reached out toward him, her voice soft, husky.

Sexy.

He took a rapid step backward.

Immediately a shuttered look fell over her features, slamming away the welcoming look that had resided there a moment before. "I'm sorry. Do you want your bed? I can get up."

He recognized her tight expression right away. God knew he'd seen it enough times in the pictures today. Uncertainty. Discomfort.

Isolation.

And he'd been the one to put that look in her eyes this time.

She withdrew the arm she'd reached out to him.

No, damn it. He wasn't going to let her withdraw from him.

He crossed until he was standing right next to her. "Actually, I would like my bed."

"Oh." She sat up. "Okay. Just let me—"

"No. I want it with you in it." Before either one of them overthought it, he reached down, took her slight weight in his arms and slid her over. Then got into the bed next to her.

He turned over onto his side then looped an arm around her waist and pulled her up against him.

For the first time since he'd gotten that message from Steele that Bree was in trouble, Tanner relaxed. She was in his house, his bed, his care.

He kissed her hair. "Go back to sleep. I just want to be with you. Even if it's just for tonight."

She didn't say anything but a few moments later began to relax against him.

And everything about it felt right.

Chapter Twenty-One

When Bree woke up a few hours later, Tanner was gone. She saw so little of him for the next three days, she was almost convinced she'd imagined the whole thing.

Imagined lying in bed with his strong arms securely around her. Imagined feeling safe and secure and cherished for the first time in her life.

She knew why Tanner hadn't been around much. He'd explained about creepy, thin guy—Steele, or whatever his real name was—and his obsession with her and the twins. Tanner and Scott had been working around the clock trying to find him.

Bree couldn't even wrap her head around it. Only she could somehow gain a psycho stalker at the same time as being hunted by a deadly organization intent on her capture or death.

She knew Tanner had questions about the Organization. That it wouldn't be long until he began to press her for info.

Rightfully so.

Because what about Melissa? Except for that panicked conversation a few nights ago, Bree hadn't heard anything from her cousin in two weeks. Had no way to hear from her.

Had she been caught when she warned Bree?

Was she even still alive?

Bree refused to accept that her cousin was dead. But she also couldn't run from the truth any longer.

Melissa couldn't defeat the Organization. It didn't matter how motivated or determined she was. She just didn't have the hacking skills to get around their system.

Michael Jeter was a computer genius. He would have backup systems and trapdoors that someone like Melissa—even as competent as she was—wouldn't be able to get around.

He was the type of computer genius no one could beat.

Except another computer genius.

Here Bree sat on the steps of a ranch in the middle of Colorado, rising sun kissing her skin, healthy babies sleeping inside a warm, sturdy house.

Hell, she even had a pregnant dog sitting beside her supplying companionship, her master out somewhere providing protection against any threat that might come her way.

Bree was living a stolen life.

She was in someone else's house, with someone else's kids, even someone else's damn dog.

Even worse, she was stealing from people she *cared* about. And she had the means to stop it all if she wasn't a coward.

Melissa couldn't stop Michael Jeter.

But Bree could.

She lifted her face to the low-lying sun, breathing in the air pungent with life. These porch steps, in less than a week, had made her feel more like she had a home—a place in the world—than her apartment in Kansas City ever had. And definitely more than any place she'd shared with her mom for a few months at a time.

But it wasn't her place. And it never would be—she would never be able to live with herself—if she didn't do what she could to help Melissa.

To ensure Christian and Beth had their mother around to raise them.

She heard Tanner pulling up long before his car parked in front of the house. He'd worked all night again to protect her, or hopefully caught a few hours' sleep at his place in town.

As Tanner's SUV door shut, a sharp whistle came from the trees on the other side of the property near the back of the house, and Corfu got up and trotted off.

"I guess Noah's babysitting duties are over for the day since you're home."

Tanner sat beside her. He was wearing his civilian clothes, including that cowboy hat that set her heart beating faster than it should. He didn't look too tired.

"He doesn't mind." He knocked her knee with his. "You okay?"

"No, I don't think so."

His browed furrowed together. "What happened?"

She wrapped both arms around her knees and pulled them to her chest. "I tried to pick up both Christian and Beth yesterday evening at the same time. They lunged for each other, and I nearly dropped them both."

He muttered a curse. "Did one of them get hurt? Hell, did *you* get hurt? Those kids weigh a ton now. And they're more active than ever."

She leaned her head on her arms and studied him. "No, I got them under control and put one of them down. But you've just made my point. They're so big. They're growing more every day."

"Um, I think babies are supposed to do that."

She looked out at the horses again. "But they're not *my* babies. Every day that I get to hold them and feed them and play with them is another their mother misses out on."

"But I thought Melissa wanted you to keep them safe

while she did whatever is needed to take down these people she works for."

Bree shook her head, hugging her legs tighter. It was time for complete honesty with Tanner.

Way past time.

"Melissa can't do it. Whatever she's doing is not going to be enough to stop them."

"How do you know?"

"Because I know who she's up against. I was part of that group before my mom got me away from them when I was thirteen."

"The Organization? That same group that you said was dangerous and would kill us all?"

She nodded.

Tanner ran a hand over his face. "I need you to tell me exactly what is going on. Exactly how you're involved and exactly what needs to be done to keep you and the kids safe."

"It's not an easy story to believe."

"Try me. *Trust me.*"

She stared out into the gathering dawn. "I never went to college. Never really went to school at all actually, after I turned thirteen. That's not to say I never had an education, just that I never went to the buildings like most other people did."

"You were homeschooled?"

"Sort of. More like, I was a genius-level hacker who could read three times as fast as most people and could visualize code twice as fast as that. So I taught myself everything I needed to know."

He nodded slowly, so she continued.

"My father died when I was just a baby, and my mom struggled to provide for us on a waitress's salary. I wasn't an easy kid. If you think I'm awkward and prickly now, you should've seen me then. When I was six, she realized I had a gift for computers."

More than a gift. So much more than a gift. A huge blessing.

And a curse.

"By the time I was eight, everyone in the entire school system for the whole county had taught me everything they knew. By that point, I was teaching them new things about coding and software development."

"You were a child prodigy. Like kids with the instruments."

"I guess, except a computer was my instrument rather than a violin or piano. But yes, I could—*can*—play it beautifully. That's how I came to the attention of Communication for All. You've heard of them?"

He took a sip of his coffee. "The charity group? Sure."

"They have schools for underprivileged children to help them learn computer skills and hopefully better their lives."

"Sounds like a perfect fit for you."

She shook her head, remembering quite clearly how excited she'd been at eight and a half to finally be around people who understood her. Who knew as much about computers as she did and didn't think she was odd.

The people at Communication for All, especially Michael Jeter, revered her.

At least at first.

"I quickly got the attention of people high up in that organization. They wanted to groom me for important things. They brought me to live at one of their schools. My mom didn't want me there by myself, so they brought her, too. All expenses paid—my mom didn't have to pay for a thing and was even able to quit her job. They even brought my cousin, Melissa, since she also had skills beyond her years."

"Sounds like an amazing opportunity. I've always heard wonderful things about Communication for All."

Bree stared straight ahead. "No doubt you have." Everybody had.

"Yeah, I mean Michael Jeter has pretty much been termed an altruistic genius by every person who's ever…" Tanner faded out. *"Jeter."*

He stood with controlled movements. She wasn't surprised he was figuring it out. Tanner was too smart, too observant, not to piece it all together.

"That guy in the alley in Denver was talking to a Mr. Jeter." Tanner turned to her. "You stiffened at the name, but I misread your body language at the time. I thought it was because of the guys with the guns. But it was because Jeter was threatening to come there personally."

"When I was eleven, I outgrew most of the instructors at Communication for All. I knew more about system development and coding than they did. I was twelve when I backdoored into their main system and…"

Her whole life had changed that day. What had started out as preteen mischief and an attempt to show off had ended in a nightmare.

One she was still trying to wake up from.

"Bree?" Tanner sat back down beside her and wrapped an arm around her, pulling her against his chest.

God, he felt so strong. Like nothing could get through him. Nothing could break him.

But everyone could be broken. A twelve-year-old Bethany had learned that very quickly.

"I found out every dirty secret the inner board of Communication for All had. They're evil, Tanner. Human trafficking, weapons and information sales. They use their humanitarian front to get into places without much scrutiny."

He stiffened. She could almost hear his mind working,

attempting to process it all. He stood up and began pacing again. "Good God."

"I know," she whispered. It was difficult to take it all in.

"Everybody can't be in on it," he finally said. "Communication for All must have a thousand employees. They couldn't keep it under wraps."

She shook her head, rubbing at the tension forming at the back of her neck. "Most of them don't know what's really going on. They are trying to achieve the admirable mission associated with Communication for All. It's a very select few, an inner core of about twenty-five people, who know the truth and are behind it all."

"And you discovered this was going on when you were twelve?"

"Yes," she whispered. "At that point they were just starting to dip their toes into utilizing cell phones for illegal data mining. Run-of-the-mill stuff at first…software that caused phones to report credit cards or bank account numbers to them. Then they expanded."

"Expanded how?"

"I didn't make up that stuff I told you in Denver. They're utilizing cell audio and video mechanisms to record data, even when cameras and microphones aren't actively running. I know you don't have a smartphone, but have you ever heard people complain about how fast the batteries run down even when they're not using them?"

He began pacing again. "Sure. All the time."

"That's the Communication for All system pulling data off their phone. Every time there's a system update, they use it to piggyback onto more phones."

He stopped and stared at her. "How many do they have now?"

"According to Melissa? Millions. And they can use those phones to record data anytime they want. To find anyone they want. It's basically making a worldwide information grid that they control. Nobody will be able to hide. And it's about to get so much larger."

"How?"

She rubbed her eyes with her fingers. "Three days from now is the International Technology Symposium in Denver. Major phone manufacturers will all be there. Communication for All will provide them with some wonderful bit of technology that will be a breakthrough of epic proportion. They'll be hailed as heroes when they offer it to manufacturers for free."

"But there's a catch."

She nodded. "The tiniest of Trojan horses. A few lines of code that would probably be missed, even if the manufacturers were suspicious and went over the coding line by line. But from such a trusted source like Communication for All that has no ulterior motive? No one will ever even suspect it."

He crossed his arms over his chest. "How do you know about it if you've been gone for ten years?"

She forced an even breath. "That Trojan horse was the last thing they tried to get me to build before my mom took me and ran. But I didn't do it. I could've, but I didn't. And it's taken them ten years to get caught back up."

"I'm surprised they didn't force you. You were only a kid. With everything they're capable of, I would think brutalizing a single child wouldn't have been out of their wheelhouse."

Even now, ten years later, bile pooled in her stomach as she thought about it. The memory of the sound of her own bones breaking a split second before the pain ripped through. Her body still woke her up in a cold sweat sometimes.

She forced the memory from her mind now as she wrapped her arms around her knees once again and pulled them against her chest.

She closed her eyes. "It wasn't beyond their capacity. They used starvation and sleep deprivation first, but then realized that wasn't conducive to me actually being able to get the Trojan horse made. So then they went with physical pain—broke my legs in three different places over the course of the year. Finally, they started torturing my mother to get me to cooperate. That worked best."

"God, Bree…"

"Bethany. Bethany Malone. That's my real name." And she hadn't been able to say it out loud in ten years. "Melissa named Beth after me. But I'm Bree now. Bethany Malone died ten years ago when she hobbled out of the Communication for All campus with a mother who was hanging on to the last grips of sanity."

Chapter Twenty-Two

Tanner wanted to grab Bree and pull her into his arms. To comfort both her and the child inside her who had suffered so much.

But the way she said it all with almost no emotion—how they tortured her and her mother—told him she wouldn't respond to comfort right now.

"My mom gave me eight hours and forty-five minutes' warning that she'd found a way to get out," Bree continued, her voice getting more and more distant. "I used that time to do as much damage to the Organization as I could. I made sure to set them back for years, while also erasing every image that had ever been taken of me or my mom. I didn't want them to be able to find us."

"That was smart of you."

"The damage I did to them in eight hours set them back *years*. I know for a fact Michael Jeter hated me after that. I wish I could've seen his face when he'd found out what I'd done."

But her own face got sadder, not happier. Tanner couldn't stay away anymore. He sat down and pulled her up against his chest. "You got out. You survived. You bested them. That's what matters."

"If I had worked that hard when they wanted me to, they wouldn't have hurt my mom. She never recovered,

Tanner." She shook her head against his chest. "She never stopped looking over her shoulder, convinced the Organization was there. Never stopped being terrified. Even at the end, she was convinced she was being betrayed and the Organization was coming to get her."

Bree rubbed her shoulder in the peculiar way he'd seen her do multiple times in the last few weeks.

"She never got over it?"

"No. We moved around all the time. Sometimes we even lived apart if she thought they might be gaining on us. Split up a lot."

Which explained why she'd wanted to do that when they were in trouble.

"Toward the end…" She trailed off, rubbing the front of her shoulder again so hard he was afraid she was going to leave a mark on her skin.

He pressed his hand over hers so it lay flat against her shirt rather than moving. "Toward the end…she hurt you?"

Bree's eyes flew to his. "She didn't mean to. She was confused. Sick. The last few weeks, she was convinced I was working for the Organization. That I was helping them take us back into captivity."

That didn't make any sense, of course, but he didn't need to point that out. Bree was well aware her mother's fears had been irrational.

"She stabbed me in the shoulder because she thought I had poisoned her. Then she ran outside and right in front of a car. Killed her instantly."

He gripped her hand in his and brought it down from a wound that was years old but obviously had never healed. Might never heal.

He brought her fingers to his lips. "She needed more help than you could give her. She had a breakdown."

"She needed a daughter who hadn't let her mother be tortured until she was never right in the mind again!"

It was the most emotion he'd ever heard out of Bree.

He pulled her against his chest and wrapped his arms around her. "No. She sacrificed to get you out of there. She wouldn't have wanted you to give the Organization what they were demanding. But her head muddied it up."

She held herself stiff for a moment before relaxing against him with a sigh. "I know. I know she wanted us out of there. I just wish we could've gotten out earlier. That I had been smart enough to figure out how to do *that* rather than just useless computer stuff."

"Useless? You formulated technology that was years before your time. And you were a child when you did it."

"And then I destroyed most of it before I left."

They sat in silence for a few minutes. Tanner wasn't sure if that had been the right call or not. But it had definitely been the only choice a teenager who'd been tortured physically, mentally and emotionally had.

"Where does Melissa fit into this?"

"Melissa didn't know what the Organization really was until recently. She lost everything." Tanner listened as Bree told him about how Melissa's fiancé had been killed and how she hid the babies so she could try to make her move against Communication for All.

"But she can't do it," Bree said. "She's not good enough. I've known that the whole time but ignored it because I've been afraid. They have to be stopped right now, and I'm the only one who can do it."

"That means coming out of hiding. I can put you in protective custody."

"No. I've been thinking about this all day. In order for this to work, I'll have to be at the symposium myself. I'll use their own system against them."

"I'll make sure you're safe." And he damn well meant it.

A soft sound came from the monitor. Beth was awake. She generally woke up from sleep first and played contentedly for a few minutes until Christian woke and made the entire world aware of his unhappiness.

Bree stood and pointed at the baby monitor. "Those kids need to grow up with their mom. Not with their emotionally stunted second cousin," she said.

Tanner stood also. "Technically, it's first cousin once removed."

Bree laughed, a beautiful sound he wanted to hear more of. "I notice you don't try to argue the *emotionally stunted* part."

He stepped closer. "You're emotionally *guarded*, not stunted. And that's completely understandable." He slid a hand under the thick brown hair at her nape. "There's absolutely nothing wrong with taking it slow. Believe me, slow can be very, very good."

He kissed her. Tenderly, aware that this woman—brilliant, brave and about to bring down a major group of criminals—had never known tender kisses. Outside of him, had probably never known any kisses at all.

He would be more than glad to show her any type of kiss she wanted to learn.

She sighed, leaning into him, her trim body brushing against his. He had to struggle to remember to remain tender and gentle.

When Bree's little tongue brushed against his lips, all thoughts of tender fled. His hands came up to cup her face, tilting her head so he had better access to those sweet lips.

He nibbled at them until they opened then deepened the kiss until it was a melding of their mouths, no space left between them. He knew he should slow things down, but Bree's arms wrapped snugly around the back of his neck weren't going to allow it anyway.

Not that he wanted to.

But still he was impossibly cognizant of the need to take

this at a speed she could handle and process. No matter how much her lips were driving him crazy.

In the end it wasn't either of them who broke the kiss, it was Christian letting the world know he was awake.

Bree let out a sigh as they broke away from each other, but at least her eyes still met his. "That kid sure can scream," she whispered.

"If it wasn't for him crying, I never would've walked down that aisle at the drugstore. But I'm glad both of them aren't like that."

She let out a sigh and tilted her head against his chest. He would've gladly stood there forever and let her lean against him. "I don't have much time to stop the Organization. I have to start right away."

"What do you need?" he said against her hair.

"A safe place to work, preferably on a government computer so I can more easily cover my tracks." She pulled back and looked up at him. "And someone to watch the twins. It's going to take every spare minute before the symposium for me to get inside the Organization's system. I won't be able to care for the babies the way they need. It nearly killed me when I was trying to do that before using the library's internet."

"That's why you were there in the middle of the night when you were supposed to be resting?" That made so much sense now.

Those green eyes widened. "How did you know?"

"I saw you there that night. I had no idea what you were doing."

She nodded. "I was trying to help Melissa. But she told me to stop and focus on the kids and let her worry about the Organization. I don't even know if she's still alive, Tanner. She might have risked it all calling me and telling me to get out of the apartment."

"I know people in federal law enforcement. Omega Sector can have someone knocking on Communication for All's door today. If she's still alive, we can get her out."

Bree thought about that for a moment. "No. If they didn't catch her, going in there will tip them off and we'll never be able to stop them. Mellie wants to be free. Wants the twins to be free. The only way that will happen is for me to stop them from the inside."

"Then we'll make it happen. Whatever you need. I'll make sure you have it. You're not alone in this anymore, Bree."

Her big green eyes blinked up at him. "I... I..." She faded off with a shrug.

He put a finger over her lips. "You don't have to know what to say. You don't even need to know what to feel right now. Let's go get those babies fed and then let you go to work so you can save the world."

Chapter Twenty-Three

After helping her feed the kids, Tanner left, telling Bree to pack up everything for the babies. She was crying by the time she got the second armful of baby stuff into the car Noah brought over.

She knew there was every possibility she might not see them again. Despite Tanner's assurances that they could handle the Organization, he and his federal law enforcement friends in Omega Sector who were waiting on standby really didn't have any idea of who they were up against.

Tanner thought he could protect her, but she still knew the odds were that she would be dead or, worse, back in the Organization's clutches by the time the symposium was done.

She couldn't live through that again.

But she couldn't do nothing any longer, either.

"You want help loading?" Noah asked. He was standing at the end of the porch, Corfu at his feet.

"No. It's not heavy. I'm just an emotional basket case."

Noah didn't try to argue or placate her. She appreciated that. "Being close to people is hard," he said. "The price is high."

"Too high?" she muttered, more to herself than him.

He answered anyway. "Almost always."

Right at this moment, she didn't disagree with him. How much simpler her life would've been if she'd never opened the door to Melissa in the first place.

She placed the last load of stuff in the car. But how much emptier.

Would it be worth it in the end?

She knew when Tanner was about to show back up by the way Noah disappeared without a word. Sure enough, a car pulled up the long driveway a few moments later.

But when she saw who it was with Tanner, Bree almost burst into tears again.

Dan and Cheryl.

When they rushed out of the car and hugged her, this time, for the first time, she hugged them back.

"Oh, sweetheart! You're okay!" Cheryl kept her arms around Bree almost in a choke hold, but Bree didn't mind. "When Tanner told us what was going on, we came right over here to help. I'm so glad you're safe."

"And I'm so glad I will eventually heal from the bruises Mrs. A's smacks gave me when she found out you were here and that I hadn't really run you out of town," Tanner muttered.

But he grinned and winked at Bree from where she remained trapped in Cheryl's arms.

"Dan and Cheryl are going to take the twins and leave town," Tanner explained.

Cheryl finally pulled back. "We're going to go visit my son and his wife in Texas. Stay completely out of the fray. Tanner explained that you're doing something important and dangerous."

"Yes."

Dan placed himself so he was between her and Tanner. "Bree, you don't have to. You can come with us and the babies. We'll hide out until this all blows over."

She reached out and grabbed Dan's hand, something

she wouldn't have been able to do a month ago. "This will never blow over. I have to make a stand here or the babies and I will never be safe."

Once the Organization uploaded the software to the phones, they would be able to find her no matter where she hid.

"Okay," Dan said. "I just wanted you to know you have a choice."

She squeezed his hand. "This is my choice."

"And I'm going to make sure she's safe," Tanner said. "If they want to get to her, they're going to have to go through me."

They all spent the next few minutes getting the babies ready for their road trip. Bree kissed them both tenderly before placing them into the car seats. Way before she was ready, they were pulling away.

Bree didn't cry. Didn't stare after the car. Didn't let herself dwell on the fact that she might never see Christian and Beth again.

Instead she pulled on every bit of strength she'd developed from years of living on her own—strength her mother had instilled in Bree before her own strength disappeared—and turned to Tanner.

"It's time to get to work."

The Organization had stolen way too much of her life. She wasn't going to let them steal any more.

TANNER HAD NEVER seen someone do what Bree could do with a computer. She had been working for nearly three days straight to try to get into Communication for All's inner computer system.

She'd tried to explain exactly what she was doing the first day, but he hadn't understood ninety percent of what she said. So he'd just tugged on her ponytail until she'd looked up from the computer screen and kissed her to shut her up.

He was pretty sure her fingers hadn't stopped typing the whole time.

The woman was completely focused on the task at hand.

He'd been tempted to distract her. To force her out of the emotionless bubble she'd encased herself in, because the bubble hadn't included him.

Any other time he would. He had no plans to let Bree shut him out just because she'd always kept people shut out in the past.

But right now that bubble was what was allowing her to function. To stay firmly committed to the task at hand and take down these murderous bastards.

They'd set up Bree's workspace in the Sunrise, since it was closed while the Andrewses were gone. She was working in the office, a space already familiar to her, which gave her access to food and a bathroom, and didn't have any windows that would allow someone to spot her.

Plus, the Andrewses' absence gave Tanner the excuse to look in on the diner without suspicion. Noah and some more of his former Special Forces friends from Wyoming were providing invisible around-the-clock security for Bree, since Tanner couldn't do it.

Tanner was being watched. He had no doubt about it. The question was, by who?

Had Steele backtracked to Risk Peak, looking for Bree? Had the Organization sent someone else to see if they could find her here?

Or maybe it was just the townspeople who were still angry with him for sending Bree off on her own, and then, worse, causing the town's favorite diner to shut down for a couple weeks because the Andrewses were so heartbroken.

Tanner could take the evil eye from the town. But he knew they were running out of time. The symposium was in just a few hours, and Bree was exhausted. She hadn't gotten more than a couple hours' sleep here and there since she started. Hadn't even stopped for a full meal.

Tanner didn't like it. Every instinct had him wanting to pamper and protect her, and teach her how to accept it.

And he would. But right now he would accept/acknowledge she was a woman on a mission and he was backup. So he would encourage her strength.

He let himself in the back door of the Sunrise like he had each day. He walked over and kissed Bree on the top of the head before removing the plates and cups piled up by the Grand County laptop she was using.

"We've got a problem," she said. Her fingers stopped typing.

That wasn't a good sign.

"How bad?"

"The Organization knows I'm in Risk Peak. They don't know who I am or what exactly I'm doing, but they know someone's pushing at them."

He muttered a curse. "We've got to get you out of here."

"I can't leave now. I'm too close to breaking through, and we're out of time. We need to leave for the symposium in no more than six hours in order for this to work." She looked up at him with those green eyes. "Tanner, I need you to buy me some time. Make them think I'm somewhere else. But they're going to be monitoring every cellular transmission anywhere they can within a fifty-mile radius of here."

Tanner pulled out his dumb phone. "This still safe?"

She nodded. "Until tomorrow. Once the Organization's new system goes live and they start piggybacking off the manufacturers' systems, then no cellular phone will be safe. Every phone will broadcast data to the Organization. But I still wouldn't use it just in case I'm wrong."

"You keep working. I'll buy you the time you need."

She gave him a tired smile before her eyes and hands were back on the laptop in front of her.

Tanner turned on the back light of the diner, his signal to Noah that they needed to meet. A few minutes later, Noah showed up. Tanner led him into the kitchen so they could talk without disturbing Bree.

"Bree says the Organization is onto her. We need to set up a decoy, get her the space and time she needs. And we should deem all cell phones no longer safe."

Noah grunted. "We can set something up at the ranch. Make them think she's there. It would give you and me the tactical advantage since we know it so well. And my team is fully capable."

Tanner had made the decision not to bring in law enforcement. Official channels meant too many modes of communication that could be monitored.

"Yeah, good. I've got my federal colleagues in Denver as soon as Bree cracks the system and we've got the proof we need that Communication for All is dirty."

Noah nodded. "One way or another, it ends today. How are we going to get our bad guys out to the ranch?"

"They don't know we're onto them," Tanner said. "So we use cell phones against them."

Noah smiled. "And then we take them out of commission. My kind of plan."

"I'm going to have to bring Ronnie in on it. I'll leave him here as guard for Bree. She's not going to notice if either of us are missing anyway. A bomb could go off and I'm not sure she would notice."

"I'll get my team out to the ranch and will be waiting for your call."

A moment later, Noah was gone.

Tanner walked back into the office and crouched down beside Bree. She stopped what she was doing and looked at him.

"We're leading them away," he said. "You keep working. I'll send Ronnie to guard but will tell him not to disturb you."

Her lips pursed. "I know I can do it, but I don't know if I can do it in *time*."

He reached over and kissed her softly. "You can."

This time when his lips met hers, she clung to him. He groaned against her mouth. "There's nothing I want to do more than stay here and kiss you, but we've both got to get to work."

"Be careful." She clutched him closer to her for just a second. "The Organization is dangerous and smart."

He smiled. "So are we. We'll buy you the time you need."

She straightened. "I won't waste it."

He pulled her in for a tight embrace and kissed the top of her head. "I know."

Her fingers were already flying on the keyboard as he walked briskly out the door.

Back at the station a few minutes later, he found Ronnie at his desk.

"Ronnie, can I see you for a second in my office?"

The deputy nodded and followed him in.

"I don't have any further updates about Steele, if that's what—"

Tanner cut him off. "I need to borrow your personal phone to make a call."

Ronnie eyed both the phone sitting on Tanner's desk and the one clipped at his waist. Probably just being in the same room with Ronnie's smartphone meant the Organization was listening, but Tanner wanted to make sure they got this message loud and clear.

"Um, sure."

"You'll understand in a minute."

Ronnie entered his password and handed the phone to Tanner. Tanner immediately punched in his brother's number.

"Dempsey."

Noah's greeting was terse. If it hadn't been for this situation, he probably wouldn't have answered at all.

"Noah, it's Tanner. I'm using Ronnie's phone because I think mine might be bugged."

Right on cue, Noah muttered a curse.

"Is Bree okay?" Tanner asked.

"Yeah. I've got to admit I never expected to see her face here again. She's looking pretty tired and hasn't gotten up from her computer since she arrived."

Good job. Give them something to make them nervous.

"I can't get home until this evening. Too many people around, and I feel like I'm being watched."

"That's fine. Like I said, she's busy with her computer stuff here in your kitchen. She's excited. Talking about bringing down some sort of organization."

Tanner winced. They were trying to buy time, not cause the Organization to bomb the ranch.

Noah was spoiling for a fight. Wanted them to send out the troops.

That was fine, because so was Tanner.

"Just keep her in my house until I can get home. Make sure she doesn't run off again."

"Will do, bro. Since nobody knows she's here, I'll just be back and forth between my place and yours."

"Okay," Tanner said. "Just keep an eye out. I don't want her running off again until we get some answers."

"Roger that." Noah disconnected the call.

Tanner looked at Ronnie but didn't hand him back his phone.

"Holy hell, boss. What exactly is going on?"

"Let's go out back and have a cigarette."

Before Ronnie could respond that neither of them

smoked, Tanner held a finger up to his lips in a gesture for quiet.

He threw the other man's phone in a drawer and led him outside.

Ronnie looked all sorts of confused. "Do you really think your phone is bugged?"

"I think it's way more than that. And I'm going to need your help."

"Providing backup at your ranch? Do you think Steele might make an attempt for Bree?"

"We've got much bigger problems than Bill Steele, or whatever his name is. And Bree is not at my ranch."

"But you and Noah just said—"

"I said that specifically for the ears that were listening. And those ears are listening to *any* cell phone, off or on. I don't have time to go into the details right now. You're just going to have to trust me."

Ronnie nodded. "What do you need me to do?"

Tanner was thankful he and Ronnie had been working together for so long. "Bree is at the Sunrise. I need you to watch over her while Noah and I do some hunting."

"Sure, I—"

They broke off from the conversation as Scott walked outside and saw them.

"You letting him in on it?" Ronnie muttered softly.

Tanner gave a short shake of his head. It wasn't that he didn't trust the kid; as a matter of fact, Scott had been almost more ferocious in the search for Steele than anyone. But Scott was leaving soon, and Tanner didn't want to put him in any unnecessary danger.

Scott gave them a friendly smile as he joined them. "Hey, somebody told me you were out here. I'm just about done with everything and will be heading out this afternoon. I'm just missing one laptop to place the final training software on. It's an older one, and no one seems to quite know where to find it."

That would be because Bree was currently using it to try to work her magic. But Tanner didn't have time to come up with a reasonable lie. He needed to get to the ranch since the plan was already in motion.

"Honestly, I'm not sure where that thing is. I'll just install the update myself once it's located."

"Oh, okay." Scott shrugged and gave a half smile. "Well, then, I guess this is goodbye. I'm moving on to Colorado Springs today."

"Thanks for your help this past week. I know I wasn't the best of company, but I appreciate you trying to help us track down Steele. That went above and beyond what you were here to do."

Scott's chubby face broke into a smile. "It was no problem. Sorry I couldn't do more to find him. He's a slippery bastard."

Was he one of the people on their way to Tanner's ranch right now?

He reached out to shake Scott's hand. "I visit different departments quite a bit. I'll try to touch base with you and see if we can go have a beer sometime."

"I'd like that."

Tanner gave both men a brief nod then hustled toward his SUV.

It was time to catch some bad guys.

Chapter Twenty-Four

Tanner may have never fought side by side with his brother in battle, but there was damn well no one else he'd rather have at his back right now when it came to protecting Bree. Having three more of Noah's highly qualified former army team members here was just a bonus.

Tanner and Noah were currently standing in the tree line, just to the side of Tanner's house. Noah had binoculars and was scoping everything out around them. Every once in a while, he would use hand gestures to signal to his teammates. None of them were willing to take a chance communicating over phones or radios.

They would have to do things old-school.

Just over an hour after Tanner made the fake phone call to Noah, the action began.

"Looks like we've got four coming in on foot from the south. They're making a stealth approach directly toward the house," Noah said after looking through his binoculars. The two of them did not have that area in their sights; Noah was reporting back whatever his team was signaling to him.

The plan was to let them come. To let them get as close as possible and think that Bree was here for as long as possible. Buy her as much time as they could.

"They're dressed in suits. Not ready for the terrain." Noah rolled his eyes. "This is almost too easy."

Tanner kept a close eye on the house. "Remember the plan. We string them along, take them down, but nobody gets killed. Make sure your people know that."

"They know. If that wasn't the case, there'd already be four suits on the ground."

A couple minutes later, they could hear an engine of a vehicle making an approach down their long driveway. Tanner brought his own binoculars up. "What a surprise. It looks like the power company has chosen today to pay a visit."

They both knew that was not the power company coming up their drive.

"We must've forgotten to pay the bill and they're coming to collect," Noah said dryly.

"Bet you five dollars they go with faulty wiring as their excuse. It looks like there's two guys in the front seat of the van. Possibly more in the back."

"The van is probably the signal for those guys in the woods to close in."

Tanner nodded. He agreed. That would be the smart play.

"Have your team take out the people coming in on foot. Make sure they aren't able to send out a signal or message. If someone gets word out, this is all for nothing."

"Roger that."

"Noah, remember, no body bags."

Noah just grinned. Tanner left him to signal the information to his team, watching the van get closer. It would be up to him and his brother to take down however many *power company* guys were coming their way.

Surprise was the best element they had. The Organization was only expecting Noah and Bree to be here, so they weren't expecting much resistance. They'd also be complacent, thinking backup in the woods was just moments away.

By the time Noah was finished communicating with his team, Tanner had a plan. "You go out there and talk to them since they're expecting you. You handle the two in the front seat, and I'll handle whatever's in the back."

"You sure? Could be a ton of trouble in the back. You're going in there blind."

"Or it could be a half dozen dancing monkeys. I can handle myself."

Noah slapped him on the shoulder. "I know it."

Noah stepping out of the shadows proved he meant it. There was no going back now. If everybody didn't hold up their end of the task—if any of these bad guys got a single call out—this was all for nothing.

As the van got closer, Tanner turned and made his way silently through the trees so that he would be able to approach from the back. He stepped closer as the vehicle pulled to a stop directly in front of Tanner's house.

Both men got out of the front in Colorado power company uniforms.

"Mr. Dempsey? We're with the power company. We've received an urgent report that the wiring in some of the houses in this area is faulty and extremely dangerous."

Ha, Noah, you owe me five dollars.

"Is that so?" Noah replied. "I've never had any problems. Not even so much as a single flicker."

Tanner made his way closer to the back of the van.

"It's good that you're not inside the house," the second man said. "We've had reports of unexpected fires. There have even been some severe injuries."

Tanner recognized that voice. It was the same one who'd called Mr. Jeter in Denver. If Tanner had had any doubt about this not being the real power company, it was completely gone now. Not that he'd had much doubt. In the twelve years he'd owned this house, the power had been out here a grand total of zero times.

Tanner took a few steps closer. It wouldn't be long before whoever was in the back came out to provide assistance.

Tanner wanted to be right at the door when they did.

"Is there anyone else inside the house, sir?" the first guy asked. "It's important they come out right now."

"Right now? It's really that dangerous?" Noah played his part well. "I have a friend doing some important work on a computer."

"Yes, sir," Denver guy said. "If you could just call your friend out right now. We can't let you go back inside. It's too dangerous."

Too dangerous for them to risk letting him out of their sights. Did they have orders to kill the would-be Bree immediately, or take her back into the Organization?

"Hey, Bree, can you come out here for a second? It's important," Noah called out.

The back van door creaked open. That must have been the cue they were waiting for. Tanner stepped to the side of the van. He and Noah would have to time this perfectly.

"Can you call her again, sir?"

"How about if I just go in there and get her. This is ridiculous. The house isn't going to blow up in the thirty seconds it takes me to get her."

"I'm sorry, we can't let you do that." Denver's voice was farther from the van, closer to Noah.

"Hey, man, get your hands off me. You don't have any right to tell me whether I can or cannot go into my own house."

There was a scuffle, and Tanner didn't wait any longer. Noah would take care of those guys. Tanner had his own bad guys to worry about. It ended up being three. Not dancing monkeys after all.

The first two were out of the vehicle and the third was on his way when Tanner rounded the back.

He immediately slammed the door against the head of the man climbing out, glancing over to make sure he was unconscious before facing the other two men.

Something jolted hard against the front of the van, and Tanner prayed it wasn't Noah.

Tanner didn't waste any time. He dived for the closest man, being sure to knock the phone out of the hand of the second guy. That bought Tanner a little time, but not much.

Fighting two men was never easy. Keeping them from using their weapons, phones or even calling out to whatever transmitting devices might pick up their voices was damned near impossible.

His flying punch connected with the first man's jaw, and he kicked out backward with his foot to land in that guy's stomach. Tanner grunted as he took a solid hook to the jaw from the first man, and saw the second man reaching for his gun from the corner of his eye. Tanner brought his elbow up and around into the face of the first man, hearing the unmistakable crack of a breaking nose.

As that guy howled, Tanner turned toward the second, diving for him to keep him from getting his weapon out. He knocked the gun from his hand and sent it skittering across the drive.

Tanner didn't hesitate. Three quick punches and the second guy was on the ground, unconscious. He jumped up, spun and a roundhouse kick to the first man had him lying next to his buddy.

The third guy, who was just starting to get his senses back after being knocked on the head by the door, groaned and began crawling toward the back of the van again.

Tanner just slammed the door against his head again, since it worked so well the first time, and watched him fall.

Noah came running around the van. "You clear?"

Tanner nodded, sucking in air to catch his breath, wincing at the blows he'd taken. Noah tossed him some zip ties and bandannas to use as gags, and soon all five men were restrained and sat up against the van. A few minutes later, the other four were dragged in by Noah's teammates, also tied and gagged.

Noah and Tanner walked so they could speak freely without the transmitters hearing them, while the rest of the team stood guard.

"It won't take the Organization long to figure out that their team is out of commission," Noah said. "Then they're going to start the hunt for Bree all over. Wiser this time, because they know we're onto them."

Tanner wiped at a little bit of blood that had formed at the corner of his lip. "I know. But I'll be leaving with Bree for Denver in a couple of hours. Hopefully it will buy us that long. Once she's into their system and has the proof we need, Omega Sector can handle the arrests from there."

Noah nodded. "I hope it's enough."

Tanner did, too. "I've got to get out of here. If not, it will raise too many questions about why I didn't go through official channels."

"Okay, take off. I'll call this in, in a little while. State that I thought someone was trying to rob me. Maybe that will buy another hour or two."

Tanner clapped Noah on the shoulder. "Thank you—to you and your team—for what you did here today."

"Are you kidding? Taking down asshole bad guys is what we live for. No thanks needed. Just bring some that are a little tougher next time."

Tanner grinned and jogged toward his SUV. He wanted to check on Bree. They may have bought some time, but that didn't mean she was out of danger. And while he trusted Ronnie, he wanted her back in his sights.

Permanently.

And wasn't that scary as hell, considering he'd only kissed the woman a handful of times and she had more locks on her emotions than Fort Knox.

He planned to unlock every single one, picking a few if he needed to.

He made it back into Risk Peak in record time, parking his car at the station, intending to go straight to the Sunrise. But Gayle caught him in the parking lot. She was still mad at him for chasing Bree out of town. Before he could say anything, she held up a hand.

"I'm not going to ask you exactly what is going on. God knows I worked long enough for your father without always having the details. I trusted him, and I trust you."

Tanner let out a breath. "I promise I'll explain when I can."

"This has something to do with that girl, doesn't it?"

He nodded, glad she hadn't said Bree's name out loud.

"Fine," Gayle continued. "I'm glad to hear you're doing the right thing by her."

"That's my plan." He gave her a nod and turned toward the diner.

"Oh, and I gave Scott the location of the last laptop like you wanted."

Tanner stopped in his tracks. "What?"

She looked confused. "He said you said it was critical that he finish this last laptop before he left. So I looked it up on that system we installed a couple of years ago when we were doing the county-wide inventory."

Tanner blew out a harsh breath. "Scott? I told him I would do it."

"Well, that's not how he understood it. He was adamant that he get a hold of it immediately. It was over at the Sunrise for some reason, so—"

"When?" His heart began to slam against his chest.

"Maybe an hour ago? I'm not sure—"

Tanner didn't listen to the rest. He ran as fast as he could toward the diner.

The enemy had been hiding in plain sight all along.

Chapter Twenty-Five

Bree grinned at the screen in front of her.

She'd done it. She'd outmaneuvered the Organization.

Take that, you rat bastards.

They thought like criminals, and ultimately that had been their downfall, providing her the way into their system. Everything the Organization did was in shadows and back channels.

They weren't expecting someone to come straight up and knock on their figurative front door. There had just been the smallest crack of an opening, the tiniest of weaknesses, ones they wouldn't even have seen because they weren't her.

But that was all that Bree needed.

Her data was saved from the computer onto a SIM card. Now all she had to do was upload it to any member of the Organization's phone in the vicinity of the Denver symposium, and when the Organization tried to pull their little stunt where they took over all the cell phones in the world, they'd be in for quite a surprise.

Instead of being the ones controlling the information about everyone else, the entire world would have all the dirty laundry about *them*.

Every compromised member of Communication for

All would be exposed. But hopefully the charity itself could live on.

Ronnie had been here with her in the office for a while, but his presence had been throwing her off, so he'd gone out into the main section of the diner. Whatever Tanner had done to gain her these last couple of hours, it had been worth it.

She sat back in her chair and grinned. They were going to take the Organization down. She never would've thought it was possible.

And couldn't even begin to think what her life might possibly be like after today. But making sure Melissa and the twins were safe was all that mattered.

"You know, when I met you, I knew you were more than a waitress, but I had no idea who you really were."

Bree turned with a gasp and found Scott standing in the door of the office.

Blood was dripping from a knife in his hand.

He held it up and inspected it. "I'm afraid Ronnie had an accident."

Bree spun around in the office that had provided her with a sense of security because it had no windows. But that also meant there were no other exits—something she hadn't even thought about until now. Her mother would've been so disappointed.

All it takes is one slipup and you're dead.

Looked like this was Bree's.

Scott took a step farther inside the room. "You know the great thing about looking like a pudgy middle schooler? Nobody tends to think of you as a threat."

Bree took a step back as he took one forward. "You work for the Organization?"

He gave her a slimy smile, and she wondered how she'd ever thought of him as charming. Then winked at her. "I was handpicked for this mission by Mr. Jeter himself when we first realized someone on the inside was keeping tabs on someone in this town."

He shook his head in wonder. "Who would've thought that the greatest hacker who ever lived was not only alive, but had started the cutest little family of her own? Where are the screaming brats? I'm sure Mr. Jeter would like to meet them."

Just the sound of Jeter's name had nausea curdling her stomach. "They're not here. They're far away from here."

"Don't worry. We'll find them." Scott wiped off the handle of the knife with a napkin and grabbed her hand before she realized what he was going to do. He forced her fingers around the handle.

She let go as soon as he released her fingers, but it was too late. Her fingerprints were already on the weapon.

"You can consider that your going-away present to Tanner. A murder weapon with your prints on it seems like a pretty good reason for you to leave town without saying goodbye, don't you think?"

"R-Ronnie is dead?"

Scott shrugged. "Will be soon, if he's not dead yet. Too bad, really, I kind of liked him. But Mr. Jeter told me to bring you straight to him. It's a big day for Communication for All, you know. Mr. Jeter is going to be a hero."

She reached over and slid the SIM card into her hand before stuffing it into her pocket. Scott was about to hand deliver her where she needed to go anyway. Maybe she could upload the data before they killed her.

Although no one was likely to just lend her their phone.

Scott grabbed her hands and slid a zip tie around her wrists, pulling it tight, and began yanking her toward the back door.

"If you yell once we're outside, I'll kill whoever comes."

Bree believed him and kept her mouth shut.

She kept it shut on the ride to Denver, trying to come

up with a plan. If she couldn't upload the data on the SIM card, no one would ever be able to gain proof about the Organization's illegal activities. They'd be untouchable.

And what about Tanner? Would he think she'd lied? Killed Ronnie?

The closer they got to Denver, the more fear seemed to swallow her whole. Panic crawled all over her body by the time Scott dragged her from an underground parking lot into a private suite that was part of the convention center.

He pushed her through the door and closed it behind him.

All she could see was Michael Jeter.

Terror slammed into her. She tried to remind herself that he was just a man, not a very big one at that. But all she could remember was the pain, the fear, the sound of her own bones breaking and her mother sobbing in pain as Jeter told her to focus. Concentrate. Do the work on the computer in front of her.

"Bethany!" Fingers snapped in front of her face, and she blinked back into the present. It was Jeter, of course. He'd never had any tolerance for people not doing exactly what he wanted at the moment he demanded it.

Who cared if they were terrified or traumatized or tortured?

Bree sucked in a deep breath, forcing oxygen into lungs that burned. She had to keep it together.

A sound caught her attention from the corner. Melissa sat on a couch crying softly. She'd obviously been beaten.

Bree's eyes flew back to Jeter as he spoke. "I'm so glad you're here, Bethany. I'm sure your cousin is, as well. We weren't sure if she knew where to find you or not."

"You bastard."

"I'm sure it must look that way to you. But you're not a child any longer. You can't use that as an excuse not to see the big picture."

She wanted to curse at him. To rage, strike him, hurt him the way he'd hurt her and the people she loved.

But there was only one way to take down the Organization today. And that was by being smart.

She held up her wrists in front of her face. "Your lackey bound my hands too tightly. Have someone cut me loose before I have permanent nerve damage. I won't be much good to you then."

Jeter's eyes narrowed. Obviously, he liked it better when she'd been cowering in fear a few moments ago. Swallowing the terror that wasn't far from the surface, she raised an eyebrow.

Your move.

Jeter gestured with his head, and the guard came over and cut her hands loose. She rubbed at her aching wrists.

"I knew it was you, Bethany. Over the last couple of days when we first spotted someone trying to piggyback on our servers, I *knew* it was you. I've always known you would come back to me."

She glanced over at the clock. There were less than ten minutes before the cell phone update went live. She had to get the data on the SIM card uploaded to a phone by then.

She turned to Jeter. "You tortured me and my mother. Why would you think I would ever come back to you?"

Jeter continued as if she hadn't spoken. "And the fact that it's today, the day that history will revere me as a hero, makes it even more fitting. You were always supposed to be here when this happened. Be by my side. That would've happened years ago if you hadn't run."

He put his hands on his hips, moving his suit jacket to the side, and she saw what she needed. On one hip sat a smartphone clipped into his belt.

On the other was a holstered gun.

Either could work.

"I'm not excited that you went and had children, Bethany. That you let some other man touch you. But don't worry, we'll use them to keep you in line this time."

Melissa began crying harder.

Praying he wouldn't stop her, Bree walked toward Melissa, sticking a hand in her pocket as she went, fishing out the tiny SIM card. She sat down by her cousin. "You're upsetting Melissa by talking about hurting innocent children, Michael."

His nostrils flared and his lips turned up a little. He liked her calling him Michael—the sense of intimacy it implied. Her stomach churned, but it was something she could use.

She covered Melissa's hands with hers. "It's okay," Bree crooned. "I'm not going to let anything happen. Crisscross, applesauce."

She pressed the SIM card into Melissa's palm as she said the words.

Melissa sniffled again, brows pulling together in confusion, but she didn't draw any attention to the SIM card.

"I'm glad you're here, Mellie. I don't think I could do this on my own. But don't cry anymore, okay?"

Melissa nodded. Bree stood and walked back toward Jeter, even though every instinct and memory told her to stay as far from him as possible.

"We could've done a lot together," she said.

He tilted his head to the side. "Oh, we still will. You're the only person who's ever come close to being my equal."

Scott snorted from the opposite side of the room, but they both ignored him. "You taught me a lot," she whispered.

Jeter's lips narrowed. "I taught you everything you know. I thought for a while that you were smarter than me, but the last few days have showed me otherwise. I was disappointed with how you came at our system, Bethany. Surely you must have realized that you couldn't shut us down remotely. What sort of genius would I be if I couldn't stop that sort of attack?"

The kind that was so conceited that a straightforward approach would slide right under his radar.

She took a step closer, and the guard cleared his throat. "Mr. Jeter…"

"She's fine," Jeter snapped, holding out a hand when the guard started to move toward them. Jeter himself closed the distance between them, reaching out to cup her cheek.

It was only by sheer strength of will that she kept herself from shuddering at his touch. She hoped Melissa was ready. They would only get one chance at this.

"You need guidance, Bethany. Discipline. You always have. I can be your greatest teacher. Together we can literally rule the world."

Even if she had had more time, she couldn't have stood one more second of hearing his voice, of feeling his hands on her.

She lunged for Jeter's waist. She knocked the cell phone off his belt and kicked it toward Melissa, praying she would understand what needed to be done.

Then Bree dived for the gun.

But Jeter had already recovered. His gun was out of his holster, in his hand and pointed at her face.

She took a step back.

"I can't tell you how disappointed I am that you did that, Bethany. And that you weren't smart enough to figure out what side of my waist the gun was on before making your move."

Melissa sobbed louder from behind her. Bree prayed it was to cover putting the SIM card into Jeter's phone.

Because they were out of time in more ways than one.

The gun remained pointed in her face. "Maybe you're not as smart as I think you are. Maybe like everyone else you're just a disappointment. Maybe I'd be better off getting rid of you right now."

"Maybe I never planned to remote hack you."

His eyes narrowed to slits. "What?"

"Mellie?"

"Done," her cousin responded.

"I'm still smarter than you, Jeter. I was when I was a kid and I am now."

For the first time, he looked worried. "Whatever you think you're going to do, you're too late. The update just went live."

Scott cursed from over in the corner. "Um, boss? We've got a problem."

Bree smiled as Scott continued to curse.

Jeter turned from her to glare at Scott. "What exactly is the problem?"

When Scott finally looked up from his phone, all color was gone from his normally ruddy cheeks. "Did you do this?"

Bree just continued to smile.

"We need to get out of here right now," Scott said. "She fooled us all. Instead of sending out our code, the update just sent out all the details about the Organization's illegal activities."

"To who?" Jeter sputtered.

"Everyone."

Bree glanced to the side as Melissa stood and held Jeter's phone out in front of her. "Looks like she's always going to be smarter than you, Jeter."

He pressed the gun against Bree's forehead. "Not if she's dead."

Chapter Twenty-Six

Scott had played them all from the beginning.

As soon as Ronnie had been taken by the ambulance, Tanner was in his vehicle, headed toward Denver. Every minute that passed seemed like an eternity.

No one from law enforcement—even the prestigious Omega Sector—could move in on Michael Jeter without a warrant. And no judge was willing to grant one on the day where Jeter was about to change the course of history by providing a huge technology breakthrough free to everyone.

And trying to explain that the huge technology breakthrough was actually part of a terrorist plot didn't go over well.

He'd called in a favor and had the lab immediately run the prints on the knife that had been used to stab Ronnie, hoping there might be a link to Jeter. But the prints had been Bree's. Or, more specifically, Bethany Malone's.

Tanner damned well knew Bree had not stabbed Ronnie. He didn't care what it looked like.

But he was on his own trying to find her. And his chances of being able to get to Jeter on this day—when he'd been the keynote speaker of a huge event a few hours ago—were slim to none.

He pulled up to the convention center downtown, parking illegally, flashing his badge at everyone until it got him to someone high enough to tell him where Michel Jeter was located.

"It's an emergency," he told a Mr. Kenyon, the manager of the building. "I need to see Jeter immediately."

Kenyon was maddeningly calm. "I have placed a call to Mr. Jeter's assistant with your request. I told him it was an emergency, but since you can't give me any other details about said emergency, I'm afraid no one seems to be taking your request seriously."

Kenyon gave Tanner a big, toothy smile. Tanner had to force himself not to punch him in it, or follow him when Kenyon turned and walked back into his office.

Tanner's fingers itched as they fell on the holster at his waist. If he pulled his weapon right now, he could get to Jeter. Get to Bree. Force Kenyon and his big smile to show him where they were.

It would be the end of his law enforcement career. But if it got Bree out of this alive, it would be worth it.

Saying a prayer, he flipped the snap off his holster.

"Save your theatrics, Dempsey," a voice said from behind him. "I can take you to Jeter without you doing time for terrorizing a building manager when this is said and done."

Tanner recognized that voice, and he had his weapon coming out of the holster anyway, spinning to face the man behind him.

Creepy, thin man. "Steele."

Steele held out his hands at shoulder height. "Actually, my name is Chris Martinez."

Tanner didn't lower his weapon. "Is that name supposed to mean something to me?"

"Perhaps if I say my full name is Christian, and that the love of my life named one of our children after me, it might ring a bell."

Now he lowered his weapon. "You're the twins' father?"

"Yes. And I worked for the Organization before they had me killed. Or almost had me killed. It's been a long recovery."

It explained some of the man's thinness. And so much else.

"I would love to answer all the three hundred questions burning in your eyes right now, but it will have to wait. I know where Jeter is."

"How?" Tanner asked.

"I'm not nearly as good as Bree with computers, but I know my way around one enough to be able to hack food services and find out where private meals are being delivered."

Tanner put his weapon back in the holster. "If you're lying, I'm arresting your ass."

Chris rolled his eyes. "I'll be happy for you to arrest me if we're still alive in a few hours."

They made their way through the hordes of people crowding the convention center for the symposium, everyone just milling around.

"They're all waiting for the big update coming in about five minutes," Chris explained. "To be here when it goes live gives them bragging rights."

"If they knew what it was really going to do, they wouldn't be so thrilled. Bree has been working day and night to try to find a way to stop Jeter. I have no idea if she finished."

They finally made it into any empty stairwell and started going down.

"If anybody can do it, it's Bree," Chris said. "Jeter has been obsessed with her for years, even when it seemed probable that she was dead. Melissa thought she was dead, too."

Tanner shook his head. "You know, when you said I

had three hundred questions for you, that was probably a little on the conservative side."

"Get us out of this alive, and I promise I'll answer all of them. As thanks for keeping my children safe."

As they walked side by side down the hall, Tanner stuck out his hand to shake. "Deal."

Chris shook then picked up speed. "This hallway isn't used by anyone but security and food services. It leads from the main suite to the underground parking for bigwigs."

"Okay."

"The room is at the end of this hall. Our best bet is probably to try to come in an air duct from the next room or to impersonate hotel staff and get them to open—" Chris stopped to look at his phone when it beeped.

"Oh, my God." The man couldn't tear his eyes from the device.

"What?"

Chris shook his head. "That was the Communication for All update. She did it. Holy hell, did she do it."

"Bree was successful?" Not that Tanner had had much doubt.

Chris was shaking his head in awe. "She just let the whole world know what the inner circle of Communication for All was up to in the most public way possible. Every single one of those bastards will be going down."

That meant...

Tanner started running. If Jeter had Bree and knew she'd just told the world all his secrets, he would kill her for sure.

Tanner grabbed the fire extinguisher on the wall. He would use it to break down the door.

"Tanner, you don't know what the situation is like in there. You may be way outgunned."

"I don't care."

Chris pulled out a gun from the back waistband of his jeans. "Then let's do this. I'll go to the left."

Tanner brought the edge of the extinguisher down on the doorknob, feeling it rip from the jamb, then kicked it as hard as he could. Chris ran into the room, gun raised, Tanner a half step behind him.

Jeter had a gun pointed at Bree but turned at the disturbance at the door. Bree didn't waste any time. She dived at Jeter while he was distracted, Melissa jumping on top of him to help her cousin.

Chris made his own dive for the guard closest to the door, while Tanner turned and raised his weapon at Scott.

"Drop it, Scott. I don't want to have to—"

Scott's eyes narrowed, and he brought his weapon up and pointed it at Tanner.

Tanner pulled the trigger, the sound barreling through the room. Scott fell back against the wall then slid down it, eyes closed. Tanner kicked the gun away from his hand and turned.

Bree and Melissa had wrested the gun from Jeter, and Melissa was pointing it at him.

"Tanner?" Bree's green eyes were huge. "Are you okay?"

He smiled at her. "Takes more than a chubby middle school kid to stop me. Are *you* okay?"

Melissa still had the gun pointing straight at Jeter's head. "You deserve to die. For what you've done. What you were going to do."

Tanner recognized that tone. The woman was going to kill Jeter.

"Mellie, no," Bree said. "Don't. Not like this."

"He's a monster. He killed Chris."

"No, he didn't, angel." Chris moved from the guard he'd knocked unconscious. "And I'd very much like it if I didn't have to come visit my wife in prison. We've got a lot of time to make up for."

Melissa froze, looking like she couldn't believe what she was seeing. "Chris?"

She handed the gun to Bree and launched herself at him.

Jeter ignored them and looked at Bree. "You're making a mistake. We're two of the greatest technological minds of this century. Together we would be unstoppable. Think about it."

"The only thing I need to think about concerning you is that neither I nor any of my loved ones will ever be hurt by you again. And that's more than enough for me." She turned to Tanner. "Captain, will you please read Mr. Jeter his rights?"

Tanner cupped her cheek. "It would be my pleasure."

Chapter Twenty-Seven

Bree had always liked her apartment in Kansas City before. But now that she was back here, she realized how lifeless it really was.

There were no gorgeous Colorado Rockies out her window. No horses, no pregnant dogs.

There were definitely no infant twins needing constant attention and care.

Melissa and Chris had gone to California to be near his family. A family who—just like Melissa—were thrilled to discover he was alive. Melissa had invited Bree to come with them, but she'd said no.

They had a lot of lost time to make up for. A lot of memories they needed to create, just the four of them, as the sweetest nuclear family.

Bree understood that, even if it did feel a little like someone was using her heart as a pincushion. One tiny little pain after another. None of them enough to really wound her, but taken all together...agonizing.

She was free now. The Organization as it had existed was no more. After all the information came out and everyone started turning on everyone else, no one had any doubt that Jeter and all his cronies would be spending the rest of their lives in prison, although at least Ronnie Kitchens had survived.

The future of Communication for All, the actual charity, was uncertain. But maybe under the right leadership it could become great again.

Bree, or Bethany Malone, if she wanted to call herself that, was free.

No one was chasing her. Hell, she could even open a social media account if she wanted to. Make friends. Talk to other people without having to worry about being hunted.

She didn't know how to do any of those things.

So she was eating cereal at her kitchen table alone. Just like she'd started. Her spoon was halfway up to her mouth when a knock came at her door.

She didn't run for a bug-out bag this time, although she still was a little uneasy. Nobody here in the city even talked to each other. Why would someone be knocking on her door?

She looked through the peephole then fell back against the door with a thud.

Tanner.

She opened the door. "Hi."

Oh, dear. He was wearing his cowboy hat. She took in the dark hair and stark jaw that needed a shave even though it was only lunchtime. Those broad shoulders and trim waist. It had only been three weeks since she'd seen him, but she couldn't stop staring.

Finally, she met his eyes. Those soft brown eyes. "Hey there," he whispered.

"Hi." She couldn't stop her smile. She stepped back so he could come in. "What are you doing here?"

He held up a small cooler. "I brought us both a slice of Mrs. A's lemon pie."

She felt her eyes grow big. "Really?"

"Yep."

She led him into the kitchen, tossing the cereal bowl in the sink and pulling out two plates. This time it was

Bree who gobbled the pie down, rather than Tanner. She was already almost finished when she realized he'd barely eaten half.

"What's wrong?"

"I want to eat it slowly. This might be the last time I get any of Mrs. Andrews's pie."

"Why? Are you leaving Risk Peak?" She couldn't imagine Tanner living anywhere else.

He nodded solemnly. "Maybe. It depends."

"On what?"

He took another small bite of his pie. "On you."

"Me?"

"Mr. and Mrs. A said I can't ever have another slice of their pie unless I talk you into coming back to Risk Peak."

She smiled and swatted at him. "No, they didn't."

He grabbed her hand and brought it up to his lips. "Oh, they did. They miss the twins, but they miss you, too. They sent me here with that pie and told me to make sure you understood how much they—how much *all* the people of Risk Peak—want you to return. They said you could have your job back, but..." He trailed off.

She stiffened. "But what?"

He shrugged. "You're a genius. I told them it's beneath you to work at a job like that when you could get any job you wanted to with computers. And..." He faded off again.

She raised an eyebrow. "Have we switched bodies or something? Since when do you have trouble getting words out instead of me?"

He gave her a half grin. "I know Risk Peak isn't for everyone. It's small. You live in a big city. But I want to get to know you. Know you now when you're not an overwhelmed single mom on the run. I want to get to know the real Bree, or Bethany, or Susan. I don't care what you call yourself as long as I can be near you."

Her eyes got big. "Oh."

"If that has to be in Denver or even here, I'm willing to do that. I can put in for a job on the force here." He looked around her place, trying not to grimace. "I can make it work."

What he meant was he *would* make it work.

For her.

To be near where she was.

When she didn't want to be here at all. She wanted to be in Risk Peak.

"But there's no pie here. Or mountains. Or horses."

She could tell that she had every single bit of his attention. "No, those things aren't here. But there are computer jobs here. And you deserve the chance to live the way you want to, Bree."

"Please call me Susan."

He laughed. That sexy, confident chuckle that did things to her insides she couldn't even begin to explain. But then he grabbed both her hands.

"You're a beautiful, intelligent woman who hasn't been given the opportunity to explore the details about herself because she's had to live in hiding."

"I want that, too. But I think I would like to try it in Risk Peak. I have no interest in working with computers right now. I might never want to again."

He shrugged. "And if so, that's okay. And I won't lie. The thought of having you in Risk Peak…everything about that feels right to me."

"You'll say whatever you have to in order to get your lemon pie privileges reinstated."

Before she could let out a squeal, she was picked up by the waist and deposited on his lap. "I'll say whatever I have to to get my *you* privileges reinstated."

She relaxed into him. She wanted that, too. "I'm new at this. I'll have to figure things out at my own pace."

"As slow as you need. For as long as you need." His lips

brushed against hers with the promise of everything that could be between them.

Lips that held the promise of *home*.

* * * * *

COMING SOON!

We really hope you enjoyed reading this book. If you're looking for more romance, be sure to head to the shops when new books are available on

Thursday 11th July

To see which titles are coming soon, please visit

millsandboon.co.uk/nextmonth